Tainted Love

Tainted Love

Soul Searchers

Book 2

NANCY MORSE

ISBN 978-1499716887

Chapter 1

New Orleans, 1803

"*D*eath is only the beginning."

That's what Nicolae said to her the last time she saw him. It was nine years ago in Paris. She and Papa had just emerged from the *Salle des Cent Suisses* where Breval had performed his Sonata in C Major for violoncello. The city was fragrant with cherry and apple blossoms, the cobbled streets lined with daffodils, and the trees along the Seine wore every shade of green. Unusual warmth lingered in the April air, and there had been no sign of the rain that came so frequently at that time of year.

"Did you enjoy the concert, Papa?" she had asked.

"Very much," her papa had replied.

Sensing an evasion, she questioned, "But?"

He hesitated. "I do so miss the way our young friend played the violoncello. Oh, to hear it again. That would be heaven. Sheer heaven."

"That's an interesting choice of words," she had commented sourly. "Considering it is on his account that you and I shall never see Heaven."

"Now Pruddy," her father had said in a conciliatory tone, "Nicolae only did what had to be done."

"I'll thank you not to mention his name to me," she had tersely replied. "Or have you forgotten what we are?"

"I haven't forgotten."

"When was the last time you sat in the sunshine?" she asked pointedly.

"When was the last time you enjoyed the beauty of the night?" he had countered. "Look around you, Pruddy. It's a beautiful night. The moon is high and the stars are shining brightly." He had drawn a deep breath into his lungs. "The air is warm and clear. And have you ever smelled anything so lovely? Why, all of Paris is blooming."

But Pru had ceased listening. Her gaze was riveted on a tall, lean figure across the square. Something inside of her froze, but it was not until he turned and saw those astonishingly green eyes from afar that the recognition slid like ice down her spine.

How he found her she didn't know. After leaving him for dead with a poker in his heart sixty-four years earlier in London, she had fled to Paris, hoping to put the whole sordid experience behind her, and had settled herself and her dear papa in a lovely little chateau just outside the city where their nocturnal pursuits would not arouse suspicion. How foolish she'd been to think she could destroy him. Oh, how she hated him.

She had grasped her papa's arm to turn him away, but the figure moved across the cobbled square like a swift dark wind and was suddenly standing beside them.

"Nicolae," James Hightower exclaimed. "What a coincidence. We were just talking about you."

Those green eyes lit up with typical conceit and a mellow voice spoke from out of the past. "My dear music master, what a pleasant surprise this is."

She had watched the exchange in tight-lipped silence. Coincidence? Surprise, pleasant or otherwise? Not likely. Of course papa would be delighted to see him. Unlike her papa, who had taken with a measure of alacrity to the exiled existence Nicolae had forced upon them, she found nothing cheerful in the dark and lonely existence to which they were consigned. In all these years she still had not gotten used to it. As if the darkness and the unsavory feeding habits weren't enough, she was always so dreadfully pale that people were forever asking her if she was ill. And there he was, looking impossibly handsome and smiling that luminous smile of his as if nothing had happened to make her hate him.

"You are looking well," James had remarked.

"Thank you. I was somewhat indisposed for a while."

"Nothing serious, I hope."

"No, no. Just an unfortunate accident with a poker."

Nicolae had nodded courteously and turned to her then. "You look surprised to see me, Prudence."

He had always called her that. Not Pru or Pruddy. Prudence. So formal and polite, when there was nothing courteous or considerate about him. He was evil personified, a clever and cunning manipulator despite the devastatingly good looks.

She studied that pale face. Did it seem a little crueler, or was it a trick of the street lamp? Through gritted teeth she told him, "I have no wish to see you after what you did to me."

His green eyes coursed over her. He smiled, a mere uplifting of one corner of his beautiful mouth, and said, "Death is only the beginning."

Wasn't it just like him to be so haughty and cruel? "Come Papa." She'd taken her papa by the arm and steered him away from Nicolae's disdainful arrogance, sifting into the crowd, trying desperately to ignore the heat rising within at the memory of the nights she had shared with that monster, when she had actually imagined him capable of possessing a soul, what seemed now like a lifetime ago.

She didn't see him again after that. Perhaps he sensed what was in the air and fled Paris. Because soon after that fateful meeting people were having their heads lopped off at an alarming rate. Even the French king's head wound up in a lunette. She'd been among the crowd in the square the day Robespierre himself, that master of terror, an intelligent but smug and self-righteous man, had ridden in the cart for his date with the guillotine to cries of "Down with the tyrant!" Master of nothing was more to the point when his head lay inside a bloody basket while his legs still wiggled behind him. The whole thing was quite distasteful.

"You cannot kill what cannot be killed," Papa had said in an attempt to assure her of their safety. But decapitation was a different matter for their kind—she'd never been able to bring herself to tell poor papa about that—and she wasn't waiting around for it. So, as France sank further into debt and a reign of terror enveloped the republic, she and Papa packed their bags and fled Paris to the new world, settling first in Boston and then New York, and finally here in New Orleans, a city of splendor and secrets too deep to reveal.

"Death is only the beginning."

Nicolae's words haunted her even now, nine years later, when that Paris night was far behind her.

The heat of the day lingered, but there was a breeze off the river on this August evening in New Orleans. Pru wrapped herself against the chill that had become so much a part of her as her footsteps took her through the seedy *Vieux Carrè* with its houses that looked more Spanish than French, and past the nine-pointed cross, a symbol of the voodoo religion, atop the Catholic church. Twining jasmine choked the brick walls all around her as she made her way across Rue Bourbon with no particular destination in mind.

It was like that, wandering aimlessly night after night in pursuit of sustenance. She damned him for doing this to her. She could feel it growing stronger, the thirst that led her on these nocturnal hunts. At the beginning, all those years ago, she had tried to ignore it, foolishly thinking she could subvert it. But as the transformation took hold, the thirst grew stronger, until it was an overpowering force she had neither the will nor the wish to control.

On this night her footsteps led her to the cemetery. The elaborate stone crypts and mausoleums lining the rows made the place look like a city of the dead. How clever of these people whose city was built on a swamp to put their dead above ground, lest buried caskets float away.

It was an appropriate place for her to be. The narrow paths and tombs offered concealment for muggers, and she might find one that wasn't drenched in liquor or didn't stink too badly. But it wasn't only for sustenance that she often found herself here. The quiet finality of the place brought a strange sense of peace and calmed her restlessness.

Here she was, seventy-three years after she'd crashed through a window and been left for dead, when Nicolae had made her the unwilling recipient of his dark gift, and she was still struggling with her evolution from mortal to immortal. Her life had become more chaotic as her humanity slowly slipped away. The worst part of it was that she wasn't more unsettled at losing that part of herself. It was funny really, how things that were once unthinkable became entirely possible when there was no choice in the matter. Nicolae had once tried to explain that to her, but she'd been mortal then and hadn't understood. Now, to her unending regret, she did.

She moved through the rows of tombs, some surrounded by rusted ironwork, running a pale hand over the stone carvings, reading the inscriptions, some in Spanish, some in French. Her acute eyesight fixed on the broken face of a stone angel on wrought iron and the carved head of a lion with a metal ring through its nose adorning one of the tombs. As she carefully picked her way through the twisted paths and over the brick and plaster strewn everywhere, skirting the crumbled corners of tombs jutting out like fingers to snag her pelisse, she stopped in her tracks. Only one such as she could have detected the nearly inaudible sound of a heartbeat and smelled the warm blood close at hand. With stealth-like cunning she crept silently forward and peered with cat's eyes into the darkness.

A man stood in the shadows at the foot of one of the tombs. For many long moments he did nothing. Then, leaning forward, he scraped a big X into the stone. He kicked his right foot backwards three times. Then he kicked the grave three times with his right foot. He knocked three times, turned to the right three times, bowed, and put his right hand over the X. His lips moved, and although his words were too soft to be heard by mortal ears, Pru's astute sense of hearing made out the man's secret wish. When he was finished, he left something at the foot of the tomb and was gone.

Pru approached the tomb. At its foot were three pennies left as an offering to whomever...or whatever...was inside. She decided to follow the man who disappeared down the street and had no trouble picking up his scent on the wind.

He didn't know he was being followed as he made his way through the streets of the city, beyond the ramparts and out into the surrounding countryside. She followed him along the river road, past the levees on both sides of the riverbank, her feet treading noiselessly over the damp ground, past an old plantation house, through the hardwood forest and deep into Bayou Saint John.

The sound of drums reverberated through the damp air and the orange glow that flickered through the trees grew brighter as she approached.

In the glow of a campfire a group of slaves congregated around a tree in the center of a clearing chanting to the syncopated rhythm of the drums. A man cloaked in a black robe drew symbols in the dust with cornmeal and poured rum on the ground.

A woman entered the circle and began to dance. She was beautiful, tall and statuesque, with curly dark hair and brown skin glowing red in the firelight. Faster and harder she moved with the rising pulse of the beat, while off to the side two men drew their knives and slit the throats of a black pig and a small goat and chopped off the head of a rooster. The blood from the pig and goat was sprinkled over the worshipers. The rooster's blood was drained into cups of green liquid and passed around for everyone to drink. The animals' bodies were thrown into a pool of bubbling mud. Many of the people jumped into the pond as well and came up drenched in the brown, oozing slime to join in the dancing.

The woman who danced at their center looked to be struck by a severe blow at the back of the head even though nothing touched her. She collapsed on the ground as if in great pain, writhing, contorting her body and shaking uncontrollably while screaming for vengeance against all those who suppressed them. One of the dancers moved too close and brushed her with his foot, whereupon the others began screaming and fell upon the offender.

The man shrank back in terror as the others surrounded him and grabbed his arms from behind. They dragged him to a tree and bound him to it. His cries carried deep into the cypress forest. The drums stopped. The beautiful woman who danced lifted herself from the ground and turned her head in his direction. The firelight glanced off her face, and even Pru who watched surreptitiously from her hidden place and who had seen much of life that was other-worldly, cringed. The woman's eyes rolled back in her head until only the whites shone through the darkness. Moving like a blind woman in a trance-like step, she approached the man bound to the tree.

Tears spilled from his eyes, leaving crooked little trails down his mud-caked cheeks. "No! Sabine! Sabine! No!"

The tortured scream dissolved into deep-throated gurgles cut hideously short when the woman he called Sabine reached forward, her hand contorted, fingers spread like grotesque talons, and grasped him by the neck.

Pru's breath caught in her throat. Was it possible she had stumbled across another of her kind about to drain a victim? Except for Nicolae and Papa, she'd never met another immortal and drew forward with morbid curiosity. But what she saw next sent a wave of revulsion through her.

In one swift motion the woman called Sabine pierced the skin of the man's breast, and driving her fingers in with superhuman strength, she ripped out his heart.

She turned to the others who stood in paralyzed silence and held up the bloody, still-beating heart in her palm for them to see. With a snarl of contempt, she bit into it, spit the piece to the ground and tossed the dead man's heart into the mud pond where it landed atop the carcass of the slaughtered pig.

Pru turned away in disgust. She'd heard about the voodoo ceremonies brought to these shores by slaves working the sugar plantations of French settlers in Saint-Domingue, but she'd never witnessed the terrifying ritual. She was reminded of the time Nicolae had taken her on one of his hunts and the sickness that welled up from her stomach at the sight of him feeding from another man's throat. It was when all her illusions of him had been shattered and she saw him for the thing he really was. Vampire. The word itself filled her with revulsion. She'd never even heard the word until she'd gone to see an alchemist about the possibility of reclaiming Nicolae's lost soul. The sinister little man told her something about reclaiming the soul through a witch's chant, but she never imagined that she would need a witch's chant one day for herself.

She was about to leave that place on the bayou when she spied the man she had followed there break away from the crowd and melt back into the forest. In the confusion of dancing and drum beats and sacrifice and murder she'd forgotten all about him and the wish she had overheard him whisper at the cemetery. She felt the hunger begin to bubble hotly inside. It was time to hunt him down and make his wish come true.

She followed him back to the city and through the angled streets. At the Place d'Armes she was glad to be a creature of the night and spared the spectacle of the public executions of disobedient slaves that were carried out in broad daylight. Was it her imagination, or could she hear the cries and moans of the dead as she hurried along?

The man stopped before the Ursuline Convent on Rue de Chartres. With slightly arched windows and rustic cornerstones, there was nothing about the building to warrant more than a passing glance. Yet the man stood transfixed, staring up at the timbered walls as if they held some secret significance, before moving on.

She passed by one of the few houses whose whitewashed brick was still intact, having escaped the fire that destroyed so many others nearly a decade before. She wrinkled her nose when her keen sense of smell picked up the lingering scent of ash and soot and shuddered at the memory of the distillery fire in London that had almost destroyed her and Nicolae all those years ago.

The hunger was building, and she was tiring of this chase. She longed to be home, safe inside the slate and tile-roofed house she shared with Papa, walled in with hand-forged wrought iron, where the midnight air carried the aroma of Belizean orchids and jasmine and not the scent of blood.

Her bonnet ribbons flapped in the breeze as she followed the man into a cobblestone alley running between the Cabildo and the cathedral. Raucous sounds issued from a tavern lining the alley, a haven for the pirates who smuggled their goods into New Orleans from the marshes of Barataria. A sign swinging above the shingled roof read *The Snapping Turtle* in peeling paint. The tower of the old cathedral shielded the alley from the light of the moon, and the delicate clang of its half-hour bells could not obscure the voices of drunken men.

The man's footsteps grew faster. He knew someone was following him. She sensed his fear as acutely as if he had screamed right beside her. It was time to strike. In a movement too swift for mortal eyes to see she surged past him, rustling the sleeve of his shirt as if a wind had passed overhead, and was waiting for him at the end of the alley.

Stepping out of the shadows, she stopped his flight.

"Good evening," she said.

He looked at her suspiciously, his ebony skin shining like glass in the moonlight, dark gaze darting about, no doubt looking for an accomplice.

"I have nothing," he said.

"I do not mean to rob you," she told him. *At least, not of your purse.*

His eyes narrowed as if with understanding, and he smiled, showing crooked white teeth.

"And I am not some bored white woman looking to couple with a slave."

"I am a free man of color," he said.

She shrugged her shoulders beneath her pelisse. "Nor that."

"Then what do you want?"

"What were you doing in the bayou?" she asked. "Do not bother to deny it. I followed you there."

"You saw?"

"Oh yes, I saw. Tell me about that woman. What is her name?"

She did not have to describe what she had seen for him to know of whom she was speaking. He swallowed hard, and answered hesitantly. "Her name is Sabine Sejour."

She could not shake the image of the woman's contorted hand, fingers flexed like talons, looking like...Lienore, the witch who had killed her mother and inhabited the body of her poor Aunt Vivienne. The witch who had nearly choked the life out of her and sent her crashing through the window. The witch who could chant the spell that would reclaim the soul she lost upon her making. "What is she?"

The man drew back in fear, reluctant to say more.

With a swift motion she reached forward and grasped him by the neck, using her inhuman strength to pull him closer. She brought her face near to his and sniffed. There was no telltale odor of alcohol or disease hovering about him. He would do. She could satisfy her burning thirst and rid the world of—what was it Nicolae called it? Oh yes, the dregs of humanity.

He clawed at her hand in an attempt to loosen the grip, and when he could not, he gave a shaky, compliant nod of the head.

She eased her strangling hold, and asked again, "What is she?"

He answered in a scratchy voice. "She is the voodoo queen."

"Where will I find this voodoo queen?"

"She sells sweetmeats in front of the Cabildo."

"Where does she live?"

"On Rue Ste. Anne, near Congo Square. But you do not want to go there."

"Oh? Why not?"

"The slaves meet there. It is a dangerous place for a white woman."

The sound of her laughter caused him to shiver. "I have no fear of them." Or of anything human. Unless, of course, it aimed a hawthorn stake at her heart. "She is a slave?"

"Voodoo queens are never slaves. They are free women of color.

"And how did she become so?"

"It is said she was brought to New Orleans from Saint-Domingue and bought her freedom by selling herbs and spells. She used to hold ceremonies at an abandoned brickyard on Rue Dumaine. Then she moved them to the bayou."

"Yes, I would imagine the residents of Rue Dumaine would not look kindly on murder in their midst. Why did she kill that man?"

He shivered. "The man came too close and touched the queen while she was dancing."

"I suppose that's as good a reason as any to have your heart ripped out," she said wryly.

"If that is all you want—"

"That is not all I want." She ran a finger along his neck, pausing at the pulse that throbbed there. Her fingers crept slowly, snugly around his neck. "I am thirsty."

"There is that place over there." He nodded nervously toward the tavern whose windows glowed from the play of candlelight within.

Pirates, she thought with distaste. She had no wish to meet one. Not that she had experienced better men than that over the years. The image of Edmund de Vere loomed, the London pewterer she almost wed, the vampire hunter who used her as bait to trap Nicolae. There were others after him, but men, she had learned, were a weak and sorry lot. Except for Nicolae, her vampire lover. There was nothing weak about him, neither in his nature nor his capacity for sexual pleasure.

"The convent," she ventured. "It means something to you, does it not?"

"I—I don't know what you mean."

She gave him a knowing look, and said, "I know what you wished for."

He stared back blankly.

"At the cemetery. Ah, I can see how you might wonder how that can be when you scarcely uttered the words." Her melodic voice belied the tightening grip at his throat. "You wished for no one to find out what you did to that nun, the one whose body you ravaged and then buried in the bayou." He sucked in his breath, and she laughed. "I can make your wish come true." But to do that she would have to kill him, and then no one would ever know his secret.

She saw a glimmer of hope spark behind his frightened eyes. In the next moment it was gone as she dragged him behind a banana tree. Her bonnet slipped from her head as she sank her fangs into his throat. The man screamed, the sound rising from the depths of his being. But the scream, as well as the sucking sounds of her mouth against his jugular, were lost amidst the boisterous voices coming from the tavern.

A gurgling sound erupted from his chest. His eyes were wide with terror. His body flailed. But it was no use. He was trapped in her inhuman embrace like a fly caught in a spider's web. She drained him to the point of death. When she had been new to this, she had often left her victims alive, although barely, until she got the hang of it, and then, like now, she finished them off.

She had tried to subsist on animal blood like Papa did. Dear, Papa who had not the nature to take a human life. But the dark hunger that rose from the pit of her being craved more than ox or chicken blood. The need that welled up from within was for human blood. As she drained the last drop of blood from the nun-murderer she wondered distractedly why she was so different from Papa and so much more like Nicolae. What had Nicolae done different when he'd made her that he had not done when he made Papa?

She dropped the lifeless body to the ground and with her foot rolled it behind the shrubbery. It would not be found until it began to stink, and then no one would want to get close enough to it to see the bite marks on the neck or notice that all the blood had been drained from it.

As her victim's warm blood coursed through her veins Pru felt a perverse satisfaction in knowing that he would never kill another innocent. The streets were a tiny bit safer now, and she was feeling the rosy flush of fresh blood tinting her cheeks. Straightening her clothes, she wiped the crimson traces from her lips and bent to retrieve her fallen bonnet. Emerging from behind the banana tree, she started back down the alley toward Rue de Royal.

The sky had turned a pale shade of violet. She breathed in deeply, drawing the sultry air into her lungs. With no street lamps, the light coming from the tavern cast a warm glow to light her way.

She was feeling strangely serene in the aftermath of her feeding. Perhaps it was the sweetness of orange blossoms lacing the air, or the thought of seeing Papa's smiling face when she returned home.

Home. There had been so many places to call home since they left London more than seventy years ago. Madrid, where women in colorful swirling dresses whispered behind their fans, "That woman, look how pale she is". Venice, where there had been no place to dispose of the drained bodies except to toss them into the canals where they floated to the top and created a mood of hysteria throughout the city. Paris, where the blood from the guillotine ran more frequently than the blood of her victims, and where she had last seen Nicolae. And now here, to the new world, where she had hoped to find a bit of the happiness that eluded her, first in Boston, then New York, and now here, in New Orleans.

New Orleans, a mystical, magical city, where one such as she could move virtually unnoticed beneath the street lamps, where the French and Spanish lived among a medley of slaves and free men of color, where people from the islands sold baskets of shiny fruit along the *banquettes* and Indians lingered up and down the levees, where arrogant Americans and old-world planters drank side by side in the taverns all along the narrow streets, where pirates sold the smuggled goods that the gentlemen purchased for their shops and homes.

To someone whose senses were heightened beyond any mortal's imagination, it was a city of sounds and smells. Church bells rang, cabriolets careened down the streets, horses' hooves clopped in the mud. Huge oleanders scented the great courtyards, wisteria grew over whitewashed walls and honeysuckle twined along wrought iron balconies. There was no shortage of unsavory characters to feed her sanguinary need, and like London's sordid East End, the seedy part of the city gave up its prey with scant notice.

Here in this city of wrought-iron lacework, of spells and potions, of beautiful women both light and dark, and men of mixed blood and pure blood, she had everything she could want—evening gowns, a shining landau to transport her and Papa about, an abundance of their favorite foods from the French market—all paid for with the money from the sale of their Spitelfields house in London and the purses she helped herself to from her victims. Yes, she had everything, except the thing she longed for most—love. Not the fatherly love lavished on her by her doting papa, nor the tainted, unchaste love Nicolae once claimed to have for her, but the love of a man who was good and honest…and mortal.

All thoughts of love vanished when the tavern door suddenly swung open as Pru was passing, throwing bright light into the alley and momentarily blinding her.

"Sortez, vous misèrable Amèricaine!"

A body came hurling out. He rolled over several times and came to a stop face down in a puddle at her feet. She hopped back to avoid falling over him.

She wasn't afraid—there was little she feared save a stake to the heart and never finding love—but the mud that splashed onto her dress leaving an unsightly blotch brought her temper immediately to the fore.

"Now you've done it!" There was no need to address him in French despite her fluency, for the man who tossed him out had called him a miserable American. "My dress is ruined. I don't suppose I can expect the likes of you to pay for the damage."

He lifted his face from the puddle and coughed. "The likes of me?" he echoed.

"Yes. You are nothing but a pirate, and everyone knows pirates have no money. How do you expect to pay for the damage?"

He planted both palms on the ground and pushed himself to his feet. As he straightened his clothing with his back to her, she realized that perhaps he wasn't such a pauper after all. He brushed the dirt from brown velvet breeches and adjusted a waistcoat of crimson damask shot with silken threads of gold and silver. Beneath it he wore a shirt of white linen whose sleeves billowed in the midnight breeze. He bent to retrieve the coat that had been tossed out after him and smoothed his palms over the ornate braid trim. A sliver of moonlight glinted off the buckles on his shoes. A ribbon held his dark shoulder-length hair tied at the back of his head. Spotting his tricorn on the ground, he swiped it up and slapped it on his head. The exotic red feather it was decorated with danced about in the breeze.

He turned to her then. "You were saying?"

The first thing she noticed was the brightly colored sash slashed diagonally across his shoulder and the knife protruding from it. A cutlass hung from the wide leather belt at his waist, the candleglow from the tavern sparking along its curved cutting edge.

"Well, I'll be," he exclaimed. "Good evening, ma'am. Stede Bonham at your service."

There was a slight cadence to his speech, a drawl and a lilting accent that were strangely appealing. He took off his hat and gave her a low, sweeping bow, although Pru could not dispel the notion that she was being sorely mocked.

She was about to voice her displeasure when he stood upright again, and just as the moon was emerging from behind a cloud, she saw his face. She controlled the impulse to moisten her lips nervously. He was appallingly handsome. Unlike Nicolae's ethereal beauty, this was a raw animal-like appeal that made her feel like she was strangling on her own breath.

There was no softness to his solidly built frame. Beneath a shelf of dark brows his eyes were gray, as bright as silver pennies, and ringed with impossibly thick lashes. His nose was straight, his chin strong. His skin was smooth and darkly tanned by the sun, and she struggled against the temptation to touch it. His face was impassive, and were it not for the smile playing teasingly across his lips, she might have judged him to be a cruel, implacable sort. In spite of the polished veneer, the gray eyes regarded her with the undisguised lust of a common pirate. And one who'd had too much drink, if his swaying posture was any indication of it.

"You, Sir, are drunk," she said disapprovingly.

He offered a lopsided smile. "Happily so," he said with a laugh. "With compliments to *la fèe verte*. But not so drunk that I don't know a beautiful woman when I see one."

She could feel the carefully controlled energy flowing through his muscles in much the same way the warm blood of the free man of color flowed through her veins. He took a step toward her and she jumped back, unsure of his motive.

"Your bonnet," he said. He reached up and straightened it upon her head. "What have you been doing to turn it half around?"

"I—I—" What could she say? She couldn't very well tell him that was drinking the blood of her latest victim, and in the struggle, her bonnet fell from her head and she put it back on in haste. "Don't change the subject," she said. "If you think to distract me from the damage you have done to my dress, think again."

"That's a delightful accent you have. English, if I'm not mistaken."

"Yes. London. Now, if you would please—"

"What are you doing out and about at this hour?"

"Sir, you ask too many questions," she said with a huff.

He laughed. It was a smooth, contagious sound from deep in his throat. "My dear departed mother used to tell me not to ask a question for fear of the answer."

"Indeed. I was merely on my way home from visiting a sick friend." Lying, which had once been so difficult, came easy to her now.

"Then you must permit me to escort you home. These streets are dangerous for a woman alone."

That's what Nicolae said to her the first time she'd met him on the London Bridge. She should have known from that experience that it was unwise to accept such offers from strangers. Look where that fateful meeting had led. But there was something about the way those gray eyes were watching her that brought warmth to her cheeks, and she heard herself say, "Very well. You may escort me home. And we will consider that an even exchange for the soiled dress." And if he attempted to lay one finger on her, no matter how handsome he was, she would devour him before he could utter a prayer to his dear departed mother.

Chapter 2

*S*tede Bonham's first impression of the woman walking beside him was of solemn eyes a dusky shade of blue, like the twilight sky just before night descends, and hair the color of dark ale, the tendrils escaping her bonnet tinted gold beneath the light of the street lamps. Her profile reflected a straight nose, a determined little chin, and lips that were firm and slightly pouted.

There was nothing noticeably strange about her features except for an alluring pallor and a rosy stain on her cheeks. She walked with uncommon grace and an unusually quiet step, her shoes making practically no sound on the damp *banquette*. It seemed almost as if she were floating, a notion no doubt fostered by *la fée verte*. The Green Fairy often made him imagine things that weren't there. He blinked his eyes to clear them. She looked innocent and yet not innocent. Fresh and naïve and yet somehow as old as time. She wasn't as starkly beautiful as some of the quadroon girls who strolled the Place d'Armes, with their dark, flirtatious eyes and pecan-colored skin, yet there was something about her that made him steal quick glances at her as they walked. It made him smile.

"How long have you been in Nawlins?" he asked.

She looked at him with unblinking eyes that seemed to hold some secret wisdom, and said, "We arrived in April."

"From where?"

"Boston, New York, and before that, Paris."

"Paris, huh? It must have been some bloodbath over there."

Pru pulled in a breath and let it out in a low sigh at the memory. It wasn't the image of all that blood that was so disturbing she still dreamed about it, but rather the sight of all those heads chopped off, a punishment striking too close to home for her comfort.

"Yes, Papa and I were fortunate to get out when we did."

"You have no other family?"

His questions summoned too many unwanted memories. "My mother is dead," she said without offering further explanation. There was no need to tell him that her mother had thrown herself off the London Bridge, or the terrifying reason that had led her to such an act.

And how could she explain about Aunt Vivienne? She had often wondered these past decades if the witch Lienore still inhabited poor Aunt Vivienne's body, or if her aunt had become a mass of moldering flesh and bones in some forgotten corner of the world.

"What about you?" she asked, hoping to shift his attention away from her past.

"I was born in the French-heavy bayou country to the south. My father gave up planting and worked his way through the Caribbean on tramp steamers and merchant vessels, learning the sea trade first hand. Later on, he set out to make a name for himself here in Nawlins, first as a clerk among the merchants who jammed the docks with sugar and cotton, and then with the importation of, well, other goods."

"You mean slaves," she said disapprovingly.

He shrugged his broad shoulders. "You do what you have to do to get by."

Oh yes, she knew all about doing what had to be done to get by. "Your mother didn't object?"

"She died when one of the trading ships brought the yellow fever over from Africa. I was ten at the time. After she was gone, he took me sailing with him. That's how I came by my love of the sea."

"So now you sail aboard a pirate ship."

"Now I'm captain of my own ship," he corrected.

She dismissed the distinction with a wave of the hand. "What's the difference? It's all plunder and pillage, isn't it?"

"Of course," he said proudly. "But that doesn't mean it's a free-for-all. We pirates have a code of conduct, you know."

Pru rolled her eyes.

"What? You don't believe me?"

"What code can there be among lawless men?"

The challenge in her tone irked him. He'd never before had to explain himself to a woman. "Well, to begin with, every man has equal voting rights and gets his fair share of the loot. Me and the quartermaster each receive two shares of a prize, the master gunner and boatswain get one and one-half shares, and all others one-quarter. Aboard my ship there's no gambling, boys or women allowed. I do not permit my men to fight one another, and if they do, their quarrel ends on shore by sword or pistol. All lights and candles are put out by eight o'clock," he said, adding mischievously, "Even pirates need their sleep. Any man who wants to drink after eight can do it up on deck."

"My, my," she said, sarcasm dripping in her tone. "And if a man does not follow the code?"

He answered simply, "I run him through with my sword."

"And just when I thought you were actually a decent sort, you prove yourself to be no better than a common killer."

He could have sent her sprawling with a disparaging remark like that, but her tenacity intrigued him, and he could not help but wonder what made her so sure of herself and unafraid. "You're wrong," he said.

"How so?"

"I'm not common."

"But you are a killer."

"When I have to be."

"Do you like killing?" she asked.

He let out a short breath. "No. I don't. There's nothing honorable in killing a man, no matter how necessary it may be."

There was something about him that drew Pru's interest in spite of herself. Perhaps because, like her, he killed out of need, and by his own admission he didn't enjoy it. They were alike in ways he could never imagine.

They fell into an easy silence, his footsteps echoing through the narrow streets. Passing by an old house on Rue Bourbon, he reached across the wrought-iron fence and snagged an orange hanging from a nearby limb. He peeled it with the knife he drew from his sash and sliced it into quarters. "Here." He held one of the slices out to her on the tip of his knife. "Come on, it's good."

Pru gingerly lifted it off the knife and bit into it, sending sweet juice squiring into the air and dribbling down her chin.

Stede laughed. "Look at you, trying so hard to be proper with orange juice rolling down your face." He popped a slice into his mouth, and reaching forward, dabbed the juice from her chin with the pad of his thumb.

"I used to be quite proper," she said, succumbing to a self-deprecating laugh.

"What happened?"

Nicolae happened. But of course she couldn't tell him about that. "It's a long story."

He offered her another slice of orange, but she shook her head, so he ate it himself. "When a woman looks like that, it's usually because of a man."

"There was someone, once."

"Were you in love with him?"

She bit back a caustic little laugh, and said adamantly, "No." But even as she said it, she knew it wasn't true. She had loved Nicolae, or at least the romanticized version she had created of him, until it all came crashing down.

"Why did that man throw you out of the tavern?" she asked.

"Well now, that's about the quickest change of subject I ever heard. All right, so you don't want to talk about it. That's fair enough. There are things in every person's life that are best kept to themselves."

More than you know, Pru thought with a grimace.

He tossed the orange peel into the darkness, and said, "I don't know how much attention you've been paying to what's going on, but President Jefferson sent his territorial governor to Nawlins and people here aren't too happy about it."

"Governor Claiborne, yes."

"The people don't like his control over the city. They don't want him telling them they can't dance and drink and gamble on Sunday. And they sure as hell don't like it that Congress has outlawed the trafficking of slaves. That hasn't stopped the French and Spanish landowners from smuggling them in, though. The people here see owning slaves as a natural thing. That's bound to make men hot under the collar. It just came down to a difference of opinion in the tavern."

"I take it you stand on the side that's against it?" she ventured.

"I never did see the right in one man owning another, and I'm not afraid to say so."

"Is there anything you are afraid of?"

"Not much. Except a hangman's noose. The Americans don't look too kindly on pirates either."

"But you're American."

"Well, sort of. My father was American. My mother was the daughter of a Creole plantation owner. She had French, Spanish, African and Indian blood in her. So I guess that makes me a little bit of everything and a whole lot of nothing. The French and Spanish don't like the Americans, and the Americans think all Louisianans are heathens in the wilderness. I come ashore now and then, but the only place I feel at home is at sea."

"When will you sail again?"

"My sloop, the *Evangeline*, is anchored in a secluded cove on the south side of Grand Terre. I was thinking to set sail in a day or two. But now…" His eyes swept over. "Now, I'm not so sure."

Pru looked at him forthrightly. The silvery aura of the moon fell across his face, lightening his gray eyes. "Why did you tell me all this? Aren't you worried I might turn you over to the American authorities?"

There was no telltale sign of worry amongst his features, just the perfection of his looks and his mouth curved upwards at the corners. He moved a bit closer and she could smell the orange he'd eaten on his breath. "Are you going to do that?"

She shifted nervously from foot to foot, and answered honestly, "No."

"I didn't think so. Just as I'm not going to tell anyone that you were in the alley tonight."

Impatiently, she replied, "I told you, I was visiting—"

"A sick friend. Yes, I remember. And was it your sick friend who left the blood on your dress?"

Pru cast a horrified look downward. The wind flicked open the folds of her pelisse to reveal droplets of blood staining the bodice of her white muslin dress. "I—I—"

"You don't have to explain," Stede told her, looking at her steadily. "Maybe some day, when we know each other better, you'll tell me what you were really doing in the alley tonight."

Unlike Nicolae, who had succumbed to a desperate need to tell her who and what he was, it wasn't likely she would ever know Stede Bonham well enough to trust him with the truth of what she'd been doing in the alley, no matter how deeply she longed for a confidant, someone in whom she could confide who loved her strongly enough not to be repelled.

"You're wondering if you can trust me."

Pru managed a smile, although her darting glance reflected her scattered thoughts. "Not at all," she said. "I'm sure you are a most trustworthy pirate."

It was more than her biting sarcasm that intrigued him. He liked beautiful women as much as the next man, but there was something about this woman that was different. Her beauty had an ethereal quality, as though not of this world, an obscure notion he would have found ridiculous were it not for those eyes that were uncommonly clear and that complexion, so translucent and smooth, with not a line on her face and only the tiniest smattering of pale blue veins hiding just beneath the surface of her skin.

The white muslin dress, so fashionable for the day, blended almost perfectly with the hue of her skin, and were it not for the mud he had splashed on its hem and the droplets of blood staining its skirt, she looked almost completely naked beneath her pelisse, kindling familiar sensation in his loins.

"Pirating is what I do," he said. "Not what I am."

She looked up at him with beautiful, unblinking eyes. "What are you?"

"A man," he answered. "Just a man."

And beneath her façade she was just a woman, with a woman's hungers and needs. She came to a sudden stop by an iron gate before one of the houses on Rue Bourbon. "This is where I live."

Stede looked past her to the house built in the Spanish style, with long galleries opening onto a lush and tranquil courtyard. In the center of the courtyard stood an immense Spanish lime tree. The fruit warmed to ripeness by the sunlight hung like small globes against the dark, verdant leaves rustling in the breeze wafting up from the river. Beyond the spreading limbs of the Spanish lime tree the yellow glow of candlelight split the darkness from one of the upstairs windows.

Pru's gaze followed his. "My papa," she explained. "He often has trouble sleeping and is up late." It wasn't a lie, not really. Her papa didn't sleep at night, only during the daylight hours, on a layer of London soil carefully spread atop his down mattress.

She turned back to Stede. "You haven't answered my question. Why did you tell me those things about yourself?"

He shrugged beneath the coat carelessly draped over one shoulder, the full sleeves of his shirt billowing in the breeze. He studied her by the light of the stars. Her complexion was so pale, and combined with the hint of fear behind her eyes, he might have been inclined to think she was in need of protection, were it not for the strength of her character. "I don't know why I told you," he answered truthfully. "You're a puzzle. An odd little thing." He watched her reaction. "Are you shocked by that?"

"I'm not as shocked as I pretend to be. Although *odd* is not how I would choose to describe myself. Different is more to the point." As she spoke, she was all too aware of his strong, warm presence drawing nearer, making her stiffen with awareness.

"I don't even know your name," he said.

She moistened her lips. "My name is Prudence Hightower."

"Such a formal-sounding name. I think I'll call you Pru." He put his hands on her shoulders and pulled her toward him. "And I think I'm going to kiss you."

His mouth came against hers in a kiss that tasted of ale and seduction. She'd known from the first moment she saw his face in the alley that she wanted to be kissed by him. Her hands came up to flatten against his chest, fingers kneading the brocade of his waistcoat like a cat flexing its paws with pleasure. A little sound came from her throat as an aching need welled up within her. It had been so long since she had been kissed like this.

His hands locked behind her, one at the back of her head, holding her mouth prisoner against his, the other with fingers splayed across her back, forcing her closer with gentle pressure until her ample breasts flattened against him. The warm rush of his breath, the thrust of his tongue, the hardness biting into her through his breeches brought back memories of carnal pleasure. No one since Nicolae had kissed her like this and made her feel the raw, pulsing hunger for more.

He bowed his face to the soft curve of her neck and pressed kisses to her flesh while a score of emotions flooded her—joy, passion, hope. She could so easily fall in love with this man whose masculine beauty took her breath away, this pirate who lived by plunder and pillage and yet whose happy-go-lucky nature overrode the dark treachery of his wayward life. With looks like his exerting a natural pull on feminine hearts, she'd be a fool to think there hadn't been other women for him, but that was all right, for there had been other men for her who benefited from Nicolae's artful teachings in the ways of pleasure. But she hadn't felt anything with any of them remotely akin to what she was feeling now with this man. Maybe it was because they shared so much in common—lawless lives, living on the fringes of society, the danger of secrets too deep to reveal.

"Pru." He whispered her name against her flesh, sending an array of goose bumps over her. "Will you let me protect you?"

She stiffened. Gripping his billowing sleeve, she pushed herself away forcibly and retreated several steps away from him. With her back pressed against the wrought-iron fence, she exclaimed, "Why do you think I need protecting?"

A long silence fell between them during which he studied her. She acted brave, and he did believe she was. But behind the bravado he sensed her sadness. Something troubled her, something so deep her blue eyes could not hide it. He lifted his shoulders in a careless shrug. "Who knows? Maybe I'm wrong about you. I just thought—"

"You thought what?" Pru cut in. "That just because I was out tonight alone I am in need of rescuing?" Oh yes, she needed rescuing, but not the kind he was suggesting. It was not her person that needed rescuing, but her soul, and until she found that witch Lienore, there was nothing any man could do to help her. She straightened her back and jut out her chin. "I'll have you know I can take care of myself."

"Excuse me for thinking otherwise." He removed his hat and swept low in a bow. "Good night, Pru."

Her hand fumbled with the gate latch as she watched him walk off into the mist that crawled in from the river. The gate creaked open. She walked up the slate path to the door, her heart fluttering wildly in her breast, caused not by the influx of fresh blood but by the devilish smile and the heated kiss of a common pirate.

Chapter 3

*J*ames Hightower burst out of the music room in a flurry of confusion. "Pruddy, have you seen my sheet music?"

Drawing the hallway curtains over the window to block out the afternoon light, Pru answered over her shoulder, "Did you look in your case?"

"My case. Yes, of course. Now I remember. I left it there last night."

"Why aren't you sleeping? You know how tired you get when you don't rest."

"I'm working on a new piece and haven't been able to sleep."

"Or feed, judging from your paler than usual complexion. You go get your music Papa, and I'll bring your decanter to the music room."

He smiled tenderly at her. "You're such a good girl, Pruddy."

Pru sighed. Her papa wouldn't think she was such a good girl if he knew she'd been careless and had almost been caught feeding a few nights ago, or that she had let herself be kissed by a man with an unsavory reputation.

The effects of the kiss lingered for days. Every night when she went out to hunt, she hoped to catch sight of Stede Bonham. She felt like a silly schoolgirl swooning over a handsome man, and not even an honorable one, but a very disreputable pirate who made his living by robbing others. Not that she was in any position to judge him. And she did, after all, have a proclivity for dangerous men.

The image of Nicolae flared suddenly in her mind. He was as dangerous as they came, a natural-born killer even if it wasn't by his own choosing. She'd be lying to herself if she denied that she missed those mesmerizing green eyes, the pale, handsome features, the beautifully slender fingers that had teased her to madness and created the most profoundly splendid music she'd ever heard.

But she didn't miss his penchant for cruelty, or that mocking voice, or the look on his face when she'd left him for dead. That looked that screamed "How could you do this to me?" haunted her dreams even to this day, decades after she had plunged a poker into his heart and fled his house in Hanover Square. It was because of him that she was a creature of the night subsisting on the blood of others. Because of him she would never find happiness with any man, not even Stede Bonham whose kiss had filled her with the promise of what might have been, if only she were human and worthy of a mortal's love.

A feeling of dejection washed over her as she picked up a decanter holding what appeared to be dark claret and carried it to the music room where her papa sat behind his beloved violoncello, his latest composition on the music stand beside him.

"Here you are Papa," she said, placing the decanter down on a rosewood table. "I'm going to the dressmaker's for a final fitting of the two dresses I ordered."

He glanced toward the window at the sliver of light that pierced an opening in the drapes.

"Don't worry," she said, guessing his thoughts. "It's an overcast day. I'll be all right. I'll stop at the market on the way home. Is there anything you'd like?"

"*Beignets*," he said. "And perhaps some pralines?"

"If I'm not back by the time Babette arrives, tell her we would like shrimp gumbo for dinner. And ask her to change the oil in the lamps. It's beginning to smell."

They could not have hoped for a better servant than Babette, a free woman of color who came each day to cook and clean. She served them delicious meals of hot boiled crawfish, and *étouffée*, a gumbo made with a dark *roux* with tomatoes and okra over rice. On Mondays she made Papa's favorite, red beans and rice. Monday was wash day and the long unattended pot allowed her to use Sunday's ham bone and let the pot simmer without having to watch over it.

The mournful strains of the violoncello sifted through the house as Pru strapped on the metal pattens to her shoes, raising them an inch to protect them from the muddy streets.

It was a sunless day as she made her way along the crowded streets, past the grog shops to the dressmaker's shop. The bell atop the door jingled when she entered.

Papa thought it appropriate to dress in black befitting their undead condition, but Pru preferred more fashionable attire. She stood motionless for the final fittings of a morning dress to be worn at home with a high-neck and long-sleeves to cover her pale throat and wrists and no embellishment, and a new evening dress, extravagantly trimmed with lace and ribbons, cut low, with short sleeves to bare her arms, both dresses high-waisted with soft, loose skirts. Although she could have chosen her dresses made in any color, she invariably chose white in all its varying shades, partly because it was the fashion of the day, but mostly to mock the purity it invoked. For if there was anything she was not, it was pure. Leaving her order with the dressmaker, she left the shop.

At the French market the vendor stalls just inside the arcade doorways were crammed with stacks of green vegetables and golden fruit, hanging sides of beef, moss-covered baskets of crabs, and cages of rabbits and fowl. The air was thick with the smell of spice and fish, spring flowers and rotting cabbage. Swatting at the flies that buzzed everywhere, she filled her basket with a sack of oysters in the shell, some Irish potatoes, two ears of husked corn, bunches of greens, and some *beignets* and pralines for Papa.

Outside, a Haitian woman with huge earrings jangling from her lobes squatted on the *banquette* selling voodoo trinkets. The woman stood, and as Pru passed, she reached out and clamped a hand over Pru's arm. "Sister," she said, "get your good luck charm."

Pru cast a heated look at the dark skin covering her own pale flesh, then stared straight at the woman, her eyes cold and arrogant. "I need no lucky charm," she hissed, "when I have these." She lifted her lips, devilishly revealing pearly white fangs, reasoning that even if the woman told others what she'd seen, it wasn't likely anyone would believe her. The woman's eyes widened, showing yellowed whites around the black pupils. Her hand fell away as she sank back into a squat.

From there, Pru stopped at the levee, skirting coops of squawking chickens and tubs filled with crabs stinking of brine, and purchased saffron, several sprigs of basil, powdered sassafras and some bay leaves sold by the Choctaws who sat silently beside their baskets. She climbed the wooden steps to a higher level of the levee to purchase dry goods from a vendor, pausing to glance at a chain of black slaves whose necks were linked with heavy rope and cast a furtive sneer at the white man who kept them in line with a black whip in his hand. She had half a mind to track him down, and if he wasn't riddled with disease or stink too badly of alcohol, sink her fangs into his neck and put an end to his brutish ways.

The streets were muddy from a morning rain and congested with pedestrians. Heavy wagons rumbled by, making a calamitous sound against the big cobblestones brought over the sea long ago by sailing ships that used them as ballast. Street merchants with pushcarts yodeled their wares. The shouts and curses of flatboat men from upriver joined the cacophony of noise. Sailors stumbled drunkenly out of back alleys. Dark-skinned women from the islands sold fruit from the baskets balanced atop their heads while their men sat on corners hawking hand-made crafts and rum. Planters from the tobacco and indigo plantations crowded the taverns.

The sun was already beating down on the sloped roofs as she crossed the Place d'Armes, the town square edging the riverfront levee, where beautiful quadroons, some no older than fourteen and fifteen, strolled beneath lace-trimmed parasols on the arms of wealthy white dandies along paths worn bare of grass.

And everywhere were the conspicuous Americans—the gamblers and the merchants, the gentlemen, rogues and Kaintocks—who migrated to the lawless swamps of Louisiana and settled in New Orleans hoping to get rich. Every day brought new clashes between arrogant Americans and old-world Creoles which usually resulted in a duel out upon the open plain just beyond the city.

New Orleans had always embraced the French way of life. Even the Spaniards who ruled for a time hadn't tried to change the flavor. But the Americans were a different breed, regarding the Creoles of French-Spanish blood as saucy tempered, lazy and lawless. New Orleans itself was like a foreign city to them. And now, with France's Bonaparte having abruptly decided to sell the territory to the United States, tempers were quick to surface.

What a strange people the Americans were, Pru griped to herself as she passed through the mud streets lined with old houses where women scrubbed the stoops with red brick dust and the smell of laundry hanging on lines filled the yards. The Americans couldn't even tell the difference between a quadroon and a Negro, or a slave and a free man.

America's army in blue uniforms and black leather shakos, its fifes and drums and its red-white-and-blue had nothing to do with her. She had her own problems, not the least of which was protecting the façade she presented to the world and the ever-constant look over her shoulder for fear that a member of the Sanctum, the centuries-old cult of avowed vampire hunters, might have discovered her true nature and come at her heart with a hawthorn stake.

The cathedral bells began to ring the hour by the time Pru returned home. The candles were lighted and the aroma of gumbo from the cooking pot filled the entire house.

She and Papa dined beneath a crystal chandelier, with Babette filling their bowls with Creole gumbo and their goblets with French wine. After dinner they retired to the music room where Papa took his place behind his beloved violoncello and Pru reclined on a silk-upholstered, claw-footed settee.

"Tell me what you think," he said excitedly as he closed his eyes and drew the bow across the strings. The music filled the room as the perfect compliment to their sumptuous meal.

When he had coaxed the final notes from his instrument, he opened his eyes. Tears aglow with candlelight rolled down his cheeks.

Pru got up and crossed the Oriental carpet to place a kiss upon his cheek. "Oh Papa, it was beautiful."

"I finished it while you were out. Yes, I'm quite happy with it. If only…" He paused and looked at her. "You know what I was going to say."

"I long to hear him play, too," she said grudgingly. She dismissed the momentary sentimentality with a wave of the hand and an edge to her tone. "But it cannot be. Who even knows where he is?"

She crossed to the rosewood table. Uncorking a decanter, she poured a deep red into two crystal goblets and handed one to him.

"Let's drink to the beautiful piece you created." She tilted her glass and clinked it against his, then took a sip of the chicken's blood, stifling the urge to wrinkle her nose, while her papa downed his in several quick swallows.

"Are you going out tonight?" James inquired from over the rim of his goblet.

"I'm tired. I think I'll stay in."

It wasn't weariness keeping her from the hunt tonight; it was disappointment. She'd gone out every night since that fateful meeting in the alley looking for him only to return home hungry, not for blood but for his kiss.

"What troubles you, Pruddy?"

Her father's voice called her away from her thoughts of Stede Bonham. "I met a man," she answered truthfully. "I thought perhaps I might see him again, but apparently not."

James Hightower gave his daughter a sympathetic look. She seemed to be having such a difficult time adjusting to an immortal state, while he had taken to it without care. But then, he was old and had already known the love that comes but once in a lifetime. He thought of his beautiful Margaret and could still hear her humming softly to herself while she wove silken fabrics in the garret room of their Spitelfields house back in London. Lovely, gay Margaret who had turned so unexpectedly disagreeable and sad. He hadn't understood what caused her to smash her loom to pieces and throw herself off the London Bridge. But then Pruddy explained that business about the witch Lienore inhabiting the body of Margaret's sister, Vivienne, and before that, of Margaret herself. No wonder Margaret had chosen death over such a cruel fate. He himself had been a victim of Lienore's wicked intentions when, in the person of Vivienne, she had tried to drain the life force from him and would have succeeded had not Nicolae come in the nick of time to snatch him from the jaws of death.

Immortality was a strange gift indeed. Yes, it made him a creature of the night, but except for the unpleasant reality of subsisting on blood, it was not without its appeal. It enabled him to play his beloved violoncello and pass on his musical knowledge to his students, albeit during evening lessons when the sun had gone down. All in all, it was not that disagreeable a state, considering that the alternative would have been the cold, finality of death.

But Pruddy was young yet, and except for her brief betrothal to the pewterer, Edmund de Vere, what chance was there for her to find true love? Not that there had been anything true about Edmund, who had revealed himself to be a member of the Sanctum and used Pruddy as bait to snare Nicolae. Edmund had turned up quite dead, and even though it was never proved, there could be little doubt that it had been at Nicolae's fangs.

James heaved a sigh when he thought of the tangled web surrounding his daughter. He had hoped she might come to love Nicolae, for then, at least she would have a companion for all eternity, but she hated Nicolae for the act that doomed her to immortality. And now there was a man, a mortal, to whom she was attracted. A dangerous liaison to be sure. Only heartache waited for one such as her falling in love with a mortal. His heart went out to his daughter, for the disappointment shone plainly on her face. Yet it was for the best, he supposed.

"Pruddy." He spoke her name tenderly. "Love will come in time."

She turned toward him, blue eyes brimming with sadness, and said in an unconvinced tone, "Yes, Papa."

He was about to say more when the door to the music room opened and Babette entered. "There's a man to see you Madame."

"Who can be calling at this hour?" James asked.

"It must be the man from the dressmaker's shop," said Pru. "He promised to have my new dresses delivered tonight."

"Must be him," said Babette. "He carries a big bundle."

"Show him in please, Babette." Pru rose and started for the door. "This will only take a few minutes Papa. Why don't you play the Prelude from Bach's Suite Number Five? I've always loved that one."

In the foyer a man was waiting, a package wrapped in brown paper draped over his arm.

"*Merci,*" Pru said as she approached. "You can leave it on the chair."

He turned to her then, and her heart leapt into her throat when she found herself looking into smiling gray eyes.

"Mr. Bonham," she exclaimed, trying hard to convey a calmness she did not feel. "What brings you here?"

"This," he replied. He placed the bundle on the chair and stood back. "Well? Aren't you going to open it?"

She hesitated.

"Hell, Pru, there's not a gator inside. It won't bite."

There it was again, that lovely cadence of speech with its strangely falling accents.

She wet her lips and moved closer, all too conscious of her heartbeat growing more erratic with each step.

"Whatever can it be?" she mused as she gingerly untied the string and opened the folds of brown paper.

She gasped.

Inside, was a dress of blue silk.

"I picked it because it reminded me of the color of your eyes," he said.

"You bought this for me?"

"I didn't exactly buy it."

She shot him a disbelieving look. "You stole it?"

Speaking proudly, he said, "We took a Spanish galleon a few months back and this was part of the loot."

Pru drew back from the dress. "Oh no, I couldn't accept it."

"Why not? I owe you a dress after splashing mud on the other one. Besides, this one was probably on its way to some wealthy plantation owner's wife upriver. She can always send for another one." He chuckled, and added, "Which I'll probably relieve her of, if I'm lucky."

Pru wasn't certain if he meant he would relieve the plantation owner's wife of the dress before it reached its destination or while she was wearing it.

The dress was quite simply the most beautiful thing she'd ever seen. Unlike the sheer muslin fabrics that were so fashionable, this was heavy silk brocade woven with silver threads that captured the light of the candles like tiny jewels. Its square neckline was cut considerably lower than all of the evening dresses in her *armoire* and meant to reveal as much of the pale flesh of her bosom as decency would allow. The sleeves were short and trimmed with the same exquisite lace adorning the hem.

"It can get mighty chilly here in Nawlins in the winter, and those muslin dresses you women like aren't suitable."

"Mr. Bonham—" she began.

He staunched her objection with a chastising look. "Now Pru, it's not nice for two people who shared a kiss to be so formal, is it?"

"That was a mistake. An error in judgment, if you will. I never meant—"

"To like it so much?" he cut in.

"Are you suggesting that I took some kind of pleasure in being kissed by a perfect stranger?"

"Not at all," he countered. "I never said I was perfect."

"Stede," she said sweetly, "thank you for the gift, but I would hardly know where to wear it."

"You can wear it when you're with me."

Pru's heart thumped in her chest. Papa's words suddenly filled her thoughts. *Love will come in time.* Could this be it? Was this the man with whom she might find love? Or was he interested only in the pleasure of relieving her of the dress?

"Didn't you say women are not allowed on board your ship?" she asked, testing him.

"That's right. I was thinking you could be with me right here in Nawlins."

Her pulse quickened. "I suppose we could meet from time to time."

"I was thinking on a more regular basis."

She tried not to show her eagerness. "Yes, I think I would like that."

"Good. I'll come by tomorrow around noon and we'll go for a ride along the river. I'd rather not be seen around town, if you don't mind." He ran a hand over his neck to remind her of the hangman's noose.

Pru prayed he couldn't hear the wild beating of her heart as she walked him to the door. "Of course. The river. That would be fine. I'll see you then."

He paused to look at her with a gaze that melted over her face. "You're a fine-looking woman, Pru."

She swallowed hard and lowered her lashes demurely.

"And who knows? Maybe one of these days you'll even trust me with whatever it is you're hiding behind those sad eyes of yours."

She opened the door, straining to keep her thoughts from showing on her face. "Good night, Stede."

"Good night, Pru." He turned to go, then stopped and turned back around, cocking his head to one side. "That's real pretty music."

She'd been so caught up in the warm sensations flooding through her she hadn't even been aware of the strains of the Prelude coming from the music room. "That's my papa. He plays the violoncello. He's quite masterful at it."

"It sounds a lot like the music I heard the last time I went to Bayou Saint John to hunt gators."

"That's not possible," Pru said. "No one plays like Papa. He was the music master back home in London."

Stede slapped his plumed hat onto his head. "Well, someone plays just like him. Heard it with my own two ears coming from one of the Creole cottages along the bank."

Chapter 4

*T*he bayou was a marshy, sluggish place where alligators floated like fallen logs and cottonmouths slithered across the dark waters. At a spot where the water curved like a crescent, tucked behind magnolia and sweet olive trees, was a small cottage.

Pru peered through the darkness at the pastel-painted exterior covered with half-timbering and mud-and-moss plastering. A wide, central chimney reached toward the night sky and starlight fell across its continuous-pitch roof and porches. A warm yellow light glowed through its louvered doors and windows.

She crept silently forward, her feet barely skimming the shell and pebble walk lined with columbine, rudbeckia and purple cone flowers. Her nose picked up the scent of the moist earth beneath a thick patch of maidenhair fern and yarrow. With her gaze sweeping in a slow arc, scanning the shadows for treachery, she approached the front porch. Her ears were tuned to the slightest sound, but all she heard was the croaking of bullfrogs in the swampy water and crickets chirping in some far-off tussock.

Stede had to be mistaken about the music. She knew of only one person who could make the violoncello come alive as if it sang with a human voice, ironic considering the person with that power wasn't even human. Could Stede's untrained ears have mistaken the Cajun fiddle for a violoncello? She was about to back away and fade into the night when the air suddenly filled with sound. She froze like a deer in the forest as the music swept over her, spiraling her back to a place and time she wanted to forget.

There was only one instrument that could create such a mournful sound, only one musician who could coax such melancholy emotion from it. Pru shut her eyes tight against the onrush of memories. She'd heard this piece played once before in a lonely garret room in Hanover Square. The Bridge of Light he had called it, composed just for her, named for the London Bridge on which they'd met and for the light he claimed she brought into his life.

Stede had been right. It was a violoncello being played, and Pru did not have to see the face of the musician to know who he was.

His music was like a siren, beckoning her to come closer. Moving now with a will outside of her own, she climbed the half-dozen steps to the gallery porch that ran the length of the façade. Before her stood French doors of cypress wood whose panels were weathered and scarred with the rough patina of age and nature. She squinted through the window panes of old crown glass and saw the distorted candle flame from within. A rusted box lock was open. Who but a vampire would keep his door unlocked in a place such as this? With a trembling hand she opened the door and stepped inside.

Two rooms filled the front of the cottage. In the parlor candles burned on a mantle that wrapped around the chimney breast and touched the wall. The ceilings were tall, drawing the hot, sultry air to the upper part of the room. The walls and woodwork were painted in a palette of yellow ochre and walnut brown.

As it had done so long ago at the house in Hanover Square, the music trapped her in its spell, drawing her closer. She passed through the front rooms, following the melodic trail to a back room dimly lit by the light of a single candle. The door was ajar. Her breath stilled as she stepped inside.

He looked dark and magnificent against the flickering candlelight. His eyes were closed, his head bent. The painted and gilded instrument that had once belonged to a king of France was held like a lover against his chest with a touch that was as tender and possessive as she knew his touch to be.

The music moved through her like blood, rich and deep and nourishing, spreading heat through her veins and life into her being. She swayed beneath its rhapsodic power. Only he could summon this depth of emotion in her with a mere passing of the bow across the strings.

He drew the music from the instrument the way he made love, passionately one moment, harshly the next, but always and ever with a consummate hand that knew how to coax the chords and notes as skillfully as it knew how to reduce her to writhing pleasure. She could have listened to him play forever, for it was only when he was creating a magical realm such as this that she did not hate him.

"I knew you would come."

His voice, that sweet, spellbinding voice though barely a whisper, was filled with the arrogance that was so much a part of him. All the old feelings of contempt and disdain came rushing back.

"How did you know I was in New Orleans?" she asked, not bothering to hide her scorn.

The music ceased.

"I merely followed the trail of bloodless corpses." He rose, removed the instrument from its endpin, and placed it carefully in its velvet-lined case. "I must say, Prudence, you're not very neat about it, are you?"

She turned her face away from those green eyes that glowed out of the darkness like emerald beacons and held the power to mesmerize, and said flippantly, "I am what you made me."

"I didn't make you to be so sloppy about it."

"I'm not here to discuss my feeding habits with you."

"Why are you here?"

"I want to know why you followed me to America."

"Oh now Prudence, self-flattery is so unbecoming."

She detested that mocking voice. "All right, if you didn't follow me, what are you doing here?"

"I've been here quite often these past few decades. The Americans were fighting their war for independence, or perhaps you were too busy cavorting about the globe to notice. The pickings were wonderful. Who was to notice another dead colonial when they were all over the place anyway? And, of course, there were all those redcoats running around. I do so love the taste of English blood."

He said this with a devious smile that would have made the color drain from her face were she not already so pale. "You'll never have a taste of my English blood again," she spat.

"Again you flatter yourself. What makes you think I want it?"

"Because I recognize that look in your eyes."

He floated toward her. "Yes," he said, looking strongly into her eyes, "I do hunger for you. That much has not changed in all these years. When I saw you in Paris, looking so beautiful beneath the lamplight, I had all I could do to restrain myself. Everything about you thrills me. Even your disdain for me. It used to be your innocence that I found so compelling. Now it is your self-assuredness, your pluck, your treachery that draws me to you."

"Do you forget that I tried to kill you for what you did to me?"

"That's something one does not forget."

"Or that I would try again?"

"Even that does not deter me. You are my creation, Prudence. You are mine."

"I will never be yours, Nicolae."

His name spilling from her lips pushed him almost beyond reason. "And if I were to take you on the floor the way we did it in the garret room in my house in Hanover Square?"

The heat rose to her face, flushing it with momentary color before receding and returning it to its deathlike pallor.

"There is my answer," he said arrogantly.

Her guard went up against the danger of his kiss and the threat of what his touch could do to her. In all the years since she fled London no man had ever made her feel as sublimely decadent as this one. He had taught her scandalous ways to make love and taken her to heights she'd never imagined possible.

She stiffened and turned quickly away. "Don't touch me."

"You weren't always so reluctant. In fact, I seem to recall our last evening in London. You were—how shall I put it—quite the little glutton for pleasure. Granted, you did plunge a poker into my heart afterwards, but not before you put on the most marvelous display of wanton sexuality I have ever experienced."

"Don't remind me," Pru huffed.

"What will your pirate think, I wonder, when he finds out you are not as innocent as you appear?"

With a gasp, Pru came forward in a rush, and in a voice angry and threatening, she warned, "Stay away from him."

"Pirate's blood doesn't interest me," he scoffed. "Not when there is so much sweeter Creole blood around for the taking. But what about you, Prudence? Are you so sure you can resist the temptation to drink from your pirate's throat?"

"I wouldn't do that."

"Of course not," he said, amused. "You will fornicate with him first. Well, that's understandable. I would be a fool to think you would remain celibate forever."

"I'll do more than that with him." Her voice held a hint of dangerous expectation.

He raised a dark, questioning brow, but even he was not prepared for her answer.

"I will fall in love with him."

A familiar look flashed through his eyes, not of petulant danger, but of a wounded animal. It was the kind of distressed confusion she'd seen before, reminding her that beneath the impenetrable exterior of the vampire lurked a human vulnerability.

He turned his face aside to hide it. "Why would you want to fall in love with a common pirate?"

"He is easy to fall in love with. He is kind and gentle and generous. He has an agreeable nature. And he is oh so good looking."

"Enough!"

"You asked."

He turned back to her. "What will happen when he finds out that you kill people and drink their blood? Will you turn him into one of us?"

"I told you I would never do that."

He went on in the same ruthless tone. "What will it be like for you then, watching him grow old and die? That's what will happen, you know."

Pru put her hands over her ears to block out his spiteful voice.

He gripped her wrists, fingers closing painfully as he pulled her hands away. "There can never be any future for you with him, or with any mortal man."

"Future?" she cried. "What future is there for me now? You robbed me of whatever future I might have had. I might have married—"

"Who? Edmund de Vere? The vampire hunter who tried to burn you alive in the distillery?" he cut in, sarcasm dripping like blood from his lips.

"I might have had children. A family of my own. Now there is nothing for me."

He reached for her in a swift, undetectable motion and pulled her hard against him. "There is me. There will always be me."

He brought his mouth down on hers in a kiss that defied all logic, reminding her with the power of his lips the undeniable fact that they were alike. The same bloodlust drove them. The same hunger for carnal pleasure.

She pulled her mouth from his. "Let go of me!" Pushing herself away with a mighty shove, she backed away from him. "I want to know something."

He turned away with a bored expression. "Don't ask me again why I did it. I told you why. You were dying, and I couldn't let that happen."

She narrowed her eyes at his strange inhuman beauty. "Oh yes," she uttered with smooth disdain, "so you made me into this...this...thing like yourself. We have already established that there is no end to your selfishness. But no, that's not it. I want to know why I am so different from Papa. Why can he exist on chicken blood when only human blood will do for me? Why is it he cannot tolerate the bright light but I can? Why am I so much like...*you*?" This last word was spoken with all the vehemence that had been festering inside of her these long decades.

His eyes caught the lingering light of the candle that had nearly burned down to its nub. He smiled, a thin curve of the mouth, and sighed. With a tight catch in his throat, he said, "When I found you lying face down in that puddle, having been thrown from the window, I knew of only one way to save you. Yes, yes, I know, call me selfish. Call me every name you can think of. But when I pierced my vein and gave you my blood to drink, I did so out of love."

He walked to the window and for several moments stood gazing out upon the reflection of the moon in the crescent of water. His eyes closed as the image came back to him of Pru draped lifelessly across his arms, the beat of her heart growing fainter and fainter. He winced as the emotion surged back as if it had been yesterday.

"I'm waiting."

Her restive voice drew him away from his thoughts. "Ah, there it is," he said, his breath falling upon the window pane, "the same impatience you showed that night when you drank from my heart."

He turned around to face her. "When Lienore, in the form of your Aunt Vivienne, had drained your father's life force to the point of death, I gave him only what he needed to survive, but you, dear Prudence, were such an impatient, greedy little thing, I could not stop you from drinking the blood I offered from my vein. When I was finally able to pull your mouth away, you had drunk far more than you should have." He sauntered over to the music case and looked down at the violoncello nestled against the red velvet. "That is why you hunger for the taste of human blood. That is why you can tolerate the bright light. That is why you are so much like…me."

To his surprise she began to laugh and he felt a rush of resentment. "You find that amusing?"

"Yes," she managed between breaths. "Yes, I do. It looks like you got more than you bargained for." The laughter died with a long, low sigh as she started for the door. "I'm tired of hating you."

He moved silently and swiftly to block her path. "Then stop."

"I have no reason to stop. I am reminded of how much I hate you every time I see a happy couple walking arm in arm. I hate you every time the grit of soil disturbs my sleep because I must travel with soil from my native London. When I am unable to preen before a mirror as all women like to do because there is no reflection, I hate you."

"And do you also hate this?" His hand caressed her breast through the thin muslin of her dress. "And this?" With his other hand he reached down and cupped the soft mound between her legs.

She stood there, silent and solemn as his hands slid over her, awakening her flesh in ways he was so good at doing. She could have pulled away, but she didn't. A calculated thought entered her mind. Why should she not take her pleasure with him? She would use him, allow him to take her to an unimaginable climax and then leave. She didn't have to love him to fulfill her sexual needs with him.

A low, protracted moan issued from his throat when she slipped her hand between their bodies and closed her fingers around his swollen phallus through the fabric of his breeches. She could have drawn it out and stroked and petted it the way she used to do. She could have dropped to her knees and taken it into her mouth the way he had taught her to do so long ago. She could have hiked up her dress and guided it into her entrance and let him thrust into her.

But suddenly an image loomed in her mind, of a pirate's handsome face and reckless smile and eyes not green but gray. She pulled back with a groan. "I can't do this."

He didn't' let go. "Why not?" His voice was a raspy plea. "You want me. I can see it in your eyes. And I want you. God, Prudence, how I want you."

She shook her head violently. "No, I don't. I can't let you do this to me." She broke away and ran to the door.

He did not follow. She paused with her hands on the French doors and turned over her shoulder to look at him. He stood there looking dejected, his mouth sulky, his eyes concealed beneath a sweep of dark lashes. But she knew him well enough to know there was much more going on inside of him. He was hurt. Well, what did he expect, that she would submit herself to him as if nothing had happened? She refused to be swayed by the pain she saw in his eyes. He was, after all, such a clever manipulator.

Pushing past the telltale weakness that had always accompanied his touch, she hissed, "I shall hate you until the day I die. Oh, that's right, I can't die, can I?"

The vulnerable moment passed swiftly and his green eyes darkened to a frigid shadow by the dying light of the candle. His voice took on a mocking note. "Save the dramatics for the stage."

"Go back to your music, Nicolae."

"Nicholas."

"What?"

"I call myself Nicholas now. It's more befitting the time and the place, don't you agree?"

"Damn you, it makes no difference to me what you call yourself." Pushing the doors open, she fled into the night.

***

She hated him. As if he didn't already hate himself.

She damned him. As if he weren't already damned to this eternal existence.

Her words rankled in his brain. He should have known that once she came to know him for what he really was her feelings of warmth and affection would change, and she would realize that what she thought was his soul was just a demon in disguise. She claimed to hate him because of what he'd done to her, but he realized with sudden clarity that she'd begun to hate him long before that.

Why had he revealed himself to her back in London all those years ago? What weakness led to such a fatal blunder to think she could be trusted with his dark secret? He should have kept his true nature to himself, used her for the pleasure she provided, drained her blood and been on his merry way, just as he'd done with all the other women over the centuries.

Only she could make him run contrary to his true nature. Only she could lift him from the eternal misery in which he was drowning, offer him hope to cling to as if it were a lifeline, and then cut him loose to drift further and further out upon a sea of loneliness. He'd been going about his life, such as it was, without care or caution, until she came along with her prim little ways, so guileless as to think him capable of possessing a soul. A silly, naïve little mouse in the clutches of a powerful predator. Until she unwittingly turned the tables on him, and then he was no longer so sure who was the one in danger.

He didn't know how it happened, only that it did. After centuries of restless yearning and finally giving up hope of ever finding it, there it was. Love. To his eternal regret he had fallen in love with her. He was hopelessly, desperately, uncharacteristically in love. Even when she plunged a poker into his heart all those years ago in London, stupidly thinking it could kill him, even then he loved her. If it had been a hawthorn stake she had used, he would have been destroyed with one last word upon his dying lips— Prudence. Not that a poker hadn't done sufficient damage. But by the time he had recovered and gotten back to his old self, she was long gone.

It hadn't been difficult picking up her trail in those early years. He wasn't exaggerating when he accused her of being a sloppy killer. She was, in the beginning at least. Now, of course, she was a much more accomplished predator. Like himself, he thought with a dash of pride, a swift and silent killer.

That's when she became difficult to find, covering her kills much more skillfully. It was only by coincidence that he'd found her in Paris, when he'd been drawn, like she and her father, to the concert. And he hadn't even known she was in New Orleans until he spied her one night moving amongst the tombs in the cemetery.

She might like to think he was in New Orleans because of her, vain little thing that she was, but in reality, it was another whose trail he had followed to these soggy bayous.

Lienore.

He'd never much minded that witch. Oh, her tactics were dreadful enough. There was something so covertly undignified about sucking the life force from an unsuspecting mortal. His method was more direct. One, two, three and they were done. No unnecessary suffering there. But ever since Prudence came up with that preposterous story about reclaiming the soul through a witch's chant, he'd been searching for the one witch powerful enough to restore the soul that was lost to him.

She was an elusive quarry, however, flitting from body to body as she was so fond of doing, draining the life force out of them, reducing them to husks of skin and bone, and then moving on to another. The last time he'd seen her was in London where she'd been inhabiting the body of Prudence's Aunt Vivienne. He hadn't the heart to tell Prudence that after Lienore hurled her out the window she fled, leaving Vivienne's body a cold and lifeless corpse that he buried in the bog. For all Prudence knew, Lienore was still within Vivienne's amply endowed body. But he knew otherwise.

After London he heard the stories whispered in dark corners by others of his kind who recognized Lienore's sinister trappings. The stories led him from one place to another, one country to the next, searching, always searching for the witch with the power to chant the spell that would reclaim his lost soul.

His search led him to America, and here to New Orleans, where voodoo worship in the steamy bayou was just the kind of thing to attract an entity as malicious as Lienore. Perhaps the ceremonies reminded her of the primitive Celtic rituals and the witchcraft she practiced in her ancient Dubh Lein. Or maybe she was attracted to the abundance of voluptuous Creole and Cajun bodies from which to choose. Whatever drew her to these marshy bayous, he sensed her presence here as keenly as he sensed the nearness of blood.

But she was an elusive creature, wrecking her malignant hatred on the mortal world. If it took all of eternity, he would find her. But when he did, how would he trick her into uttering the spell? And if he succeeded and was able to reclaim his lost soul, what difference would it make if Prudence refused to join him in mortality as she had once refused his dark gift?

Prudence again. Always it came back to Prudence. The thought of her loving another man sent him into a ferociously jealous rage. He was tempted to find her pirate and snap his neck like a twig, but if he did that, Prudence would only hate him more than she already did. There was nothing he could do except cling to the hope that her infatuation would run its course. And when it did, when her pirate lover learned what she was and turned his back on her, he would be there to pick up the pieces of her broken heart.

He wasn't about to give up, not when he had waited centuries for someone like her to come along. Someone who saw him for what he was underneath the blood and gore, a man, just a man. She hadn't always hated him. Those nights in London when he had played his music for her, music she claimed could only come from the soul, she hadn't known then that he was a soulless creature, and yet she had seen something in him that no one else saw. If she could just see beyond the gloom and shadow of their existence and embrace the dark gift, she might come to appreciate it and, in time, maybe even come to love him. He would wait. What choice did he have?

The more he thought about it, however, the angrier he became until the anger surged through him like a tidal wave, washing away all logic and reason. He tried to fight it but it was no use. He longed for peace, the kind he'd briefly known all those years ago in London when the music master's daughter had reached out to him and he had found in that timid mouse of a woman a chance at the happiness that eluded him for centuries.

With a low moan, he shut his eyes tight to block out the images springing from out of the past. Images of Prudence, so tender and trusting, meekly surrendering to his powers. But she was no longer as humble and submissive as she'd been in those days. She had come into her full powers and was a force to be reckoned with. The timid mouse was now a tigress with claws sharp enough to kill his hope. They were equals now, and he only loved her more for it.

He shook with frustration. Her pirate would never love her the way he did. To love someone for who you thought they were was a fool's love. To see someone for who and what they really were and to love them not only in spite of it but because of it, that was a love worth having. Why couldn't she see that? He wanted to kill. To wreck vengeance against a world that shut him out of its glorious light and kept him a creature of the darkness, unworthy of love.

As he stalked about the cottage a different kind of lust began to seep slowly, insidiously into his being. This was a powerful lust that had nothing to do with Prudence, a lust over which he had no control and would not wait. He could feel it growing steadier and stronger inside of him. His thoughts shifted menacingly from Prudence to the one thing he could not survive without. Blood.

Chapter 5

The curricle followed the river road past the columned galleries of the Creole houses built of cypress standing amid lush gardens and trees dripping with Spanish moss, and the white pillared houses of the sugar planters with their accompanying mills and rows of slave quarters.

Stede's hands were relaxed on the reins as he led the high-stepping horse along the curving road, following the twists and turns of the river. Seated beside him in the two-wheeled carriage, wearing the dress he had plundered from the Spanish galleon, Pru remarked, "Please don't tell me you plundered this carriage, too."

He laughed. "No, it's mine."

"Where do you live when you're not pirating?"

Delighting in her forthright manner, he answered, "I have a cottage just outside of town."

Pockets of fog rolled off the river to wrap spidery tendrils around the trees rooted in the pliant bank. They rode under a dense canopy formed by ancient live oaks. With no bright sunlight to fear, and a parasol handy just in case, Pru sat back, relaxing in the warm, sultry air to the steady clop, clop of the horse's hooves.

"I brought something for you in case you're hungry," he said. Reaching behind him, he drew out a small box and placed it in her lap. She opened the lid and smiled. Inside, were several *beignets*, fresh and still warm. The aroma of the puff pastry and powdered sugar was too much to ignore. She reached for one, but he stopped her. "You might want to take your gloves off for those."

Drawing off the gloves that reached to her elbows, she selected one took a bite.

"Hey, what about me?"

She offered the box to him.

"I can't take my hands off the reins. You'll have to feed it to me. Well, come on. You don't want me to starve, do you?"

She happily obliged by holding a *beignet* to his mouth. When he got down to the last bite, he surprised her by licking the powdered sugar from her fingers. The tickling sensation turned more intimate when he drew her forefinger into his mouth and gently sucked on it. A pleasurable sensation shot through Pru at the familiarity of his act, and though she wished it would go on, she became flustered and pulled her hand away.

He smiled that infectious, boyish smile of his, and said, "Have I told you how pretty you look today?"

"Yes. Several times, in fact."

"Well, it bears repeating. I was right choosing that dress for you. It matches the color of your eyes so well. You're a beautiful woman, Pru. Much too beautiful to be wearing white all the time. You're so pale, white doesn't do you justice. I say leave the white to the virgins."

Pru sucked in her breath at that, but before she could voice her offence, he went on in a casual voice. "I could tell right off. A woman doesn't have that look in her eyes unless she's been with a man. Don't get me wrong, it's all right with me. With a virgin it's usually no, no, no, when what she really means is yes, yes, yes. No thanks. I'll take a woman any day who knows what she wants. One who says yes and means it."

"Is that why you've invited me on this ride today?" Pru asked.

He looked at her with an expression of utter truth on his face. "Hell no. I asked you because I wanted your company. Although..." His eyes sparkled devilishly. "Watching you eat that thing sure does put some wicked thoughts in my head."

For an instant she thought she might slap him for his impudence, but she broke out in laughter instead. They understood each other perfectly.

Grasping the reins in one hand, with his free hand he reached for hers.

With her shoulder touching his, she reveled in the strength and warmth of him.

"Your hand is so cold," he said.

Pru stiffened, and her guard went up around her. She now regretted having removed her gloves.

The fog that came off the river shrouded the trees. "Maybe it's the fog," he said. "It'll burn off soon enough."

But the cold would never go away, Pru thought dismally. It was one of the first things she had noticed about Nicolae, or Nicholas, or whatever he was calling himself these days. She had naively thought he was ill, and even when he'd been burning up with passion as though a fire raged within, still his skin had been cold to the touch. He had explained it all to her, telling her the chilling story of the night he was made into the creature that he was, playing upon her sympathy. But Stede was neither a gullible fool nor likely to be swayed by her sorry tale. She didn't want to tell him that after a kill, with fresh blood pumping through her, she was as warm as fresh-baked bread, so in anticipation of the fog burning off, she said, "There's something about the fog and mist from the river that makes me feel cold all the time."

An impish smile played across his lips and his fingers tightened suggestively around hers. "We'll have to see what we can do about that."

Despite her inner warnings, her hand in his felt like the most natural thing in the world. "I thought you couldn't take your hands off the reins."

"I lied."

She settled back, feeling secure in the warmth of his hand. "Where are we going?"

"To a spot I know."

The sun peeked through the dense canopy to dapple the winding river road. Stede appeared to know exactly where he was going, and Pru caught herself wondering how many other women he had driven to the spot he knew. She told herself it didn't matter. After all, neither of them were innocents. And yet, the though of him making love to another woman filled her with uncharacteristic jealousy. Even more unsettling was the possibility that he had been in love with any of them. Would he…could he…ever fall in love with her?

He guided the carriage to a spot along the levee and pulled up on the reins. Jumping out, he went around to her side. His hands going around her waist as he lifted her down sent a little tremor through her.

"Come on," he said," we can sit down over there." He led her to a grassy spot beneath the spreading limbs of a live oak.

The voluminous skirt of Pru's dress cascaded over the ground like a waterfall when she sat down. Stede dropped to the ground beside her and leaned back on his elbows.

"I like coming down to the river," he said. "There's something magical about the way the water moves in the sunlight. It makes me homesick for the smell of the sea."

The gentle slush of the water was like a lullaby, a soft, lulling sound that calmed even Pru's restless heart.

He liked the smell of the sea and the taste of *beignets*. But there was so much more about him that she wanted to know. Did he drop sugar cubes into his coffee? Did he put his right boot on before the left?

"Have you brothers or sisters?" she asked.

Stede shook his head. Plucking a blade of grass, he touched it to his lips. "When I was a boy, I'd sneak off from doing my chores and head over to one of the big plantations to watch the slaves chop the cane with their big knives and haul it in big-wheeled carts pulled by mules over to the sugar house. During the fall harvest they grind the cane day and night. Some of it they make into syrup that they sell, but most of it is made into sugar. There's nothing like the smell of fall in the air and the sweet smell of the sugar cane and syrup. Except maybe the smell of the sea and the salt spray washing over the *Evangeline's* decks. And the smell of a woman." His look turned pensive and his voice lowered. "It's funny how something like a smell can bring back memories."

Pru's heart lurched. So, there had been a woman in his past, not just any woman at any port, but one who put that look of bittersweet remembering on his face.

"Yes," she said softly, "it's like that for me and strawberries."

She would be forever haunted by the smell of the sweet, ripe strawberries she tasted at Nicolae's house all those years ago when she'd gone there to hear him play the piece he finished for her papa.

Papa had been too ill to complete the composition or to play his beloved violoncello. Of course, she didn't know at the time that the reason was because Lienore, in the form of poor Aunt Vivienne, was slowly and insidiously draining his life. Nor could she have known that the sweet taste of strawberries would lead to scandalous pleasure at the hands of a clever debaucher and how her life would be drastically altered by the events of that night.

"What was she like?" she ventured.

"Who?"

"The woman you loved."

He tapped the blade of grass against his lips as though contemplating whether or not to share the memory with her. "Women don't usually want to hear about the other women in a man's life." He gave her a sidelong glance and a teasing smile. "But something tells me you're not like other women."

He lay back in the grass and let the past flow over him like the sultry river breeze. "Her name was Evangeline. Her father was a wealthy Creole landowner and her mother was from the *gens de coleur libres,* the free people of color. You probably know some."

"Yes, my servant, Babette." But it wasn't Babette's image that sprang into Pru's mind. It was that of the free man of color who had murdered the nun and into whose throat she sank her fangs. "Was Evangeline very beautiful?"

"She had skin like glass and hair that fell in dark waves to her waist. If there was anything on this earth that could have kept me from going to sea, it would have been her. But not just because of her beauty. She had spirit and intelligence, and when she laughed, it was like a sound from heaven. I know that must sound crazy to you."

"No, it doesn't sound crazy at all." The closest thing to heaven Pru had ever experienced was the music that flowed from Nicolae's violoncello, but to tell Stede about it would have led to telling him things she dared not reveal. "You and she never married?"

In a voice tinged with bitterness, he said, "She was fifteen, the age when a girl's mother goes in search of a wealthy benefactor for her daughter. It wouldn't have been so bad if she at least had gone to a man who could love her as much as I did, but her mother chose instead a fat, balding, pompous planter from upriver who was old enough to be her grandfather. She wept in my arms the night before he took her away."

"Why didn't you run away with her?"

"She would never have shamed her mother like that. No, the contract was sealed and there was nothing she could do about it."

"And you never saw her again?"

"Oh, I saw her all right. The day they buried her. Her tomb is in the St. Louis Cemetery. Her life must have been too much to bear, so she started going into the bayou at night with the old man's slaves and taking part in their voodoo ceremonies."

"And her husband found out about it?"

"Husband?" he echoed. "Hell, they were never married. When the old man found out she was going into the bayou at night, I guess he was afraid she'd become a voodoo queen like her mother."

"Her mother?" Pru asked, her suspicion piqued.

"Sabine Sejour. The most powerful voodoo queen in Nawlins."

Pru shuddered. Yes, she supposed a woman who would rip the heart out of a man would have no qualms about selling her daughter to the highest bidder. "I've heard of her," she said, without revealing the sordid details of what she knew.

"Who hasn't?" he said dryly.

"Tell me about her."

"Much of it is common knowledge. Don Ramon de Lopez, a sugarcane planter from Santo Domingo, brought her to Nawlins and kept her as his mistress. When he died, she bought her freedom and married Jean Laveau and was known for the big galas at her home on Rue Royale. When Laveau died, she married a Creole landowner and moved upriver with him. She probably picked up her voodoo magic in Saint-Domingue with the other slaves. There was some talk that she'd taken up with one of the slaves who was a voodoo priest. When she returned to Nawlins, she told fortunes and made charms and potions. There were other voodoo queens but she got rid of them by hexing them until she was the only one left. If you ever need a spell or potion or some good *gris-gris*, she's the one to go to."

"What happened to Evangeline's father?"

"He'd been sick for a long time. Nobody could figure it out. He just grew weaker and weaker and finally just died. It was as if he just gave up living. Who knows? Maybe he knew what his wife was up to."

Pru practically choked on her gasp. Just like her papa and Aunt Vivienne and...Lienore.

"Pru? What's the matter? Did my story upset you?" He sat up and wound an arm around her shoulders. "I'm sorry. I didn't mean to turn the day all dark and gloomy with my story. Look. The sun is peeking through the clouds."

She turned her gaze to the late afternoon sunlight that glittered across the water and managed a weak smile. "You named your ship after her."

"Yes. After her death I took to the sea in an old brig I'd bought with my own money. About two weeks out we overtook a French ship, relieved her of her cargo and sent the captain and crew overboard." He shrugged, and explained, "I was in a black mood that day. Anyway, the brig had a deep draft and was able to ride storms and deal with the rough open waters, but she was slow, so I kept the French sloop for myself. She's small and fast and just what I need to get in, get the goods and get out. Now, instead of a French flag, she flies a black flag, and no one who sees her ever forgets she's Stede Bonham's ship."

He studied her closely, noting that her eyes were downcast as if unable to look at him. "You don't approve of what I did to the captain and crew, do you?"

This was the first indication that there was a dark and dangerous side to him. She answered truthfully, "It seems a little harsh."

In an effort to brighten the sullen mood that had fallen over them he pointed overhead to the tree under which they sat, and said, "Did you know that when the live oaks shed their old leaves and put on their new ones at the same time, it means spring is very near? This old tree is probably two hundred years old. Can you imagine anything living that long?"

Inwardly, Pru groaned. Was there nothing they could talk about that did not lead down this dangerous path? Vampires lived that long, and longer. She herself had been living now, both alive and dead, for nearly a century, and Nicolae far longer than that. If it weren't so hideously sad, she might have laughed.

"Stede, let's not talk about the past."

"You're right. There's just one more thing." He took her hand in his and gripped it tightly as he stared into her eyes. "I didn't think I could love anyone as much as I loved Evangeline, but now I'm not so sure." He leaned forward, bringing his head close to hers, and kissed her lightly on the lips.

Her joy surged at the possibility that he might love her. She drew his breath into her being and returned with equal ardor the deepening kiss.

He laid her back against a soft carpet of grass and slid his body on top of hers. "Don't worry," he said, nuzzling her neck, "nobody ever comes to this spot.

Oh, how long it had been since she'd been laid bare to a man, when she had ached for a man's eyes upon her, his hands all over her, his heat filling her up to bursting.

He was a considerate lover, with a slow and steady hand that gentled her for a long, loving time and lips that glided over her skin like skaters on ice. She opened her eyes and gazed at the dark lashes so close to her face, and beyond the green canopy to white wisps of clouds riding in a sapphire sky. Evening was coming upon them, cool and sweet, bathing the land in an opalescent light.

She squirmed beneath his hand that delved deep into her bodice to caress her breasts while his tongue sought the recesses of her mouth, delving in and out like a consummate lover. All around her she could hear the rushing of the river and the sounds of far-off voices of the men on the flatboats coming from throughout the Mississippi Valley with their bounty of goods. The hot green scent of summer rose from the ground, mingling with the ambrosia of his skin, filling her with unspeakable delight.

This was not a mad rush at passion or the heated demands of a selfish lover, but a tender union nearly bringing her to tears. Having been initiated by a lover as harsh and demanding as Nicolae, she never imagined how sweet it could be. All the lovemaking of the past shrank to nothing against the sublime loveliness of this pirate's touch.

When he reached beneath her skirt to cup the silky softness at the apex of her thighs, she felt suddenly shy and apprehensive. His fingers caressed her intimately as his lips pressed wet kisses to her temples, her cheekbones, and the corners of her mouth. She could feel him fumbling with his breeches to extricate his arousal. He pushed her skirt up past her hips and she felt his hardness brush her thighs.

She cried out when he came into her in one swift, sure move, not from pain but from the sheer joy of it, as though she were being taken for the very first time.

Gripping the woven fabric of the breeches at his flanks, she shut her eyes tight and held on to him until she felt him burst within her at the same time that her own climax washed over her. Panting, they clung to each other, thrusting and writhing in the grass.

Her carnal needs had grown so strong over the decades that the thirst to satisfy her sexual cravings had become almost as great as the blood lust over which she had no control. She had known other men intimately through the decades. Nicolae, her vampire lover, was notoriously expert at pleasuring a woman. Others were no more than boys, sweet and fumbling. Some were big and strongly built, some slender and beautiful. Some were men of power and means and some had not a penny to their names. Some she drank from. Some she let live.

But never had she found a man worth loving...until now. Stede Bonham's happy-go-lucky nature and infectious smile were rare treats indeed, and she'd be lying to herself if she said she didn't find his way of life a little bit thrilling, although she could have done without the knowledge that he had killed the captain and crew of the French ship. Aside from that, he was handsome and reckless and personable.

Lying in her pirate's arms in the aftermath of their lovemaking, she felt satisfied, and for the moment, unmindful of the danger of loving a man who was all too mortal.

And yet, although she was sated and satisfied from their lovemaking, she did not have that thoroughly ravished feeling as she had each time Nicolae had taken her, and she felt a little disappointed over it. Stede's was a safe kind of intercourse; Nicolae's was wild and dangerous.

Rolling toward Stede, she placed a kiss on his lips. "Do you think I'm terribly wicked?"

He opened his eyes and looked at her. His face was washed in the glow of sunset that accentuated the handsome boyish features. "I like a woman who knows what she wants." He smiled crookedly. "I have a feeling there's more to you than meets the eye. Next time we'll go to my cottage and you can show me just how wicked you are."

"Next time?"

"Are you free tomorrow night?"

She smiled suggestively.

"Good. I'll send my carriage to pick you up. We'll have dinner, and then, well…" His words trailed off discreetly.

As much as Pru craved his flesh, she wanted so much more than that. "Stede, if all you want is the pleasure of a woman's body, there are so many others to choose from."

"Hey now," he said, disengaging himself and sitting up. "It's not like that. At least not with you. You're right, beautiful women are everywhere. And I'd be lying if I said I don't want your body, but I want more than that from you."

Her lashes fluttered demurely, and she dared to ask, "What do you want?"

"I want to know how you like to be touched. I want to know what you look like in the morning when you wake up. What makes you angry. What makes you happy. What secrets you're hiding. I want it all. Hell, Pru, it's happening so fast. I don't know where all this is leading, but I sure would like to find out."

Pru's heart sang even as a small voice at the back of her mind cautioned against revealing too much of herself until she was sure Stede Bonham could be trusted with her dark secret.

The lights of the old French city lay before them, and the moon hung like a silver disk over the cypresses as the carriage rolled in from the bayou road. It stopped before the house on Rue Bourbon. Stede jumped down and hurried to the other side to help Pru out. Before she could take her leave, he pulled her into his arms and kissed her. His arms were reluctant to let her go. "Tomorrow, then?"

"Tomorrow," she whispered.

She watched him climb back aboard and give the horse a tap of the whip, her heart aflutter as the carriage disappeared down the street.

Chapter 6

The fronds of the banana trees rustled against the galleries running the length of the house, and the courtyard ground was littered with the fallen, ripened fruit of the old lime tree.

Looking up, Pru saw two figures seated on the balcony, the parlor doors open behind them. The fragrance of honeysuckle and orange blossoms filled the air, but it was the perfume of a different sort that chilled her as if a dark wind has passed overhead. She would recognize that sweet, smooth-flowing, evil scent anywhere.

Inside, a sliver of yellow light came from beneath the French doors that opened onto the parlor. Beyond the dark polished wood she heard the clinking of crystal glasses. All thoughts of the tree-lined levee in the moonlight and Stede's silky touch vanished when she threw open the doors.

The parlor was dimly lit by a single candle whose flame danced when she entered, casting shadows across the plaster ceiling. The heavy velvet drapes of the gallery windows were drawn tight. Across the room two figures were silhouetted on the balcony, the dark red blood in their glasses glistening like garnets in the moonlight. What was *he* doing here?

She stood motionless for several moments watching him drain his glass. His movements were elegant and deceiving. There was a noticeable flush on his pale and perfect features, proof that he had recently fed on human blood and not the chicken blood her papa offered from the decanter. No doubt, he was as warm as toast after his killing.

He shifted slightly in his chair. "Are you going to stand there all night, Prudence?"

The sound of his voice, arrogant and mocking, forced movement into her limbs. She came forward across the Oriental carpet to join them on the balcony.

The breeze from the river blew up the ends of her hair. She had not bothered to sweep it up and put the pins back in to hold it in place. The burnished strands, tangled by Stede's fingers, hung long and loose down her back.

"There you are, Pruddy," her papa said. "Did you have a pleasant day, dear?"

Twisting the stem of his glass between his long, elegant fingers, Nicolae cast an all-consuming look over her, and said, "I would venture to guess you had a satisfying day. Although perhaps not as thoroughly satisfying as you might have wished?"

His ability to pinpoint her innermost thoughts made her cringe. She'd always felt stark naked before him, even when fully clothed.

She bent to place a kiss on her papa's cheek. "Yes, Papa, I had an exhilarating day." She aimed a scornful look at Nicolae and saw a lean muscle jump in his cheek, proof that her well-aimed barb hit its target.

"Won't you join us?" James said. "We were just toasting the delightful coincidence of all of us being in New Orleans at the same time."

"How serendipitous," she remarked sourly.

"Nicholas was giving me pointers on how best to live within the confines of our condition."

"Nicholas?" she echoed.

"Our young friend prefers to be called Nicholas now, and we must respect that."

Those green eyes sparkled arrogantly. "We must adapt to the times, Prudence."

She heaved an exasperated sigh. "Like I said, I don't care what you call yourself."

James lifted an inquisitive brow. "Like you said?"

"It's nothing Papa."

"Honestly, how you two do go on." James got up and turned toward the parlor. "I'm going to fetch my latest composition. Do try to be good until I get back."

Pru smiled sweetly. "Yes, Papa."

When he was gone, Nicholas asked, "Do you think he suspects?"

"Suspects what?"

"What you were doing today." He lifted his face and sniffed the air. "I can smell it on you.

"Nicolae, if you—" She stopped abruptly when he turned his face away from her. "Very well, *Nicholas*," she relented with biting sarcasm. Knowing it was useless to deny what she'd been doing, she warned, "If you breathe one word to him, I'll—"

"You'll what? Hate me even more than you already do?"

"*That* would not be possible."

He got up and sauntered to the railing. "You'll just have to trust me to keep your little secret."

She came to stand beside him and cast a disdainful glance over him.

He was dressed impeccably in a frock coat of dark taupe cut velvet with floral silk embroidery meant to look like lace along the edges, matching velvet breeches and a lace jabot at his neck. An ivory silk waistcoat embroidered with bright gold threads captured the starlight. His profile etched against the night was so sublimely beautiful she might have forgotten what a scoundrel he really was.

His was an ethereal beauty, almost as if it had descended from Heaven, refined and perfect down to arch of his brows and the curve of his lips. He'd put on weight and muscle since those nights in London. No longer fragile-looking, now he exuded a visible robustness to match his immortal strength.

How different his pallid handsomeness and tall, well-formed physique was compared to Stede Bonham's stockiness and sun-browned appeal.

Her voice drifted into the stillness. "I'd no sooner trust you than Satan."

He turned his head and looked at her with those astonishingly green eyes that held the power to turn her to liquid with a mere glance. "One day, Prudence, you're going to have need of me. And I don't mean just for the pleasure that only I can give you." He lifted his hand from the iron railing and caressed her breast through the silken fabric of her dress.

"You see?" he went on. "Even now, you do not pull away. Do you remember what it was like for us? Don't tell me you don't dream about it. Long for it. Can your pirate take you to the heights you have been to with me?" At the drawing in of her breath, he chuckled deep in his chest. "I didn't think so." He withdrew his hand. "You and I aren't finished using each other in the most delicious ways."

"You're disgusting," she spat as she flinched away.

"You never thought I was disgusting when I was deep inside of you."

"If I ever come to you, Nicholas, make no mistake, it will be only for that. I will use you and then discard you like yesterday's newspaper."

There was a time when the wince in his beautiful eyes would have made her regret her harsh words, but it didn't now. She wasn't the same timid little creature he'd known in London who took orders blindly from a callous fiancé, avoided confrontation with her outspoken and frivolous Aunt Vivienne, and who succumbed to the otherworldly charms of a vampire. The cold reality of the life he had forced upon her—the dark gift, he called it—had sharpened her edges. She no longer needed others to pave her way. Over the preceding decades she had become self-reliant to a fault, choosing her lovers instead of them choosing her, draining her victims without remorse and following no man's orders. Yes, she might come to him of her own free will, but only to copulate, only when she was burning with the physical need which, like blood, gave her life meaning. She would writhe beneath his thrusting body, taking from him the raw animal power she knew she would never get from Stede Bonham, withholding from him the one thing he wanted above all else. Her love. That was her power over him, and she wielded it like a mighty sword.

"I may want you and need you, but I'll never love you."

In a bored tone, he said, "You have made that abundantly clear on more than one occasion."

She turned to go. "When you're finished with Papa, come to my room. I must speak to you about something important."

Chapter 7

She sat at the vanity, running a hairbrush through her burnished locks, when there drifted into her nostrils not the rot and decay of what one would expect of the undead, but the sweet, alluring fragrance of the vampire. Looking up, she saw nothing in the mirror, not even her own reflection. How many times over the long decades had she gone to the mirror, hoping against hope of seeing something there—a light or a glimmer—something that would remind her of herself? Now, as she had done hundreds of times, she pushed herself away dejectedly and rose.

The muslin dressing gown she wore was lined only in the bodice, the rest sheer enough to show the outline of her legs in the moonlight slanting through the open window. In the glow of the candles the off-white color had an ever-so-slight tint of blue.

His gaze fell upon the small French knot buttons at each side of her bosom, the swell of heaving white flesh accentuated by the high waist and low-cut neckline. He licked his lips, and said from the shadows, "Why Prudence, if I didn't know better, I'd say you invited me here with the intention of seducing me."

"Don't flatter yourself," she said dryly.

He removed his frock coat and tossed it carelessly aside. Passing noiselessly from out of the shadows he sat down on an upholstered chair. The candlelight glimmered over the silken threads of his waistcoat and illuminated the green glow of his eyes. "Of course not. Why would I do that? You'll flatter me quite nicely when you come to me."

She knew the picture she presented in her sheer dressing gown and felt a sense of triumph in the way his eyes raked over her. "Don't be so sure of yourself."

"But I have reason to be. Do you recall that time in London when I said you would come to me of your own free will, and you did?"

The memory flashed through her mind despite the passage of more than seventy years. Her papa had been wasting away, victim of Lienore in the guise of Aunt Vivienne, and Nicolae, which was what he'd been calling himself back then, had claimed to be able to save him. All he had demanded in return was that she come to him of her own free will. And she had, partly in desperation to save her papa, partly because— She tried to block it from her mind, but his words from that night came back to taunt her—cold, hard, irrefutable. *"You are here because you cannot deny what you feel. Just as I cannot deny what I am."* She hadn't grasped the full extent of his meaning until he taught her things that night, shameful, scandalous things, and then, as if that wasn't enough, revealed the terrible truth of what he was.

"I was different then," she said defensively.

"Oh my, yes. You were so prim and proper. So, how shall I put it, unworldly. I, of course, was accustomed to women who were more experienced, but there was something about your virginal innocence that intrigued me. You were such an avid pupil. So hungry to learn all the little tricks and positions. Do you still enjoy doing it like the wolves?"

"You were a very good teacher," she said. "Imagine how delighted my pirate will be by all I learned from you."

That wiped the smile from his face in a hurry. It wasn't just lovemaking tricks he'd taught her. She had also learned from him how to cut and slash down to the heart.

"You said you wanted to speak to me about something important. What is it? I don't have all night. Well, actually, I do, but unless you're going to spread your legs for me or tell me something of monumental importance, I have other places to be."

Ignoring his biting sarcasm, she said, "Have you heard of a woman named Sabine Sejour?"

He sighed with disinterest. "The voodoo priestess."

"She was married to a wealthy Creole landowner who died under mysterious circumstance."

"One of my victims, perhaps?"

"It was not his blood that was drained. It was his life. Slowly and surely. Just like Papa's was all those years ago. And we know who was responsible for that."

A spark of interest ignited in his eyes, turning them from a dark forest green to the color of raw jewels. His lips mouthed the name *Lienore* as he slowly worked the information over in his mind.

"I've seen her," Pru said. "In the bayou. She's beautiful."

He edged forward in his seat. "Lienore chooses only the most beautiful bodies to inhabit." His gaze moved over hers with sly relish, pausing to appreciate the generous breasts pressing against the thin fabric.

"She ripped the heart out of a man."

"She's a nasty thing."

"Nasty? You call ripping a man's heart out nasty? I call it evil."

"Don't forget there are some who would call us evil," he pointed out.

"There's not a day that goes by that I forget," she replied bitterly. "But even you do not kill out of evil."

"How charitable of you."

"Creatures like us cannot help what we are. You told me that once. I didn't understand it then the way I do now. Do you relish the kill? Do you derive joy from it?"

He sank back against the chair. "No," he admitted. "I do not."

"Nor do I. Even when I drain a criminal or a murderer I tell myself I am ridding the world of human garbage, but deep down inside a part of me cries for the loss, not just of another life, but of something within myself that was once human. But that thing I saw in the bayou took pleasure in the kill. I tell you, Nicholas, she held the beating heart in her hand as if it were a trophy."

He glanced up at her, suspicion darkening his eyes. "How did you find out about her?"

"I followed one of my victims to the bayou and watched the terrible ceremony."

"No, I mean how did you find out about the Creole landowner?"

"A friend told me," she said evasively.

He nodded with terse understanding. "Your pirate."

"Yes. But what difference does it make?"

"Does he know what she is?"

"He knows only that she's the mother of a girl he loved."

"Love." The word spilled from his lips like poison.

"Never mind that," Pru said. "It's Lienore. I just know it is."

He got up and walked across the room to the widow. For a long time he stood looking out at the lights that twinkled like stars from the tall French windows of the Spanish colonial houses along Rue Bourbon. He breathed in deeply, filling his being with the scent of oleanders and jasmine, and said without emotion, "What does it matter if it is her?"

Pru rushed up to him in disbelief. "Nicholas, you remember what the alchemist in Clapham said. Only a witch as strong as Lienore can chant the words that will restore our souls."

"Ah, yes, the alchemist. He did so want to unlock the mystery of eternal life. I wonder what became of him."

"As I recall," she said sourly, "you turned him into the undead."

He turned toward her with a devilish smile. "It was the least I could do. But don't feel too sorry for him, Prudence. Don't forget that he wanted to capture me and perform ungodly experiments on me."

Pru's mind raced back to the day she had gone to see the alchemist in the hope of finding a means of reclaiming Nicholas' lost soul. The wizened little man had given her an elixir for her ailing papa and read something from an ancient tome about how a spell chanted by a powerful witch might reclaim what was lost. She'd been appalled by the rat's head she'd seen suspended in a vinegar solution in his laboratory and had gotten herself out of there with all due haste. It had been only Nicholas' lost soul she'd been worried about at the time. Now, of course, it was her own and her papa's. To be human again, to bask in the glorious light of day, to feel her own blood racing through her veins, to love a man like Stede Bonham and be loved back.

"The chant, Nicholas. We must go back to London and find the book that holds the Reclamation Chant. And then we must find a way to make her speak it."

His breath fell against the glass. "It is written in a combination of Gypsy-Romani Romanian and must be spoken as such."

She looked askance at him. "How do you kow that? You didn't see the book."

"I did more than see it, dear Prudence. I took it."

"You mean you stole the Book of Chants from him?"

"Oh, don't pretend to be so shocked. I'm sure your pirate has done his share of stealing. Besides, when I went back to the house in Clapham, our undead alchemist had departed for parts unknown, leaving everything behind. I remembered what you told me about the book from which he read. I found it and thought it might come in handy one day."

"And it looks like that day has arrived. What?" she questioned when she saw the skeptical look on his face. "We need only find a way to trick Sabine into speaking it."

"If the voodoo priestess really is Lienore. We don't know that for certain."

"There's only one way to find out."

He flashed her a warning look. "Stay away from her, Prudence. If it is Lienore, she'll know you for what you are."

"Of course, she will. I remember how Aunt Vivienne detested you because she, or rather Lienore, knew you for what you are." She pulled in a ragged sigh as a thought suddenly occurred to her. "If Lienore is inhabiting Sabine's body, then Aunt Vivienne must be..."

"Dead," he put in.

"I wonder when. How."

"It happened that night." Her eyes turned upon him as he spoke. "You had been through so much I didn't have the heart to tell you then, but I suppose enough time has passed for you to know the truth."

"You choose which truths to tell me and which ones to conceal?" Her temper rose with each word.

"What good would it have done to tell you that your aunt died the night Lienore hurled you through the window? Or that I found her body beside the bed and buried it in the bog? Would knowing have made you feel any better?"

"You didn't hide the truth from me for my sake," she said accusingly. "You did it for yourself so that I wouldn't hate you more than I already did. You always were a selfish beast."

"Ah, well, such is the nature of the undead. In any event, nothing I can say will sway you, so think of me what you will."

"Thank you, Nicholas. I'm so glad I have your permission to choose my own thoughts."

He had a petulant look on his face, like that of a child who has been scolded for stealing pennies. "I have another confession to make," he said.

Pru rolled her eyes. "I can hardly wait to hear it."

"I've been following Lienore's trail for decades. All clues led here."

"So, you're not in New Orleans because of me?"

"Not everything I do is about you, Prudence. Not that seeing you again after all these years isn't delightful, even when you're hating me. I suspected she was here. I just didn't know who she was inhabiting."

His skin jumped when he felt her hand on his sleeve. Even now, after all this time, she had the ability to affect him in ways physical and emotional.

"We must act." Her fingers tightened over his arm for emphasis.

"*We* will do nothing," he told her. "I'll look into this." He saw the familiar tilt of her chin, a sign of defiance.

"Sabine may recognize me for what I am," Pru said, "but she won't know that I know who she really is. And besides, I was mortal back then. If she remembers me at all, it is as a mortal, not as this."

He wrenched free and spun her around to face him. "If Sabine is Lienore, she'll know exactly how to destroy you. I almost lost you once. I won't take the chance of losing you for good."

Pru recognized the human vulnerability behind the sulferous glare of the vampire's eyes. "Why do you persist when you know it can never be?"

"Because of everything I have lost—my humanity, my soul—the one thing remaining is my hope that one day you will love me."

Sometimes it was impossible to hate him. Despite his amoral character and selfish nature, he hungered for love. She forced herself to remember the tale he told her back in London of the terrible night of his making, more than three hundred years ago, when a creature called Vlad Tepes had slaughtered his family and left him neither dead nor alive, but somewhere in between. He'd been in love with a girl from the village in his native Carpathians, but the wedding and their future were never to be, brutally stolen on a snowy Romanian night that changed his life forever.

Oh, how she wanted to hate him, but when he was looking at her with that lost and lonely look on his face, those green eyes beseeching hers, she was filled with an emotion that was neither love nor hate, but something that had no name.

She lifted her hand and cupped his cheek and felt a lean muscle jump beneath her touch. His flesh used to be so cold to the touch, but that was when she was human and had the warmth of human blood coursing through her veins. But she was like him now, and the feel of his skin against her palm was neither cold nor warm, alive nor dead. It was just the tactile translation of need pulsating beneath her fingertips.

His hand closed over hers, the fingers long and slender and familiar. For a moment she was reminded of the magical music those fingers produced, the aching vulnerability of the man in each note he played. And the dizzying heights of pleasure those fingers had taken her to, the inhumanly spectacular sex of the vampire.

She felt a familiar pulsing in her loins, not the throb of anticipation for a human lover, but the frenetic beating of expectation for the pandemonium she knew awaited in the vampire's arms.

Her eyes gazed at him steadily, giving no hint of her thoughts, yet he knew that look. For many long moments neither of them spoke nor moved. And then there came from the floor below the strains of the violoncello, wafting like a sultry breeze through the tall windows and into the room, a haunting emotion-filled rhapsody that wrapped itself around them and drew them toward one another.

His arms came around her to pull her up against the silk of his waistcoat. A single sound, a strangled groan, split the music in two as his mouth came down over hers. He drew one hand through her hair, weaving his fingers through the ale-colored tresses, then pausing at the small of her back, spreading his palm against the sheer muslin fabric and holding her like that with the peaks of her breasts pressed against his chest.

He reached into the thin bodice of her dressing gown to cup her breasts, the alabaster skin surrendering to his touch. The lush promise that awaited, the desperate yielding, the gutteral moan that spilled from her throat when he pinched her nipple, drove him past reason. It made no difference if she hated him as long as he could have her like this.

It was too late for either of them to turn back. He swept her up into his arms and carried her to the bed. Dropping her onto the feather mattress, he hung above her on braced arms, a triumphant little smile curving his lips as he gazed down at her.

"Do you want me?" he asked hoarsely.

"Yes," came her breathless reply. "Do to me what you used to do." Her head fell back, exposing the beautiful white throat from which he had drank all those years ago, and the mouth into which he had spilled his own immortal blood opened, the little pink tongue darting out from between lips that were reddened by his kiss.

He wanted to take her slowly, to prolong the bruising pleasure and make her remember how it used to be between them. Once, a long time ago, he had mesmerized her into dropping to her knees and using her mouth to bring him to the very peak of erotic fulfillment. When she had abandoned her prudish nature in favor of pure, unadulterated carnal bliss, she had come to enjoy bestowing that gift upon him as much as he enjoyed receiving it. He asked it of her now by sliding smoothy and insinuatingy up the length of her body until his hips were level with her face. His erection pounded at his breeches, begging for release, but he needed to cast no hypnotic spell over her this time. She greedily obliged. Hastily she undid the buttons and shoved her hand into the velvet opening to grasp his phallus and draw it out. Like the hungry little creature she was, she brought it to her lips and took it into her mouth, stimulating him orally until he thought he would explode. His sanity was rapidly deserting him. His body was on a short fuse about to discharge at any moment.

The slow and steady rhythm brought him to the brink. "Enough," he mumbled in a harsh breath.

It took all of his willpower to withdraw before filling her mouth with his demon seed. Sliding back down her body, he bent his head and kissed her throat as he pushed her deeper into the feather mattress. He pulled her dressing gown upward, tugging at the delicate muslin with frantic hands. When she was bared to him from the waist down, he spead his palm over her belly, caressing the roundness before plunging downward to delve between her legs. A sound of excitement spilled from her lips as her legs fell open.

He kissed her breast through the muslin, his tongue wetting the fabric, finding her nipple and drawing it between his teeth, nipping until she arched and whimpered beneath him, while his fingers slid into the silky crevice and she closed her legs tightly on his probing hand.

His tongue slid to her belly, swirling around her naval before moving lower, licking and tasting the cool, smooth flesh. Her fingers were in his hair, grasping the silken locks with heated pressure, urging him lower still. When his mouth came to that place that burned with fierce desire, she thrust her hips upwards to meet his searching tongue. The first time he had done this to her she had burned with shame, but that was before she knew the exquisite pleasure of being kissed so intimately, and now she demanded it, holding his head hard against her moist, pink lips.

She was panting when he lifted himself and brought his head back up to hers. He kissed her, and she tasted herself upon his mouth. "Does your pirate do it like that?" he teased.

Looking into his desire-narrowed eyes, she smiled and said, "I'll find out tomorrow night."

Her callous response drew the effect she was seeking. She wanted to feel the raw animal potency of him, to be taken by the vampire with the strength of a hundred mortal men, to revel in his powerful invasion. She ached for her body to be full of him, to feel his molten energy consuming her until she was incapable of thought and all that remained was the sensation.

With a gutteral groan, he pushed himself between her legs and thrust harshly into her.

"Yes," she cried, "Yes, like that. Oh, Nicholas."

Her moist heat swallowed him up, and he lost himself inside of her. With strength unmatched by mortal men he pumped his hips, slamming himself against the nub of her wanton desire.

She clawed at his back, her own immortal strength shredding the delicate threads of his waistcoat. Wrapping her legs around him, she matched each frenetic thrust. Lost in sexual frenzy, she heard the music that streamed like moonlight through the window. The chords reached deep down into her being, filling up the place where her soul had once resided, just like the creature filled her body with his potent lust, lifting her higher and higher until her whole body shuddered and shook.

In that moment of mindless passion his muffled groan forced her eyes open. Tilting her head back, she looked up at him. His face was slanted downward, dark hair spilling over his forehead. The eyes that were the most beautiful shade of green she had ever seen were now a deep yellow-gold as the moment of release came upon him. She had seen him like this once before when, in the throes of passion, he had taken on the appearance of a wolf. It had frightened her then. It excited her now. She clutched him tighter as he thrust with animalistic potency, losing all control as he spilled himself into her.

Afterwards, she lay in his arms spiraling back to earth. When the sheen of perspiration had evaported from her flesh, she got up.

"I don't want Papa to know you were here," she said, her voice husky with sated desire. "You can leave by the window. I'm sure you'll have no trouble finding your way down to the street."

"Am I leaving so soon?" he asked lazily from the bed, his head against the rumpled pillow.

"I got what I wanted from you. There's no need to prolong this visit." She stole a peek at him. His phallus was still very much erect, proof of his sustainable prowess.

"So much for sentimentality," he muttered. Rising, he pulled up the breeches he had not bothered to remove and buttoned the fall front. "The window. Yes, it should be no trouble at all." He moved across the room with the grace and stealth of a jungle cat. "By the way, Prudence," he said as he reached for his frock coat and shrugged into it, "when you're fornicating with your pirate tomorrow night, how will he react, I wonder, when he looks into the eyes of the wolf?"

Pru sat down at the vanity and ran a brush through her tangled hair. "That won't happen," she said confidently.

A look of infinite cunning crossed his face. "You think not? Your eyes turn a lovely shade of gold when you come. Didn't you know?"

She slammed the hairbrush down and swiveled on the vanity seat to face him. "That's not true."

"How would you know?" he chided. "Can you see yourself?" He grasped the edges of the window and turned back to look at her. The impact of what he'd just said settled over her like a shroud, tugging her mouth downward into a frown.

"That blue dress you were wearing earlier is very lovely. I always said colors suit you. I'm so glad you gave up those somber hues you used to wear. White may be fashionable, but it does nothing for your complexion."

"Thank you," she said rigidly. "It was a gift."

"From him?"

She answered without hesitation. "Yes."

He stiffened, but made no move to leave. "Did you let him penetrate you?" he asked against the darkness.

He may have been able to detect the scent of sex on her, but even his astute powers could not tell the extent to which her lovemaking with Stede had taken beneath the moss-draped limbs of the live oak tree.

Her voice drifted cold and harsh from across the room. "With pleasure."

He turned his face away to hide his wince. "Two men in one night. I must commend you on your insatiable appetite, Prudence."

"And what about you?" she said accusingly, gesturing to his breeches that stood out against his erection. "How many women will it take for your appetite to be appeased?"

He shrugged in a grandiose manner. "Two, three. One never knows. I'm only just getting started for the night. After all, the way to a man's heart is through his loins."

He gripped the window and swung one leg over the sill. "There was a time when you were afraid to bear the child of a vampire, yet tonight you let me spill my seed in you. And no doubt your pirate's seed is still within."

"I take the necessary precautions," she said.

"That's reassuring." And with that, he was gone, slipping out the window like mist from the river.

Pru rushed to the window and watched him make his way down the plastered side of the house like a nimble spider.

With an anguished groan, his last words reverberated in her mind like pistol shots. *Two men in one night.* He was angry at her for that, but no more so than she was at herself. What respectable woman did such a thing? But how respectable was a creature of the night who subsisted on blood and sex even if it was through no fault of her own?

She closed the window and leaned her forehead against the glass, feeling miserable and confused. In Stede's arms she'd felt modest and innocent, like the virgin she used to be. In Nicholas's arms she felt wild and uninhibited. The two facets of her sexual self seemed to contradict one another, and yet both were a part of her—the vulnerable young immortal who longed for emotional love from her partner, and the wanton vampire with uncontrollable urgings for whom love only got in the way.

She lifted her head distressingly as another thought flashed through her mind. Was it true what Nicholas said about the vampire's eyes at the moment of climax? None of the mortal lovers she'd had over the decades made mention of it, partly because most of them did not live beyond their coupling, but mostly because she had the habit of closing her eyes at the moment of orgasm, imagining that the man penetrating her was the vampire she hated.

Would she ever be free of him? Tomorrow night, would it be the mortal's face she saw in the midst of lovemaking or the vampire's? She put her palm on her forehead, trying to think. She could feign illness when Stede's carriage came to pick her up and decline to go. Even as she pondered it, however, she knew she would go, for there was more than physical gratification at stake. There was the possibility of finding the kind of love she had always dreamed of.

Yet still too many questions lingered in the humid, cloying air. Would Stede love her if he knew what she was? Would he be able to be with a woman who remained young while he withered and grew old? If she offered him the gift of immortality, would he take it? The path toward winning the pirate's love would be long and winding, like the river road. The seeds had already been sewn beneath a centuries-old live oak tree. Tomorrow night she would indeed show him how wicked she could be. After all, like Nicholas said, the way to a man's heart was through his loins.

What about the vampire's loins? She was under no illusion that a creature as potent and vital as he would not hesitate to sate his lust with scores of other women. She didn't care how many women he bedded. The thought of other women laying themselves bare to his intimate kisses and the surging power of his body aroused only a glimmer of jealousy. But the possibility that he might actually love one of them produced a heartburning resentment. She didn't want his love, yet she didn't want him to love anyone but her.

Chapter 8

*T*he morning sunlight gleamed on the rosewood furnishings in the parlor, across the dark polished floor, and onto the staircase that pirouetted to the upper gallery when Pru opened the drapes. Papa was still sleeping, so there was no harm in letting a little light into the room. She barely squinted against the rays that fell across her face, frowning as she recalled Nicholas's explanation for why she was able to withstand the sunlight when her papa wasn't.

Turning from the window and thoughts of that scoundrel, she went to the dining room where Babette carried in breakfast of hot spoon bread, veal hash, fig preserves, and steaming coffee.

She had the whole day to think about the coming night with Stede, hours in which to daydream and dare to hope for the love that eluded her. And to plan. Yes, she had to plan wisely, from the selection of her dress to the style of her hair. Every detail had to be carefully calculated to achieve the desired result.

The way to a man's heart is through his loins.

With Nicholas's words in mind, after breakfast she went to the rosewood *armoire* in her bedroom and perused the gowns inside. After much consideration, she opted for a short-sleeved, high-waisted dress of light pink, the soft hue innocent-looking although not quite virginal. Stede claimed not to mind that she wasn't a virgin, yet men were such simpleminded creatures, and she had yet to meet one who did not fantasize about being the first to deflower a woman. If she could not give him that, at least she could give him the appearance of it.

Later that evening, Pru sat at the dressing table running a brush through her hair, but rather than fashion it in a bun with loose waves as was the fashion of the day, she left it suggestively long and loose over her shoulders and down her back, sweeping a pink ribbon up under the burnished tresses and tying it in a simple bow atop her head as the perfect compliment to the virginal-looking dress.

The wall clock struck the hour just as carriage wheels sounded on the street outside the front gate. Clasping a thin chain necklace around her neck, she slipped her feet into velvet slippers, swirled a golden-colored shawl around her shoulders, and left the house.

The carriage door was held open for her by a striking figure of a man in a perfectly fitting frockcoat. He was tall in a city of short men. His skin was the color of honey and his hair was tightly kinked and blond. A quadroon, Pru thought as she climbed inside. Eyes almost as blue as her own beneath a shelf of eyebrows matching his hair regarded her with a measure of suspicion as he turned away and took his place atop the perch.

He steered the carriage's high-stepping horse down the narrow cobbled streets to the river road. From there, it was a short ride with the moon peeking between spreading boughs to a house on the outskirts of the city bordering the swamp.

It was a two story structure with a sloping roof of red tiles and a garden on one side. The ragged leaves of banana trees rustled against the wooden walls, and a wild array of red roses cascaded over a fence of iron lacework. The tall quadroon held open an impressive gate for Pru to pass through, his expression stony except for the pale eyes that washed over her just as he turned to climb back aboard the carriage and drive it to the carriageway to the rear of the cottage.

Pru hesitated at the front entrance to smooth the skirt of her dress with her palms. Before her stood a door with thick panes of cut glass and an immense knocker in the form of a cherub. Lifting it, she rapped several times. It was one of those cool summer evenings so prevalent in New Orleans during the heady days of early September, and she drew the shawl tighter around herself against the chill as she waited.

It was only moments before her knocking was answered. A Creole woman led her up a curving staircase and across a wide hallway of marble tiles into a drawing room, and then left without a word, closing the French doors behind her.

While she waited, Pru looked around. The room was huge, with heavy portieres dividing it from an adjoining room and pale golden draperies at the widows. Framed pictures of pastoral scenes hung about the white walls. Thankfully, there were no mirrors. The divans and chairs were upholstered in gold and blue. A French clock sat on a carved marble mantel. An enormous chandelier hung from the ceiling, each crystal sparkling like diamonds from the candles' glow. This was not what she expected of a pirate, common or otherwise.

He was nothing like the dusty pirates she saw about town in their shabby coats and stockings, or the sailors who flooded the taverns whenever their ships docked in the harbor whose clothes were sewn out of worn sail canvas, or those who minced about town in silver-buckled high-heeled shoes, clad in plundered, often mismatched, garments and sporting gaudy ear pendants. Indeed, the clothes Stede had been wearing when he was tossed out of the tavern, and those he wore the afternoon they drove to the river, although flamboyant, were tasteful and costly. What, she wondered, made him so different from the others?

But whatever uncertainty Pru had over the source of Stede Bonham's resources was dashed when the French doors opened behind her.

"Pru."

The sound of her name quickened her pulse. Swallowing hard, she turned around.

Tonight he was dressed in a shirt of fine linen opened deeply at the neck with handmade lace cascading off the cuffs and tight-weaved woolen breeches whose below-the-knee buttons disappeared into the tops of black leather boots with fancy stitching.

His boot heels clicked against the marble tiles as he came forward. Taking her hand in his, he lifted it to his lips and pressed a kiss to it. "You look real pretty tonight. Just like a pink rose."

She saw the way his eyes devoured her and lowered her lashes demurely, confident that winning his heart would be an easy task.

"Thank you, Stede." She lifted her gaze to meet and hold his for several moments before looking away. "I was admiring the room. You have very elegant taste."

He laughed. "You mean for a pirate?"

"I mean for anyone. Although, I didn't know pirates could afford such luxury."

"My ventures have been profitable," he said.

Pru smiled coyly. "So it would seem." She suspected there was more to it than he was willing to say, but that was all right with her. She wouldn't press him to reveal the nature of his ventures. After all, she had secrets of her own to protect. And besides, she wasn't sure she wanted to know.

"How did you come to own this house?" she asked.

He uncorked a decanter and poured wine into two crystal glasses, saying as he did, "The previous owner received a land grant and settled an indigo plantation on the river north of the city. This was where he kept his—" He paused, deciding how to delicately explain the situation.

"His mistress?" Pru ventured.

"Ah, yes." He placed a glass in her hand. "He was quite wealthy and set her up here rather than in a little one-story house on Rue du Rampart where most white men set up their quadroon mistresses. That's the way it's done here. You won't find any self-respecting Creole who doesn't have a quadroon sweetheart. The arrangement often continues for years, and when broken by his marriage to a white woman or for some other reason, the mistress usually receives compensation to set her up in business. Most of them become hairdressers or nurses and are eventually forgotten. He left the house to her when he married and moved upriver with his white wife. They say she died of a broken heart. Every quadroon woman thinks her partner will prove an exception to the rule of desertion."

"How sad for the daughters of quadroon mothers," Pru muttered.

"Not nearly as sad as it is for sons of quadroon mothers. Those boys can't even marry women of their own color who cry *'ils sont si degoutants'*. They're either shipped off to France or they marry women whose skin is darker than their own."

Pru contemplated the Bordeaux in her glass, the deep red glowing like garnets in the candlelight, and frowned at the thought of a quadroon girl calling a quadroon man disgusting. Such things as skin color were trivial compared to the stigma she carried.

"Your servant," she said. "The one who drove the carriage. He is quadroon, is he not?"

"Christophe? Yes."

"There is something disquieting about him. I could not put my finger on it, but perhaps that's it. I take it, then, he is not married?"

"Christophe is as free as a bird. There was someone once. He doesn't talk about her, but when a man loves as strongly as I loved Evangeline, you recognize it in another."

A feeling of resentment pulsed through Pru at the mention of the young quadroon girl Stede had loved. Would he ever be able to put his love for Evangeline in the past where it belonged and love her in the here and now? It was becoming more and more urgent as she felt herself filling up with emotion for him. Having never been in love, she didn't know how it could happen in such a brief span of time, but she could not ignore the yearning deep down inside, not for just any man, but for this one.

Nicholas would call it lust, and there was some truth to that. The crazy notion of marriage sprang into her mind. But first things first. She had to get Stede Bonham to fall in love with her. Judging from the lust she saw in the gray eyes looking at her from over the rim of his glass could love be far behind? A wild hope invaded her heart. Perhaps then she could reveal the truth of what she was and convince him to join her in immortality.

The room suddenly filled with the aroma of spices. "It smells like dinner is ready," he said. Lifting the glass from Pru's hand, he set it down beside his own on a small round table. Offering his arm, he walked her across the room, swept aside the portieres and escorted her into a dining room aglow with candlelight.

They dined on crawfish *etouffèe* simmering in a blond *roux* with tomato sauce over rice.

"This is delicious," Pru remarked, grateful it was not a meat dish dripping with blood.

Stede grinned at her from across the table. "I like to see a woman with a healthy appetite."

"This isn't the only thing I have an appetite for," she said with a devilish twinkle in her eyes.

He froze in mid motion with a piece of crawfish half-way to his mouth.

She slanted a half glance at him and could tell by his expression that her comment had hit its target. "I'm hoping there will be a delicious dessert."

He chuckled. "I can ask Delphine to make some hot chocolate to ruddy up your cheeks."

"Oh? Do my cheeks need color?" she asked innocently. "It must be the weather here. It's so hot it tends to drain the color from my face."

"You haven't been in Nawlins that long. You'll get used to the heat."

"There seems to be so much going on in the city," she said, adroitly shifting the subject away from the unusual paleness of her skin.

"The French Colonial Prefect arrived in March to receive the province on behalf of France from the Spanish Governor," he said as he ate. "But instead, a French ship arrived with notice that the Americans were negotiating for the whole damn territory. The Spanish troops are sailing for Havana. I'm sure you saw the battalions of men patrolling the city to protect it from rioting and looting."

"Now that you mention it, I have heard a cannon fired every night."

His look soured. "In the Place d'Armes they fire the cannon to signal an eight o'clock curfew for sailors to return to their ships."

"You do not strike me as the kind of man who adheres to curfews."

He acknowledged her insight with a smile.

"I am given to understand that the Creoles place a high premium on honor," she said. "Why, just the other day I observed two men quarreling over a matter of etiquette, a venial sin against politeness, if you ask me." It had been late one evening after she had fed at the cemetery, while strolling the deserted streets, but she didn't say that. "I half expected them to strike some blows."

"Quarrels among Creoles never end in fisticuffs," he said. "An unwritten law in Nawlins society forbids it. Those kinds of altercations are settled by duels."

Pru looked up from her plate. "How primitive."

"It's been going on for decades. During the French and Spanish days most of the duels were fought in a cleared space behind the Cathedral. These days the ground beneath a grove of giant live oaks outside of the city has seen its share of spilled blood."

"And you?" Pru questioned. "Have you ever engaged in a duel?"

"I know nothing of this dueling business," he replied.

"But I am under the impression that no gentleman can refuse a challenge."

"I'm not a gentleman," he said, smiling. "I'm only a pirate."

"And quite an enterprising one, it would seem."

"Is there anything you need or want?" he asked. "I have connections to obtain any number of things."

"Papa and I are quite comfortable," Pru replied. "But if anything comes to mind, I'll be sure to let you know."

There it was again, that suggestive tone of her voice that made him stare at her. "Pru, I do believe you're teasing me, and doing a fine job of it."

She placed her fork down beside the dish and looked at him seductively from beneath her lashes. "Why, Mr. Bonham, I don't know what you mean."

The swipe of his tongue over his lips as if he were gazing at a mouth-watering morsel told Pru she was making headway. Pushing her plate away, she sat back in her chair, and running her fingers suggestively up and down the glass, she said, "I'm quite full. I can't imagine what more I could possibly put into my mouth."

There was a time when such saucy banter would have mortified her just to hear it, but she was no longer the timid little mortal she used to be. The one good thing about her preternatural state, she thought as she watched his reaction, was the freedom it brought to say and do whatever she pleased.

Stede swallowed hard as his eyes devoured that delectable mouth. He could well imagine what he'd like to put into it. Rising from his seat, he said roughly, "Let's go out on the gallery."

Outside, the swamp rose in misty tatters. Moss-hung cypresses seemed to float against the night sky, and the languid air filled with the sounds of crickets. Candles burning in the upstairs parlor sent soft yellow light skimming across the imported rosewood furnishings and through the French windows, sifting through the lace curtains and spilling out into the night, casting a shimmer over the wisteria that clung to the shutters.

Stede walked to the edge of the gallery and stared out into the darkness. "Sometimes I sit out here for hours just thinking."

"And what do you think about?" she ventured.

"Oh, lots of things. Why we're born who we are and why we're so afraid of dying."

"How do we know we weren't as afraid of being born as we are of dying?"

"What do you know of such things?" he jested.

"Of being born, nothing."

He looked at her askance. "Of dying?"

She hesitated. "My mother died in London many years ago, and my papa was close to death before recovering. And my Aunt Vivienne died. And the young man to whom I was betrothed." And herself. She died. She was dead. Could he not tell? Could he not sense it in his pirate's soul? "I know no more of dying than anyone else, I suppose." The lie was thick in her throat. "You have had your share of it. Your mother of yellow fever. Your father. Evangeline."

The name caused him to wince. "I'll tell you what does not die."

Pru stiffened. With dark foreboding she wondered if he knew about vampires.

"Love," he muttered. "Love doesn't die."

Her muscles relaxed, yet she felt a rush of doubt. "Are you saying Evangeline was the only woman you could ever love?"

"It takes just one bad experience to teach a man that love is for fools," he scoffed.

She came close. Toying with the buttons on his shirt, she peered up at him and asked, "And me? What are your feelings for me?"

His breathing quickened. "There isn't a man alive who wouldn't sell his soul to be with you," he said.

This was not the impression he gave yesterday when they'd made love beneath the live oak when he professed to want to know her so much better. "For what? An evening or two of pleasure?" She affected a frivolous laugh. "What about forever?"

"Forever is a very long time," Stede remarked.

Didn't she know that only too well?

"As the Creoles are fond of saying," he went on, "he who takes a partner takes a master." He reached for her and drew her into his arms. "But let's not talk about such things."

She softened at his touch and pressed a cheek to his shoulder. "Forgive me," she said. "I did not mean to imply that your feelings for me should go beyond an accommodating friendship."

"There, that's better." His eyes caught the starlight and his mouth curved up at one corner. "Who knows what tomorrow will bring? If there's one thing I've learned from a lifetime of running at sea, it's to live for the moment. And at this moment I think you know what I want."

Yes, she knew what he wanted. What all men want. She would show him what she could do, how she could make him feel, how she could make him desire only her, and in his desire, gain his love.

Forcing his evasion to the back of her mind, she pressed herself against him and felt the bite of his arousal through his breeches. He was already hot for her.

Her lips parted and her eyelashes brushed downward as his arm slid around her waist.

His kiss was gentle at first, a slow and warm movement over her lips. His free hand slipped down to press her tighter against him. She stirred her hips, responding provocatively as his arm tightened at her waist and his mouth opened over hers. He tasted of wine and lust and smelled of the sea, a heady combination that brought the hot need surging up from the depths of her being. She wanted to bury her face in his dark hair and feel his big hands on her body. Her breath changed at the feel of his body's excitement. She wanted to please him, to lay herself bare to him, to do all the things she knew he wanted, hoping it would be enough to secure his love.

A desperate longing spread through her body, coursing from the possession of her mouth down to her breasts pinned against the hard wall of his chest, across her belly and to that place between her thighs that was moist and hot and aching for him.

He pushed her hair back, twining the silken tresses around his fingers as he kissed her throat. Tugging the fabric of her bodice downward, he buried his face in the generous curve of her breasts, nuzzling the soft, white flesh. With moves that grew rougher and more frantic, he forced the fabric off her shoulders, exposing her breasts to the damp swamp air. His tongue swirled around her nipples, first one, then the other, drawing each into his mouth in turn until they were swelling with pleasure.

He could have taken her right there on the gallery, and she would have let him, but instead he lifted his face and pressed a kiss to her hair.

"God, Pru," he rasped, "You're driving me crazy."

She opened her eyes and peered up at him. Her heart beat faster.

The expression on his face was loving, lips drawn back in a serene smile.

The way to a man's heart is through his loins.

"Let's go inside," she whispered seductively.

His tongue darted out to sweep across his lips at the suggestive tone. "What'd you have in mind?" he drawled.

"I'm sure I can think of something," she cooed.

Her breasts disappeared into her bodice as she pulled the fabric back up over her shoulders. Taking his hand, she was about to lead him back inside when a throat nervously cleared behind them.

"Pardonnez-moi."

Stede groaned audibly. "What is it, Delphine?"

"A man to see you, monsieur," she said, her English heavily accented, her eyes shifting to Pru.

"Who is it?"

Her gaze darted away. "I do not know. But he has a face like, how do you say it, *une figure de pomme cuite."*

"There's only one man I know with a face like a baked apple. Wait for me, Pru. I'll be right back," he said, running his thumb down her spine. "Delphine, will you show Pru to my room?"

In the few short months she'd been in New Orleans Pru found the Creole way of life very different from that of Boston and New York and back home in London, where guests were received in parlors and never saw a bedroom unless someone was ill. But here, guests were invited into the most comfortable room which was invariably the bedroom. And this one was as well appointed as any fashionable London or Boston parlor.

The focal point was the fireplace. Sitting atop the mantle were a fancy gilt clock and two Derbyshire vases. Placed upon the ornate wooden paneling above the mantle was a painting depicting the eruption of Mount Vesuvius and hand colored engravings of camellias. A mahogany *armoire* stood against one wall. The bed was an impressive four-poster piled with feather mattresses. Beside the bed was a night stand with a black- and gold-veined marble top. An argand lamp, brighter than half a dozen candles, with a wick that required less trimming, threw light across the beamed ceiling and over the carpet. The smell of burning oil caused Pru to wrinkle her nose as her gaze moved around the room.

Then she saw it—the mirror, plumed and gilded—and drew a long, shuddering breath. What if Stede chanced to look in the mirror and saw no reflection of her in the glass? What if he again questioned the coolness of her skin and commented on her unusual paleness? She would stick to her story of the mist like blood upon a rusty knife and hope to divert him with coyness and caresses. A thought flitted across her mind of how much easier it was to be with Nicholas with whom there was no need to pretend nor fear her undead state being discovered.

She shoved her disquieting thoughts aside and went to the French window where the night pulsed with insects and sounds breathed from out of the deep heart of the swamp. The whispered voices of men, sharp and clear to her astute senses, drew her closer. A voice she did not recognize spoke with a desperate note.

The anger curdled in Stede's throat when he answered. "Let them try to dismantle my operation." His whispered words carried across the still night with the ease of sound skimming across water. "The Americans don't have an army big enough to protect their coast, much less have the audacity to attack me. Besides, technically, we're not pirates. My men carry their letters of marque from Cartegena. We're men of the open sea."

She knew by the hard strike of his boot heels against the flagstones that he was pacing. "The excessive customs taxes charged to move my trade down river was depleting my income," he complained, bitterness rifling the merry ring of his voice that she was accustomed to hearing. "That's why I moved my operation to Barataria in the first place. And now, Claiborne is complaining about pirates attacking American merchantmen. Damn that Virginian. You'd think he has enough to deal with trying to Americanize the city. I've ordered my men not to attack American vessels. Can I help it if one greedy sonofabitch hungry for gold bullion ransacked an outgoing American ship? They hanged him and that should have been the end of it, but being in charge means I have to accept blame for the crimes of my men. Very well, then. Go back to the island and ready the siege guns. If Claiborne sends troops to Grand Terre, we'll be ready for them. But first, there's something else I want you to do."

His voice dropped to a conspiratorial timbre as he walked with his cohort in the direction of the swamp.

Pru cocked her head to hear them better, but her attention was diverted from their conversation to the sweet aroma that suddenly filled the room. She sucked in her breath and whirled around.

He was sitting in one of the chairs flanking the fireplace, one leg crossed over the other, staring moodily at her from across the room.

She came forward in a rush. "What are you doing here?"

Tapping his fingers on the arm of the splat back chair, he mused, "It's quite comfortable. Louis Philippe, if I'm not mistaken."

"Never mind the décor," she seethed. "I asked you a question. What are you doing here?"

A guilty look flashed across those ethereally handsome features. "I was curious about your pirate."

"You mean you're spying on us," she charged in a furious whisper.

"I had no idea you were here," he said. "Really."

She cast him an appalled look. "How did you get in? Did you crawl up the side of the house like a spider?" She shivered. "Such nasty little creatures, they are."

"I don't appreciate your mocking talents," he complained, the beautiful curve of his mouth shadowed in the lamplight. "But no, I didn't climb up the side of the house. Let's just say the mist from the river isn't the only vapor that can infiltrate a room."

"Oh, you are insufferable."

"Have you recently fed, or is it your disdain for me that brings such a delightful flush to your otherwise pallid cheeks?"

She squeezed her eyes shut, hoping that when she opened them, he would be gone. But he was still there, watching her with those magnificent green eyes and that lazy, knowing look that made her want to scream. Forcing a level tone, she said, "Nicholas, please, I have no wish to spar with you tonight. You must leave. He'll be back any moment."

"To do what? Ravish you with his big, brutish hands? Really, Prudence, couldn't you have chosen someone more refined?"

"Like who? You?"

"Well, now that you mention it."

She hurried to the window and glanced out. Two figures were silhouetted against the night, their heads bent close in conversation. Safe for the moment, she whirled back around and demanded, "I want you to leave."

"Not unless you leave with me."

She stood rigid and adamant.

"Then I will remain right here, as invisible as the mist, and watch while you and your pirate fornicate on that garish bed of his."

"You wouldn't!"

But the diabolical gleam in his green eyes told her otherwise.

"You truly are an evil man." She gathered up her skirts in her hands and started for the door. "Very well. You can stay. I'll leave. You cannot follow me everywhere. I will make love with him and there's nothing you can do about it."

"Has he told you he loves you?"

She froze with her hand on the door latch. Slowly, she turned to face him.

His look was petulant and dangerous, his voice dripping like honey from across the room. "Ah, I didn't think so. Oh, well, you can always obtain a love potion, I suppose, or purchase some *gris-gris* for luck. Something tells me you're going to need it."

Flinging open the door, she rushed out. In the downstairs parlor she stopped only to retrieve the shawl she'd left over the back of a chair. Twirling it around her shoulders, she marched past Delphine and out the door.

Outside, a bright moon cast a ghostly light over the land. At the sound of the front door slamming shut, Stede looked up and saw her standing on the gallery. With a muffled curse, he sent his cohort disappearing into the shadows and strode toward the house.

"Pru, I'm sorry. I didn't mean to take so long. It was business."

"Yes, I know."

"You know?" he questioned.

"I mean, I assumed."

"Come now, let's go back inside." He reached for her elbow to escort her into the house, but she drew back.

"Not tonight, Stede. Would you call for Christophe? I'd like to go home."

"Aw, Pru, don't be made at me."

"It's not you." It was that miserable creature upstairs. The one who haunted her. "I have developed a terrible headache."

"All right." Disappointment rang in his tone. "I'll have Christophe bring the carriage. I'll take you home myself."

Upstairs, in the lavishly appointed bedroom, Nicholas stood at the French window watching as the carriage disappeared down the winding road that led back to the city.

He wasn't a man given to regrets, except, of course, for the one great regret of his life—his immortality. He tried to cast out the doubt over whether he'd done the right thing in taking Prudence's mortality. Yes, she hated him for it, and in truth maybe he did regret it for all the grief it had caused him.

His life, such as it was, had been perfectly under control before he met her. Why did she have to come along to fill him with such uncertainty, to make him hunger for more than blood and to suffer the pain of rejection? She would make good on her word to make love again with her pirate, and she was right that there wasn't anything he could do about it. For decades he had known of her intimacies with mortal men, each one like a hawthorn stake driven into his vulnerable heart. Yet what could he do except stand by and wait for her love to shine its light on him?

He should have abandoned her years ago. She was too much trouble, with her scorn and disdain, those damn blue eyes that made him do stupid things, and the infernal feistiness she had acquired since her making. The timid little mouse that had captured his fancy was now a formidable equal. She might not yet have acquired the power to transform into mist or assume the visage of a bat or a wolf—in time that would come—but her tongue was as sharp as a blade and her hunting skills were as deadly as his own.

He knew her so well—better perhaps than she knew herself. Like him, she longed for love. If only she would look toward him and the love they might share through eternity. He knew the feel of her through silk, the way her lashes swept down over her eyes whenever she tried to mask her emotions, the way her voice deepened when she hurled vehemence at him, as if to emphasize a hatred she did not truly feel.

For more than seventy years he'd been waiting for her to come to the realization that they were meant for each other. As much as it pained him to see her with her pirate lover, he would wait a hundred years and more. What was a century or two to a man with all of eternity ahead of him?

With that sobering thought in mind, he turned from the window and glanced about the room. Where to begin?

The *armoire*, yes. He crossed the room with noiseless steps and stood before the mahogany *armoire*. A touch of the latch opened the door. His gaze raked over the clothing inside, the garments too costly to belong to a common pirate. But there was nothing common about Stede Bonham, was there? Prudence had been too busy hurling her hatred at him to notice, but the conversation he'd overhead outside the window confirmed there was more to this pirate than met the eye. But how much more? Was he merely a businessman operating a meager enterprise, or was he the commander of an army of leathery buccaneers who sailed the seas for plunder, bringing back spoils to sell for a price, raping ships at sea and harvesting the booty? Ah, well, who was he to judge how a man earned his keep?

He was about to turn away when a familiar odor crept into his nostrils. His brow furrowed. Was that garlic? Dropping to his knees, he rummaged through the contents on the floor of the *armoire*, and drew back in horror at the discovery of a black bag tucked away in the farthest corner.

Gingerly, he lifted it out and set it down on the floor. For an immortal afraid of nothing, he hesitated, fearful of what was inside. His pale hands fairly shook as he opened it, and his mouth tightened at the sight of the hawthorn stake, the vial of holy water, the string of garlic, and the wooden mallet—tools of a seasoned vampire hunter.

Chapter 9

"*I*t's not possible!" Pru wailed. "You're just saying that to destroy my chances with him."

"Are you so sure of your pirate? I tell you, he is hiding a dangerous secret."

Yes, she had sensed as much, but certainly not this. "How can he be what you claim he is? He has no brothers, so how can he be a first born son?"

"Who is to say his younger siblings didn't die in childhood? Just because he has no living brothers does not mean he was an only child."

The tale of the Sanctum, a secret society of vampire slayers comprised of the first born sons of first born sons, tolled like a distant bell in Pru's mind. "So what?" she argued. "Even if there were younger brothers, there are many first born sons who know nothing about our kind."

His disbelieving laughter filled the room. "Can you be so blind? The bag, Prudence. How do you explain the bag I found in the *armoire*?"

"You will say anything to malign him in the hope that I won't fall in love with him. But it's too late. I'm already in love with him. I love him. Do you hear me, Nicholas. I love him. For the first time in my life I'm in love, and I won't allow you to ruin it for me."

His strange inhuman beauty looked distressed under the onslaught of her words. "He is a hunter," he said weakly. "He can destroy you."

"You are the only thing that can destroy me," she exclaimed. "You and your demon love."

Her barb hurt, as it was intended to do. There was a time when it wasn't in her nature to be cruel. When had she acquired the ability to wound so deeply? Her insides shuddered with empathy, and for a moment she felt almost sorry for him. Blinking back the weakness, she leveled a long, hard look at him.

He stood by the window, silhouetted against the light of the moon that shone through the panes of glass, looking melancholy—a dangerous misconception for one as wicked as he—his face pale, his green eyes darkened to icy shadows in the candlelight.

"Have you anything else to say?" she said tersely.

"Only this. I love you, Prudence. I would give my soul, if I had one, not to love you, for loving you has brought me nothing but heartache and pain." He paused to weigh his words, his voice hardening. "But mark my words. The day will come when you will love me. All the mortal lovers in the world cannot give you what I alone can give you. One day you'll realize that and come to me, and I'll be waiting."

"I have told you before and I'll say it again. I will never love you."

In a rush of wind that rustled the curtains he was standing before her. "Enough," he said forcefully, taking her in his arms and seizing her face in one cruel hand. "Deny me the love I crave, but you will never deny me this." He stroked her face and reached down into the bodice of her dressing gown to caress her heavy, full breasts and felt her quicken like lightning at his touch.

She gasped when he buried his fingers in her hair and drew her head back for a savage kiss.

Great shafts of evening light bathed the room and fell across the silken threads of the woven coverlet as he forced her to the bed.

He took her with alarming suddenness while the candles sulked and sputtered within their bronze holders.

When they were finished using each other for the carnal satisfaction they could derive nowhere else, he rose from the bed and straightened his trousers.

"Remember that," he said with a malicious grin, his molten green eyes fixed on her as she lay naked and panting on the bed, "the next time you fornicate with your pirate."

She rolled onto her side and propped herself up on one elbow. "Any animal can copulate." Her voice was heavy with sated desire. "What does that have to do with love?" A sense of savage triumph swept through her at his wince, all but imperceptible except to one watching so closely.

He strode across the room with panther-like grace, quick and deadly. "I will kill him if I must."

Pru's voice stilled him at the door. "If you kill him, you kill me, as surely as it is possible to do so."

She heard him mutter under his breath before wrenching the door open and disappearing.

After he was gone, she sank back onto the mattress and stared up at the ceiling. The fury that had flooded her earlier ebbed, and she felt herself dissolving into tears. This could not be happening. Of all the mortal men on earth, how was it possible that she had gotten involved with two hunters, first the pewterer, Edmund de Vere, and now the pirate, Stede Bonham? Long into the night she wrestled with her thoughts. Nicholas was jealous, that's all. He would say and do anything to keep her to himself.

She could not deny the pull he had on her. Never had she seen a man more beautiful. The moonlight caressed his face, etching his cheekbones, sharpening the strong line of his jaw, brightening the emerald of his eyes. His thick, black hair felt like ribbons of silk in her grasping fingers. And that mouth that brought her such infinite satisfaction, beautiful whether it bore a smile or a sneer. Sex with him was like no other, hard, driving, punishing sex that awakened every nerve. It was lust at its most primal.

And yet, lust was not love. Lust was for the moment. Love was forever. Or at least that's how it was supposed to be. How she envisioned it with Stede Bonham.

But what if what Nicholas said was true, and Stede really was a member of the Sanctum? There had to be a way to find out. She could reveal her true nature to him to test his reaction, but if he was a hunter, it could very well mean a stake driven into her heart. Even asking subtle questions might arouse his suspicions and put her in jeopardy. If only he were in love with her. Men in love often overlooked a woman's shortcomings. But judging from what he'd said the night she was at his house, he wasn't likely to fall in love so easily. She had to find a way to make him fall in love with her.

In a fit of despair she got up and went to the window and watched as one by one the candles and whale oil lamps in the houses along Rue Bourbon went out. She felt lost and lonely. Soon it would be dawn, but not even the light of day could chase away the bleakness she felt within.

She moved back from the window, the darkness following her, and threw herself down on the bed and wept into her pillow. Eventually, she fell into a sleep so deep it had a sound of its own.

Shafts of pale sunlight poured through the tall leaded window, pooling on the floor. With the new day came the answer to Pru's heartache, and it was Nicholas who had unwittingly provided it.

Chapter 10

*O*verhead, the sky faded from blue to pale violet. The twilight air was sultry and oppressive and scented with the pink and white blooms of oleander as Pru made her way through the narrow, muddy streets of the *Vieux Carre* where the remains of a few of the old French houses with their sloped roofs and cracked plaster stood between the Spanish facades.

She found the cottage on Rue Ste. Anne, a few steps from Rue du Rampart and Congo Square. It sat low to the ground and had a roof of red tiles. Banana and fig trees afforded a degree of privacy from the alley that was crisscrossed with lines of cord for hanging laundry. A tangled growth of rose bushes gave the place an untamed appearance.

When her rap upon the door brought no response, she followed a flagstone path to the rear of the cottage, where the aroma of marjoram and bay leaves drifted into the air from a small brick building whose window glass was broken and patched with cloth. Drawing in a supportive breath, she balled her fist and knocked on the door.

The woman who answered did not have the demonic appearance of the powerful *voodooienne* Pru had witnessed in the bayou. She wore an ankle-length skirt made from an assortment of colorful kerchiefs sewn together. A heavy cord of blue twined kerchiefs was knotted at her waist. Her dark curly hair was tucked into a bright red *tignon*, the ends knotted high atop her head. Huge golden hoops swung from her lobes and bracelets of gold jangled at her wrists.

At the sight of the white woman with unusually pale skin she recoiled, her ringed hand going to her throat to catch a breath. "You are not the slave who comes to clean my cottage," she said.

Pru suppressed a tremble at the weight of those black eyes upon her. "Madame Sejour, I would like to engage your services."

Her eyes narrowed. "To fashion your hair, perhaps? That is what I do for the white women."

Pru shook her head.

The look on that beautiful black face changed from suspicion to curiosity. "Come in." The bells at her ankles tinkled as she led the way inside. She gestured to a cypress table laden with sweet potatoes, collard greens and a basket of fresh eggs, and pulled out a chair whose seat was stuffed with Spanish moss and horsehair, and said brusquely, "You can sit."

Pru sat down and glanced around as she unloosened the strings of her bonnet.

Copper kettles simmered inside the open hearth. Atop the mantle was a breadbox and a pair of globes housing brass candlesticks. A live chicken roamed the room, head bobbing as it clucked. Two blue jays squawked inside a bird cage hung from the beamed ceiling. A butter churn and sugar chest stood on either side of a beehive oven. The kitchen was filled with the smell of baked bread, beans bubbling in the kettle, and red hot coals.

The woman bent to retrieve a pot from the back of the oven. "I put the beans in here so that they cook slowly overnight." Drawing out the pot, she hung it over the coals in the hearth.

The cooking fire glowed red along her face. She looked for all the world like a simple Creole woman sweating over a pot of red beans and rice. But Pru knew better than to be misled. Into her mind sprang the image of the woman who had danced to the beat of the drums in the misty bayou and then ripped out the heart of a man. But it was more than the power of a voodoo queen that cautioned Pru to tread carefully. It was the tale of an ancient witch sacrificed on a stone alter when the world was young, a witch with the power to suck the life out of a mortal's body, a witch who held the key to reclaiming a lost soul. The witch's name hovered like a coward on the periphery of Pru's consciousness, fearful of forming into cogent thought. Her eyes never left the woman. Was the ancient witch now inhabiting the body of Sabine Sejour?

"I make them myself," Sabine said when she turned and caught Pru staring. "My *tignon*. I see you are admiring it."

Pru met the woman's black eyes and did not flinch. "It's lovely."

"There was a time when the white ladies did not like to see the *gens de coleur libres* with diamonds and pearls woven into their beautiful hair," she said as she turned back to the pot of beans and stirred it with a long iron spoon. "Gifts from their wealthy white gentlemen. So it was decreed that a woman of color must wear the *tignon*. Most are of cotton, but I make mine of fine silk. I think they make us look even more beautiful." She lifted her head proudly as she spoke, lengthening the smooth column of her neck, her delicately chiseled features gleaming by the light of the fire.

"But you did not come to my cottage to admire my *tignons*." She flicked a look at Pru from over a slender shoulder. "And you are much too well bred to dine on red beans and rice."

"On the contrary," Pru said. "Our servant prepares it for us every Monday. It is one of my papa's favorite dishes."

"Your papa, he is Creole?"

Inwardly, Pru went aghast at having spoken without thinking. If Sabine was the witch, would she remember the old English music master whose life she attempted to drain for the unpardonable sin of creating beautiful music? "No. He is not."

Sabine set the spoon aside, turned around, and padded across the brick floor in bare feet, kicking the chicken out of her way as she did. With an indignant squawk and a flurry of feathers it landed across the room. Coming close to Pru, she asked, "Have we met before?"

Tossing someone through a window wasn't nearly as memorable as tearing a man's heart out, Pru thought with veiled disgust. "I don't see how that's possible. We only recently arrived in New Orleans."

"And where did you live before this?"

"Paris."

"That does not sound like a French accent to me. More like English."

"Yes, we are English." She caught the breath in her throat. An inner voice cautioned against revealing too much to this witch in Creole clothing.

"You do have a familiar look about you, though," Sabine said.

Pru forced a laugh. "The English all look alike."

"Eh, *bien*, at least you are not a *stupide Amèricaine*. They are so crude and bad-mannered. All they care about is making money." She raised a suspicious brow. "What do you care about, eh? Why are you here?"

"I am in need some *gris-gris*."

Sabine's dark eyes brightened. "The whites come to me for oils and powders and my little bags. What is it you desire?"

"A love potion."

Her look soured, and she said disapprovingly, "So, you have a young man and would like him to fall madly in love with you."

Pru inclined her head, feigning shyness. "I would like that very much."

"Are you in love with him?"

"I think so."

"An honest answer for one as cunning as yourself."

"I don't know what you mean."

"Oh, I think you do. Tell me, do you wish the potion to make your young man fall in love with you or to distract him when you bite him?"

"Madame Sejour, what are you suggesting?"

"Do not deny it. You are a blood drinker. I knew it the instant you walked through my door."

Nicholas was right when he said the witch would know her for what she was. But it also confirmed that she did not recognize her as the music master's daughter, because the young woman hurled through the window that terrible night had been very much mortal. Feeling bolder, Pru said, "I cannot help what I am." Unlike the witch, she caused no harm to innocents. "I want only for a certain man to fall in love with me."

"Men are such pitiful creatures. Often, they are blind to a woman's flaws and will overlook even the most obvious ones. It would serve him right if you drained him of every drop of blood."

Aunt Vivienne had once voiced a similar disparaging remark about men, minus the part about blood. Of course, it hadn't been Aunt Vivienne at all, but this loathsome entity that harbored a hatred of all men since the night centuries ago in ancient Dubh Lein when she'd been sacrificed at the hands of men.

"I have no intention of draining him of his blood. I want only for him to love me as a man loves a woman."

"Love," Sabine huffed. "It is a sickness worse than yellow fever and the cholera. Ach! I would take the fever's convulsions any day to the pain of falling in love."

"Be that as it may, will you make the potion for me?"

"I will make it for a price. Come back in two days and you will have your potion."

Pru hesitated. "It is not enough that he should desire my body. I want him to fall deeply in love with me, so much in love that he would never hurt me."

"I will make the potion and he will fall in love, but there is no potion that can protect you from love's pain."

"I will take my chances," Pru said, turning to leave.

"Does your young man know what you are?" Sabine asked as she walked with Pru to the door.

"No, he does not."

"And will you tell him?"

"Perhaps, one day, when I am certain of his love."

Sabine opened the door and sniffed the air. "The fever comes at this time of year. Last year it was very bad. People walked with pale lips and feverish eyes. And the dead were everywhere. Everyone kept their doors shut and their windows sealed with tar paper. The rich fled to their plantations. I was so busy making my little bags of camphor and herbs for protection, there was no time for grief. I would make you one, but your kind does not fear sickness, eh?"

The sound of tom-toms reverberated from the square. "The dancing has begun."

"You must be eager to join them. I'm sorry for keeping you," Pru said as she stepped outside.

"I do not dance in Congo Square," Sabine said, her eyes flashing with fire. "I do my dancing in the bayou."

Oh yes, Pru thought with a shiver, *your dancing and your killing.*

Sabine walked outside in her bare feet to the edge of the alley way and looked toward the sound from which the drumbeats were coming.

"The French feared an uprising and prevented the slaves from assembling. Slaves were not even permitted off their plantations. The Spanish governors were no better. .The *Amèricaines* .let the slaves dance to keep them happy. Maybe they are not so *stupide* after all, eh? Have you seen the dancing?"

"No, I have not."

"You will find them dancing on Rue du Rampart or Rue Orleans. Even the old brickyard on Rue Dumaine. But try Congo Square. It attracts almost as many white watchers as dancers. That is where you will find Squier, the Bamboula dancer. Go now, and return in two days for your potion."

"You are more than kind, Madame," Pru forced herself to say. She turned to leave, but before she could take a step, the voodoo queen's voice whispered at her ear.

"Be careful, blood-drinker," she warned, her voice vibrating with menace. "There are those who live only to destroy you. Some are closer than you think."

The mist was beginning to roll in from the river as Pru walked along the street in the pale light.

The voodoo queen's words beat in her mind like the drums coming from Congo Square. *There are those who live only to destroy you. Some are closer than you think.*

Was the woman alluding to herself? Pru had not failed to notice the way Sabine had recoiled upon first seeing her, in much the same way Aunt Vivienne had recoiled at the sight of Nicholas. And Sabine Sejour was a beautiful woman. Hadn't Nicholas told her that Lienore chose only the beautiful ones to inhabit? But what if Nicholas was right and the hunter who could destroy her was Stede Bonham? Her only hope was that Stede would not harm her if he loved her.

Oh, yes, she would return in two days for the love potion. First, she would gain Stede's love, and then she would find a way to get Lienore-Sabine to chant the words to reclaim her soul and restore her mortal state.

Assembled beneath the sycamores in the square, the slaves were dancing a calinda, the men strutting in the cast-off finery of their masters, whirling to the rhythm of the drums, the women in dotted calico and brightly colored Madras *tignons*, hips and shoulders swaying and feet barely moving.

To Pru, the movements looked eerily similar to what she had witnessed in the bayou, part primitive dance from the African jungle, part *contre-danses* of the French. But there was little chance here of anyone having their heart ripped out.

As the sun went down and the stars came out, the tempo increased, the drums and tom-toms beat steadily, and the high-pitched wind instruments wailed and whined.

It was then, when night had fallen and the faces of the dancers shone like black glass in the torchlight, that Squier appeared. A gigantic man, he leaped higher and shouted louder than any of the other slaves. In his giant fists he wielded beef bones, rattling them upon the head of one of the drums with a mighty roar as he cried "Badoum! Badoum!"

Pru stood among the throng, watching the dancing, feeling the rhythm of the drums pulsing through her as the big African slave weaved and stamped and shook the ground under the sycamores.

"He is magnificent, isn't he?"

A familiar voice startled her, and turning, she found Nicholas standing close behind her, his sweet preternatural scent mingling with the sweating bodies of the dancers and the burning torches lining the square.

"But I would not try drinking from him. He is sure to put up a good fight and is big enough to do some damage even to ones as strong as us. Besides, it would be a shame to deprive the world of such a specimen."

"Are you following me?" she asked with a huff.

"Not at all. I often come to the square to watch the dancing."

She could tell by the rosy flush upon his cheeks that he had recently fed. "By way of the *Vieux Carre*, I suppose."

He grinned. "Yes, that is where I like to dine. There's such a selection on the menu in that part of town."

She turned away from the dancers and started down the street. Nicholas fell into an easy stride beside her.

People were out, and carriage after carriage passed them coming in from the river road. The ragged leaves of banana trees fanned the galleries of the inner courtyards of the houses lining the street. On the balconies figures sat silhouetted against the candlelight shining through the high windows, pewter smoke curling from the men's cigars and fans fluttering before the faces of the women.

"Look at them" Nicholas mused, nodding toward the people who crowded the *banquettes*. "There is so much diversity in this city—French and Spanish, free people of color and those of mixed blood, Indians and planters, sailors off the ships in the harbor. Here, a vampire can walk the evening streets virtually unnoticed among the throng of exotic characters. There, do you see? They scarcely look at us as they rush by. This city was made for us, Prudence, with its wealth of dastardly throats upon which to feed. Why, just this evening I followed a man into the Sure Enuf Hotel where he paid a picayune to deflower a young girl brought in off the street. I wrenched him off of her in the nick of time and sent her off with a stern warning never to go near the place again. And then I escorted him into one of the city's many dark alleys and made certain he would never do it again. His demise will no doubt be attributed to the bands of robbers that roam the streets unless, of course, one looks closely and spots the bite wounds on his neck. But fortunately for us, people have an aversion to getting too close to the dead."

"It may interest you to know that I have spoken with Sabine Sejour," she said. "I was right. It is the witch Lienore." The flash of fury she expected from him did not materialize. "What? No lecture from you? Are you feeling ill?"

"I'm quite well, thank you," he said. "And what good would a lecture do except to waste words on a stubborn woman like you? When did you ever heed my words about anything?"

"At last you are beginning to understand me," Pru said, unable to contain a laugh.

"I always enjoyed the sound of your laughter," he said. "It's good to hear it again. At least you're not hating me at the moment. I'll take any bit of levity I can get from you."

She was tempted to argue not to confuse a moment of lightness with tolerance, but she kept the saucy reply to herself. What was the point of angering him when she could feel his tension simmering in the sultry air?

"Aren't you the least bit curious about what I learned about the voodoo queen?" she asked.

"Not really."

Was he toying with her? He was such a clever game-player. "There is something *I* am curious about," she said.

"I can hardly wait to hear it," he replied sardonically.

"You know full well that Lienore can chant the words that will restore our souls, yet you do not express any interest in what I have learned, nor have you taken it upon yourself to find out anything about her on your own. Why is that, I wonder?"

"Why do you assume I have done nothing to find out on my own?

"I assume nothing. If you had found out anything, you would have come to me with it, to prove me wrong if she is not Lienore, or to hatch a plan if she is."

"Why should I be so eager to reclaim a soul?" he asked. "What good would a soul do me, anyway?"

"What a contradictory fellow you are. And here I thought reclaiming your lost soul would have been high on your list of priorities."

She looked at him through the moonlight that sifted through the moss-hung trees beneath which they strolled. He was so beautiful with the tips of his midnight hair rustled by the river breeze, his emerald eyes shining brightly in the swaying light, and his mouth full and somber. With the bloodlust abated for the time being, for a haunting instant he looked like a fallen angel whose emotions could so easy shatter.

And yet there was something about his expression that gave her pause. As the silence between them lengthened, a slow realization dawned on her. Her eyes narrowed upon his face.

"You don't want to find Lienore and make her chant the words, do you? You don't want to reclaim your soul at all." She stopped in her tracks. "Good God, Nicholas, why?"

The angel spread his tarnished wings when he bitterly complained, "God was not so good when he forced this existence upon me."

"Don't be sacrilegious," she admonished. "And don't change the subject. Are you telling me you don't want your soul back? You don't want to be mortal again?"

"There was a time when that was all I wanted. Every waking hour, each moment of my existence was focused on that which I had lost. But it changed."

"When?"

"When you came into my life. At first I wanted to be mortal again so that you wouldn't fear or despise me. Then I was forced to give you the dark gift, and— Oh Prudence, don't look at me like that. We've been over this. I couldn't let you die. I had to turn you into the undead, and in doing so, deprive you of your soul. We became alike, you and me, two soulless creatures. Don't you see, Prudence? We can go on forever like this together, discovering new places and things. We don't need our souls for that. We don't need our souls for anything as long as we have each other."

She turned away from him, saying with an audible groan, "It cannot be," and continued on down the street.

His lips compressed into a thin line. "Oh, that's right, the pirate."

When she looked again at him, his expression was black and scowling. "It has nothing to do with him. If it were not him, it would be someone else. Someone mortal. For that is what I wish above all else to be. Mortal. I don't want to live forever. Who knows what lies beyond this century or the next? Perhaps it will be something so terrible we will wish we were dead. But we cannot die. We cannot escape this prison of immortality." Her back stiffened and her chin shot up in typical defiance. "You may not want to reclaim your soul, Nicholas, but I want mine back."

"Is that why you went to see the voodoo queen?"

She saw past his anger to the hurt inside and did not wish to wound him further by telling him that she had gone to Sabine Sejour for a love potion. "Yes," she lied. "That is why I went to see her."

Like a sullen child, he asked grudgingly, "And you are convinced she is Lienore?"

"She displays all the symptoms. A beautiful host to inhabit, a hatred of men, an aversion to me no matter how hard she tried to hide it."

"But you are not certain." He said it matter-of-factly, annoyingly able to read her doubt.

"Not completely certain, no," Pru admitted.

"And have you come up with a clever plan to trick her into uttering the words you long to hear?"

She detested that mocking tone. "No, I haven't. But the next time you come to see Papa, I'd like you to bring the book that holds the ancient chant, the one you took from the alchemist's house."

"As you wish. But what if your pirate plunges a stake through your heart before you can trick Lienore into chanting the words to reclaim your soul? Have you thought about that, sweet Prudence?" His mouth curved up at one corner as if he had just delivered the decisive blow in their game of parry and thrust.

She quickened her pace, but his long, graceful strides would not allow to get too far ahead of him. "He is dangerous," Nicholas said tautly. "How can I make you see that?"

"I see only a man so jealous he would do anything to thwart a rival. You dare not kill him for fear of my loathing, so you seek to demean him in my eyes."

He looked dark and magnificent as he glared down at her. "The bag, Prudence," he sharply reminded her.

"How do I know you did not place it there yourself?"

The threat in his eyes caught the starlight. "You don't."

This was the Nicholas she knew, the clever manipulator, the angel from hell. Each time she thought she saw a vague humanity in him, he shattered the illusion by revealing his true nature. The man she once thought him to be never existed. This was what he was, this creature, this vampire who had made her and would never let her go.

His lips curled in a cruel smile. "From the look on your face, it appears we understand each other perfectly."

As she watched him cross the street and walk off into the night, his footsteps making nary a sound, it wasn't so much his uncanny ability to read the thoughts written upon her face that made Pru feel as if she were strangling. It was the doubts that plagued her, each one like a hand at her throat squeezing tighter and tighter. Did Nicholas place the black bag in the *armoire*? Was Stede a vampire hunter who would destroy her if he knew what she was? Was Sabine Sejour the ancient witch Lienore? Would the potion bring her the love she longed for?

As she turned onto Rue Bourbon she heard the music of the violoncello streaming from the open windows of her house, and smiled through her gloom. Papa was playing his beloved instrument. At the gate, she paused with a pale hand on the latch, listening for a moment as the music floated out into the night. Her eyesight pierced the impenetrable darkness under the spreading limbs of the Spanish lime tree and moved slowly upwards to the warm yellow light emanating from the parlor.

Into her mind sprang an image, not of her papa, but of another seated before the instrument, cradling its curved body against his chest, midnight hair falling across his brow, green eyes closed to the magic of the music. When she hated him as much as she did, why was it his image that tortured her thoughts? Why was it his music that transcended heaven and hell and carried her to a place that could not be described with words, music she had once thought could only come from the depths of one's soul. But that was before she knew him for the soulless creature he was and her own soul had been wrenched from her being. Oh, yes, she hated him down to her bones, and all the sweet music in the world would not change that.

Forcing the image from her mind, she opened the gate and hurried up the walk that was strewn with fallen leaves and the shriveled fruit of the lime tree.

Chapter 11

*T*he marshes and bayous of Barataria were as beautiful as they were deadly. It was a blue-green jungle of moss-hanging cypresses and tall marsh grass where fat cottonmouths slithered through the iridescent water and alligators lay partially submerged like fallen logs on the soggy banks.

A man could get lost in this untamed wilderness and wander until he died of starvation or madness, but Stede Bonham knew every inch of the impenetrable, hot, ever-muggy mass with its quicksand traps and undertows.

Confident that all those American soldiers quartered in their forts up and down the Mississippi would never find him and his stash of plundered goods, he had established ingress routes to the marshes of Barataria where his fleet of barges hewn from cypress trunks shuttled merchandise back and forth to New Orleans. The barges were unloaded below the city and the goods put on pirogues which moved through Bayou St. John beyond the stations of the pesky United States Customs. The freight was then unloaded on the banks and placed in wagons for delivery to the city's shop owners.

Stede was proud of the entrepreneurial ingenuity that had enabled him to rise to the top of his illicit profession, avoid tariffs and capitalize on the lion's share of the trade. And with his siege guns in place around Grand Terre, there was little threat from the Americans to dismantle the operation he had spent years building.

But Stede was not content to sail the high seas with his letter of marque under the legal pretext of plundering Spanish shipping and transporting the pillaged merchandise to the city. The trip by water from Barataria to New Orleans could take as much as a week, longer if the weather did not cooperate. The delays could leave the merchants' store shelves empty and foodstuffs rotting before he could get them to the French market. And although he himself did not traffic in slaves, many of his men did, and if the barges carrying slaves did not arrive on schedule, his operation was in jeopardy from irate plantation owners unable to harvest their crops.

To avoid risking the wrath of the men upon whom his profits depended, he devised a clever scheme to create a chain of retail outlets where the public could browse the endless supply of furniture, clothing, the latest silks and finest embroideries, fruits and vegetables, wine and cheese, and medicines, purchase the contraband goods at handsomely reduced prices, and carry them home in their own wagons. All that remained was to build the outlets and set his ambitious plan in motion.

On this sun-bright day in mid-September, from his stronghold on Grand Terre, he relaxed in a red-clothed hammock strung between the ragged leaves of two banana trees. Grasped lazily in his hand was a glass of green liquid that he lifted frequently to his lips. The caws of gulls flying overhead brought his gaze skyward. With a lopsided grin, he glanced at the banner of Cartegena flying over the island, flapping in the breeze that blew ever-constant from the Gulf.

"*Bos*?"

He turned his head lazily toward the voice that spoke and blinked hard in an effort to see past the intoxicating haze that enveloped him. He laughed. "Delphine's right," he said, his speech slurred by the effects of the drink. "You do look like a baked apple." He took another swallow from the glass. "Ah, *la fée verte*," he said, licking his lips. "She may have sold my Evangeline to the highest bidder, but damn if that voodoo bitch doesn't make the best Green Fairy in town."

He struggled to sit up. The hammock rocked and overturned, sending him to the sand. He rose unsteadily to his feet and stood swaying over his shadow. "Did you do what I asked you to do?"

"Yeah, *bos*."

"And what did you find out?"

"I followed her to the cottage of the voodoo queen."

Stede took a stumbling step forward, his expression clouded. "How long was she there?"

"Not long. From there she stopped at the square to watch the dancing. She was joined by a man."

The fog lifted a little from Stede's eyes. "What did he look like?"

"That's hard to say."

"Try," Stede tersely suggested.

"Tall. Well built. Dark hair. I didn't get a good look at his face, but I got a glimpse of his eyes as he turned away. Green, they were. Bright and cold. Made me shiver down to my bones. He moved like the wind, noiseless and fast. When they parted on the corner of Rue Bourbon, he disappeared before I even knew he was gone."

"And the woman? What did she do?"

"She stood at the gate for a bit and then went inside."

Stede digested it all with a calculating look. "Ready the *Evangeline*," he ordered.

"Where are we headed, *bos*?"

"Honduras. There's a Spanish fort in Omoa that guards the silver shipments from the pines of Tegucigalpa to overseas destinations. Once they put to sea, those ships are fair game. Call the men away from their mistresses and tell them to be ready at dawn."

He sent the man away with a wave of the hand and started up the beach, his bare feet leaving staggered footprints in the sand, the bottle dangling from his fingers. He staggered past the warehouse that contained the plundered goods and the barracoon where the slaves were quartered awaiting sale, to the brick two-story house facing the Gulf.

Passing through the wide arched doors to his office, he sank down into a chair and stared morosely at the papers on his desk. Given his humble beginnings, he was well-dressed, well-read, spoke four languages fluently and could discuss politics with ease. He knew the unique habits and customs of the city, the lay of the land populated by Creoles and Cajuns, found company among merchants and bankers, and had under his thumb a fleet of fifty sailing vessels and an army of buccaneers. All in all, he considered himself a pretty smart fellow. Yet despite all this, he could not unravel the mystery surrounding one enigmatic woman.

What was she doing at the voodoo queen's cottage? Had she gone there for some *gris-gris*? But for what purpose?

He thought back to their first meeting when she appeared in the alley with a blood stain on her dress. She was as mysterious as she was beautiful. She was a woman who seemed to know what she wanted, if their coupling under the live oak along the riverbank was any indication of it. And even that had marked her as different from any other woman he knew, not because she made no attempt to disguise the fact that she was not a virgin, but because of the strength she had exhibited during their lovemaking. He would not have thought a woman as slender and pale and fragile-looking to be so physically strong. It had both delighted and shocked him.

There was something decidedly unnerving about her that he could not put his finger on. She had come to his cottage outside the city for an evening of pleasure only to leave in haste. Could she have overheard his conversation outside and been displeased by it? She would have to possess an extraordinary ability to hear whispers from afar, which was impossible...unless...

As a boy growing up, he heard the stories the old Cajuns told of the Rougarou, creatures that prowled the swamps. It was whispered that they could read thoughts and hear far-off conversations, that they had the strength of twenty men and could wing like bats across the face of the moon and lope through the marsh like wolves, that they transformed others by sucking their blood at night and returned to human form at sunrise.

What if the creature was a full-breasted, voluptuous woman with a beautiful face, hair the color of ale, eyes as blue as a cloudless sky, and skin as pale as milk?

And what about the man who accompanied her, the one whose footsteps made no sound and whose eyes made a hardened buccaneer shiver down to his bones? The Cajuns, descendants of French settlers exiled from their land, brought to the swamps of Louisiana ancient legends. One such legend carried across the ocean from France was about a creature that drank the blood of humans. The tales swelled with each generation's telling, but one feature was invariably the same. The creature had eyes that were bright and cold and green.

Stede laughed nervously. What was he thinking? It was the voodoo queen's elixir that brought such outrageous thoughts to his mind. It wouldn't be the first time he had imagined things while drinking the green liquid.

Still swirling from the effects of *la fèe verte*, he got up and went to the window. The blush of a red sun wrapped its glow around the island, and the drumbeat of the surf had settled into a calm lapping on the sandy shore. The bay was busy with schooners and sloops, some coming in with merchandise, others going out to plunder. The sight of full masts squared and triangular silhouetted against the horizon in the purple twilight never failed to excite him. It was time to leave the swamps and bayous he knew so well and take to the sea.

His thoughts drifted back to the plucky Englishwoman whose flesh, though cold to the touch, stoked the flames of his desire like no woman had done since Evangeline. The thought of the young quadroon girl he had loved and lost filled him with a sense of longing. He was older now and had seen enough of the world to be cynical and somewhat jaded, yet the longing never left him. It was a simple enough longing—to find a woman to love and settle down with, perhaps here on Grand Terre or in one of the old Spanish houses in the heart of the city, with great banana trees stroking the courtyard gallery where he would sit in the dusky evenings smoking a cigar to the gentle press of his wife's hand in his while she chattered on about things women are so fond of chattering about. Through the tall windows he would hear the sound of his children playing in the parlor while a hound dozed peacefully at his feet.

Was Pru that woman? He could not deny that she stirred something inside of him, but he was not sure if it was his heart or his loins. He thought again of the Cajun myth and told himself that stranger things than Rougarou lurked in the tangled swamp. Was Prudence Hightower, with her pale, cold skin and nocturnal wanderings, part of the myth? Was that the secret she was guarding?

Or perhaps it was the aftereffects of the Green Fairy that had him entertaining such notions. Granted, the drink did put wild thoughts in his mind and even caused him to see things that weren't really there. Nevertheless, he'd come to rely on it to take him away from the hard, unscrupulous life he'd chosen. He glanced at the bottle on the desk, and frowned. It was nearly empty. He'd better send word to Christophe to go to the voodoo queen to obtain more.

His thoughts hardened around the voodoo queen, the mother of his lost beloved. With no more daughters to sell to the highest bidder, what mischief was that evil wench up to these days?

***

In the cottage on Rue Ste. Anne Sabine Sejour stood over the kettle, her brown skin flecked with perspiration. She had ground the fennel seeds, coriander and cloves with a mortar and pestle, soaked the mixture in distilled wine, and allowed it to steep for two weeks. Now, she strained it through a muslin cloth and added the anise, wormwood and a sprinkling of herbs. The water was added, and there it was, *la fée verte*, just the way her customers liked it.

The oils from the herbs infused the spirit, and the herbs gave it a green color. Too strong a dose of wormwood could cause convulsions and even death, but why take the chance of losing a paying customer? In just the right dose, however, it would produce hallucinations not lurid enough to drive a man insane but strong enough to make him imagine he was seeing things.

Men were nothing but trouble, she huffed to herself as she bottled the green liquid. She'd had her fill of men with their petty little minds. She had paid the ultimate price at the hands of men. They thought they put an end to her when they sacrificed her on an altar of stone in the ancient land, all for the sin of lying in the bracken with another woman by the light of the Beltaine fires. Who were they to tell her who she could or could not lie with? Little could they have known all those centuries ago that they could not destroy a witch as powerful as herself. In their haste to destroy her they had provided her with an eternity in which to cavort, inhabiting the bodies of the most beautiful, taking lovers young and old to satisfy her insatiable lust. She could still recall the sound of their laughter as they plunged the blade into her beating heart. But it was she who was laughing now, for they were long gone, having passed into oblivion, forgotten as if they never existed, while she was here, preparing the Green Fairy inside the body of this beautiful voodoo queen.

When she finished decanting the green liquid into the bottle, she turned her attention to the love potion the blood-drinker wanted to make her young man fall in love with her. Withdrawing several unopened magnolia buds from a dark glass jar, she put them into two cups of rainwater saved from the first rain in May and a quart of vinegar and boiled it down until all the liquid was gone. Into this she put several drops of lavender and rose oil for attraction, strained the mixture and sweetened it with honey. But the buds and the oils of the voodoo recipe were nothing, she thought with malice, unless accompanied by an incantation to increase the magical energy.

Her voice rumbled in her throat, building in pitch and frenzy until the chant burst forth in a lurid mixture of English and words from her ancient Dubh Lein that shook the walls of the small cottage.

"Lig an glacadóir a deochanna an potion cithfholcadh an giver le grá ar emotion," she chanted, the lilt of the ancient tongue she carried since her birth growing stronger. And then in English, "Let the receiver who drinks this potion shower the giver with love's emotion." Over and over she chanted the spell as the body of the voodoo queen swayed and rocked and Lienore's power surged forth.

When the chanting and the dancing were over, she collapsed in a chair. Making magic always wore her out, but at least the pretty blood-drinker would have the potion she asked for. There was something about the young woman that looked vaguely familiar, but then, there had been so many pretty faces over the centuries.

She had no use for blood-drinkers. They were so predictable and obvious. Her method was much more clever. She didn't need to drink blood when she had a whole body in which to reside, slowly eating away the mortal fiber until all that remained was a husk of skin and bones. And then she gleefully moved on to another. There had been so many beautiful, voluptuous bodies to inhabit over the centuries, and a wealth of them right here in the misty bayous and cobbled streets of this city in the new world.

She'd been flitting around, a mere gust of vapor on the wind, searching for just the right body to inhabit when she spotted the Creole woman dancing among the slaves upriver. Skin the color of warm molasses, full lips, pendulous breasts and accommodating hips had attracted her attention, and in less than a heartbeat she'd made herself at home.

What a combination they made—the voodoo queen making *gris-gris* with the help of spells chanted by an ancient witch—the likes of which this soggy land had never seen.

The evil *gris-gris* she concocted was unrivaled even among the voodoo spells from Saint-Domingue. Not even the Maroons, known for their magical powers, could compare. She knew the evil *gris-gris* well—the powdered head of a snake to cause blindness, a doll stuck with pins to bring death, little bags stuffed with dog or cat hair to bring misfortune. When people came to her asking for such things, she sent them away. She had no time for the trivial insults and slights that made them want to get even with the offenders. In the privacy of her Creole cottage, however, with no one watching or listening, in the form of the infamous voodoo queen, she could wreck havoc on the unsuspecting populace.

She had her own special brand of *gris-gris* for those she wanted to destroy. And if anyone caused her insult, she needed no ancient spell or voodoo trick to exact punishment, just the inhuman strength of one such as herself. That miserable devil who had danced too close to her in the bayou was proof of that. It wasn't often she exhibited her physical powers to watchers, but that night in the bayou, as the slaves had danced to the rhythm drums, they'd been too inebriated with her green elixir to know if what they witnessed really happened.

She led the dusk-to-dawn rituals in the bayou, with bonfires, dancing, orgies and animal sacrifice, often writhing to the beat of the drums with a snake wrapped around her body to the shock and lurid delight of the slaves. But the ceremonies on Bayou St. John were nothing more than showy displays of magic at its most primitive, and this voodoo queen whose body she inhabited relied on amulets and charms, fortune-telling and hexes, and *gris-gris* for this and *gris-gris* for that. This was nothing like the diabolical magic she herself made when she was still mortal and worshipped the Goddess. Her power then and now was undaunted, relentless, and merciless.

A knock upon her door drew her thoughts away from voodoo ceremonies in the bayou. She adjusted her *tignon* as she got up and went to answer it.

A disapproving frown tugged at the corners of her mouth when she saw who it was.

"Oh, it's you, Christophe," she said curtly. "Come in. The drink is ready." She didn't like the way the quadroon looked at her with those watery blue eyes, as if he expected something, although what it was, she could not imagine as she swished away, the bells tinkling at her ankles. "And stop looking at me like you haven't eaten in days. Isn't that miserable pirate feeding you well enough?"

"He is good to me," Christophe replied.

"No doubt when he has enough *la fèe verte* in him."

"What have you got against him?" he asked.

Other than the fact that he is a man? she huffed to herself. Or that he was once in love with the daughter of the voodoo queen and made such a nuisance of himself over it that the foolish girl killed herself? Everyone, the voodoo queen included, thought it was the plantation owner who killed her, but Lienore knew otherwise. She could smell the stench of suicide through the decades.

She shrugged her elegant shoulders. *"Qui sait?* Maybe I don't like his face." She leveled a hard look at him. "Or yours. Take the drink and leave the money on the table."

He placed a gold doubloon on the table and hesitated. "Sabine." His blue eyes held an unspoken plea.

"Go away. You are nothing to her."

"Her?" he questioned.

"To me," she quickly corrected. "Now shoo. Or I will put a hex on you."

Christophe shook his head. "There was a time—" he began.

"Do not speak to me of times that were," she cut in with sharp reproach.

"It all changed when you went upriver," he lamented.

It changed long before that, on a night in May by the light of the Beltaine fires, she thought viciously.

"When you returned, you were, I don't know, different."

"Not different. Better. So much better."

"How can you say better when before you were a loving woman and now it seems that you hate everything?"

"Not everything," she replied. "I love this body." She ran her hands seductively over her full breasts and the curve of her hips and smiled with satisfaction at the loud catch in his throat. "You want to touch, don't you, *cher?*" she teased.

He moved toward her, but she floated away as if on a cloud. "I will not give this beautiful body to a slave."

"But I am not a slave. You of all people should know that."

"Ah yes, *un homme libre de couleur. Eh bien*, not even your free hands will touch this body." She moved away from him with a sneer of disdain. "Now go. I have to finish a love potion for some foolish woman who thinks she needs the love of a man, although it won't do her any good, I can tell you."

Christophe hung his head and muttered, "I had the love of a good woman once."

"Ah, but your woman was mortal. This one is not."

His head snapped up. "What's this you say?"

"You are surprised? You should not be. Where else but here, in this city of the night, can the undead walk among us unnoticed?"

His blue eyes sparked with interest. "Where will I find this creature?"

She cocked her head at him and asked suspiciously, "What do you want with her?"

"It is not for me that I ask," he answered evasively.

She contemplated her reply before speaking. She could have told him to wait as the blood-drinker would be arriving shortly for her potion. Then he could follow her and he would know exactly where to find her. Were the creature a man she would have obliged him. But why should she aid in the destruction of a woman? A vampire, yes, but a woman nevertheless. "I do not know," she said at length. "And if I did, I would not tell you."

"You do not fear her?" he asked.

The light from the hearth softened the features of her strong, lovely face when she laughed, but the sound was cold and carried no mirth. "I fear nothing. I am—" She paused. Ancient, powerful, incapable of being destroyed. "I am the *voodooienne*."

She seemed to grow taller with every word she spoke. He blinked his eyes several times and backed away. The door flew open behind him and a wind rushed in, not like that from the river, but such as he had never felt before. It shook the walls and rattled the copper pots hanging over the hearth. Unnerved, he ran out. His footsteps flew over the flagstone path, down the alley and out to the cobbled street.

In his haste to flee, Christophe ran right past the woman coming down the street, not noticing the tendrils of ale-colored hair that escaped from her bonnet and the blue eyes that flashed as she jumped aside for him to pass.

Chapter 12

*I*nto Pru's nostrils wafted the aroma of peanuts cooking in the confectionary vats, malts from the ale houses, ripened fruit from the open-air market, spices from the levee, the tang of fish from the wharves, and the odor of fear emanating from the man who rushed past her on the *banquette*. She glanced over her shoulder at Christophe's retreating back and wondered what had frightened him as she lifted her skirt to cross the muddy street on her way to the cottage on Rue Ste. Anne.

"I thought your kind doesn't come out in daylight."

There was something insolent and cunning in the voodoo queen's face when she answered Pru's knock on her door. She was dressed in a kimono, wore slippers on her feet, and her tightly kinked hair was tucked carelessly beneath a blood-red *tignon*.

"I tolerate the sunlight quite well, thank you," Pru said.

The woman made a little sound, not quite a laugh. "*Eh bien.*"

"Forgive me, Madame Sejour," Pru said when it looked to her as if the woman had just awakened. "I did not mean to disturb you. I would come back another time, but—"

"But you are in need of the potion."

"I do not necessarily believe in any of this, you understand, but I do so desire the love of this man, I am willing to try anything."

"You do not flatter me, blood-drinker."

"I beg your pardon. I meant no insult."

The same hand that had ripped out the heart of a man dismissed the remark with a negligent wave. "I have heard worse. Come in. Besides, you are not disturbing me. I've already had a visitor." She shook her head ruefully. "What men will not do for *la fée verte*. A steady customer sent his man by for it. If you ask me, he drinks too much of it. It will be his undoing. Not that I care. He deserves whatever happens to him."

Pru watched her shuffle across the brick floor and shifted uncomfortably from foot to foot. Here she was, in the home of an ancient witch bent on revenge against life itself. The witch hid her hatred well, but it was there, festering like an open wound that defied healing. But Pru harbored hatred of her own, not against men or the mortal life she left behind, but against the eternity that stretched before her like a great abyss. Without a soul there was nothing to look forward to except untold centuries of always longing for love. Oh, yes, she'd use the love potion on Stede Bonham, but except for the chance that he would not destroy her if he loved her, what good would it do for him to grow old while she never died? The thought that there was no future for her with any mortal man drove her to distraction and hardened her resolve to trick the witch into chanting the spell that would reclaim her soul and restore her mortality.

But how would she do it? The witch was clever and would see through any trick she might devise. She had to find a way to gain her trust. And then it came to her, a thought so sly and intriguing she could have clapped her hands with glee. She smiled at her own deviousness, and a vow pierced her thoughts with the sharp intent of a killing blade. The witch would pay for what she did to her and to her dear mama and poor Aunt Vivienne. She would extract from the witch the chant and then find a way to destroy her.

The cathedral bells began to ring the hour, snapping Pru out of her vengeful thoughts.

"This is what you seek," Sabine said of the vial of dark glass she held in her hand. "The *gris-gris* will hold your man to you."

"I do not wish to hold him prisoner," Pru said. "Only that he fall in love with me."

"He who drinks this potion will fall in love with the giver," Sabine assured her.

With Nicolas's warning rankling in her mind, Pru dared to ask, "And would the man who drinks this potion ever harm me?"

"He who drinks the potion will cause the giver no harm. Pour it into his wine so that he does not detect the flavor of the herbs," Sabine suggested, "and you will have the love you seek."

Pru clutched the vial to her breast, feeling hopeful. Reaching into her pocket, she withdrew the coins to pay for the potion and laid them on the table, noticing the gold doubloon sparkling in the ray of sunshine that fell across it from the open window. A pirate's currency. The image of Christophe rushing down the street flashed through her mind, and Sabine's remark of a customer having sent his man to see her made Pru wonder.

"What is this *la fée verte* you speak of?" she asked.

Sabine gave a derisive snort. "It is an elixir I make that some men cannot do without. It makes them, how do you say it?" She lifted her hand and whirled a finger beside her head to indicate madness.

"Are they dangerous when they drink it?"

"Mostly they are just *stupide*. Some see things that aren't there. Some fall into ruin. And some are very dangerous."

"And the customer who sent his man to you for some, is he dangerous?"

"Any man who pretends to be what he is not is dangerous."

The cryptic reply made Pru shudder. Was she talking about Stede? Was he only pretending to be a pirate? Was it all just a crazy coincidence? Sabine's warning flared suddenly in her mind. *"There are those who live only to destroy you. Some are closer than you think."*

"Madame Sejour, there is something more I would ask of you."

That brown hand with the strength to tear out a heart closed around the coins on the table and a dark brow lifted with curiosity.

"I would have you teach me the ways of voodoo."

"What's this? I thought you said you don't believe in it."

"Perhaps I spoke too hastily. I will admit I am intrigued. I can pay you handsomely for teaching me."

The voodoo queen's dark eyes narrowed with suspicion. "You wish to take my place as *voodooienne*?"

"Oh, no. Never that. There can be only one queen, and your powers are far superior to whatever feeble spells I could ever work."

The flattery tempered Sabine's suspecting gaze. "Why do you want to learn?"

"Only for the good I can do. You know what I am. I seek only to atone for an existence that was forced upon me." A sly thought came to her, and she added with feigned innocence, "If you have ever had anything forced upon you or taken from you, then you understand."

Sabine's lovely face darkened with distress, and Pru felt a measure of triumph in knowing that her words had struck their target. From all Nicholas had told her about Lienore, the existence that had been forced upon her was far worse than Pru's lot. At least she still had her own body whereas, without a host, Lienore was vapor, nothing more than invisible matter floating in the air, like the deadly yellow fever borne on a foul wind.

There was a deep pause. Was the voodoo queen fearful of being supplanted by another powerful entity despite Pru's assurance to the contrary? Was she jealous of a younger woman? She seemed to be undecided. Then she nodded. "I might be persuaded to teach you."

"When can we begin?" Pru asked, trying to keep her eagerness from showing.

"Come back tomorrow."

She left the voodoo queen's cottage, her thoughts fragmented into a hundred pieces. Questions tore like bats through her mind. Had Christophe been to Sabine's cottage to obtain the elixir? Was Stede under the influence of *la fée verte*? He did not appear to be intoxicated the day they drove to the river, nor the evening at his cottage, although she could not say the same for the night he was tossed out of the tavern. And what about Nicholas's claim that Stede was a hunter? There had to be an explanation for the black bag Nicholas found in the *armoire*. Was she truly in danger from the man whose love she craved? Was it all a trick that Nicholas was playing on her? Did the *voodooienne* hold the key to reclaiming her lost soul? To find out, she had set the wheels in motion, and there was no turning back.

Chapter 13

September brought thunderstorms to the city. Beyond the tall windows of the house on Rue Bourbon rain lashed the streets, thunder boomed like cannon fire, and lightening streaked the sky.

Inside the second floor bedroom, the crystal drops of the chandelier scattered candlelight over the room as Pru sat at the dressing table, carefully pouring the contents of the brown glass vial into a decanter of wine.

A soft knock upon her door drew her head up.

"Pruddy?"

She quickly secreted the vial in the drawer of her dressing table and answered the melodic ring of her papa's voice. "Come in, Papa."

James Hightower entered with a candle, the light bobbing with his noiseless footsteps across the floorboards. He set the candle on the windowsill and gazed out the rain-splattered pane. "You're not going out tonight, are you, Pruddy?"

"Yes, Papa. I had planned on it." *To take the love potion to Stede's house*, she thought, holding back the tide of emotion that accompanied the thought of him and the possibilities to come.

"Would you consider changing your plans? I have invited company for the evening."

She swiveled to face him. The shifting candle glow cast her expression of disapproval in shadow and light. "You know how I feel about him," she said with disdain. "Why did you invite him?"

"Pruddy, you are not the only person in this house. I live here, too. And I can invite anyone I want to visit with me in my home."

Even though he spoke softly, Pru felt thoroughly chastised. "You're right, Papa. I'm sorry."

"Besides, he and I have been working on a new piece together, and tonight we will play the completed composition. I would most like your opinion of it."

Her gaze shifted to the decanter of wine that held the secret love potion. She was eager to get on with her plan to deliver it to Stede and could almost feel his arms going around her and hear his lilting drawl whisper how much he loved her. Biting back her disappointment, she said, "Very well, Papa. I won't go out this evening." Tomorrow, she vowed. Tomorrow Stede would drink the wine and she would have the love she desired.

"Have I ever told you that you have your mother's look?" he asked, drawing her thoughts away from the promise of Stede's love.

"Yes, Papa, many times. I have the same color hair and eyes and similar facial structure."

"Not just the physical resemblance," he said, coming forward. "That look on your face just now, faintly chastising, reminds me so much of her."

"I wish I could see it, too," she said. "It would make me feel closer to her." She cast a quick glance back at the mirror above the dressing table in which no reflection shone, not that of her father standing behind her nor of her own to remind her of the mother she lost all those years ago. Something hardened inside of her. Lienore had driven her mother to take her own life, and Nicholas had taken Pru's mortality. If it was the last thing she did she would get even with them both.

She turned back to her papa. His face was flushed, and she realized he must have recently fed from the decanter of chicken's blood she filled for him daily and hid in the rosewood cupboard away from Babette's prying eyes. It was good to see him smiling again. For so long after her mother's death he had walked around in a morass of despair. And then Aunt Vivienne, in the form of that evil witch Lienore, had slowly and insidiously drained the life from him. She supposed she should be grateful to Nicholas for saving her dear papa from the brink of death by infusing him with his vampire blood, but she hated that rogue too much to find any words of thanks for him.

"Papa," she ventured, "would you want to be mortal again?"

He looked at her curiously. "That's an odd question, Pruddy. I must say I haven't considered it. Why do you ask?"

"No reason. I'm just curious. If words could be uttered that would give you the chance to live again as a mortal man, would you take it?"

She watched him for a long, measured moment as he considered how to answer. At length he said, "Once before you asked me if immortality were offered to me whether I take it."

"I remember," she said quietly. "You told me that such a gift could only come from Satan."

"That was before I knew our young friend's true nature and that only his generosity could save me," he said.

"Generosity?" she echoed. "You mean selfishness, don't you?"

"How was it selfish to save a dying old man?" he asked with a half-frown upon his face. "To give me back my life so that I can play the music I so love?"

It was his way of getting to her, she wanted to say, but she could not deny that it did her heart good to see her papa playing his beloved violoncello again. Her face flushed a little, as much as her pallid complexion would allow, as it did whenever she thought of that scoundrel. "He is a sinner," she said. "He is utterly and shamelessly immoral."

"That may be," James replied. "But I wish to have him dine with us tonight and to play the new piece we have been working on." He bent forward to brush a lock of hair from her face and sweep a pale finger across her cheek.

She felt the brush of his callused pad from a lifetime of pressing his instrument's strings, and stifled her vexation. "You are playing your music again, so for that I am grateful."

"You were always a good girl, Pruddy," he said amiably. He walked with soundless steps to the sill, picked up the candle, and gave her a warm smile as he left the room.

Good girl, indeed. Pru made a face. Why couldn't he see that she had changed and was capable of making her own decisions, particularly about whose company she did not welcome? She sighed. Papa still regarded her as a little girl, as all fathers regarded their daughters, she supposed. He'd always been so absorbed in his music she wondered if he'd even been aware of her transformation from child to girl and girl to woman.

Now that he had his music again, did he notice the ways in which immortality had changed her? Perhaps it was better if he did not, for he would not be pleased if he knew of her dalliances with men, not to mention the dangerous charade on which she was about to embark to reclaim a lost soul.

She had left behind the drudgery of the day-to-day obedience that was her life in London all those years ago when her mortality was wrenched from her. Now she was poised to enter a world of darkness and jungle-born magic, where goats and black pigs were sacrificed in voodoo rituals and green elixirs led men to the brink of madness. No, Papa would not approve at all. But that was the least of Pru's worries. She shuddered to think what Nicholas would do when he found out.

***

The selfish rogue Pru detested lay with his head pillowed in the smooth curve of the neck of a lovely young quadroon. The rain that had battered the narrow streets all day turning the black, loamy soil into greasy and slippery masses of mud had slackened to a steady patter of drops against the windows of the slope-roofed cottage on Rue du Rampart to which she had taken him.

Earlier in the evening he had visited a little roulette house to do some gambling among the river men, draining one blustering barbarian of his money as well as his blood. With the Kentuckians swarming down the Mississippi to loot the city, there was a wealth of throats from which to feed. To the Creoles they were coarse and vulgar brutes who terrorized the town. To him, they were a ready meal.

With the river man's blood pulsing through his veins, he left the roulette house and had gone in search of a whore to ease the pulsing in his loins. He found this little beauty aboard one of the flatboats transformed into a rude bagnio. It was not as sumptuously appointed as some of the bath houses he had frequented in Europe, but it would do for his purpose. She was young—he guessed her to be not more than sixteen—and well schooled in the art of pleasure.

She led him to a narrow cubicle built into the cargo box and lifted her calico dress, beneath which she wore nothing at all, although he suspected that her lack of under garments was not due as much to facilitate a hasty intercourse as it was to her downtrodden existence, if her slippers that were badly scuffed and run down at the heel were any indication of her sorry state of affairs.

What a clever little strumpet she was, holding his potently erect phallus between her thighs to simulate intercourse without penetration. But his appetite was so great this evening that he had curbed the impulse to snap her neck for using such a trick.

When he suggested that they leave the flatboat for more comfortable quarters, she took him to her little cottage, where he lay now atop the wafer-thin mattress on her bed, having climaxed all over her velvet thighs and threadbare sheet, casting a negligent glance around the room that was sparsely and crudely furnished. He felt sorry for her, and as she slid her curvy body down the length of his and drew his still erect phallus into her mouth, he wondered fleetingly how she had come to this sorry state so young in life. It surprised him that he felt anything at all for her, when there was a time he would have ravaged her without feeling a smidgen of emotion.

She could have been any whore at any time at any bordello. It didn't matter to him. As long as his sexual appetite was appeased, he wasn't particular. He would have preferred to sate his lust with Prudence, but she was being most disagreeable and he was not in the mood for her waspish tongue. He had no one but himself to blame for it, he supposed, although secretly he delighted in Prudence's extraordinary appetite for pleasure.

"Oh, monsieur," the young whore exclaimed when he came a second time and still retained a robust erection.

He pushed her away and got up. "If you were any good at what you do, I might have been satisfied," he said, more harshly than intended as he pulled on his trousers. Thinking of Prudence and how much she hated him always made him irritable.

"I'm sorry, monsieur. I meant only to please you."

Nicholas finished buttoning his shirt and turned back to her. Her eyes were downcast and her face drooped with humiliation. When the only thing she had to give was this, he'd made her feel worthless. He was ashamed of himself for it.

The mattress sagged when he knelt upon it with one knee and leaned forward to place a finger beneath her chin and guide her eyes to his. "And please me you did."

"But—" Her gaze dropped to the place on his trousers that stood out against his erection.

"Never mind that," he said. "It's a physical ailment."

Her face brightened a little. "Is there nothing that will cure it?" she asked innocently.

Yes, there was, and it waited for him on Rue Bourbon.

He reached into his pocket and withdrew a few coins which he tossed onto the bed.

"This very generous of you," the little whore exclaimed.

"I don't want you going back to that place," he said as he strode to the door. "It's unsafe for you."

"But I must work."

"Why are you not dancing at the quadroon balls? You are pretty enough. Your mother should be able to find a wealthy white man."

He'd been to one such ball himself searching for amusement, only to find a long line of young Creole dandies dressed in long coats of gray and boots with fancy stitching, waiting their turns for the *contre-danses* with the quadroon belles, while the girls' mothers sat behind lace-trimmed fans, determining which man would make a suitable match for their daughters. On the night he was there a dispute had arisen between an arrogant American who had demanded that the musicians play English *contre-danses* instead of French and the Creole youths who drew sword-canes to cries of *"Contre-danses francaises!"* It was all so disagreeable that he never returned, preferring to sate his lust among the city's whores.

"The cholera took *maman*," she said sadly. "I work to feed myself."

"You can work for me," he said.

She jumped from the bed, her small breasts bobbing as she ran to him, and threw herself against him. "Oh, *merci, merci*. I will please you all day, every day."

"Yes, I believe you will." What better way to make his beloved Prudence jealous than to bring another woman into his life? "Pack your things. I'll have a carriage sent for you in the morning. There's one more thing." He looked down into her eager face. "What's your name?"

"Marie."

"No more tricks, Marie," he said, waving a stern finger. "I'll not spill myself all over your pretty legs. Go down to the levee and obtain a good supply of the herbs you'll need to avoid pregnancy. I won't be the cause of you conceiving a child." Or a mortal bearing the offspring of the undead. Those nasty little creatures invariably set out to destroy their parents.

"*Oui, oui.* The seeds of Queen Ann's lace work well."

He looked at her wryly. "Who taught you these things?"

"Madame Sejour," she answered.

"The voodoo queen?"

"*Oui.* She and *maman* were like sisters until—" She paused to pull in a breath.

"Until the cholera," he muttered.

"Their friendship ended long before the cholera took *maman*. Madame Sejour became..." She shrugged her bare shoulders. "Different."

Nicholas lifted an inquisitive brow. "How so?"

The sputtering candle cast the room in shifting darkness, but his keen eyesight saw the goose bumps that raced over her naked flesh. "I do not know," she said. "When I was a little girl, she was loving and kind. And then, she was not. When *maman* died, Madame came to me and said '*cher*, I will teach you the things you must know to woo men and destroy them.' I said if that is what I must do, I will do it. But only to make money to feed myself, not to destroy anyone."

"And what did she say to that?"

"She laughed, and said that when I am used by enough men, I will want to destroy them all. I do not understand what she meant by that. Do you, monsieur?"

If Sabine Sejour was indeed inhabited by that evil witch Lienore, he knew full well what she meant. "No," he lied, "I cannot imagine. Tell me, Marie, how long has your mother been dead?"

"Two years."

"And you have been selling your body to those ruffians since you were fourteen? How dreadful. Well, there will be no more of that. And enough of this monsieur stuff. You will call me Nicholas. That is my name. Now run along and put on some clothes. As lovely as you are without them, I wouldn't want you to catch cold."

"But what about you, Nicholas?" she sweetly inquired. "Your skin is so cold. You are sick, maybe?"

He thought back to those nights in London with Prudence, when he had initiated her into the world of vampire sex and she had asked him if he was ill due to the coldness of his flesh.

"I am plagued by an illness you cannot understand," he replied. "One for which there is no cure."

"Ah, I see," she murmured with false understanding. "Like the illness that keeps you so hard." Her hand slid between them to cup his phallus. "I will have to work very hard to satisfy you."

There was nothing in the mortal world that could satisfy him, Nicholas thought bitterly as he nudged her hand away. Not the tight pink lips between her thighs, nor the sweet lips of her mouth, providing a momentary sating of animal lust, nothing more, nothing less.

There was only one thing that could satisfy him deep within his being, and it was the blue-eyed immortal who hated him. He left the little whore and went out into the night, his footsteps against the wooden planks of the *banquette* making no sound as he turned the corner and headed in the direction of Rue Bourbon.

Chapter 14

*B*abette answered the knock at the door and showed Nicholas into the parlor where James was seated on an upholstered settee reading the day's edition of *Moniteur de la Louisiane.*

"It's a good thing you are fluent in French," Nicholas remarked of the French-language newspaper.

"Ah, my friend, how good of you to come." James placed the newspaper aside and rose to greet him with a handshake. "Yes, my years in Paris prepared me well."

Gesturing toward the newspaper, Nicholas inquired, "Anything interesting?"

"It seems every day there are new hostilities between the Creoles and Americans. Just now I was reading an account of a ball in which a group of Americans insisted that the musicians play a jig instead of the cotillions the Creoles prefer. It caused quite a row."

"During the thirty years of Spanish rule, the Creoles were never forced to dance the fandango," Nicholas said. "The same respect should be shown by the newly-arriving Americans. But enough of that. I have been counting the hours until this evening. I took the liberty of sending my instrument on ahead. Has it safely arrived?"

"Yes. It's waiting for us in the music room. I trust you've had a pleasant day."

With the little quadroon whore in mind, Nicholas replied, "It has been somewhat satisfying, but not nearly as pleasurable as this evening promises to be." *If Prudence will let me devour her,* he thought licentiously. "And where is your daughter?"

"She'll be down in a while."

Nicholas nodded knowingly. "It took some convincing on your part to get her to join us, didn't it?"

"A bit," James confessed. "I'm afraid she is still quite peeved over what she perceives as the injustice you did to her."

"Is there nothing I can do to atone for the sin of saving her life?" Nicholas lamented.

James shook his head. "I don't understand it. She used to be such an agreeable girl."

"Immortality does strange things to us all," Nicholas said. "Personally, I prefer her this way." Eager to spread her legs.

"What way is that?" James asked.

"Capable and resourceful, of course," he said, masking his scandalous thoughts behind an air of nonchalance.

"Well, my capable and resourceful daughter grows unhappier every day. She thinks I do not notice, but I do. She bemoans the prospect of never finding true love."

"Love is often where we least expect to find it." He was a prime example. In all the centuries since his making he had never imagined falling in love, least of all with prim little Prudence Hightower. "Love," he said with a sigh of dismay, "is a sickness full of woes."

"It sounds as if you've had your share of love," James observed.

"I have. The unrequited kind."

"I say, you're not in love with my daughter, are you?"

"Of course not." He hoped his too-quick response did not register with his friend.

"That's good," James said. "For it seems my daughter has found a suitor she is enamored with."

Nicholas stiffened. The pirate again. "And is her suitor equally enamored?"

"I would not know."

"You don't sound pleased."

"What good can come from falling in love with a mortal? Although, to hear my daughter speak, she is determined to be mortal again." He looked askance at Nicholas. "It's impossible, isn't it?"

"Nothing is impossible," Nicholas answered. "You and I and Prudence and others of our kind are proof of that."

He was hesitant to tell James about the tome he removed from the alchemist's bookshelf in London all those years ago, the one that held the chant to reclaim lost souls. "And if there was the possibility of regaining your mortality, however slight that chance might be, would you take it?"

"Prudence asked me the same question earlier this evening. Now that I've had a chance to think about it, I must confess I'm content with things as they are."

"I'm relieved to hear it," Nicholas said with a chuckle. "I would hate to lose a friend. Among the undead, friends are hard to find."

"How many others of our kind are there? Surely, we cannot be the only vampires on earth."

"It's a thought I pondered in those first decades after my making," Nicholas said, "when I felt lost and abandoned and so utterly alone. But they're out there. You do not hunt when the sun goes down, so it's understandable that you would not have encountered them. In my nocturnal wanderings I have caught glimpses of them. I just never felt the need to befriend any of them. Perhaps it's because they remind me too much of myself.

"I cannot help but wonder what became of that evil witch who tried to kill me."

"Oh, I'm sure she hopped into someone, somewhere," Nicholas said evasively. What good would it do to tell him that Lienore was close at hand? "Tell me, did Prudence say how she would go about regaining her mortality?"

"No. Just some nonsense about uttering words that could make me mortal again. My daughter's imagination is quite fertile."

"Indeed," Nicholas responded. But his casual reply belied his suspicion that Prudence was up to something.

***

The music brought her out of her pique and lured her downstairs. She found her father and Nicholas in the music room seated behind his instruments. She didn't relish seeing Nicholas, but as she stood in the doorway listening, the music soothed her troubled mind and calmed her bewildering feelings toward him.

She thought back to the time so long ago when she thought music such as his could only come from the depth of his soul. His music then and now filled a place in her heart that felt empty and bereft. It nourished her spirit and lifted her on wings of beauty to places not found in the ordinary world of mortals or the dark abyss of the undead.

She came forward without making a sound to disturb them. Her papa's eyes were closed and he wasn't aware of her presence, but Nicholas lifted his head slightly and gave her a sweet, sublime smile. One would never guess from it that he was such a dangerous man, Pru thought as she sat down in a chair before the fireplace. She rested her elbows on the arms of the chair and closed her eyes. When playing his violoncello and creating his exalted, noble music, it was easy to imagine him not as a monster, but as a man, as human and vulnerable as any mortal.

She forced herself to keep her eyes shut, not daring to gaze upon him for fear of the emotions his beauty would stir inside of her. It was when he was seated behind his instrument, holding it to his breast as if it were a lover, running the bow passionately across the strings, eyes closed, dark head bowed, that the impact of his looks was most striking. Try as she might, however, she could not prevent her eyelids from fluttering open and gazing upon him as he played.

The firelight lovingly caressed his face, sharpening the line of his jaw, etching his cheekbones to perfection, deepening the shadow of the dusky lashes fanning his pale cheeks. His hair fell across his brow in thick locks, and a thousand little lights seemed to hover around his mouth. His expression shifted, from almost angelic, to tragic and torn, savage and hostile, depending upon the mood of the passage being played. He wasn't just playing the music; he was the music.

The composition closed with Nicholas drawing his bow across the strings in a final plaintive chord while her papa brought it to an end in his own distinctive style.

The silence that followed was deafening. For several moments no one spoke. Pru looked at her papa and could tell by the look in his eyes that the piece had drained the energy from him. He may have been immortal, but he was still an old man.

Nicholas flicked the locks of hair from his eyes and rose. "Prudence, how good of you to join us."

James opened his eyes and smiled at her from across the room. "Did you hear it, Pruddy?" he asked eagerly.

"Yes, Papa. It was wonderful. You played beautifully."

"And what about our young friend here?"

She flicked a contemptuous glance at Nicholas. "You too," she said grudgingly.

"How kind of you to notice," Nicholas replied as he rose from behind his instrument.

"I dare say a little sherry would be just the thing to celebrate our collaboration," said James. "Pruddy, would you do the honors and pour three glasses?"

"Of course, Papa."

She went to a small round table upon which sat a crystal decanter. Removing the stopper, she poured the sherry. She carried a glass to her father and placed it in his thin, veined hand. The other she handed to Nicholas whose beautiful, strong fingers brushed hers as they closed around the glass. She felt a cold current pulse through her and pulled her hand away, shocked that so simple a gesture could produce such unwanted sensations.

Lifting her glass, she said, "To a beautiful collaboration between teacher and pupil. Do you have any plans for the piece? I hear a big celebration is planned to commemorate the purchase of the territory. Perhaps you could debut it during the festivities."

"From what I read in the newspaper," said James, "the American purchase is not looked upon too kindly by the Creoles."

Nicholas sipped his sherry and said with a laugh, "That's quite an understatement. Poor Laussat. Before the French Prefect even learned to appreciate a good gumbo, Bonaparte sold the territory out from under him. Many citizens still long for Louisiana to become a French colony again. I doubt the festivities will be all that festive."

"But we are neither American nor Creole," Pru said.

"You're quite right, Prudence. We're not like them. In more ways than one."

Pru frowned at the pointed reminder. "You're so good at stating the obvious."

"Now, Pruddy," James said in a lightly admonishing tone. "Let's have none of that this evening." He lifted his brows and said wistfully, "I do so wish for us all to get along."

She tore her disdainful look away from Nicholas's smug smile and focused her attention on swirling the sherry in her glass. What was it about that rogue that had her hating him one moment and drawn to him the next? It was the music, she told herself. But from a corner of her heart a small voice whispered words she did not wish to hear, telling her it was more than the passing of a bow across the strings that drew her to him like a moth to a savage flame. It was his animal magnetism, his ability to shift seamlessly from refined gentleman to heartless rogue to cunning immortal. He could be playful and yet devious, solicitous yet mocking, with a boyish exuberance and intelligence as keen as Satan's. Possessing appallingly good looks, he could have had his pick of any woman anywhere, yet to her dismay, he had set his sights on her. She might have been flattered were she not so determined to loathe him.

"So, tell me, Nicholas. What have you been up to these days?" she said conversationally.

"Nothing quite as intriguing as what you have been up to, I'm sure."

Bristling at the faint insolent smile on his lips she tersely replied, "I don't know what you mean."

There was a flash of mockery in his laughter. "Oh, Prudence, when did you become so humorless? I was jesting, of course."

In the shimmer of firelight she saw the knowing glint in his eyes. He knew what she was up to, flashed through her mind. She controlled the urge to moisten her lips nervously. At least he had the decency not to bring up the matter of the voodoo queen. She looked from his impassive face to her papa's, and breathed a sigh of relief to see nothing in those kindly old features to suggested he suspected anything.

After an hour of trivial conversation had passed, Pru made the mistake of suggesting that they go outside for a bit of air. Her papa sighed, a little too conveniently heavy, she thought, and said, "I'm tired, Pruddy. Why don't you two run along?"

She knew what that sly old fox was up to. He clearly disapproved of her liaison with Stede Bonham and made no secret of his fondness for Nicholas. A quick look at Nicholas and the smirk of satisfaction on his handsome face made her cringe.

"Good evening, then, my friend," Nicholas said to James. "I'll send my man around in the morning to pick up my instrument. Come, Prudence, the night awaits."

The night was cool, and the candlelight poured from the open doors. An early evening rain had left the air sultry and sweetly scented, with drops glistening upon the leaves of the Spanish lime tree like tiny diamonds in the starlight.

He leaned against a pillar at the end of the gallery and said, "Are you thirsty? Perhaps we could go hunting together. You know what they say. The vampires who hunt together stay together."

"Certainly not!"

"Well then, perhaps another activity," he said, smiling devilishly.

"You're out of luck," she coldly informed him. "I have no intention of coupling with you tonight."

"It wasn't you I had in mind."

"Oh?" she ventured, trying hard to impart disinterest. "Who then?"

"My paramour."

"Your what?"

"My—"

"I heard you," she snapped. She eyed him suspiciously. The silvery aura of a full moon fell across his face, lighting a pale fire in those green eyes. "What game are you up to?"

"No game at all. If you don't want my love, there's someone who does. Her name is Marie, and she's quite lovely."

"What a beast you are," she uttered with disgust.

He replied cynically, "That may be, but it's not of my choosing."

She brushed his claim of innocence aside with a scowling look. "You may have been the victim of that creature who made you, but every sinister thing you do is of your own making."

In a monotonous drone, he said, "How many times must I tell you I cannot help what I am?"

"Are you going to drain her?"

"Are you going to drain your pirate?"

"Is she in love with you?"

"Is your pirate in love with you?"

"Does she know what you are?"

"Does your pirate know what you are?"

"Would you please stop doing that? You sound like a parrot, for goodness sake."

"And you sound like a spoiled child," Nicholas shot back. "Why don't you just admit that you are beside yourself with jealousy?"

"A mortal emotion," she huffed. "And I'm not mortal, or have you conveniently forgotten that?"

Nicholas rolled his eyes. "You may not be mortal, but your humanity is showing."

The air had grown suddenly stale with bitterness. "I lost my humanity thanks to you," she muttered as she turned away from him.

"You hate me, and you're jealous of my paramour. Those are human emotions. No, you haven't lost your humanity, Prudence. Your soul, but not your humanity. And speaking of your soul, your father tells me you mentioned something about words that could be uttered to regain mortality."

She felt the weight of his eyes upon her as he waited for her response. "Did you bring the book?" she asked

"Yes. I left it in the parlor for you. What are you going to do with it?"

"Nothing. I wish to study it, that's all."

"How do you plan to get her to chant the words?"

It was futile for her to deny it. He was much too astute and would see through any subterfuge. "I will get her to trust me," she answered, not daring not reveal the extent of her plans.

"Prudence," he said warningly.

When she turned back to him, she saw the rigid unease in his posture. His jaw was set, and his lips were compressed in a tight line. His dark brows were drawn in a scowl. Beneath them, his green eyes shot fire.

"Go home and frighten your Marie with that look," she said. "You do not frighten me."

"Yes, Marie is waiting for me. And where is your pirate?"

She hadn't seen Stede in days. Where was he? At his cottage? Aboard the *Evangeline*? She had to see him and give him the potion-laced wine.

Forcing the thought from her mind lest it show itself on her face, she said dismissively, "You can leave now. Your paramour is waiting."

He turned toward the French doors. "Be careful, Prudence. Do not turn your back on the hunter or the voodoo queen." And then he was gone, his foreboding words lingering in the sultry air.

Nicholas was right. She was jealous, and it was jealousy that made her say the harsh things she regretted now as she walked to the edge of the gallery and peered out over the railing. She searched the street below looking for a sign of his panther-like stride pulsing with feral grace, but he had evaporated into the shadows, leaving only the sweet scent of the vampire to taunt her.

There was no sport in hurting him. He was powerful and fearless and yet so easily wounded by her words. But it was more than the aching vulnerability in his eyes that made her regret her harshness. Even when hating him, her fingers ached to touch the cool skin of his breast beneath his linen shirt and do the things she knew he liked that would make his body shudder and quake.

She knew every inch of that well-knit body and craved the stroke of his hand and the hard, driving, animalistic possession that made every nerve scream for sweet release the way only he could do. In his arms she felt wicked and weak and free. Yes, free, even though trapped in this prison of immortality from which there was no escape, save the implausibly dangerous charade on which she was about to embark.

Her head ached with confusion. She didn't want his love, she thought dully, and yet she could not imagine life without the pleasure she found in his arms. How it took all modesty and virtue from her, although in truth she gave it up so easily. How it offered momentary respite from the impulses she could not control. How afterwards she would lie in his arms, sated, remembering only the bliss, until reality reared its menacing head and she was reminded once again of the miserable existence he had forced upon her.

He was forever taunting her, as he did this evening by disclosing the existence of his paramour. Indeed. Was the girl as lovely as he intimated? Was it true that she craved his love? There had been untold numbers of women for him over the centuries, but Pru had never been aware of him inviting any of them to live with him.

The wind murmured off the river. It was time to go hunting. But first, she would go to the cottage on the bayou and see this Marie for herself. It was curiosity, she told herself. She had nothing to worry about, for it wasn't likely the girl's path would ever cross with hers.

Chapter 15

She prowled the narrow streets for hours, alone with her thoughts and plans and the secret fantasies she dared tell no one. Her quiet footsteps took her to the tree-lined levee where it was easy to pick the pockets of men lying drunk in the alleys. From there, she turned in the direction of the bayou, to the small Creole cottage sitting at a bend in the crescent of water, nearly obscured by magnolia and sweet olive trees.

The light of a single tarnished candle lit the cottage within. As she approached, she heard a woman's voice softly humming. She crept stealthily up the steps and peered through the window.

A lithe figure in a white dressing gown moved about the room. Her hair was down, reaching nearly to her waist. When she turned, Pru could see her arms, slender and honey-colored, and the press of her small breasts against the thin fabric. Her eyes were large and brown beneath a shelf of fine, black lashes. Nicholas was right; she was lovely. And young. A dainty little creature soon to lose her shimmering youth, to wither and die like the commonest weed in the garden. Whereas, she would remain youthful and vibrant forever, and for the first time since her making, Pru did not hate her lot in life. That, she supposed, was what jealousy did, put notions in her head that were otherwise repugnant. A wicked thought came to her. She could slip in without a sound and overpower the girl and drain every drop of blood from her veins.

It would serve Nicholas right to deprive him of his pretty quadroon. He would be terribly angry, of course. She could just picture him drawing himself up to an unimaginable height, green eyes molten, face contorted with rage. But the thought vanished like morning mist on the river. She would not kill the girl, not because she feared his wrath, because she didn't, but because she was not a wanton killer.

Sniffing the air, she detected no hint of the sweet intoxicating fragrance that invariably accompanied his presence. He was most likely out devouring his latest victim, having left his little paramour for later consumption of a different sort. The girl's odor came to her on a bayou breeze, and she drew back at the scent of sex. So, he had already had her this evening. Once? Twice? Insatiable beast that he was. Why should it matter to her who he bedded? She had more important things on her mind. Hugging the decanter of potion-laced wine to her breast, she left the cottage on the bayou.

She hadn't seen Stede since the night she feigned a headache and he drove her home. They hadn't spoken much on the dark, winding river road leading back to town. She had sucked in her breath at the strength of his hands that went around her waist to lift her down from the carriage, craving the feel of those strong fingers burning into her flesh. He had kissed her briefly but passionately at her front door before bowing low and taking his leave. If Nicholas had not shown up unexpectedly and uninvited to thwart her plans, she would now be basking in the love of her mortal.

The moon was peeking through the moss-hung cypresses when she arrived at Stede's house bordering the swamp. She expected Delphine to answer her knock, but when the door swung open, it was Christophe's tall form standing in the doorway, silhouetted by the candlelight within.

"Is he in?" she inquired. "He's not expecting me, but I thought—"

"He's not here," the lanky quadroon said abruptly.

She sought to mask her disappointment. "I see. And may I ask when you expect him to return?"

"I didn't ask, and he didn't say."

She didn't like the way those unblinking eyes looked at her. "Very well. Would you tell him that I called?"

He allowed a long silence to pass before answering with a negligent shrug. "I'll tell him."

"That's very good of you," Pru said, unable to keep the caustic tone out of her voice.

He stepped back and closed the door.

There was something about that man that made the hairs at the back of Pru's neck stand on end. Those watery blue eyes regarded her a little too closely, and his abrupt manners left something to be desired. He clearly did not like her, although what sort of opinion he might have formed about someone he did not know was beyond her. Did he sense something unusual about her, or worse, something unnatural?

She turned away from the swamp and headed back to the narrow streets of the old city. Through the high windows of the old French houses candlelight from crystal chandeliers played across the plaster ceilings and lamp-lit courtyards nestled behind whitewashed walls. It was well past the hour when decent folk were out and about, and she was burning with the physical need to drink. She turned in the direction of the cemetery, where she often found peace from her disturbing thoughts among the crypts, and sometimes a meal. A rat scurried across the *banquette* in front of her. She might have fed easily from it, but rats were such repugnant creatures. Somewhere nearby a dog howled at the moon, but she'd always had a fondness for dogs and could not bring herself to feed from a furry canine throat.

Her dear papa was spared the gory details of the hunt. For him, chicken blood or ox blood was sufficient to satisfy his sanguinary needs. But she subsisted on the salty blood of humans, and although she was in love with her mortal nature and clung to the memory of her former life and the hope of regaining her lost soul, she could not deny that the hunt had developed into a game for her, a game of superhuman strength and otherworldly power at which she excelled. She could fulfill her thirst and eradicate an unsavory character all in the same bite.

A movement from the shadows caught her eye. It was the *padre* exiting the cathedral. She recognized his round brim hat and rounder belly. What was he doing out at this hour?

The stars were small and faint in a sky of deep midnight blue, and the air was muggy and fragrant as she followed his penguin-like gait through the narrow streets to the riverfront where the immigrants lived. He stopped at a little slope-roofed house whose cracked and blistered plaster showed the moldering brick beneath. Weeds grew knee-high along its foundation, and the shutters sat askew on windows of broken glass.

She watched from behind a tree as he waddled to the front door along a walkway where weeds erupted through cracks in the stone. A shaft of yellow light split the darkness when his knock was answered and the door opened. He stepped inside, sealing off the light.

Pru was about to turn away when she heard a pitiful cry from within the house. She stood stark still in the moonlight and cocked her head to the side, listening. There it was again, a desperate sound, like a whine, a moan, and a plea all combined. In the blink of an eye she was at the window, peering into the dimly lit interior.

A woman cowered against the wall, eyes wide, face as pale as plaster. A long, unbearable moment passed in which the inevitable bore down upon the woman and her expression changed from revulsion to mute understanding.

He reached for her waist, but instead of flinching away, she stood motionless. Pru heard the pounding of the woman's heart succumb to the dull thud of resignation and saw a curtain descend over her eyes, and she knew the woman was willing herself far, far away from the assault that was about to happen and which had obviously happened many times before.

Pru drew back in horror. Her heart, unfed and thirsting, pounded. Without forethought, she found herself inside the house, having burst through the door with enough force to shatter the rotting timber.

With pants pooled at his ankles, the astonished *padre* whirled around and found himself looking into ferocious blue eyes. He stumbled back in horror, but his fate was sealed. With one hand she lifted him off the floor and flung him against the wall. As the woman cowered in a corner, she fell upon him, twisting his head to one side to expose a fleshy throat, and sank her fangs deep into his jugular, bonnet ribbons flapping with each great, gulping swallow.

When she was done, she lifted herself from his bulbous body and wiped the blood from her lips with the back of her hand. The *padre* stared fixedly, his mouth frozen in gaping surprise, his lascivious heart having taken its final beat.

Pru felt no remorse for what she had done, no shame or guilt to have rid the world of one such as him. A sudden thought came to her. She knows! Her gaze swung to the woman.

"Is he—is he—?" the woman stammered.

"Yes," Pru said flatly. She delved into her pocket and withdrew the coins she had filched from the pockets of men in the alley. "Here," she said, pressing the coins into the woman's hand. "Take these." Now that the *padre* was dispatched, she didn't want the woman to have to resort to selling herself to drunken sailors just off their ships. "There will be more every month on the condition that you tell no one what you saw here tonight." She squeezed the woman's hand for emphasis. "Do you understand what I am telling you?"

Whether out of fear or the prospect of a monthly income, the woman gave a pained nod of the head. Confident she'd made her point, Pru turned back to her kill. Casting a sneer down at the *padre's* rotund, now drained, body, she hoisted him up and slung him over her shoulder. He smelled of incense and tallow as she carried him to the door. Peeking out and seeing no one about, she moved with superhuman speed through the quagmire of riverfront streets and squalid alleys. On the outskirts of the city she dropped the bloodless body into a bog.

From deep in the swamp she heard the beating of drums, and light from a fire flickered faintly through the oaks and cypresses. With the image of Sabine Sejour writhing in a trace-like state and ripping the heart out of a man's chest fresh in her mind, she stayed only long enough to watch the muck swallow up the *padre's* body. Come morning, the parishioners would no doubt be wondering where he was when he failed to show up for his Godly sermon.

Pru smoothed the wrinkles from her skirt and brushed off her hands. Having rid the world of one more heinous character, she fancied herself quite the avenging angel as she made her way back to town.

The light from the oil lamps swinging from projected arms nailed to wooden posts lit her way along the constricting streets. As she neared the alley between the Cabildo and the cathedral where she'd had her first encounter with Stede Bonham, it occurred to her that he might be at *The Snapping Turtle* getting drunk with his cohorts. Hopefully, he wasn't stirring up trouble to get himself tossed out again.

Judging from the volume of sound coming from the tavern, the men inside had consumed copious amounts of raw whiskey and beer. A stealthy peek through a dirty window revealed a low-beamed room populated by an assortment of men in various stages of inebriation—a flatboat bully with a red turkey feather bobbing in his cap, a gambler whose frilled, loose collared shirt was partly concealed by a fancy vest of unspeakable gaudiness, sailors in short pants, buttoned jackets and knee-high stockings secured with garters, pirates with colorful sashes across their chests and big gold buckles on their belts. Stede was not among them.

"I'm a pizen wolf Kaintuck and chock-full of fight!" the flatboat man shouted.

"I can wrastle a gator and chew off the ear of a panther!" another boasted.

"But can ya swim five miles to shore when yer ship's been sunk by the Spaniards?" another chimed in. "Aye, that's what I did when the *Evangeline* went down."

One by one the voices died as he told his tale.

"We was cruising off Omoa when we spotted two Spanish merchant vessels. It was cloudy and visibility was low that night. *Bos* says we can take 'em. They looked to be runnin' away, but then they made some lantern signals and turned back. Turns out they was armed Spanish warships and returned heavy fire. The *Evangeline* put up a good fight, but she was no match. Them bastards came aboard, took the *bos* and killed the rest of the crew. I was up front pissin' off the bow, so I jumped overboard. Then they scuttled the ship."

"They took him to the Fortress of San Fernando," said the gambler. "I've heard of it. The Spaniards built it to protect the coast and shipments bound from the mines of Tegucigalpa to Spain from attack by pirates. Sounds like your captain wasn't so smart to get himself caught and his ship sunk."

"More like he was drunk," the seaman bitterly complained. "The *bos* likes his green drink."

"Ah, *la feè verte*," the gambler exclaimed. "The ruin of many a good fellow. They probably hung him by now."

"They're more likely to torture him first," said one of the others.

Outside, Pru sank back against the weathered timbers of the tavern, her fist going to her mouth to stifle a sob. The thought of Stede being tortured in a Spanish prison was unbearable. With silent, trance-like steps she left the alley, the tears that tumbled down her cheeks glistening in the light from the oil lamps.

Back home, coal burned in the grates to chase away the autumn chill, and the chords of her papa's violoncello floated through the house. Rather than stop by the music room, she went straight upstairs. In her bedroom she heaved an involuntary sigh, shuddering with uncertainty over Stede's predicament. What were the Spaniards doing to him?

She flung herself down on the bed with its billowy hangings, not daring to let her thoughts go that way. It would do him no good for her to fret and worry. What he needed from her was action. But what could she do? To sail to the fortress would take days...days which Stede did not have...and her preternatural powers were not yet strong enough to transform into a bat and fly across the water. There was one, however, whose powers were already forceful and robust. But did she dare approach him for this?

Chapter 16

"You want me to do what!"

Pru knew he'd be angry, but she underestimated the ferocity of his outrage. Pushing back the hood of the chintz cloak that swung from her shoulders, she bit back a cringe. "I'm not yet strong enough to transform or I'd do it myself."

"So, you don't mock my talents when it suits you."

"Oh, that." She offered a guilty little smile at the way she had ridiculed him when she accused him of crawling up the side of Stede's house.

"Yes, that," he said petulantly. "You want me to use my transformative powers to save him? And what would you have me transform into? Not a nasty little creature like a spider." It was his turn to mock her, and he did so with relish. "Wait. Let me guess. A bat. Yes, of course. You would have me transform into a bat and wing my way across the water to the Spanish fortress. And then what? Mist? Yes, that would get me past the guards without being seen." His look turned menacing. "And then, perhaps a wolf, to tear out the throat of your vampire hunter."

"He's not, I tell you," she exclaimed.

"Oh, Prudence. You have such beautiful blue eyes. If only you would open them to see what is as plain as the nose on your face. Or will you finally believe it when he plunges a stake into your heart? You realize, of course, that if it comes to that, I will devour him limb from limb."

"Nicholas, please, I didn't come here to argue with you."

"No, you came here to beg for my help. I have just one question for you, dear Prudence. What are you willing to give me in return?"

She covered her eyes with her hands, knowing full well what he was asking. "You truly are an evil man."

He rolled his eyes. "As you have so often reminded me. But everything has a price."

"Aren't you afraid of what your paramour will think?"

"Not at all. Marie is well aware that my appetite is too great for her alone to satisfy."

"Well, I am not comfortable with her being in the next room."

"You're quite right." The flame from the whale oil lamp swayed as he strode across the room with a graceful, almost feline quality. He opened the door and called, "Marie!"

The pretty quadroon girl appeared.

"I want you to take the carriage and go into town."

"What for?" she asked.

"I am in need of some wine. Yes, that's it, wine."

"But I filled the decanter only yesterday."

"Well, I would like it filled again. And here," he said, pressing coins into her hand. "Buy yourself a pretty lace fan."

When Marie was gone, he turned back to Pru, his smile fading to a frown. "Is your pirate that important to you that you would come out in broad daylight to appeal to me to save him?"

"I'm not afraid of the sunlight," she said.

His gaze traversed her cloak of chocolate brown with a cream and turquoise floral print whose hood was deeply pleated and lined with cream silk. "At least you had the good sense not to wear one of your silly bonnets. Bonnets are never seen on the streets. I think a graceful veil is so much more fashionable."

"Nor do I care what you think."

"How you have changed," he mused. "What happened to that timid little creature who was so afraid to speak her mind?"

"You made me into what I am today," she said broodingly.

"Yes, I did. And as my creation, you will always belong to me."

Pru sucked in her breath at his audacity. "The only place I will belong to you, Nicholas, is in your dreams."

"And in my bed. And that is precisely where I want you. Unless, you have changed your mind about needing my help in rescuing your pirate from the Spaniards."

For a moment, she battled with herself over whether or not to give him what he wanted. But the dismal fact was that without his help Stede would be executed. Over the slow, predictable rumble of her conscience she relented.

"Where is your bedroom?"

"Upstairs. First door on the right. But I've changed my mind. We can do it right here."

He stood there with a self-satisfied smirk on his face as if he had just checkmated her in a game of chess, and then walked with a lazy, assured stride to an armchair and sat down, crossing one leg casually over the other. "Take off your cloak and make yourself comfortable."

Unfastening the cloak, she draped it across the back of a chair.

"And now," he said, his tone dropping to a low, lusty timbre, "take off the rest of your clothes."

It wasn't that he hadn't seen every inch of her naked body many times before, but to disrobe before his hungry eyes added a new dimension to the usual course of their sexual encounters and made her a little giddy.

The only sound in the room was that of his breathing, strong and even from deep in his chest. A swamp breeze rustled the branches of the trees and billowed the curtains at the open window. She took a long breath. "You wish to be entertained?"

The spark in his eyes gave the answer.

"And then will you do what I have asked?"

His voice was low and threatening. "You dare to bargain with me?"

"Everything has a price."

"I can't say I like having my words echoed back at me," he complained. "But very well. Do your best to entertain me, and I'll do my best to do what you asked."

He was such a clever liar that it was entirely possible he had no intention of helping her save Stede, but at this point, he was her only hope.

Unfastening the hooks of her dress, she nudged the high-waisted bodice off each shoulder. The soft muslin fell to her waist and then slid like rainwater to the floor, pooling at her ankles. Stepping out of it, she gathered it up and held it against her naked shoulders, the fabric outlining her legs and the curve of her hips.

The fixed expression of want and desire in his green eyes and the tongue that swept across his lips to moisten them made her bolder. Her fingers opened and the dress fluttered to the floor.

The white slippery silk-satin slip she wore beneath the dress gave a smooth line when the muslin flowed over it, but with the dress lying in a heap on the floorboards, it provided scant protection from his lustful stare. She shimmied out of it and was about to send it to the floor to accompany the dress when, acting on impulse, she tossed it to him.

He caught it in one hand. Drawing it to his face, he ran the incredibly soft fabric across his cheek and breathed in the scent of her that clung to it.

Having always thought her figure imperfect with its pendulous breasts atop such a narrow waist, she opted for stays that were lighter and longer and not as heavily boned as the ones she used to wear. Although they gave a smooth shape to her gently-flaring hips, they also emphasized the generous curve of her breasts. The tips of her nipples and the circles of dark flesh around them showed through the fabric. Slowly, teasingly she loosened the lacings of the stays. It dropped away. The candlelight fell upon the satin weight of her breasts, drawing his gaze like hungry predators.

She was enjoying the effect it had on him. His complexion was florid, as though he had recently fed. There was a catch in his throat, and his fingers twitched involuntarily in his lap. He may have been the one giving the commands, but she was the one in control. And once again she felt a surge of triumph in knowing that she could seduce the powerful vampire and reduce him to liquid.

Slipping her feet out of her shoes, she was dressed now only in stockings of knitted cotton held up by garters mid-thigh, exposing the soft white flesh of her upper thighs and the triangle of darkly curled hair at the apex. Her breasts swung forward as she bent to slowly and seductively roll the stockings down the length of each leg, followed by the garters. She was glad now that she had decided against donning pantaloons, for even though they provided warmth against the autumn chill, they would have been most inappropriate for this evening's unexpected entertainment.

For several long moments he just stared at her, licking his lips with anticipation. "Turn around so that I might admire all of you."

She turned slowly away from him, and though she could not see him, she felt the heat of his gaze upon her backside. She thought back to the first time she'd been with him, when he had initiated her into the scandalous pleasures of the flesh by lifting her and impaling her on his phallus. How many times since that first night had his hands cupped her buttocks and traced circles around the dimples at the base of her spine? How many nights had she dreamed of his cold, strong fingers stroking the cleft and the brush of his lips across the pale, round flesh?

"Come to me."

His voice called her away from her thoughts and back to him. There was no need to mesmerize her as there had been that first time. She turned willingly and walked with languid movements to where he sat. From the look on his handsome face, he was straining to hold himself in check. In a low voice, with just the barest movement of her lips, she said, "What would you like?"

Clearing his throat, he said hoarsely, "I would like you to undress me."

She smiled at his sharp intake of breath when her breasts brushed his face as she leaned forward and touched the skin at the back of his neck where his hair was tied with a ribbon. The ebony locks came loose, spilling to his shoulders as the ribbon fluttered to the floor. Her hands moved through his hair, fingers crushing the thick, glossy locks, before sliding across his shoulders to play with the buttons on his linen shirt. Hooking a finger in the placket, she drew him to his feet.

He stood before her, a tall, strongly built presence whose green eyes burned with need and despair. A wild yearning seized her for the tyranny of his touch. She longed to bury her face in his tangled hair and worship his bigness, to feel him filling her up with his inhuman strength. But he remained motionless as she undid the buttons that ran half-way down his shirt and drew it up over his head. His legs clad in buff-colored leather breeches tied and buttoned at the knees and tucked into the tops of shiny black Hessian boots were braced slightly apart. She had only to reach down to cup the swelling that was so evident beneath the leather, but she held back from the impulse. This was a game to him, a game to be prolonged until it became unbearable.

Dropping to her knees before him, she lifted his leg. As he steadied himself with hands on her shoulders, she pulled off one boot, then the other one. She rose, sliding sinuously up the length of his body until she was once again standing before him, her hard tiny nipples brushing the bare skin of his chest.

With deliberate slowness she unbuttoned his breeches. He stood as still as a statue, the breath trapped in his chest as she slid the supple leather past his narrow hips and down the length of his corded thighs.

She stole a look at him. He looked dark and magnificent in the late afternoon light that slanted through the window. His lids were closed. The sweeping lashes too beautiful to belong to a man almost touched the pale skin beneath his eyes.

And then, it was as if something released inside of him. Tilting his head toward her, he breathed heat against the nape of her neck, and lifting one hand, cupped the silken weight of her breast and ran his thumb over the nipple.

He moaned, the sound like that of a wounded animal, when she wrapped her fingers around that part of him that was hard and throbbing.

With her other hand she caught his and guided it to the moist hair between her legs and clenched her teeth when his fingers slid into the pulsing opening.

It seemed to go on forever, this game between them of give and take, of pleasing and hurting.

He put his arm around her, his body drawing closer to hers until there was no space left between them. The strength with which he held her might have crushed her, he was so strong, but she could not deny the excitement of being in his arms and was powerless to stop it. Inclining her backwards, he kissed her. His lips were cool and yet a fire seemed to pass through them that burned to the deepest part of her. If it were possible for her to die, she might have done so right then and there, and it would have been a delirious death. At this moment nothing mattered, not even the pirate whose love she craved. Later she would feel guilt for that, but not now as the pandemonium radiated from the center of her all through her limbs and all she could think about was drowning in the vampire's lust.

"Do you want me?" His breath was heavy and warm against her lips, his kiss deep and demanding.

She tried to say something, but his mouth smothered hers, his tongue diving deep in the kiss, giving her no opportunity to verbalize a response.

Lifting his head, he gazed at her with fiery green eyes and rasped, "Show me," as he guided her to the freshly swept floorboards.

Covering her body with his, cold flesh pressing against cold flesh, his weight spread her legs, moaning as he went in.

He was frenzied, unable to hold back, kissing her neck and her shoulders and returning again and again to her mouth, his fingers bruising the tender flesh of her buttocks as he pulled her fiercely upwards and against his frantic thrusting.

Her head fell back against the floorboards and she drew in a sharp breath, surrendering to his conquest, reveling in the superhuman strength that forced her body to respond.

She buried her face in his shoulder as he pumped his hips, taking full possession of her with all the power that was in him. And she, mindful only of the searing sensations, pushed forward, inviting, demanding, lost in the ecstasy of his invasion, full and hard.

He groaned and whimpered as one final savage thrust pushed him over the edge, and gazing up at him, she saw the golden eyes of the wolf beneath his half-lowered lids.

She closed her eyes as her own release washed over her, wave upon wave of unbridled pleasure culminating in an explosive tremor that rocked her to her core.

His breath rushed into her ear. "Look into my eyes."

She arched against his embrace and in a haze of passion heeded his command.

"What do you see?"

In his orbs a reflection shimmered that no mirror could capture, of eyes not blue but yellow-gold. Her eyes. The eyes of a wolf.

The breeze felt cool on her arms as she lay with her back pressed against his chest, her legs tucked beneath his. The light beyond the window was fading to twilight. It was that time of day that was no longer day and not quite night. Along the river road the sun was sinking behind moss-laden oaks, the fires of voodoo ceremonies were ignited on the bayou, and the tall windows of the houses in town were flickering with light from lamps lit with fish oil, bear fat and pelican grease.

He nibbled insinuatingly at her ear. "Do you believe me now about your eyes?"

She gave a little sigh, and nestling closer to him, murmured "Um-hmm." She felt lost and euphoric and, for the moment, uncaring that he'd been right.

Nestling closer to her, he murmured, "Did I ever tell you about the time I invented champagne? It was, oh, let me think, sixteen ninety-three I believe. I was feeling lost and lonely owing to my unfortunate set of circumstances and sought refuge with the Benedictine monks at the Abbey of Hautvillers near Epernay in France. The monks were quite adept at bottling wine. One of them, Dom Perignon, was in charge of the cellar. After doing a little experimentation of my own, I suggested to him to make a second fermentation process in the bottle, and it was that which produced those delightful bubbles. The English will take their credit for its invention and, of course, the French, but no, it was me. Despite the fact that I had invented the most marvelous drink, when the monks discovered that I had been tampering with their wine, they were furious, so I spread wings and flew out of there in a hurry. You can do it, you know."

"Do what?" she asked with a laugh. "Make champagne?"

He sighed at her sarcasm. "Transform. You're strong enough. You just don't know how. Shall I teach you?"

Disentangling herself from his embrace, she sat up and turned around to look at him. "You mean I can transform into a bat?"

"If you choose. And what a lovely little bat you would make." Leaning forward, he lifted her breast in his hand and kissed the satin flesh. "Shall we give it another go?" he teased.

She brushed his hand aside and squirmed away from him. "Would I be able to fly to the fortress?"

He stiffened, and the passionate haze that lingered in the aftermath of their lovemaking dissipated in the terrible clarity of the situation. "You weren't thinking about your pirate a little while ago when it was me who was inside of you."

She slanted a haughty look at him. "Don't be so sure about that."

He shoved himself away from her. "You take such delight in wounding me," he brooded as he got up and went in search of his clothes.

Pru regretted her quip, but more than that, she could not afford to anger him, not when she so desperately needed his help. "All right," she admitted, "if you must know, I wasn't thinking about him when we were…you know."

"Are you ashamed to say it? We were fucking, Pru. Fucking. Like all animals do."

"Must you be so crude?"

"All right, we engaged in searing, passionate lovemaking. Is that more suitable for your feigned modesty?"

"You're insufferable."

"I try."

Ignoring his proud grin, she said, "While I admit it was you I was thinking about during it, you should not presume that it was anything more than the basic need to couple which, as you say, all animals do."

That wiped the grin from his face. He pulled his shirt on over his head with an angry gesture, nearly ripping the seams and leaving the buttons undone as he shoved his legs back into the leather breeches. "Fine. Have it your way. You feel absolutely nothing for me. You've made that perfectly clear."

She got up and went to him. Drawing near, arms going around his waist, she said in a low purr, "Nicholas, don't be that way. You know I have feelings for you."

He suppressed the tremble aroused by the press of her breasts, soft and provocative, against his chest, and closed his eyes to gain some mental balance. "You mean hatred and disdain?"

"Well, yes, that. But there are times when I have affection for you, too. My feelings for you are complicated. Don't ask me to put them in perspective." She reached up on tiptoes and placed an unexpected kiss upon his lips. "Now, be a good vampire and teach me how to transform."

"I'll teach you, but not today. Marie will be back soon. Besides, you won't have it mastered soon enough to save your pirate."

Releasing him, she spun away and gathered up her garments from the floor. The seduction in her voice was replaced by a curt, matter-of-fact tone. "Then you'll have to do it for me."

He flopped down in the chair, sulking as he pulled on his boots. "I hate the thought of going to that place with all those nasty tropical diseases."

"Since when are you afraid of disease?

I'm not," he asserted. "But that does not mean I enjoy watching others succumb."

His response didn't surprise her. When he wasn't being purposely cruel, he could be quite sensitive. She wasn't lying when she told him that at times she had affection for him. Her head fairly ached with confusion over her feelings for him. Hatred. Disdain. Affection. What else? Surely not love. Never love. Not when there was someone else—a mortal—whose love she craved.

"And what do you plan on doing while I'm winging my way to the fortress?" he asked.

Pru shifted uncomfortably, not daring to tell him of her plan to gain the trust of the voodoo queen. "Oh, I don't know. I'm sure I'll think of something."

Chapter 17

The smell of boiling yellow soap and hot charcoal filled the air when Pru returned to the cottage on Rue Ste. Anne the morning after her encounter with Nicholas. Satisfied that he was on his way to rescue Stede from the Spaniards, albeit not out of kindness, she could concentrate on working her way into the voodoo queen's confidence. Nicholas might not want his soul back, but she wanted hers, and this was the only way she knew to get it.

Beyond the gate she could see the figure of Sabine Sejour hunched over the washtub in the yard, and called to her. The voodoo queen straightened up, wiping the suds from her hands on her apron as she came forward.

"So, you have come to learn the ways of voodoo."

Pru smiled courteously. "Yes, as I told you, I am eager to learn."

Unlatching the gate, Sabine said, "Every leader must have a successor, so maybe you will be mine, eh? Come in."

She followed the woman into the yard, past the clouds of white smoke rising from the tub, noticing the white skirt brushing her ankles, the white *tignon*, and arms the color of warm molasses covered with gold bracelets.

"Sit." Sabine pointed to the stoop and sat down beside Pru, drawing her knees up to her chest and winding her arms around them. "You will come with me to Bayou St. John Saturday night. Then you will see."

Pru dared not reveal that she had already been to the bayou and seen the dreadful spectacle. "There is one thing we must agree on," she said. "I will not harm another person."

Sabine slanted a suspicious look at her from narrowed black eyes. "What makes you say that?"

"Nothing," she lied. "I just wanted to be clear about my intentions."

"Good *gris-gris*, yes, I understand. I myself am a good Catholic and do no evil work."

Now, who is lying? Pru thought, careful to maintain a level look lest her thoughts show on her face.

"You will come here every day for lessons and then on Saturday and I will take you to the place of the ceremony. You will watch and learn." Her dark eyes moved over Pru idly but thoroughly. "Yes, I think you will make a good *voodooienne*. The mortals will feel your power." The gold bracelets jangled when she pushed herself up from the stoop. "Go now. The washboard is calling me."

She walked with Pru to the gate, and as she slid a slender finger beneath the latch, she said, "Do you have a name, blood-drinker?"

"It's Prudence." She prayed the name would have no meaning to her. "And what may I call you?"

"You may call me—"

Sabine? Lienore? A queer tingle went through Pru's body as she waited for a reply.

"You may call me *maman*."

The word rankled in Pru's brain. She had only one mother, the one that evil witch Lienore had driven to her death from the London Bridge all those years ago. She fought to keep a tone of revulsion from her voice. "As you wish, *maman*."

***

Moonlight shimmered along the moss that hung from the twisted branches of the live oak trees and rippled across the dark waters of Bayou St. John. Pitches of flame from a giant fire leapt toward the sky and gleamed upon the brown naked flesh of the dancers.

An area was cleared at the bayou's edge and a small wooden platform erected. Seated on a high-backed chair atop the platform, looking for all the world like a queen on a throne, was Sabine Sejour.

Tonight she wore a dress of scarlet kerchiefs sewn together. A red shawl with long, cord-like fringes draped over her statuesque form, and a blood-red *tignon* covered her hair. Her feet were bare, and the bells at her ankles tinkled as she tapped them in time to the beating of the drums. Heavy gold chains jangled around her neck and rested upon her bosom. Her arms were covered wrist to elbows in gold bracelets that sparkled almost angrily in the firelight.

Pru slid forward in her chair set below Sabine's, blue eyes wide and staring at the dancers. One strapping male dancer in particular drew her attention. Clad only in a red loincloth, he danced to the rhythm of the drums. It was only when he danced close to where she sat that Pru drew back. Thick black lines tattooed on his forehead looked like writhing snakes, and the bracelets around his wrists were fashioned from what looked to be human bones.

During their weekday lessons Sabine had told her how the voodoo religion had been brought from Africa to Saint-Dominque, and from there to this new land and to New Orleans when revolution on the island had driven many of the natives out, and that the religion was older than Christianity. For tonight's ceremony she'd been given a snow-white camisole to wear that fell to her knees and had been instructed to leave her hair unbound and her feet bare. She was to remain quiet and not say anything or join in the dancing.

Watching out in the open and not hidden behind the trees brought the ceremony into sharp focus, and for the first time Pru asked herself if she really wanted to become a part of this ancient darkness.

The thought was smothered when Pru watched a man approach the platform and hand Sabine a cup which he filled with a strangely glowing green liquid. Sabine drank in long, measured swallows and then passed the cup to Pru. Again it was filled. Pru looked skeptically down into the cup.

"It is only *la fèe verte*," Sabine said as she placed a finger beneath the cup and tilted it toward Pru's lips.

The taste was strangely pleasing, and she drained the cup. The man smiled through yellowed teeth and filled it again. Soon, Pru was seeing out of haze-filled eyes, and her body swayed to the rhythm of the drums.

Sabine leaned close and whispered, "Not now, *cher*. Your time for dancing will come."

Just then, the big dancer let out an inhuman cry. One of the women shrieked and fell to the ground, but no one paid any attention to her as the male dancer launched into inaudible mumbling, raising his arms to the heavens as if calling upon ancient gods.

The drums throbbed and the dancing grew more frenzied, and suddenly, as if on cue, it all stopped. Two men stepped out of the shadows into the circle of firelight carrying a large box. They placed it on the ground and then slowly backed away, bowing. The male dancer came forward and withdrew from the box a cage fashioned out of reeds. Inside, was the Vodu, a thick-bodied snake.

The shawl fell from Sabine's shoulders when she rose from her throne and walked barefoot to the cage. Lifting one foot, she brought it down upon the cage to the wild shouts and cheers from the crowd. Then, grasping the hand of the male dancer, they both began to twist and convulse. One by one the others joined in, until they all formed a circle of writhing, twisting bodies. The circle then broke and became a chain, undulating and slithering like a serpent around the fire, the lurid light of the flames gleaming across faces with eyes rolled back in their heads.

Withdrawing her hand, Sabine broke the chain, the others falling away like loose links scattering across the ground. Drawing near to the cage, she lifted the reed door, and reaching in with both hands, withdrew the snake. A hush fell over the dancers as Sabine lifted the serpent above her head, held it there for a few moments and then draped it around her shoulders. She began to spin, around and around, faster and faster. Words poured from her mouth, words no one could understand, but which Pru recognized with shock as the language she'd heard chanted long ago in London, the language of ancient Dubh Lein. The figure dancing and chanting and spinning wildly before the fire was not the voodoo queen Sabine Sejour, but the witch, Lienore.

While she wailed on and on, the big male dancer led a black goat into the circle. With one sweep of his knife he slit the throat of the goat and held a cup beneath the dripping blood. He offered the cup first to the queen, who stopped her chanting and spinning to take a sip. The people crowded around with cups to catch the blood of the goat, licking the scarlet stain from their mouths.

Pru watched the spectacle with eyes that grew even wider when Sabine approached, the snake still draped around her shoulders and offered her the cup. "Drink and be blessed."

Drinking the blood of thieves and murderers was one thing, but Pru had no desire to drink the blood of the goat. She accepted the cup and brought it to her lips and waited until Sabine turned away to rejoin the others before overturning the cup and spilling the goat's blood on the ground.

The throbbing of the tom-toms continued long into the night as the dancing grew wilder. People were falling to the ground, their clothes in shreds, blood glistening on their bodies. Eventually, clouds began to roll in from the river, obscuring the face of the moon, and the fire gradually died to a few smoldering embers. Couples began disappearing into the shadows. Sabine wandered back to the platform, and nodding toward the clumps of trees from which came wild moans and cries of sexual frenzy, she said to Pru, "They need no love potion for that." Reaching for Pru's hand, she drew her to her feet and draped something over Pru's shoulders.

The weight of it was heavy. Pru felt it moving against her skin and wanted to scream, but no sound emerged. She shivered and flailed her arms wildly in an attempt to shake it off, the way one does when walking unexpectedly into a spider's web. Panicked, she grabbed for it. Her fingers touched something soft and warm. It was not the body of the snake, but the woolen shawl that covered her shoulders.

Sabine laughed. "The Vodu is back in his cage."

"It felt so real."

"The green drink can make us see things that are not there," Sabine said knowingly. "Come, *cher*. It is time to go."

They left the bayou and walked back to town. "You saw many things tonight," Sabine said. "Do you have questions for your *maman*."

The trance that had overtaken Pru during the frenetic ceremony was beginning to fade. Had she really seen the people tearing and clawing at each other or had she only imagined it? "The snake," she said.

"The Vodu is a symbol of the ancient religion. It is no different from praying in the cathedral before the statues of the saints, eh? The dancing, the sacrifice, even the love-making, it is all a form of worship, is it not? And speaking of love, did you give your young man the potion?"

Stede. The very thought of him was a sharp reminder of why she was here in the first place pretending to cozy up to the witch she despised. "Not yet. He is away." Nicholas would bring him back to her. He had to, now that she had paid his price.

She left Sabine at the cottage on Rue Ste. Anne and continued on her way, passing through the *Vieux Carrè* with its pastel-painted houses, iron lacework and lovely courtyards. She was in no hurry to return home. Drawing the shawl tighter about herself to hide the chemise and ward off the autumn chill, she picked her way through the narrow, muddy streets, trying to make sense of all she had witnessed tonight on the bayou. At least she had managed to wedge herself into the voodoo queen's life. Where it would lead remained to be seen. Although, at the moment, it was difficult to concentrate on what the future held when the pain in her head that had begun as a dull ache escalated to a merciless throbbing as if she'd been drugged, and all she could think of was crawling into bed.

The next morning, she washed and dressed and went downstairs to make coffee in the kitchen, when there came a rapping at the door. Her first wishful thought was that it was Stede, but she knew it was too soon for him to be back. A tall Negro stood at her door. She might not have recognized him in the dull morning light were it not for the snake-like tattoos slithering across his forehead.

"From Madame Sejour," he said, placing a small box in her hand.

Closing the door, Pru carried the box to the kitchen and removed the lid. Inside, among other things, was a black candle.

"To exact revenge," Sabine explained later that day when Pru went again to the cottage on Rue Ste. Anne.

"And the chicken feathers?" Pru asked.

"You can put them inside the pillow of an enemy for revenge."

"And what do the bags contain?"

"Powders and dust from graves for protection."

Pru laughed. "What would I need protection from?"

"Not what. Who."

Her laughter died. "You still think someone close to me will cause me harm?"

In a voice riddled with bitterness, Sabine said, "There are always men who want nothing more than to see a woman destroyed."

A man. But which one? Not the one whose safe return she prayed for.

From the voodoo queen she learned how to make good *gris-gris* and which herbs and powders to put into the chamois skin bags, careful to follow Sabine's instructions and not handle the bags too much. She learned how to make evil *gris-gris*, too—a tiny black casket containing a small doll stuck with pins and left on a doorstep would bring death to someone within, or a mixture of Jimson weed and the powdered head of a snake would cause blindness. Just in case, Sabine said, although Pru claimed she would never use it.

"Eh, bien," Sabine said with a shrug. "The good *gris-gris* will bring you enough power and money."

It was neither power nor money she wanted, just the love of the mortal pirate with the infectious laugh and happy-go-lucky nature. Had Nicholas made it into the fortress to rescue her beloved? Had he kept his part of the bargain?

Chapter 18

$\mathcal{T}$he coral and limestone walls of the fortress reflected the moonlight. In the tower, the bats hanging upside down from their perches in the beamed ceiling unfolded their finger-like wings and rose in a great swarm. With a thunderous flapping, they flew out the narrow unshuttered window and headed for the mangroves surrounding the fortress in search of an evening meal. They moved as one, winging their way across the sky and darkening the face of the moon. The soldiers on patrol did not notice the lone bat that peeled off from the others and winged its way back to the fortress.

Flying back into the tower, it alighted on the stone floor that was cold and thick with droppings. It took a few steps on its membraned wings, nose pads twitching and pointy ears straining for sounds. As it moved forward, its wings lengthened, taking on the appearance of arms, and its hind legs grew longer, stretching into flesh and bone. Each awkward step became more graceful until, within moments, the bat transformed into a man, fully clothed and determined as he strode across the floor.

The heavy oak door, bolted from the outside, was no match for his inhuman strength. Without breaking stride, he thrust out his hand and knocked it off its rusted hinges, splintering the timbers. He climbed through the shattered door, snagging his sleeve on a piece of broken wood, cursing Prudence for asking this of him, but mostly himself for being so besotted with that miserable little vampire that he would jump through hoops for her like a pet dog.

And why? So that she could have her pirate? Why couldn't she see that only pain and heartache would come from loving a mortal, not to mention the possible destruction from loving this particular one?

What was it about Prudence that drew members of the Sanctum to her like flies to honey? First, Edmund de Vere, the London pewterer who had used her as bait to destroy him and who he'd been happy to dispatch, and now Stede Bonham who was stupid enough to get himself caught by the Spaniards.

His anger intensified as he followed the winding stone corridors. Not only did he not want to be in this fetid pit of misery, but it had been two days since he'd fed and his insides were burning up with thirst.

He stopped in his tracks at the sounds of voices coming from around the next corner. Into his nostrils wafted the scent of human blood. The aroma maddened him.

He winced at the prick of eye teeth lengthening through his gums. It didn't hurt; it was more like the feel of biting down on a *beignet* that had been left to harden. Flexing his lips over the fully extended fangs, he poked his head around the corner and peered at the Spanish soldiers.

There were two of them, donned in short jackets of blue cloth with red cuffs and collars, blue breeches and buckled shoes. They had cartridge pouches and bandoliers slung across their chests. Their muskets rested against the stone wall.

He shook his head at the half-savage Spaniards who lacked the *savoir faire* of the French and the civility of the Creoles. But a meal was a meal, and in this place he could not be picky.

"Buenos nochas, soldados."

The soldiers turned in unison at the silky smooth voice that spoke from behind and stared at the tall, languid figure gliding toward them. One of them reached for his musket, but before he could lift it to his shoulder, the stranger threw him against the stone wall. Seeing this, the other soldier drew a bone-handle knife from his belt to defend himself, but it was useless against the force that came at him like a cold, dark wind, grabbed him by the neck and lifted him off the ground.

"¿Donde estàn los prisioneros."

With feet dangling, the petrified soldier told him between choking breaths where to find the prisoners. He clutched the knife so tight that the blade cut into the flesh of his hand, drawing blood. His clenched fingers were pried open and the knife thrown into the shadows. Then he watched with bulging eyes as the strange man lifted his hand and licked it clean of blood. Seconds later, he was robbed of his last breath and drained of every ounce of blood in his body.

Nicholas dropped the bloodless body to the ground and removed the black neckerchief from his victim and was wiping the crimson stain from his lips with it when the soldier he had hurled against the wall regained consciousness. Stepping over the body of the dead soldier, he reached down and grasped the other's head in both hands. With a quick twist he snapped his neck like a dried twig. Feeling robust from the warm blood coursing through his veins, he continued on his way.

He felt no remorse for what he did, just the cold, irrefutable knowledge that if he hadn't acted, they would have tried to kill him, not that he could be killed, of course, save with a hawthorn stake to the heart. But it wasn't as if he couldn't be harmed. It had taken him quite a while to recover when his sweet Prudence had plunged a poker into his heart all those years ago in London, and he hadn't been about to find out what kind of damage the Spaniards could inflict.

Prudence. The thought of her at this moment both excited and infuriated him. Who but she would have had been bold enough to attempt to kill him? And who but she would he have forgiven for it? Not that she had always been so daring. When he met her, she'd been a timid little mouse afraid to speak her mind or give in to the passion he sensed brimming just beneath her placid surface. It had been a delight to initiate her into the pleasures of the flesh. As he followed the dead soldier's directions to a steep stairway and descended the narrow, winding stone steps, he thought about how she had taken to his lessons, and how her timidity had turned into the self-confidence of a seasoned courtesan, and he felt a surge of pride at having been the instrument behind her transformation. It hurt him that she thought of him as her enemy. If only he could convince her that the real enemy was the mortal he was here to rescue.

It occurred to him that he could simply kill the pirate and tell Prudence that he died trying to escape, but he could not take the chance that she would see through his lie and hate him even more than she already did. He had no choice but to help the mortal who was a rival for her love.

He found the place where the prisoners were kept by following his nose. The smell of human waste and fear led him to a dungeon in the subterranean depths of the fortress. A lone Spanish soldier sat before a thick iron door, his chair tilted back against the wall, hands folded across a bulging belly, asleep. Nicholas heaved an impatient sigh. He'd done enough killing for one day. Closing his eyes, he focused all of his thoughts and energy on transforming.

The soldier shuddered in his sleep when a cool mist passed over him and disappeared beneath the iron door.

Once inside the dungeon, the mist solidified into human form. Shaking himself off, Nicholas prowled the row of iron-barred cells, wrinkling his nose at the smell. He found the pirate in a cell at the far-end of the corridor and stood for a moment looking at him.

His wrists were shackled in iron rings embedded in the stone wall. His body slumped forward as far as it could go, head hanging down, dark, tangled hair obscuring his face. His breathing was labored.

"What she sees in you I will never know."

Stede lifted his head at the voice that spoke from somewhere close by. His hair was plastered to his face, and he blinked glassy eyes at the tall figure of a man inside the cell. His voice emerged as a rusty sound from the back of his throat. "How did you—?"

"Never mind that," Nicholas said in a harsh whisper. "And keep your voice down. "We don't want that fat excuse for a soldier to hear us."

Stede straightened his back, wincing from the pain of bruised muscles "Who are you?" he rasped.

"I'm a friend of Prudence Hightower's."

"Pru? I—" He lost his voice in a choking cough. "I don't understand."

"You will. Later. Right now, I have to get you out of here."

Swallowing and trying to take control of his faltering voice, Stede asked, "Did you bring the keys?"

"No. There wasn't time."

Stede rattled the chains. "Then how are you going to get me out of these things?"

"Like this." Nicholas grasped the chains in his hands, and with a mighty pull they came loose from the stone that held them. Ignoring Stede's wide-eyed astonishment, he knelt on one knee, dragged the manacles toward him and snapped them open, freeing Stede's wrists. At any other time the sight of blood staining a mortal's flesh would have enticed him, but having already fed, and not wishing to see the hatred in a certain pair of blue eyes, he refrained from the impulse to draw the bloody wrists to his mouth for a taste. "Can you stand?"

"It's been a while, but I think so." Pushing himself up from the vermin-infested ground, Stede rose shakily to his feet. He took a step and stumbled and would have fallen had Nicholas not reached out in time to steady him.

"Do you want me to carry you?" Nicholas asked.

"Hell no. Just give me a minute."

"Be quick about it," Nicholas griped. "We haven't got all night." It was just a matter of time before the bodies of the dead soldiers were discovered, but he didn't want to tell him that.

Stede took a few faltering steps. "I think I can make it now." He clutched his belly as a fierce pain shot through it. "Damn those Spaniards." Gathering what strength was left in his battered body, he walked unassisted to the door of the cell.

"Stand back." Lifting a leg, Nicholas crashed his boot against the bars. The door swung open with a squeal of rusted hinges and slammed against the stone wall.

"Great," Stede muttered. "That's sure to bring them running."

"There's just one of them," Nicholas said. "And I'll take care of him."

Sure enough, the crash of the iron bars against the stone wall roused the sleeping guard. They could hear the jangle of the key ring as he opened the big iron door and stepped inside.

Stede blinked his eyes at the torchlight that spilled in from the outer corridor and felt a cool breeze rush past him. One moment Nicholas was standing beside him, and in the next moment he was at the door, propelling the guard backwards and out of sight. The torch went out, throwing everything into darkness. There came the sound of thrashing about, followed by a muffled groan and a thud, and then silence.

Poking his head back in, Nicholas urged, "Come on. Let's get out of here."

A wave of excitement washed over Stede as he followed Nicholas out the door. He did not get more than a few feet when he tripped over something in the darkened corridor. His belly tightened at the sight of the guard lying motionless on the cold stone floor. "Is he—?"

"He's alive," Nicholas answered curtly. "But I suspect he'll have a massive headache when he wakes up."

Stepping over the prostrate body, fueled by the promise of freedom, Stede's limbs came alive with deadly energy. Matching Nicholas now stride for stride, the two raced down the darkened corridors and up the winding stone steps. Behind them they heard shouting and the stomping of boots as the Spaniards discovered the two dead bodies.

"This way," Nicholas urged. They could not leave the way he had entered, but he had thought of that. Fortunately, none of the Spaniards had paid any attention to the little brown bat that flitted about the night before, familiarizing itself with the best possible way out of the fortress. With the Spaniards hot on their heels, they raced toward it now.

***

The sun was emerging behind the treetops and the air was thick and humid beneath the mangroves when they stopped to rest along the shore.

Breathing hard, Stede sank to the ground, his back pressed against the trunk of one of the massive trees. "I can't wait to get aboard the *Evangeline*."

"The ship went down," Nicholas said flatly.

"The *Evangeline*? Scuttled?" Stede turned disbelieving eyes toward the water, as if he expected to see his vessel's sails furled against her masts.

"So the story goes."

Stede tore his eyes from the water and looked up at the tall, imposing figure standing over him. Lit from behind, the sunlight burst all around him like a halo. But there was nothing angelic about those green eyes. He thought back to the day on Grand Terre when one of his men had described this man's eyes as bright and cold and evil-looking. Suppressing a shudder, he asked, "How did you do those things you did?"

"I'll tell you later," Nicholas replied, although he had no intention of doing any such thing. "Here, drink this." Into Stede's hands he thrust the bottle of green liquid that he brought along and secreted in this spot. With enough of the drink in him, the pirate would never know if what he had seen was real or if he only imagined it.

Stede drank greedily, then ran a torn and soiled sleeve across his mouth. "I sure did miss this stuff in that place."

"From what I heard, it was this stuff that got you into that place," Nicholas commented sourly. "You seem to be overly fond of it."

"We all do what we must to survive," Stede replied. He lifted the bottle to his mouth and drank again. "These mangroves, for instance. They survive in hot, muddy conditions that other trees don't like. They take the salt spray and deal with swollen rivers and violent storms. Me, I drink to survive the memory of someone I loved and lost. I don't suppose you'd know about doing what you must to survive."

Nicholas replied with a bitter laugh under his breath. "Don't be so sure about that."

"When I get back to Nawlins," Stede went on, his speech slurring, "the first thing I'm gonna do is have me a big bowl of gumbo."

"And what about Prudence?"

"You say Pru sent you?"

"Prudence," Nicholas said, stressing her full name. "Yes."

"I wonder what she's been up to since I left."

That makes two of us, Nicholas thought, recalling that she was acting funny during their last encounter, as if she were keeping some great secret.

"I'll have to find another ship.

"Sorry. I can't help you there," Nicholas replied. It annoyed him that Prudence was merely an afterthought in the pirate's mind, while she was his entire world. "I stole one of the Spaniard's horses. It's tethered just over there in the bushes. You'd better get going. You want to get back to that bowl of gumbo."

"What about you?" Stede asked.

"Don't worry about me. I got here. I can get back."

Stede grunted with pain as he pushed himself away from the tree and got to his feet, tripping over a mangrove root.

Overhead, a flock of brightly colored macaws flew from tree to tree and a giant egret winged its way across the brightening sky.

Thrusting his foot into the stirrup of the Spanish saddle, Stede mounted and grasped the reins. He looked down at Nicholas and said, "I don't even know your name."

"My name is Nicholas."

"How can I ever repay you for what you have done?"

"Perhaps there is a way. I have taken a little quadroon whore into my home. I've grown tired of her but I don't want to return her to the flatboat where I found her and the life she had before. You could take her off my hands."

Stede swayed in the saddle. "It would be my pleasure."

"Good. Her name is Marie. She's quite lovely. I'll send her over. She'll be waiting for you when you get back to New Orleans. She'll bring you many hours of pleasure. Go now. I have done my part. The rest is up to you."

"I am in your debt. If ever you have need of me, you have only to ask."

Feeling pleased with himself, Nicholas stood back and watched Stede trot off into the forest.

His ploy worked. As much as he was loathe to admit it, Prudence was right whenever she accused him of doing things only for himself. It wasn't for her benefit that he had gone through all the trouble of freeing the pirate. And he certainly hadn't done it for the pirate. No indeed. He did it for himself. For when Prudence discovered that Stede Bonham was dallying with the lovely Marie, she was sure to break things off with him. And what better shoulder for her to cry upon than his own?

There was, however, something that troubled him. He had always relied upon his astute senses to alert him to the proximity of a hunter, and yet, except for a nasty smell from languishing for days in the dungeon, nothing about the pirate had alarmed him. The man was careless and reckless to a fault and had a penchant for the absinthe that would one day be his ruin, but Nicholas was now quite certain that he was not a member of the accursed Sanctum. But how did that explain the existence of the black bag? If it was not the pirate's, then who did it belong to?

Chapter 19

On a dark and chilly day in late November, in the Hall of the Cabildo, the French Colonial Prefect received the keys to the city from the Spanish Governor, despite word having arrived in July that Louisiana had been purchased by the United States for the sum of sixty million francs.

Tensions were high as the citizens of New Orleans awaited the arrival of the American commissioners and their troops. The Creoles were angry over the Americans' threat to close down the balls that were so much a part of the life of the city. As were the African slaves who gathered on Sundays on the green by the swamp and rocked the city with their dancing. The Americans, accustomed to quiet Sabbaths, viewed the city as a haven of depravity and dancing.

In the parlor in the house on Rue Bourbon, Pru poured more coal on the fire to ward off the evening chill.

"New Orleans is a tinderbox ready to ignite," James Hightower said as he sipped the blood in his glass. "I wonder what the Americans will do about the slaves. Everywhere you look you see the result of slave labor—in the carpentry, the ironwork, the cultivated fields outside of the city. Slave dealers are on every corner." He shook his head. "Such a nasty business."

Pru prodded the fire with an iron poker, recalling the night she met Stede Bonham and the disagreement over slavery that had gotten him tossed out of *The Snapping Turtle*. Heaving a sigh, she said, "It seems no one can decide who wants this territory. The Spaniards, the French, the Americans."

"The Americans will prevail," James said. "They cannot be stopped. They are coming to make money. I hate to think our days in New Orleans may be nearing an end."

Pru glanced up at him. "We can't leave this city."

"Why not?"

Because Stede has not returned, she wanted to say. "Because we have traveled all over the globe. It's time we settled down permanently."

Her papa looked at her from over the rim of his glass. "Isn't it you who is constantly complaining about the conditions here? Mud, mud, mud. That's all I hear from you. Wouldn't you rather be someplace that isn't as soggy as this?"

She drew in an uncertain breath. "Where would we go?"

"Why not home?"

"To London? You would trade the mud of these streets for the fog of those?"

He shrugged.

"And what about Nicholas? I thought you enjoy his company."

"Indeed I do. Although something tells me I would not be the only one who would miss him."

Pru rolled her eyes. "Oh, Papa, you're letting your imagination run away with you. It's not likely Nicholas and I will ever be as you wish us to be." *Besides*, she thought mutinously, *I am in love with someone else.*

It had been days since she swallowed her pride and went begging to Nicholas to help free Stede. Her anxiety mounted as she awaited word from him.

"There are too many memories in London," she said, hoping to divert the subject from the unlikely possibility that she and Nicholas would ever become the couple her papa wished them to be. "I have no desire to return there. I'm quite content to remain here. The Americans can be coarse and vulgar, and none of them understand a word of French or Spanish, but here we can move about freely and undetected, and I suspect that in time New Orleans will become as refined as Boston or Paris."

Her papa laughed. "Now whose imagination is running away with them? No, my dear Pruddy, this city on the delta is destined to remain a place of gambling dens, cabarets, balls and brothels. And men bent on pleasure will always find a way to profit."

She crossed the room, her feet treading noiselessly over the carpet, and bent to pinch her papa's cheek. "You are sounding very philosophical tonight."

He smiled sheepishly and was about to respond when there came a rapping upon their door.

"Who can be out on a rainy night like this?" James wondered.

Pru straightened. "I'll get it." Her breath rushed into her throat as she forced herself to walk calmly to double French doors. In the hallway her pace quickened until she was running. She stopped short to catch her breath and assume a casual pose as she opened the door.

"Why Prudence," Nicholas scoffed as he strode inside, "were you in that great a hurry to see me that you ran all the way to the door?"

He looked wind-tossed and robust and smelled of the night and the rain, and despite the sarcasm dripping from his voice, his smile was luminous.

"It's about time you showed up," she said irritably. "When did you get back?"

"Two days ago."

Her hand went out to catch his arm, fingers tightening over the wet woolen sleeve of his greatcoat to halt his steps. "Two days ago?" she echoed. "And you're only just now coming by?"

Looking down at her hand, he covered it with the cool press of his and pried her fingers loose from his arm. "I've been busy."

Pru bit back the urge to wince at his immeasurable strength, not because he was hurting her, but to deprive him of the satisfaction of seeing it. She flashed him a heated look. "If I haven't told you lately how much I hate you, I'm telling you now."

He lifted his wet lashes. His eyes sparkled with mischief and candlelight. "I'd love to go to your room so you can show me just how much you hate me."

"That's not likely to happen. And can you please stop thinking about yourself for a minute, and tell me about Stede? Did you—"

"Yes," he cut in with a bored tone.

"And is he—"

"Your pirate is on his way back to New Orleans."

The tension that had been steadily mounting since she learned of Stede's imprisonment escaped in a muffled moan. "Thank God."

"It wasn't God who winged his way over there, stole a horse, broke the chains and manacles, and was forced to kill two soldiers in the process."

"And for that you shall have my eternal gratitude."

"It's not your gratitude I want."

"I'm not going upstairs with you," she reiterated.

"That's not all I want from you, and you know it. Once, a very long time ago, I almost wed a girl from my village. I believe I told you about it. Since then, I haven't thought about marrying, but I could be persuaded." There was an earnest plea in his eyes. "When are you going to admit that we belong together?"

She gave him a withered look. "Now you sound like Papa."

"At least I'm not the only one who thinks we were meant for each other."

"What a preposterous thought," she said with a laugh. "Even if I were crazy enough to marry you, where would we ever find a priest to perform a wedding ceremony to unite the undead in holy matrimony?"

"The *padre?*" he suggested. "I hear he is quite an unusual fellow."

"Unusual is hardly the word I would use to describe him." She gave a guilty little smile. "Anyway, I don't think it's likely he will be performing any more ceremonies."

"Prudence," he exclaimed. "You didn't."

"I was hungry."

Raindrops fell from the shoulders of his coat when he accepted her explanation with a shrug. His mouth tightened, and he forced a laugh, "You're right. It was a preposterous thought."

"I'm glad you agree. Your co-conspirator is in the parlor. I'm certain he's eager to see you."

"Where are you going?" he asked, when she turned away.

"To see Stede, of course."

"You won't find him there."

She stared at him, alarmed.

"But you said—"

"I said your pirate is on his way back, but unless his horse has sprouted wings, it will take some time for him to get here."

He watched her spin off. "Prudence, wait. There's something about your pirate that I must tell you."

"I don't wish to hear any more of your disparaging remarks about him."

"It's not what you think."

"You don't know what I think," she responded. "Or have you added mind reading to your list of special talents? I'll wait a day or two and then I'll surprise him."

He heaved a black sigh, muttering under his breath as he followed her into the parlor, "I think you're the one who is in for a surprise."

Chapter 20

*P*ru swirled her cloak around her shoulders and drew the hood up over her head. Taking the decanter of potion-laced wine, she left the house.

As she steered the carriage bay down the narrow streets that led out of the city, the hood fell back. The sky was overcast, and there was no need to worry about the sun's rays on her pale skin. Her hair streamed out behind her on a river breeze, a few ale-colored locks whipping about her face as she drove by the sugarcane plantations with their columned houses and slave villages and past the colorful Creole cottages dotting the winding river road.

She was anxious to see Stede and give him the potion so that they could get on with their life together as she envisioned it. Perhaps then he would turn away from the drink that had gotten him into so much trouble. People could change, she told herself, and with her love and support, there was nothing standing in their way. Except for his love of the sea. And, of course, Nicholas.

Nicholas. Would she ever be free of him? Free of those haunting green eyes, that melodic voice, the power of his music, and the touch of his hand that threw her pulse into a frenzy?

Was he thinking of marriage now? He might have sounded cavalier when he suggested it, but the vulnerable look in his eyes, of fragile emotions so easily broken, spoke volumes. She'd be crazy to think they could have a life together as husband and wife, and he was even crazier for suggesting it.

She recalled the tale he told about his life as a young mortal man on the threshold of marriage to a girl in his village, and how one night, after hunting wolves in the snowy Carpathians, his life had been forever altered. His darkness had come at the fangs of a Transylvanian prince called Draculea. Hers had come at the fangs of a handsome Romanian wolf hunter.

She hated him. She didn't hate him. Her mind pitched and swirled, much as the *Evangeline* must have done before the sea swallowed her, she thought miserably. No doubt Stede was already making plans to secure another ship and resume his swashbuckling ways. She had to deliver the potion before he disappeared again and she lost him forever.

When she reached Stede's house on the outskirts of the city, Christophe appeared to lead her horse through the carriageway. She proceeded up the steps to the front door, glancing back over her shoulder to catch the quadroon's watery blue eyes fixed heavily on her. She wasn't afraid of him—she could easily snap his body in two—but there was something about him that set her nerves on edge.

She lifted the knocker and gave it several raps. Delphine answered and stepped aside for her to enter.

"Has he returned yet?" Pru asked.

"*Oui*," Delphine said solemnly. "But the Spaniards, they beat monsieur. He is sleeping."

"I'll just go up to see him for a moment. I won't disturb him."

Upstairs, she followed the cinnabar runner to Stede's room and gently pushed open the door. The argand lamp threw soft light across the walls. She walked softly to the four-poster. Nicholas had not told her about this, but even if he had, it could not have prepared her for what she saw.

Stede lay sleeping, his body cradled by the feather mattress, dark hair tangled about a face that was swollen with purple bruises.

Her hand flew to her mouth to catch a sob. She longed to touch him, to sweep back the dark lock that slanted across his brow, but dared not awaken him. For several minutes she stared down at him, her heart breaking over what he had endured. Tearing her gaze from his battered face, she backed away slowly.

As she walked to the door, her gaze strayed to the *armoire*. She wet her lips, wondering if the black bag Nicholas claimed to have found was still there. Did she dare look?

Listening for the deep and heavy sound of Stede's breathing, she went to the *armoire*, quietly opened the door, and rummaged through the contents. The bag wasn't there. She stifled the urge to laugh with relief.

Closing the door softly behind her, she left the room and headed for the staircase. Nicholas had some explaining to do. She couldn't wait to tell that scoundrel what she thought of his outrageous accusation against Stede. Vampire hunter indeed.

As she descended the stairs, a sound drew her attention away from her thoughts. Something inside of her tightened. She knew that sound. She followed it downstairs to the parlor. Parting the portieres, she peeked into the dining room. A girl in a white dress was humming to herself as she set the table.

It was Marie, she realized with a start, the young quadroon girl Nicholas had taken in to live with him. What was she doing here?

Pru stepped into the dining room and approached her. "Good day, Marie."

The girl turned and smiled sweetly. *"Bonjour."*

"I was under the impression that you are living with Nicholas as his…his…friend."

"That was before he gave me to Monsieur Bonham."

"Gave?" Pru practically choked on the word.

"Nicholas has been so good to me. I would do anything for him. Even come here to live."

"Live? How long have you been here?"

"Four days."

So that's what Nicholas had been busy doing. Is this what he had wanted to tell her the other evening? Fury flooded her. "And what did he send you here to do? Cook? Clean?"

"Whatever Monsieur Bonham needs," Marie replied.

At the moment Stede was incapacitated and unable to take full advantage of Marie's charms, but he would soon be back to his robust self, and that, Pru realized, was what Nicholas was planning on. Well, she would beat that scoundrel at his own game.

She withdrew the decanter of potion-laced wine from beneath her cloak. "Would you be a good girl, Marie, and do something for me? The moment Monsieur Bonham wakes up, you must fill a glass with this wine and give it to him. And see that he drinks it. It contains good *gris-gris* that will help him regain his strength."

"Did you get it from the Madame Sejour?" Marie asked.

"Yes. She prepared it especially for him. It will speed his recovery."

There was not a minute to lose. She had to get Stede to drink the potion as soon as possible. Pressing the decanter into the girl's hands, she said, "Do you promise you will do this for me?"

"Oh, *oui*."

Pru gave her a warm smile, and dropping her voice to a gently warning whisper, said, "But you must tell no one about it. Not Delphine or Christophe, and certainly not Nicholas."

"I cannot lie to Nicholas," Marie objected. "He has never lied to me."

"Then you do not know him," Pru muttered, but her sarcasm was lost on the girl. "Besides, it's not really a lie. This can be our little secret."

The thought of being part of a conspiracy seemed to please the girl. "Very well, I will tell no one. I promise."

Pru left Stede's house and turned the carriage bay's head toward the city, confident that by this time tomorrow her pirate would be thoroughly in love with her, and there was nothing Nicholas could do about it.

Chapter 21

When Stede failed to come the following day, Pru attributed it to his weakened condition from the beating he'd taken at the hands of the Spanish soldiers. When he didn't come all that week, she told herself he was busy making preparations to secure another ship and resume command of his enterprise. But as another week went by, she began to worry. Aunt Vivienne used to say that men in love made such fools of themselves and that a besotted fool would do anything to be with his beloved. So, where was Stede? Not wanting to appear to be the clinging type, she judiciously refrained from going again to his house outside the city, instead waiting for word from him.

To take her mind off it, she threw herself into her lessons with Sabine Sejour. She still declined to dance in Congo Square and offered convincing excuses not to accompany Sabine to Bayou St. John. But she did wrap her head in a *tignon* and accompany her to the homes of white women where Sabine dressed and coifed their hair.

"They are so *stupide*," Sabine complained. "They think I am deaf and do not hear the things they say to each other. Oh, the things I could tell you." Sabine taught her how to do their hair, cautioning her to remain mute. "If you speak, they will see you as a human being, and then, just like this—" She snapped her fingers in the air. "You will be out. And even if the way they want their hair done makes them look like creatures from the swamp, you must never tell them."

Pru learned her lessons well, and little by little worked her way into the voodoo queen's confidence. All that remained was to think of a way to get the witch to chant the words to restore her soul so that she might begin her life with Stede.

On a cloudy Saturday morning in December she donned a woolen cloak and went out to do some shopping. From the open doors of the cathedral came the chants of High Mass, without the *padre*, Pru thought with grim amusement as she passed the ten-columned building. While crossing a street, she had to jump out of the way of a landau and skirted the *banquettes* that creaked with pedestrian traffic. The city was a noisy place, with carriage wheels squealing, horses' hooves clopping in the mud, and the medley of languages on every corner—French, mostly, although English was fast catching up, and Greek and Spanish and German and Irish. And, of course, Creole, which no one but the Creoles could understand. The only quiet place, it seemed, was the river, where ships floated noiselessly against the currents, sails making slow arcs against the sky and the waters of the Mississippi sloshing against the levee.

There was a pale light in the sky, and the sunlight struggling to break through the clouds that splashed down upon the turrets of the cathedral. A crowd of people in the Place d'Armes drew Pru toward the square lining the riverfront levee where a ceremony of some sort was taking place.

Standing among the throng, her hood pulled low over her head, she watched as the French tricolor was slowly lowered and the American flag was raised. Through gaps in the crowd she recognized the figures of William Claiborne and General James Wilkinson, the new commissioners of the territory, as they officially took possession of it in the name of the United States of America.

From their balcony perch, Claiborne loudly declared, "I assure all the residents of Louisiana that their property, rights and religion will be respected."

Celebratory salvos boomed from the forts surrounding the city, and the Americans in the crowd waved their hats, crying "Huzzah!"

The French and Spanish residents stood by in bitter silence. The French governor who had arrived in March to take charge of the colony, only to turn it over to the Americans, burst into tears.

An American in bay rum and cutaway coat stated loudly that the Creoles were like the Mississippi River, and that both should either flow peacefully or be stopped altogether. To which an enraged Creole responded, "Sir, I will never allow the Mississippi to be insulted in my presence," and flung his glove in the American's face, inciting the crowd. The military guard unsheathed their bayonets and rifles and pressed in among the crowd. The American takeover could not have begun any worse.

Pru was bumped and jostled as she fought her way through the hostile crowd. From between the crushing bodies a hand reached out to snag her arm.

It was Nicholas, wind-swept hair blowing about his handsome face, the green of his eyes dark and murky on this cloudless day.

"Are you all right?" he asked.

"Quite," she replied. "Although I can't say the same for the Creoles."

He drew her away, turning over his shoulder to glance back at the crowd. "They fear their way of life is being threatened. They're like children, unprepared for the complexities of liberty, and I doubt the Americans will give them a voice in the government of—what did Claiborne call it—oh yes, the Territory of Orleans. The Spaniards, too, are furious. It's a wonder they haven't all departed for Texas. Only the Americans are pleased. It's just a matter of time before they come swarming into Louisiana, lured by ambition, cheap land and posts in the new territorial government. The Americans are a hardy breed. It will be interesting to see what they make of this city."

They left the angry crowd behind. "I was on my way to a coffee house where the lower classes like to amuse themselves," he said. "Would you care to join me?"

"I think not," Pru coolly replied.

"If you prefer, we could go to one of the cafès frequented by Creoles who refuse to admit that their precious New Orleans is now in American hands. We could sit in a dark corner," he teased, moving forward to press a thigh against hers.

"I don't want to go anywhere with you," she exclaimed, eyes flashing with fire as she flinched away.

He nodded with understanding. "You've been to see your pirate."

"I take it that's what you were alluding to the other evening. But your plan to lure Stede away from me and into Marie's arms has failed," she said tauntingly.

"Has it, now?"

"Yes. I'm going there tonight. He should be sufficiently healed by now, and we can begin our life together."

"Is that what he told you?'

"Not exactly."

"Yet you seem very sure of it."

She was sure of the potion, but she did not want to give Nicholas the satisfaction of knowing that she had won Stede's love through any means other than her own merit. "As sure as I am that Stede is not a member of the Sanctum. I looked in the *armoire*," she said hotly. "There was no black bag. You lied about it just to make me doubt him."

"I didn't lie. There was a black bag. I saw it."

Pru was unmoved. "You might be able to fool Marie into believing you are not a liar, but you'll never fool me."

"Go to your pirate, then," he said with disgust. "How much will he love you when he learns what you are? And he will. It's just a matter of time."

He pivoted on his boot heels and stormed off, his greatcoat whipping about his legs in the wind.

She hated quarreling with him. Even when she pressed her advantage she never felt very triumphant. At times like that he looked fierce and menacing, much like what his victims must see in their last moments. But what others saw as the work of the devil, she saw as false bravado. Worse was the look in his eyes whenever one of her barbs struck a sensitive nerve. For all his inhuman strength, with centuries of living behind him, he was as vulnerable as any mortal, with emotions so easily shattered and dreams squashed.

Muttering to herself, she made her way along the levee where barges, keel boats and flatboats discharged their cargoes, and headed upstream to the French market. Heavy wagons rumbled by, but all she could think about was the look on his face when she told him about starting a life with Stede and all she could hear was the sound of his voice that he had kept low to keep from breaking.

As she crossed the Rue Condè, she looked up from her disquieting thoughts to find her path blocked by a shabbily dressed American infused with the afternoon's festivities and, from the smell of him, too much whiskey. She stood tall, squaring her shoulders and refusing to budge from the *banquette* into the muddy street.

The uncouth flatboat man hurled slurred obscenities at her in a pitiful smattering of French.

Pru's eyes darkened with anger to stormy blue. "It is not that you mistake me for Creole that I find insulting," she hissed in English, "but that you dare to speak to any woman like that."

He replied with a drunken smirk, "So you're not one of those fancified Frenchies?"

"No," Pru replied evenly.

His bleary gaze washed over her. "No self-respecting white woman would be seen here. What are you, anyway?"

"I am your worst nightmare."

In a movement too quick for human eyes to detect, she flew at him, knocking him off the *banquette*.

He landed on his belly in the street and looked up with a face covered in mud. "Why you—!"

Casting a rapid look around to make sure no one was watching, Pru reached down, and with one hand circling his throat lifted the American from the mud, cutting off the rest of his words. He coughed and sputtered, partly from the superhuman grip she exerted and partly from a mouthful of mud.

She smiled, revealing sharpened eye teeth, and watched his expression change from anger to abject fear. "Don't ever speak to a woman like that again. Because if you do, I will find you. Do you understand what I'm telling you?"

When he struggled to form words, she told him, "A simple nod will do."

He managed an affirmative shake of the head.

Satisfied that she'd made her point, she sent him sprawling with a backwards shove. Her fangs retracted as she cast a sneer down at him. Delving into her pocket, she withdrew a picayune and tossed it down to him. "Go get a drink. I think you need it," she taunted, and turned and walked away.

Her mood was growing darker by the minute, caused first by Nicholas alternating between insane arrogance and little-boy-lost, and then the American displaying an appalling lack of manners. If he hadn't stunk so badly of whiskey, she might have dragged him behind one of the market stalls and drained every ounce of blood from his body. She was inclined to agree with Sabine who regarded the Americans as uncivilized. From what Sabine told her, even the duels they fought were barbaric. Not content to answer a challenge with a pistol, they often faced one another with squirrel rifles. The code of honor that was the lifeblood of Creole society and which hung in the sultry air like the refrain of a song was unknown to them.

Her spirits lifted when she thought of Stede, although she could not help but feel a twinge of guilt over the manner in which she had secured his love. *Well, no matter*, she thought, dismissing her culpable actions. *I did, after all, save his life.*

At the French market the Choctaws sat in silence on their blankets beside their trinkets, and the fishmongers fought for the attention of the servants who converged upon the stalls each day with empty baskets. Pru filled her basket with vegetables and spices for Babette's cooking pot and was on her way out when she bumped into Delphine.

The Creole woman drew back.

Pru presumed it was due to the color of her skin, more strikingly pale in the daylight than when lit by candlelight as it had been that night at Stede's house. "Delphine, how good it is to see you." She stared straight into her eyes, holding her gaze for several long moments before releasing it. "I won't keep you. I'm sure you're eager to get back to the house to prepare the evening meal for Stede. He is well, I take it?"

"I do not know," Delphine replied.

Pru sensed something amiss in the almost imperceptible hesitation in her tone. Looking down at the basket on the woman's arm, she remarked, "That does not look like enough food to feed a man with a healthy appetite."

"It is enough for me."

"Only you?" Pru inquired, her eyes narrowing. "What about Stede?"

"He is gone."

The word ricocheted off Pru's brain like the crack of a dueling pistol. "Gone? Where?"

"Where he always goes. To the island."

Pru laughed, a little nervously. Of course, she thought with a measure of relief. No doubt he went to Grand Terre to put his pirating venture back into action. "When did he leave?"

"Three days ago."

Three days, without a word to her? She felt a dull thud of panic and fought to keep it from infiltrating her voice. "Did he say when he would be back?"

Delphine shook her head.

Drawing in a breath, telling herself that there was nothing to worry about, Pru ventured, "What about Marie?"

"Marie went with him."

"I—I beg your pardon?" she stammered.

"When I went to his room to tell him dinner was ready, they were drinking wine and laughing. They left together the next morning."

Bewildered, Pru mumbled a vague "Good day," and left.

She was unaware of the cacophony of sounds rising all around her as she made her way back along the levee and past the mud puddle where she'd last seen the rude American. At the Place d'Armes most of the crowd had dispersed, with only a few revelers milling about to celebrate the American takeover. Her steps quickened until she was running. The hood fell back from her head, and her hair flew out behind her in a wave as thoughts converged on her like a swarm of angry bees. What was she to make of this latest turn of events? Was it her wine that Stede drank? And if it was, why hadn't he come to her to profess his love? Well, she huffed on a desperate note, almost out of breath, she would get to the bottom of this.

Chapter 22

*I*t was a two-day journey by barge and pirogue through the twisting bayous and marshes to Grand Terre. When at last the pirogue thudded against the shore, Pru paid the transport fee and got out, glad to have her feet again on solid ground. The breeze was stiff and tinged with salt. Waves foamed behind her as she made her way along the sandy beach in the direction the boatman pointed. All around her was a Garden of Eden of lush oaks, palm trees and blue-green lagoons. Oleanders scented the air and brown pelicans flapped their wings to the drumbeat of the roaring surf.

As she approached the two story house facing the open Gulf, she heard music drifting on the wind and a familiar voice crooning in English.

"I stepped aboard my rolling ship
beneath the morning sun
And rode the waves for fortune's gold
until the evening come
But where was love, no friend to me,
My life felt doomed to fail
Until I met my one true love
A dark-eyed quadroon girl."

The music was unaccomplished, unlike the majesty of Nicholas's music, yet the haunting song beckoned. Like a whisper draws one closer, she moved toward it, and in a distant part of her mind she thought this must be what it's like for the moth unable to resist the temptation of the flame.

A she rounded the corner of the house, her footsteps came to a halt in the sand. There was Stede, lying lazily in a red-clothed hammock strung between two banana trees, strumming a mandolin, the rhythmic cadence of his voice soft, lazy and lusty. Pru smiled and was about to call to him when a movement caught her eye.

Someone was lying beside him in the hammock. A dark-haired girl raised herself up from his side and rolled on top of him, silencing the song with a lingering kiss on the lips.

It was Marie.

The mandolin dropped to the sand as his arms went around her, hugging her close and kissing her back with ardor.

Pru's astute sense of hearing picked up the words he whispered against the girl's mouth. Words of love.

A gull screamed overhead.

Pru staggered back.

One true love. A dark-eyed quadroon girl.

The words of the song rumbled like thunder in her mind. He loves another, came to her with the force of a sudden blow. Her stomach heaved, and she fought down the bile that threatened to spill from her mouth. This couldn't be happening. Anger curdled in her throat. Inside, she howled with rage. How vile to long for the love of a man who loved someone else. She turned and ran.

The sand flew up from under her footsteps as she raced toward the beach. From out of a thatch of saw palmettos a figure emerged. Without stopping, she thrust out her arm and with the flat of her palm to his chest knocked him out of the way. The wind blew her hair in her face. Hot tears stung her eyes. She had to get away. She had to get off this island. But how? The boatman who had brought her here had disappeared into the marshes by now.

Nothing was as important to her as getting away. Nothing. Not Stede nor the love she would never have from him. She ran blindly, her eyesight hazed by tears, focusing all her energy on escaping the heartache that lay on every palm frond and in every grain of sand of this accursed island.

As she ran something strange began to happen. She felt it first in her fingertips, a dull sensation that spread to her arms. Looking down, she screamed to find that her arms had taken the form of wings, with thin membranes for fingers and webbing stretched between them.

She stumbled as her legs grew shorter. Dark brown fur sprouted in patches and spread across her whole body. Her ears lengthened, and her nose flattened until it was just a nub with a flap over it. Her whole body was a mass of vibrations steering her toward the shore. With the water within sight, she rose into the air, higher and higher, wings flapping, weaving and diving. The island receded behind foam and salt spray as the little brown bat winged its way over the water.

Across an evening sky of pale violet the small creature, scarcely noticeable in the dim yellow light from the lamp posts, flitted through the mean and narrow city streets and over the spacious gardens of the *Vieux Carrè*. Turning a lampless corner, it came to rest in the branches of the Spanish lime tree in the courtyard of the slope-roofed house on Rue Bourbon.

Her first awareness was of the melodic strains of the violoncello wafting through the tall French windows. Like awakening from a deep sleep, she was unsure in those first few moments if she was indeed awake or trapped in a dream. She reached up absently to sweep away a leafy branch that brushed her cheek. The leaves rustled all around her, and peering out into the darkness, she gasped to see the second-floor gallery at eye level. A glance downward revealed the ground far below. Dear God, she thought with a start, how did she wind up in the tree?

It took some doing to shimmy along the branch upon which she was perched and carefully climb her way down, going from limb to limb, and finally sliding to the ground with both arms wrapped around the trunk. She would never look at that old lime tree in the same way, she grumbled to herself as her footsteps clicked on the flagstones.

She came to a stop, staring mutely at the house as the first patter of raindrops fell against her face. Dazed and confused, her mind teeming with questions, she opened the door and went inside.

The music stopped.

"Pruddy, is that you?" her papa's voice called from the parlor.

"Yes, Papa." She fought for a level tone.

"We have been waiting for you."

We? Pru closed her eyes in anguish. Why did Nicholas have to be here? Wishing the night would swallow her up, she took a deep breath and opened the double doors to the parlor.

"Did you hear it, Pruddy? Nicholas has created the most wonderful piece."

"Yes," she said dully. "I heard it on my way in. It's too disturbing. It won't sell."

She didn't catch the look her papa and Nicholas exchanged as she went to the decanter. With hands that shook she poured herself a glass of sherry.

"That's not very charitable of you," James said.

Downing the sherry, she turned to face them. Her thick lashes almost brushed her pale cheeks when she lowered her lids and said distractedly, "I'm sorry, Papa."

"Pruddy, are you all right? You look like you've just fallen out of a tree, for goodness sake."

If only he knew how accurate his observation was, she thought, aghast. "Why Papa, I don't know what you mean."

Nicholas rose and came toward her. "I think he means this," he said, plucking a twig from her disheveled hair and casting a look down at her torn and soiled dress.

She shrank away from him. "That's absurd. What would I be doing in a tree?"

He gave her a sly smile before turning away.

"You're looking a bit ill," James said.

With a wave of the hand she dismissed his concern. "I drank from someone infused with too much absinthe. I didn't realize it in time. It has given me a dreadful headache. I think I'll go to bed now. I'll be fine in the morning."

"Yes dear, a good night's sleep is just what you need."

He seemed to be satisfied with her explanation, although a hasty peek at Nicholas revealed a skeptical smirk on that handsome face.

***

"Absinthe? Really, Prudence. Do you expect me to believe that you could not detect it on your victim before you drank?"

Staring out the rain-splattered window at nothing in particular, she said dully, "I don't expect you to believe anything. And I don't recall inviting you to my room."

"Nevertheless," he said with a sigh, "I'm here."

He moved smoothly across the room to stand beside her at the window. Drawing aside the velvet drape with one finger, he looked out at the glow of crystal chandeliers shining through the tall windows of the Spanish houses lining the street. He tilted his head toward her and sniffed her hair. She smelled of the night wind and the sea. "You must have been very angry."

She looked at him. There was an ethereal quality in the sensual line of his mouth, the straight nose and elegant jaw, the dark hair falling in silken locks over his forehead, and those lashes, longer and thicker than hers. He was so utterly and appallingly beautiful that at times it was almost possible to forget what a scoundrel he could be. "Why would you say that?"

"Because it is only when we are at our most volatile that we are able to transform. It must be nature's way of assuring that we don't transform indiscriminately. Do you want to tell me about it?"

She hesitated.

He gave her a knowing smile. "You didn't climb up a tree for your own amusement. You flew there."

She drew in a heavy sigh and walked to the bed and sat down on the edge with great care, as if unsure of the mere act of sitting. She searched for words to explain what she herself did not understand. "It was the strangest thing. I was running, and then, all of a sudden…" She stopped, uncertain, and looked at him helplessly.

"It began in the fingertips," he suggested.

"Yes."

He moved toward her with feral grace. "It spread to your arms and then to your legs."

"Yes, yes," she breathed, scarcely able to contain her disbelief. "That's exactly it."

"It's not as if you can feel the wings growing or the fur sprouting or the ears lengthening," he said. "It's more like something you sense happening from somewhere deep down inside. You hate it, yet you can't stop it. You have no real memory of what transpires after that, how you get from one place to another, only that you somehow arrive at your destination. Well, not in a tree, perhaps. But you'll get the hang of it. The thing is the transformation only happens when the anger builds so strongly that it manifests itself in this way. I gave up trying to figure it out centuries ago."

"And the wolf?"

"Ah, now that's a little different. Whenever I have transformed into *lup*, as we call it in my native Romania, it was out of irrational anger, yes, but more out of a need for revenge, sometimes against another, sometimes against life itself. Vengeance, blind, terrible vengeance drives that transformation. It's not something I'm particularly proud of, and I have tried to control it, really I have. But some things are out of my control, like the need for blood, and my love for you." He gave a quick little laugh at the sharp look she slanted up at him. "Yes, I know, you think me incapable of love, vile monster that I am, but I do love. Many things, in fact. I love the sound of the cathedral bells in the morning. I love the smell of chicory and the sweet taste of strawberries. I love the music I make that lifts me from the wretched depths of my reality to a place where I can almost believe that anything is possible." The feather mattress sagged when he sat down beside her. "And I love you sweet Prudence. More than I thought I could love any other being. And for that I am paying a terrible price."

She turned her head and looked into his green eyes. "How so?"

"Every time you scoff at my love or reject me it's like a stake driven to the core of my heart. Only this stake does not end my existence. It deepens the agony and prolongs the ache."

Oh yes, she knew that feeling. Seeing Stede with his arms around another woman and professing his love felt like a stake to her heart, driven so deep that in mere moments her faith in love was destroyed as surely as Nicholas had destroyed her mortality all those years ago.

"And the mist?" she ventured.

"Standard power for a vampire, requiring more practice than innate ability. Appearing as a small cloud or a wisp of fog has its distinct advantages, although one is vulnerable to wind currents, and it's somewhat taxing to switch between mist and corporeal form. I use it primarily as a means of infiltration. It came in handy when I rescued your pirate from the Spanish fortress."

He watched her carefully as he spoke and saw the wince in her eyes, an indication that he had struck a sensitive nerve. "I take it all did not go well with your pirate."

She jumped to her feet and glared at him. "You know it did not. It went exactly as you planned when you sent Marie to him. You knew he would fall in love with her."

"You give me too much credit," he protested.

"You're right about that," she said. "I do give you too much credit. For having any honor. There's no honor in you."

"Do you really think I can control people falling in love? If your pirate fell in love with Marie, it was not of my doing."

"But you sent her to him."

"Only because I thought you might not want him if you found him with another woman. I had no idea it would be him who would not want—" His words stopped abruptly when he saw the warning look flash in her eyes. "Are you certain he is in love with the girl?"

She answered stiffly, "Quite." Caught in a web of despair, she was heartbroken to the core and angry beyond endurance.

He fell back on the mattress, fingers laced behind his head. "Well," he said, watching her carefully, "I can't imagine how it happened. Except that people do tend to fall in love."

He noticed instantly the change in her demeanor. The eyes that had flashed heat at him only moments ago now could not look his way. He knew guilt when he saw it. "Be reasonable, Prudence."

"Am I not being reasonable?" she asked, even though she knew she was not. As devious and heartless as he was, he was not to blame for this. No, something had gone wrong with the love potion. She felt his steady, impatient stare. "All right," she relented, "so you had nothing to do with it."

"Thanks for that, at least." He rose from the bed. The candles in the sconces flickered as he strode across the room. At the door he paused to look back at her. "You deserve better than him."

"And I suppose you think that's you."

A shadow of distress passed over his face. "I hoped that I would be. That you and I—" He stumbled to a halt. "No matter," he resumed. "I can wait. I have all the time in the world."

When he was gone, she returned to the window and looked for his tall, well-built form to appear on the street below. The rain that had begun as a gentle patter was now coming down in earnest. He emerged beneath the dim yellow glow of a lamp post. She watched as he stopped to pull up the collar of his coat before continuing on down the street.

Chapter 23

*T*he sun was struggling to break through the lingering clouds, and the streets were black with slush from last night's rain. Pru skirted the ditches overflowing with sewage, and was heading toward Rue du Rampart where the *banquettes* were sturdier, when she heard the drums of the Sunday bamboula in the square.

Beneath the sycamores the earth was stomped bare by dancing feet. More than a hundred people were gathered, mostly slaves, dancing and singing and squirming like snakes in a pit. Two men crouched on their haunches, holding between their knees round drums that they beat with the heels of their hands, while an old African strummed the fingerboard of a stringed instrument. The drum beats, the squeal of the strings, and the chanting of voices in the African tongue, created a hypnotic, savage frenzy not unlike the spectacle Pru had witnessed in the bayou, only without a fat-bodied snake and the sacrifice of a goat.

A few blocks away the cathedral bells began to ring the hour, and one by one the street lamps were lit, radiating an incandescent glow over the bodies of the dancers, half-naked despite the growing chill in the air as dusk descended over the city. Pru watched for a little longer and then walked away. She hadn't come to this part of town to watch the dancing. She came for answers.

Inside the cottage on Rue Ste. Anne the voodoo queen sat quietly in the parlor, her sleek black neck bent as she worked with something in her lap and rocked back and forth in her chair, the embers of a dying fire reflected in the cold beauty of her face.

Sabine answered Pru's knock and held the door ajar for her to enter. Pulling a shawl tighter around herself, she said, "Wait here. I will bring in more wood."

When she was gone, Pru looked at the object Sabine left on the chair. It was a doll made out of brown cloth. Spanish moss stuck out from the edges of its arms and legs, the seams were sewn with neat backhand stitches, and it had little black beads for eyes. Its stuffed body was pierced with pins and nails.

"It is cold," Sabine said when she came back in. She piled the wood high on the fire. The flames sprang up, flooding the room with warmth and lurid orange light. "Sit, and tell me what brings you here."

Pru undid the clasp on her cloak and swirled it from her shoulders. "It's the potion," she said. "It didn't work."

Arching a skeptical brow, Sabine asked, "Did you give it to him?"

"I brought it to his house, but he was sleeping, so I left it with instructions for his…servant…to give it to him the moment he awoke."

"But you did not give it to him yourself?"

"No. I thought coming from me it would make him fall in love with me."

"You did not heed my words. You were not the giver. You did not hand it to him as you were meant to. The servant girl did. And she is the one your man fell in love with." She said this last part in a flat, knowing voice. "That was a very *stupide* thing to do."

Pru received the reprimand with a crestfallen look. "Is there anything that can be done?"

Sabine shrugged. "There is always something that can be done, eh?" Her eyes strayed to the rocking chair upon whose seat was the cloth doll. "Or you could burn a black candle. That will also bring death and destruction.

"I do not wish to kill the girl."

"Who said anything about the girl? It is the man you should destroy."

"What?" Pru exclaimed, horrified. "I love him."

"Then burn a brown candle. That's not as evil as a black one."

"I swore I would only use good *gris-gris*. With the way I am forced to exist I already have much to atone for. Besides, why would I want to destroy him over something that was not of his doing?"

"Because he is a man, that is why, and from my experience, all men are not to be trusted. Do not be so sure that it was not of his doing. My potions work when the receiver wants it to work…even if he does not realize it. Sometimes it works. Sometimes it does not." She stopped and tapped her chin thoughtfully "You could put stale bread in little pots of water and place them in every corner of your room. That would soak up your bad luck with men. As for this one, no, *cher*, there is nothing that can be done. But if I were you, I would consider myself lucky to be free of the rat."

It wasn't Stede's fault he fell in love with Marie, and it wasn't Marie's fault for giving him the wine as Pru had asked her to do. She had no one but herself to blame for it. She'd already had Stede's affection. Who was to say it would not have turned into deep abiding love if only she'd had the patience to wait instead of resorting to a voodoo trick?

Something Nicholas said loomed suddenly in Pru's mind. *"I have all the time in the world."* As one immortal longing for another, he was right. But she was an immortal who longed for a flesh and blood man, a mortal who would notice that she was not growing older and question it. Not to mention the possibility she still refused to believe that he was a hunter and would destroy her if he knew what she was. On the one hand, time was something she had too much of. She might not be able to gain Stede's love, but she was more determined than ever to regain her lost soul so that something like this would never happen again. And for that, time was something she did not have.

She slanted a sly look at Sabine. "Perhaps there is a way." Lowering her voice, she spoke in a whisper that hinted of conspiracy. "Once, a long time ago, a man—an alchemist—gave me a very old book. In this book he said was a chant that could restore something that has been lost."

"Ah, so there you go," said Sabine. "Speak the words."

"He told me the words can only be spoken by a woman with strong power. I didn't pay him much mind, but now that I think of it, I have the book, and you have the power. Would you do it, *maman*? Would you speak the words?"

Pru hoped the half-truth she just told was believable. There was a book, and it did contain a chant. But she wisely kept to herself that it was her soul she wanted to recapture, and that the words had to be spoken by a powerful witch. She held her breath waiting for Sabine's reply.

"What language is it in? French?"

"No. It's an old language that I don't recognize. But I'm certain you'll be able to read it. All you'd have to do is recite the words exactly as they appear in the book. It doesn't matter what they mean. Probably some silly nonsense about falling in love. I don't know—I'm not sure—it's my only hope. Please, *maman*." Pru prayed the false anguish she conveyed was convincing.

Sabine's expression reflected her uncertainty. "I think it is a waste of time, but bring the book to me."

Pru left the cottage on Rue Ste. Anne feeling the first real glimmer of hope. There was no way to know for certain if the chant would work—after all, the love potion had gone awry—but she had to try. A cabriolet rolled past her, the wooden wheels churning mud on her cloak, but she scarcely noticed as her mind forged ahead with thoughts and plans.

Her first thought was of her papa. Unlike her, he had taken to his undead state with ease. Now, he could play his beloved violoncello until the end of time, and having experienced that once-in-a-lifetime love with her mother, he had neither the need nor the desire to find love again. All in all, he was well suited to immortality, and her hints to him of possibly regaining his mortality had been met with a lackluster response. She would explain to him as best she could why it was so important to her that she become mortal again—why the prospect of growing old did not frighten her nearly as much as the prospect of going through eternity without someone to love. No doubt, it would be painful for him to watch her grow older and one day die, but difficult choices were not without consequences, and she was prepared to face whatever came her way. He was a fair and decent man, and in the end she was confident he would understand.

Nicholas, on the other hand, was a different matter. Why was he so stubborn about clinging to his immortality? By his own admission he hated the thought of subsisting on the blood of others which necessitated the taking of lives, no matter how vile they were.

He had wanted her to join him in immortality, claiming to be in love with her—if indeed it was possible for that scoundrel to love anything but himself. Her rejection of his dark gift all those years ago had wounded him deeply. Then he forced it upon her, claiming he did it only to save her life, but what kind of life was this that caused her to lurk in shadows and drink from the throats of others? Oh yes, he was happily content to be undead now that she was also undead. He wanted a playmate with whom he could cavort through eternity, someone like him who understood the uncontrollable urge for blood, while all she wanted was to put this behind her and become a normal human again. And if that meant withering and dying, so be it. To live one lifetime with the love of one man meant more to her than a million lifetimes. Why couldn't he understand that?

As she walked down the wide alley alongside the cathedral, she could hear the voices of humans like whisperings from the far corners of the city and smell the sweat from their pores and the perfume scenting their bodies. Giddy, fearful, and apprehensive all at the same time, she rounded the corner of Rue Bourbon and stood stock-still in the shadows, her eyes growing wide and gathering light from the lamp post at the sight of a familiar figure standing outside the wrought-iron gate to her house.

Chapter 24

*E*ven before she saw his face in the silvery moonlight she smelled the absinthe.

Torn by an impulse to run to him, a warning voice at the back of her mind cautioned her against it. He held something at his side. Was it the stake he intended to drive through her heart?

He turned then and saw her. "Pru, you do have a knack for sneaking up on a man real quiet-like." The soft lilt of his voice and the southern cadence of his speech worked in harmony to muddle her senses, and the lingering traces of the beating he'd taken at the hands of the Spaniards tugged at the heart she was trying desperately to harden against him.

"Hello, Stede."

He looked so fine in breeches of velvet in a rich crimson color. His damask coat, open to the cool night air, was decorated with braid trim along its edges. Beneath it he wore a black silk waistcoat whose silver threads caught the light and a satin sash slashed diagonally across his chest. A heavy, curved cutlass with its deadly cutting edge hung from the leather belt at his waist. On his feet he wore black leather boots reaching to his knees. The red feather adorning his tricorn swayed in the evening breeze.

She struggled to maintain a steady voice that would not betray the rapid beat of her pulse. "What are you doing here?"

"Waiting for you. I knocked on your door, but your father said you were out. Now I see where you get your pale complexion from."

"How long have you been here?" She spoke up quickly, hoping to divert the subject away from the hue of her skin.

"Longer than I'd wait for any other woman."

The smile he flashed threatened her resolve to be on her guard. "I can't imagine why," she said, trying to sound flippant.

"I brought these for you." From his side he lifted not a hawthorn stake but a bouquet of flowers.

"They're lovely," she said of the irises whose deep blue was like the midnight sky. "Thank you."

"They grow wild in the swamp. The color reminded me of your eyes, the way they get sometimes, like now."

"Yes, I've been told my eyes get darker when I'm angry."

"You must be mighty angry at me, then, because your eyes are as dark as those flowers."

"What would I have to be angry about?" Pru asked, testing him.

"One of my men saw you on the island," he replied suggestively.

She ran a finger along the top of the wrought iron gate. "I was there, yes. I was concerned about you. I hadn't heard from you since your return from the fortress, and when Delphine told me you'd gone to the island, I thought I would go there to see if you needed anything. But it appeared you had everything you needed."

"If you're talking about Marie, I don't know what came over me."

"Are you in love with her?" The bluntness of her question surprised even her.

He hesitated, but the look on his face confirmed what she already knew.

"Then why are you here?"

"I can't get you out of my mind." He offered a guilty little smile, his handsomeness affecting her more than she cared to admit. "Marie is pretty, but she's not as, shall we say, spirited as you."

Pru bit back the temper his remark provoked. "I am no man's whore," she said heatedly. But even as she said it, she longed to lay herself bare to him and feel his possession as she had that day under the live oak.

"That's not how it is with you," he claimed.

"Oh? And how is it with me?"

"I can't rightly say. You're different."

"You got that right," she muttered under her breath. "I can't accommodate you, Stede. Perhaps it would be best if you returned to Marie."

"I understand. I guess what I really came here for was to thank you for helping me. If you hadn't sent your friend to the fortress, I never would have made it back to Nawlins."

And to Marie, she thought ruefully. "Nicholas is very thorough," she said. "I'm glad he could be of help."

"I have to tell you, though, he's an odd one. In fact, the whole damn experience was odd. There I was, shackled in chains, and suddenly the cell filled with mist. At first I thought it was off the water, but it didn't smell of brine or salt. It was the rarest scent I ever smelled. The next thing I remember was being outside. There was a figure standing over me." He rubbed his eyes and shook his head, as if trying to dislodge the image draped like a cobweb over his mind. "I remember thinking what a fine-looking thief. But he wasn't a thief, and if he was, I had nothing for him to steal. He helped me to my feet and led me to a horse he'd stolen from the Spaniards. When I was mounted, he looked up at me and said, 'I have done my part. The rest is up to you.' I wonder what he meant by that."

That was like Nicholas, doing only what she had asked of him and nothing more. It didn't matter to him if the Spaniards went after Stede and recaptured him, although how many of them Nicholas had left alive was open to question.

"Did he say anything else?" Pru asked.

"No. But I'll never forget the way he looked at me. His eyes were green and bright. And maybe it was my imagination—he did give me something to drink which I admit may have confused me— but I thought I saw hatred in them. Now, why would a man who hated me have gone through all that trouble to save me?"

Why, indeed? Pru huffed to herself. And how clever of Nicholas to give Stede something to drink—absinthe, no doubt—to make him unsure of the events of his rescue.

"I'm sure he gave you something to drink to fortify yourself for the long ride home. You do seem to have a fondness for drink," she added sourly. "If I'm not mistaken, isn't that what got you captured by the Spaniards in the first place?"

He gave her a half-smile. "How you find out about that?"

"I overheard the men at *The Snapping Turtle* talking about your capture."

"What were you doing in the alley at night all by yourself? Tending a sick friend again?"

He was referring to their first meeting outside *The Snapping Turtle* when she drank from the throat of the nun-killer. "I was on my way home from visiting a friend and cut through the alley to save time."

"There you go again," he said, "being evasive. I thought we had become good enough friends by now where you could be honest with me."

She opened her mouth, breathing unevenly as she cast about for something to say. "Honesty is a two-way street," she replied at last. "Is there something you would like to tell me?" She strengthened herself for his admission of being a vampire hunter.

"Like what?" Stede asked. "I take it you already know how I make my living, so there's no secret there."

"What are you?"

"I don't take your meaning."

"Oh, I think you do."

"All right," he said impatiently, "so I fell in love with her. I couldn't help myself, Pru. It just happened."

"Being struck by lightning just happens," she said tersely.

His gray eyes darkened like shadows in the candlelight that fell from the tall windows of the house. "You're talking in riddles," he complained.

Pru felt herself quaking with confusion. If he was a member of the Sanctum, surely he knew what she was. Yet she had the distinct feeling that he did not. Something was amiss. She thought back to the black bag Nicholas adamantly claimed he saw in the *armoire*.

"The tale of your capture was not all I overheard at *The Snapping Turtle*," she said, averting her gaze so that he would not detect the lie she was about to utter. "It was a flatboat man from upriver who told it. A coarse fellow, judging from his speech. Anyway, he spoke of a story he heard from a Saint-Domingue slave about creatures that drink from the throats of the living." She forced a laugh. "It sounded quite preposterous, of course. But it got me to wondering. I have never encountered such creatures, but you have sailed all over the world. Have you ever come across such things?"

"The Cajuns tell of strange creatures they call Rougarou living in the swamp. But I've never seen one."

"What would you do if you did encounter one?"

"Run like my pants were on fire. My neck has enough to worry about from the hangman's noose."

He said this without a hint of guile in his tone, and every instinct she owned told her he was not a vampire hunter. She should have been relieved, but the knowledge of his innocence only stoked the flames of her agony. If only she had not allowed Nicholas to plant the seeds of doubt in her mind. If only she had not acted impulsively and gone to the voodoo queen for a love potion to protect her from a man she needed no protection from. If only she had allowed love to follow its natural course. If only...if only...Anger convulsed her and she bunched her fists at her sides. What a fool she was.

He was looking at her with starlight in his eyes. "I have a new ship, the *Marie's Fortune*. She's a fast ten-gun sloop. I won't be flying under a black flag, though. It was Marie who suggested that I fly a red flag, *jolie rouge*, with a dagger on one side of the skull for battle and a heart on the other side for life. She sewed it for me herself."

A farewell whispered through the trees. The anger faded, and Pru felt cold and sick. *I have truly lost him*, flashed through her mind.

"I'll be sailing in a few days."

"And Marie?"

"I set her up in my house outside the city. I wouldn't mind if you looked in on her once in a while until I get back. She told me how kind you were to her."

Kind, yes, when I could have...should have... killed her with one swift bite. "I'll do what I can," she forced herself to say.

He leaned forward and placed a light kiss on her lips. "Maybe one day you'll tell me what secrets you're hiding." The red feather fluttered when he removed his tricorn and bowed to her. "Farewell, Pru." Flashing a boyish smile, he moved past her and started down the street.

"Stede?"

He stopped and glanced back at her.

"Why did you take her in when Nicholas sent her to you? You didn't have to. You could have said no."

He shrugged his broad shoulders. "Hell, Pru, I've never been able to say no to a pretty woman. And she reminded me of my Evangeline." The scent of absinthe receded as he disappeared into the sweet-smelling mist.

She stood at the gate, tears threatening to spill from her eyes. The mist off the river chilled her body to the bone. Again and again she heard his voice. "Farewell," he had said. *Farewell to love and happiness*, she thought with despair.

With tear-glazed eyes she looked at the flowers clutched in her hand. Her fingers opened and they fell to the ground. She opened the gate and made her way numbly along the flagstones and went inside.

Out upon the street the flowers that were the color of the evening sky were picked up like weeds and scattered on the wind.

Chapter 25

*N*icholas lay on his bed, a layer of soil from his native homeland spread beneath the mattress of moss. No sleeping in a coffin for him, thank you very much. Although where that tired old myth came from was a mystery. No more a mystery, however, than how a creature like him could have fallen so hopelessly in love with Prudence Hightower.

In her mortal state she'd been so unlike any woman he'd ever known. Prim and decent and chaste to a fault. Not that she wasn't brave about some things, like the way she hadn't turned and run when he had revealed his true nature to her, and the devilish delight with which she had taken to carnal pleasure.

He recalled the first time he touched her. Her flesh fluttered with modesty but his astute senses detected the passion dwelling deep within. He had smelled it on her and heard the rapid beating of her heart without placing an ear to her chest. She had taken to it like a duck to water, or, more precisely, like a lioness to the kill.

Just thinking about it brought liquid heat to his loins. If he lived to be a thousand years old—and by all indications it looked as if he would—he would never have his fill of her. He'd given up long ago trying to figure out why she had this effect on him.

As he lay there, he imagined her standing at the foot of the bed, naked and smiling, hair like dark polished gold spilling over her shoulders and across her breasts, blue eyes peering at him seductively through thick black lashes as she swept aside her hair to reveal heavy breasts and a soft, white belly.

If she were there right now, he would rise and go to her. He would take her hand and lead her to the bed and push her down and watch the moss mattress conform to her shape, narrowing at the waist and gently flaring at the hips. He would touch her lightly at first, and feel her flesh flutter as it had that very first time. She would sigh and arch her back. He would wind an arm beneath her and draw her upwards to meet his kiss. And the warm, sweet taste of her would grow hotter and more demanding until she was kissing him back with otherworldly power known only to those of their kind. She would open for him, hands grasping his buttocks to pull him into the sanctuary of her body. Her breath would come rapid and uneven as she drew him in deeper and deeper and the pumping grew harder and faster. And if it were possible for him to die, that was where he would wish it to be—embedded in the velvet warmth of the only woman who understood him. And it was that understanding which lifted his lust to a higher plane and made him feel the one thing that he both craved and feared—love.

But what good was love when it was given and not returned? His face darkened with distress. Why couldn't she see that they were meant for each other? He knew not how it was possible, but somehow, long before he had come into existence, fate had decreed that his heart would be captured by a timid little mouse with the heart of a lioness.

Before she came along, he had not thought much about life beyond the moment, and even less about a future that stretched to eternity. His life had been without purpose, flashing from day to day, decade to decade, century to century, like riding a runaway stallion, hurdling over obstacles and splashing through decisions as if nothing mattered. And nothing did. Until her.

It had come as a revelation. He had rebelled and ranted against it. So unaccustomed to love was he that the prospect of it frightened him. That someone like he, a creature of the night, could love someone like her, so pure and untouched by darkness, had to be the work of the devil. Surely, God, who had turned a deaf ear to his prayers for mortality, had no hand in it. Or had He? Whatever the source, there it was. He loved her. As thoroughly and completely as it was possible to love anything. And she, in all her tempestuous passion, loved another man.

His plan to drive a wedge between her and the pirate had worked, albeit not as he anticipated. Who would have guessed that the pirate would fall in love with the quadroon whore? But as he had swirled around Pru and the pirate in vapor form witnessing their touching farewell, he had not failed to notice the look on her face as the pirate left her standing alone at the gate. A furious howl had sliced through his sanity. Would she ever look upon him with the same expression of love with which she gazed after the departing mortal?

Now that the pirate was no longer a rival and clearly not the possessor of the black bag, Nicholas could put aside his malicious thoughts of sucking the life out of him and turn his attention toward whoever had placed the black bag in the *armoire*. It had to be someone who knew the pirate's movements and was aware of his long absences away from the house outside the city. Someone who knew of his penchant for absinthe, and that when wrapped in the fog accompanying the binges he was not likely to notice the bag at the back of the *armoire*. Who was he, who was he? echoed through his mind.

But a hunter in the vicinity was not the only thing that troubled him. Prudence's association with the voodoo queen was the cause of much anxiety. Having followed Prudence to the voodoo queen's cottage, he could guess what she was up to. His mind raged with unanswered questions. How was she going to get the witch to chant the words from the book? Did he dare join her in this crazy endeavor? And if they somehow managed to regain their lost souls, would they be restored to their original mortal states? It had never been done before. Who knew what they would become? And if she did not love him now, what were his chances that she would love him then? He had to stop her from attempting this foolish thing, for her sake, as well as his own.

***

A single candle burned low in the cottage on Rue Ste. Anne. Finding the door ajar, Pru pushed it open and peered inside.

She recognized the tall, lean figure standing in the center of the room even though his face was concealed in shadow.

"Christophe! What are you doing here?"

Slowly, he turned and looked at her, his watery blue gaze washing over her. "Monsieur sent me to buy the green drink."

"I would think he's had quite enough of that," she remarked sourly as she came into the room.

"There are some things a man cannot do without," he said. "For him it is the green drink."

"I've had my fill of things men cannot do without," she griped. Blood, absinthe, what difference did it make? She glanced around and asked impatiently, "Where is Sabine?"

"In the bayou dancing to the voodoo drums," he replied with bitterness.

She looked at him closely. "I take it you do not approve."

"It is beneath her."

"You know her well enough to know that?"

"I did. Once. A long time ago."

Within his doleful reply she sensed a carefully guarded a secret. What was he not saying?

"I know why you are here," he said. "You seek a potion or a spell that will bind Monsieur to you."

A brittle laugh spilled from Pru's lips. "I tried that. But the potion Sabine gave me didn't work. I am here for a different reason."

She came forward and withdrew the book from beneath her cloak. Placing it on the table, she ran her hand over the worn and cracked leather. "Within these pages are the words that will restore to me something I lost. They must be spoken by a woman with great power. A woman like Sabine." A musty odor rushed into the air when she opened the book to the tattered page containing the chant.

The moonlight that came through the window fell upon his head of crinkly blond hair as he bent his head for a closer look and squinted his eyes to see better against the dimming candlelight. "She does not know that language."

"It is not necessary that she understand what she is reading," Pru explained "Only that she speak the words as they are written."

"Will the chant restore to me what I have lost?" he asked.

Pru shrugged and answered slyly, "That depends on what you have lost."

"I knew Sabine when we were young. She was not the way she is now. She was a happy woman, not the hateful person she has become."

His eyes misted as he spoke, and it was then that she realized his secret. He'd been in love with Sabine in their younger days, and he still was. It was their lost love that he wished to reclaim.

"It is as if something evil has jumped inside of her."

More than you can know, Pru thought. *An ancient witch with the ability to jump in and out of mortal bodies inhabits your beloved and has turned her into someone whose nature you no longer recognize.* "I wouldn't know about that," she said evasively.

Pru recognized the longing in Christophe's eyes for someone beyond his reach, just as Stede was beyond hers, and sheer desperation prompted her to use it to her own advantage. "If you will help me get her to chant the words, it is possible that what you lost will come back to you." The words were a reclamation chant to reclaim a lost soul, not a lost love. And as far as she knew, once Lienore exited a body, there was nothing left but a corpse. But enlisting his aid was worth a try.

Christophe walked with heavy steps to the door.

Scooping the tome up from the table, Pru blew out the candle, and followed him from the cottage.

A wind off the river chilled the night air. As they left Rue Ste. Anne and crossed onto Rue Condè, he warned, "Be on your guard."

She looked up at him. The light from a street lamp made his close-cropped hair look like a halo around his head. The white and black blood in his veins combined to make him rather handsome. It was curious that she'd never noticed that before. "Why do you give me this warning?"

He met her gaze, staring at her for a moment. "Monsieur told me that he fears the one with the green eyes might harm you."

"Nicholas? Nicholas is my—" What could she say? Lover? Yes. Friend? Perhaps. "He would not harm me." Her hand went out to catch his arm, pale fingers tightening over the sleeve of his coat. "Do not cross him, Christophe. He carries a heavy burden and can be very dangerous."

"There is something unnatural about him."

She forced a laugh and said dismissively, "There is something unnatural about all of us."

He lowered his voice to a bare whisper. "The Saint-Domingue slaves tell stories about the undead that walk among us."

Affecting a careless shrug, she said, "I would be afraid if I believed in such things, but I do not."

"If you have seen the ceremony in the bayou, you would know that all things evil are possible. She tells me things. Things that should never be told. She told me about the house on Rue Bourbon."

A tightness formed in Pru's chest as he spoke.

"She said the undead live there, and she has sworn to destroy them."

Pru was aghast. She shook her head disbelievingly. "Sabine told you this?"

"Sabine? No," he said. "I am talking about Delphine."

Delphine. Delphine. The name ricocheted off Pru's mind like a pistol shot. She had never considered that a hunter would be anything other than a first born son of a first born son, and least of all a woman with a sweet smile masking the heart of a cold-blooded killer.

"The servant of the house told her of their strange ways," he said.

Babette!

"Apparently, the servant helped herself to some wine from a decanter. But it was not wine. It was blood."

"That is preposterous. Delphine has been listening to too many slave stories."

"That may be," he conceded.

"I have to go." She turned quickly away.

"If such creatures do exist," he went on, "they are safe for now. Delphine is upriver visiting her brother. Come with me to the bayou and bring your book. I will help you get Sabine to say the words."

Pru hesitated.

He held out his hand, palm up, beckoning with his fingers. "Come," he urged.

The temptation was too great to ignore. Putting aside her disquieting feelings about him, she followed him down the street and into the mist.

Chapter 26

A full moon flickered through the branches of the cypresses, casting an eerie glow over the bayou.

Dressed in blue calico, the points of her *tignon* sticking straight up, golden earrings glittering in the firelight, the voodoo queen writhed to the throbbing rhythm of the drums. Draped over her shoulders like a deadly shawl was a black water moccasin whose venom had been removed.

Her head bobbed from side to side. Her eyes rolled back in her head exposing the whites. "Papa LaBas! Papa LaBas!" she cried over and over again in a voice that was not her own. Lifting the snake from her shoulders and holding it aloft, she whirled around and around, faster and faster.

Some in the crowd shrank in terror. Others moaned. One man fled into the swamp.

"She calls to the devil," Christophe whispered.

Standing beside him watching the spectacle, Pru shuddered. "She must have protected herself with good *gris-gris* to summon such an entity."

The voodoo queen stopped whirling, and with the serpent held high over her head, she approached the circle of onlookers. "Fear not, my children," she said, strutting before them. "I will protect you. Papa LaBas will not dare to harm you. Dance! Dance!"

"Maman! Maman!" they cried.

As the others stepped into the ring of light to join in the dancing, she wrapped the snake around her shoulders and sprinted away, twisting and writhing.

A lean black man wearing only a loincloth appeared out of the crowd with dark green bottles of rum. As she danced, the voodoo queen seized one bottle, pulled out the cork with her teeth and drank in long, deep swallows. Swaying from side to side, infused now not only with the heat of the dance and the tom-toms but with the power of rum, she went from dancer to dancer, holding the snake's head out to them so that each in turn might kiss it.

She went around the circle, and then stopped. A lopsided smile formed on her lips. "It is time for you to take up the dance."

Pru looked into those dark eyes that were wild and bright and fixed upon her. "*Maman*, I am not ready."

A look of hostility crossed that beautiful black face when she noticed Christophe standing beside Pru. "What are you doing here?"

"I have come to watch and to learn," he replied.

Her gaze swung back to Pru. "Come, *cher*, do not be afraid. I have taught you all there is to know." She called for the bottle of rum and thrust it at Pru. "Drink this and you will be ready."

With her purpose of getting Sabine to chant the words in mind, Pru grasped the bottle and tilted it to her lips. She choked as the fiery liquor ran down her throat. After several swallows, she lowered the bottle, but Sabine laughed and forced it back to her mouth, clinking the glass against her teeth and urging her to keep drinking as she unclasped Pru's cloak and let it slide to the ground.

Pru felt the world beginning to tilt. "*Maman*, I brought the book for you."

"And I have something for you." As she said this, Sabine unwound the snake from her shoulders and lifted it over Pru's head.

"*Maman*, the book."

"Later."

The weight of the serpent came down on Pru's shoulders. Somewhere in a distant part of her mind she wanted to scream. *No! No! I don't want to dance. Take this thing off me!* But no words emerged.

Sabine took her hand and drew her forward.

Her vision hazed, Pru handed the book to Christophe and stepped into the circle.

She moved slowly at first, as if caught in a dream, scarcely knowing what she was doing. Watching Sabine, she emulated her movements to the howls and moans of the dancers. Her legs felt rubbery and she thought she would collapse. Somehow, she remained upright as the vibrations of the tom-toms sifted through her body, growing stronger and steadier and more frenetic. Something was happening to her. It was no longer possible to tell if the wails and moans, the sound of shredding garments, and the erratic breathing came from those around her or from herself. Somewhere in the frenzied mist that enveloped her she thought she heard Sabine laughing and the voodoo queen's voice close to her ear chanting in words she did not recognize, words of an ancient language.

Pru's body quivered and trembled. Lifting the snake from her shoulders, she held it aloft as she whirled around and around, lending her voice to the cries of the others. "Ye! Oh! Oh!"

The same man who had appeared with the bottles of rum jumped into the circle. In his hand he held a rooster by its feet, its wings flapping madly in distress. To the cries and screams of the crowd he bit into rooster's neck, severing its head from its body. With blood gushing from his mouth and over his chest, he flung the dead fowl to the ground.

He approached Pru where she danced, lifted the Vodu from her and returned it to its reed cage. Then he sprang at her, his loincloth whipping up in the breeze to reveal a fully erect phallus. Winding an arm about her waist, he gyrated against her to cheers of "Ye! Ye!" from the crowd. People were falling to the ground all around her, men atop women, writhing in sexual frenzy to the savage rhythm of the drums.

Pru's head fell back, and her arms dropped to her sides. She could have snapped his spine like a twig and sank her fangs into his jugular, but a dark ecstasy had overtaken her. She felt energized and yet exhausted, excited and yet repelled. "The rum…the rum…" She was only dimly aware of breathing the words. "Wh—what have y— you done to me?"

His blood-stained face split into a grin, and in a sing-song way he chanted, "Rum flavored with jimson weed and rubbed against a black cat with one white foot." The high-pitched sound of his laugher echoed over the tom-toms and out across the still waters of the bayou.

Christophe stood on the perimeter of the circle, watching the spectacle with a sneer curling his upper lip. When the voodoo queen approached, his face went expressionless, betraying none of his revulsion. Nodding toward Pru who danced with wild abandon, he said slyly, "*Mon Dieu*. Look at her. She is *magnifique*. She dances better than all of them."

The firelight caught in the beads of perspiration dotting Sabine's ebony skin. "I have taught her well."

"Too well perhaps."

"It is me they come to see. I hold the power."

"For now."

"What is that you say?"

"She can have her pick of any man. White, Negro, mixed blood, rich, poor. See how they all lust after her. How long will it be before they throw you over for her?" Whether it was true or not, he need only plant the seed of doubt. "Why take the chance that she will be the one they come to see?" he said, pressing the point. "That she will be the new *voodooienne* who holds the power?"

He saw her features harden as jealousy wrapped its fingers around her black heart, and used it as his opportunity to strike. "I am speaking now not to Sabine Sejour, but to the one who holds her captive." He knew his words struck their mark when malicious eyes turned on him, eyes that did not belong to Sabine Sejour. "The voodoo queen is not worthy of you," he said urgently. "But that one is. She is young and beautiful."

Lienore screamed. Pulling the *tignon* from her head, she tore at her hair, not the flaming red tresses that had once spilled down her back but the coarse black locks of the voodoo queen. "Young and beautiful," she cried. "As I once was."

Knowing it was no longer Sabine to whom he was speaking, Christophe bent his head close to hers and whispered, "Think what you can do in such a body."

She hated him because he was a man, but more so because he was right. All the *gris-gris* and voodoo spells and dancing in the world would not give her the power that the blood-drinker could give her. Her eyes burned with unearthly fire when they turned toward Pru. Oh, the mischief she could make inhabiting that body. "Yes, yes," she hissed. "I will do it."

She began to chant in a high, toneless wail, calling upon the ancient goddess for the power to slip out of this mortal body as easily as she had slipped into it. The harsh melody rose to a shriek. There came a shuddering through the branches of the trees, and a great womanly form appeared in the night sky, its arms open wide.

Lienore's face twisted, and her large black eyes turned fiery red before going opaque. Her body contorted. From her lips spewed words about the Mother-right and the Goddess and things no living man could comprehend. Eyes bulging, she gave out with a shrill cry. "Goddess, Mother!" Between the moan of the wind and the roar of the night, she heard an ancient voice. *Come to me. Leave the spent body behind. Come.* With a final shriek, she collapsed on the ground.

Christophe recoiled at the foul-smelling mist that wafted from the prostrate body and hovered over it for a moment before rising into the air. It swirled on invisible currents this way and that as if searching for something. Then, gathering itself into a ball of vapor, it shot off in the direction of the dancers.

Unaware of the danger hurling her way, wrapped tightly in the arms of the nearly-naked voodoo dancer, Pru opened her eyes and saw not the blood-stained grin of a man who had bitten the head off a rooster but the face of the pirate she had loved and lost. His lips were at her neck. His hand was at her breast. His erection bit into her She wound her arms around him, her heart crying, Stede. Stede.

From somewhere overhead she heard a stirring and then a cold wind descended from on high. Closer it came, chilling her naturally cool flesh. She shivered at the feel of icy fingers stroking her cheek. The drums, the frenzy, the hands of the dancer, the threatening touch of evil—she felt high above it all, alone and far removed.

Words came to her mind as clearly as if spoken. *Open for me. Let me in. Open…Open.*

She felt herself falling. Everything grew murky. Something tugged at her arms and banged relentlessly on her chest. She had only to open herself to it and the torment would stop. The voice grew stronger…angrier…more demanding.

Open!

Open!

Pru's will was fast slipping.

The faceless menace gave a triumphant cry just as it was about to infiltrate its newest host.

Suddenly, a savage, snarling creature sprang into the circle.

People screamed in terror and ran about wildly to escape the snapping jaws of a wolf.

With fangs bared, it leapt into the air and came at Pru and the male dancer, knocking them to the ground with its giant paws.

The vaporous ball that had swarmed over Pru only moments ago spun off in wild confusion.

The wolf pounced on the dancer, ripping the flesh from his throat with its razor-sharp fangs. Holding the lifeless body in its mouth, it gave it a vicious shake and flung it into the air. It landed with a thud on the ground at the feet of the horrified dancers.

Women screamed. Men begged for their lives. The wolf snarled viciously, sending them stumbling into the alligator-infested swamp.

When the circle was cleared of voodoo dancers, the wolf turned its vicious eyes toward Pru who lay unconscious on the ground. As it loped toward her, its legs lengthened, the gray fur bristling over its body disappeared, the fangs receded, and its eyes of gold turned to green. Wiping the blood from his mouth with the back of his sleeve, he knelt beside her, brushed the hair from her face, stroked her cheek, and lifted her into his arms.

A hunter's moon broke through the twisted branches of the cypress trees, casting the bayou into lurid light. As he carried her away from the place of voodoo worship, he walked right past the lanky Creole man who crouched on the ground, face buried in his hands and shoulders wracked with sobs, beside the body of the dead voodoo queen.

Snagged in the moss hanging from a cypress limb, a ball of vapor flashed angrily and disappeared with a hollow scream into the night.

Chapter 27

*J*ames was seated on the sofa, one leg crossed over the other, reading the newspaper, when the French doors opened and Pru entered the parlor. Her feet barely skimmed the Oriental carpet spread over the floorboards as she crossed the room. Pulling an armchair up before the fire, she sat down and stared morosely into the flames.

He laid the newspaper aside. "Are you all right, Pruddy?"

Drawn from her tortured silence, she answered, "Yes, Papa."

He glanced at the clock on the mantle. "I wonder what's keeping Babette."

Pru heaved a belabored sigh. "You might as well know, Papa. I let Babette go."

"But why? Good servants are hard to come by."

"I caught her stealing." It was a lie, of course. She dared not tell him that self-preservation had forced her to follow Babette home and dispose of her with a quick and painless snap of the neck. She felt remorse for what she'd done and had reproached herself severely. Nevertheless, it had been too risky to let her live, for there was no telling who else besides Delphine she had told of her discovery.

"Ah, well," James said with a sigh, "in that case you did the right thing." He picked up the newspaper. "I was reading the most lurid story when you came in. The body of one of the slaves from the Fronteneau plantation was found several nights ago in Bayou St. John with his neck torn to pieces. Witnesses claim it was done by a wolf. I did not know there were wolves in the bayou."

"It was probably a feral dog," Pru replied, suppressing the truth. "From what I have heard of those voodoo ceremonies in the bayou, the people are often intoxicated. I'm surprised they didn't claim to see flying monkeys."

Bits and pieces from that night flashed back to her like lightning in a storm-filled sky, illuminating the darkness for terrible moments of clarity.

Through the cobwebs shrouding her memory she remembered the blood-stained smile of the dancer and his voice saying something about rum flavored with jimson weed. The rum was no doubt the cause of her head aching all the next day, and Sabine taught her that the leaves of the tall herb plant, when brewed into tea, could cause hallucinations, so the jimson weed explained why she had vague notions of seeing Stede's image.

Her body trembled as memories from that night converged on her—of Sabine urging her to dance, the weight of the serpent around her shoulders, the wild abandon of the dance, the flames of the fire leaping high into the night sky, the struggling, fluttering form of the black rooster, the shameful liberties taken by the half-naked slave, the strange whirring overhead, and a fierce voice demanding that she open...open.

And then it was as if the world had caught fire. People were running and screaming. She must have fainted, for the next thing she knew, she was lying in her own bed with the coverlet drawn to her chin, and Nicholas was standing over her. No, it wasn't a feral dog or a flying monkey that terrified the dancers and tore the throat out of that slave. The witness accounts were accurate; it was a wolf. Just not any kind of wolf they could ever imagine.

"Rougarou."

She turned her face from the flames and looked at her papa questioningly.

"It's a legend the slaves tell about a creature that lives in the swamp," he said. "Some say it's a man. Some say it's a wolf. Some say it's both."

We have more dangerous things than that to worry about, Pru thought, recalling what Christophe told her about Delphine. "Papa," she said suddenly, "I think we should leave this place."

He tilted the newspaper and studied her from over its top. "You haven't been yourself for days. Have you had another row with Nicholas?"

She wanted to run to him and put her head in his lap the way she used to do when she was a little girl and something had frightened her. He would stroke her hair and tell her that everything would be all right. But everything was not all right.

"Nicholas has nothing to do with it," she said.

Although, in reality, Nicholas had everything to do with it. If it weren't for him, she wouldn't be this half-dead thing in search of mortal love, nor would she have gone to Sabine Sejour seeking a love potion and wound up dancing to voodoo drums in the bayou. "There's too much darkness here. I want to go somewhere gay and exciting."

"Nonsense," he scoffed. "I dare say in the coming years the Americans will add their own unique brand of gaiety to the city. Wasn't it you who said you did not want to leave this city?"

"I've changed my mind," she said. Now that there was no future with Stede Bonham, and with the danger of a hunter close at hand, what was the point in staying? "And I seem to recall that not so long ago you said that our days in New Orleans might be nearing an end."

"I'm quite content where we are," he said. "I rather like the masquerades and fancy-dress balls. Besides, where would we go?"

"I had thought to return to Paris."

"Where you had to go to great lengths to make your kills unnoticed," he reminded her. "Here in New Orleans there is so much crime and fever I doubt anyone notices a drained body here and there."

She expelled a resolute huff. "It was just a thought."

"Our main concern at the moment is finding a replacement for Babette. Her red beans and rice cannot be equaled, and I cannot imagine having to brew my own tea."

"You won't have to, Papa. I'll do it for you."

After a long moment, he said, "I fear something is causing you much distress. Is it about the young man? The mortal? I had not the heart to tell you that I saw no good coming of your friendship with him."

Yes, she wanted to cry. Yes, it was about Stede, and a misguided attempt to procure his love and how it had gone terribly wrong.

It was about secret lessons with the voodoo queen.

It was about love potions and drug-infused rum.

It was about servants discovering decanters of chicken blood.

It was about the ever-present threat of a hawthorn stake through the heart, or a fire, or any number of ways to destroy their kind.

It was about the tainted love of a vampire whose touch, despite everything, she craved as strongly as she craved the taste of blood.

Affecting an uncaring tone, she said, "That friendship has ended."

She rose and went to the window to pull the drapes tighter, shutting out the light on this pale afternoon. "There, that's better." On her way to the door, she announced, "I'm going out for a while. I need to see Nicholas about something."

He raised a speculative eyebrow. "Are you feeling more cordial toward him, Pruddy?"

"Of course not," she said, dashing the hopeful optimism she heard in his voice.

***

Marie answered the knock on the door and stepped aside as Pru swept in.

"Is she here?"

"She?" the girl asked, perplexed by the urgency of the question.

"Delphine. Has she returned?"

"Oh, *oui*. She returned this morning."

Uncertain of what she would say...or do...to Delphine, Pru said curtly, "Tell her I wish to see her."

"I cannot."

"Marie, I'm in no mood—" she began.

"She is not here," the girl spoke up. "She packed her bag and left."

Pru looked at the girl who had stolen Stede's heart. She wore a winter dress of dark blue wool, the high neck adorned with a silver brooch. Her cheeks bore a pale blush, giving her a luminous look, almost like that of marble. Her hair was parted in the middle and hung down her back in long ebony waves. Her eyes were large and liquid and brimming with innocence despite everything she'd experienced in her young life. It was easy to see how a man could fall hopelessly in love with her even without the aid of a potion.

Pru tried hard to hate her, but found that she could not. A peculiar sensation passed through her, and she realized that, despite everything, she felt sorry for her. As much as it pained her to know that Stede's heart belonged to this young quadroon, she had to admit to herself that it was all for the best. After all, a man who spent most of his time at sea or inebriated would not be an easy man to love.

"Do you know where she went?" Pru asked.

"She said something about seeking employment elsewhere."

It was then Pru noticed the lace draped over Marie's arm and the needle and thread in her hand, and looked past her to the windows decorated with panels of lace.

"I want to make everything pretty for him," Marie said shyly.

"Do you expect him any time soon?" Even now, knowing that he was lost to her, she could not help but cling to the vague thought that things might have been different if only she had not interfered.

"I do not know when he will return," Marie replied, adding with a crestfallen look, Or even if he will."

"He will return," Pru offered reluctantly. "He loves you too much to stay away." *And you remind him of his Evangeline*, she thought with regret.

The wind carried the ringing of the cathedral bells over the treetops. Marie lifted her head and listened. "Angelus," she murmured. "You must pardon me. It is time for my prayers."

"Yes, I'm sure you have much to pray for."

"Will you join me?"

Her face devoid of expression, Pru replied, "I think not." She lifted the soft mass of her skirts and turned toward the door. Prayers, she huffed to herself, were merely a repetition of words, some spoken aloud, some whispered inwardly, whose sole purpose was to go unanswered.

Marie's touch at her arm stopped her.

"When I was a little girl, my *maman* told me that the love we seek is right before us. We have only to open our eyes to see it."

If that was Marie's way of consoling her for losing Stede's love, Pru was hardly comforted by it. She gave the girl an unconvinced smile and left. In time, she would no longer be prey to dreams of Stede Bonham. The dream would grow thinner and disappear altogether. Until then, her eyes were wide open, and love was nowhere in sight, and all the prayers in the world would not change that.

Chapter 28

The smell of coal burning in the grates mingled with the odor of swamp decay. The live oaks surrounding the cottage were still full and green, but the ragged fronds of the banana tree were frost-burned, the lush ferns leading to the porch steps struggled under a winter chill, and the honeysuckle shuddered against the weathered timbers. Even the music that streamed from the cottage infiltrated the swamp with icy undertones.

She found him seated behind his violoncello. His eyes were closed, his dark head bent. The pads of his fingers pressed the strings as he drew the bow across them with his other perfectly formed hand. She told herself it was the music that caused her to linger silently in the doorway, watching him. But in truth it was the sight of him. The misty light from the window lovingly caressed his face, sharpening the strong line of his jaw, etching finely-shaped cheekbones, and lathering his thick, glossy hair. His striking combination of beauty and roughness trapped her. There was an insolence in that face, something cunning and dangerous and utterly beautiful.

"It's a new piece. Do you like it?" He spoke without lifting his head, the music flowing from his fingertips.

At her unrelenting silence the music stopped. He looked up and frowned. Nodding to the basket swinging from her arm, he asked, "Going shopping?"

"I had thought to do some shopping, yes."

"Then why are you here?"

She walked into the room, the flounce of her dress brushing the hardwood planks of the floor. Unclasping her cloak, she laid it aside. "We have to talk."

He got up from behind his instrument. "I'm tired of talking to you," he said sullenly. "Nothing I say makes any difference." He forced his gaze away from the press of her breasts against the high-waisted bodice of her dress. Placing the instrument in its velvet lined case, he went to the fire and poked a stick in the coals until its tip was glowing, then carried it to a rosewood table where a candle sat askew in a brass holder.

"Why can't they make these things so that they don't have to be trimmed countless times in one evening?" he griped as he nipped the wick on the tallow candle and it sputtered to life. "And the ones made of animal fat smell abominably. Maybe one day I'll be able to sit comfortably in a lit room at night without gagging and choking." A wretched weakness came over him whenever she was near, and despite the ire behind his complaint, the flickering candle revealed the pain in his eyes.

Her heart, so accustomed to hardening against him, softened. She walked silently toward him. Taking his hands in hers, she held them together and stared into his eyes for a hint of common emotion. "We're not so very different, you and I," she said. "We both love strongly. Unfortunately, we love the wrong people." She slid one hand upwards to clasp the back of his neck, and bringing his face to hers, she kissed him.

He was the first to break away. "You mean the ones we love don't love us," he said, his voice savage and low.

"That's one way to put it."

"Is there any other way?"

She shivered, partly from the coals that were growing cold, but mostly from the ice encrusting his words, and released him, suggesting, "Hadn't you better throw more coal in the grate?"

He had never run from anything before—not from the wolves he hunted in his homeland all those centuries ago when he'd been mortal and the future looked bright, and not from the hunters who lurked in dark corners intent on destroying him now that he was no longer a mortal man and eternity looked long and hopeless. Yet he wanted to run now, as far away as he could from this degrading emotion he felt for her.

He looked away from that face that had captured his fancy since the first time he'd seen her. What was the year? he thought absently as he went to the grate and poured into the dying embers more coal from a bucket. Seventeen-thirty. As if he could ever forget.

At the touch of her hand running seductively up and down his back he drew in his breath. Every instinct in him responded as he turned back to her. "I thought you wanted to talk," he said roughly.

"We can talk later."

He groaned. "Why are you doing this to me?"

"Because I can. Because I want to." She raised her eyes to his with a sweep of dark lashes, and although her voice was scarcely a whisper, it trembled with despair and desperation. "Help me forget."

It didn't matter to him if she was using him to forget about the pirate. Nothing mattered if he could have her. Yes, he would help her forget…everything except him.

A breeze stirred the dark leaves beyond the window as she moved into his arms. His breath sang against her lips, hot and uneven as he pressed his mouth to hers. His fingers spread across her cheek, holding her mouth prisoner to a kiss that was both tender and cruel. When he felt her straining for breath, he pulled his mouth from hers.

They were both breathing deeply, staring into each other's eyes. He drew a breath deep inside himself and let it go almost fatalistically. "I want you in my bed."

She smiled, a faint acquiescence.

He snuffed the candle only recently lit. The odor of the extinguished wick filled the air as he took her by the hand and led her to his room.

He sat her down on the massive four-poster draped with brocaded tapestries. The feather mattress sagged with his weight when he sat beside her and turned her toward him. He reached up and withdrew the pins from her hair, letting them scatter on the floor. Putting his hand under the heavy mantle that fell to her shoulders, he lifted the silken locks to his face and breathed in the essence of her. For several moments he toyed with her hair, spreading the strands with his fingers before brushing them behind her ears and gazing at her for long time. Her face was so angelic it was hard to imagine it belonged to a seasoned killer. Like himself, he thought with a mixture of pride and regret. So much like himself.

He couldn't remember when he had begun to fantasize about her—the timeless perfection of her face, the fragrant waves of burnished hair, flesh so creamy and warm when mortal, now as cold and smooth as alabaster, eyes as blue as a cloudless sky, her cool, silken presence.

She had become so much a part of him that he no longer knew where he ended and she began. And yet, she claimed to hate him. But it was with a measure of satisfaction that he knew there was one thing about him she did not hate—his touch.

Muted light peeked through the tangled branches of the cypress and oak trees and slanted into the room, illuminating his face and the hungry look in his eyes as he returned to her and drew her to her feet.

His hands went around her to slowly and deliberately undo the fabric-covered buttons of her dress one by one. She made a little sound when he tugged at the bodice. It slipped off her shoulders and settled at her waist and then slid past her hips to pool around her ankles, followed by the plain white shift beneath.

Dropping to his knees before her, he ran his hands over the knitted cotton of her stockings, following the curve of her calves to the bare white skin at the tops of her garters, fingers brushing the coarse dark curls to seek the hidden folds between her legs. Spreading the moist pink lips with his thumbs, he brought his face forward and began a torturous exploration with his mouth of her innermost places. His tongue swirled against the heat, then settled upon the swollen nub.

She whimpered, arching against him, fingers splaying in his dark hair, clasping him to her. He made it last, teasing her and tasting her until she thought she would go mad. The stone-cold heart with which she defended herself against him was melting like an icicle in the heat.

Sensing her moment of total surrender, he drew his face away and rose to stand before her. His hands went to her breasts. Lifting their weight in his palms, he buried his face in the deep valley between them, then brought his mouth to each one in turn, suckling on the engorged nipples, using his teeth to draw ragged moans of pain and pleasure from her.

Her hands were all over him now, tearing at his linen shirt, sending the bone buttons spinning off into the darkness and ripping the seams. Unable to wait, she tugged at the buttons at the top of his fall front and shoved her hand into his breeches and wrapped her fingers around that part of him that was all heat and hardness. She stroked him and pumped him, teasing, tickling, tenderly at first, then harsher. She knew the punishing pleasure was hurting him, but he didn't try to stop her.

Kneeling before him, she crushed her face against him, feeling the scratch of woolen breeches on her cheek. Her eyes widened at the erect phallus that thrust its head out at her, its tip glistening with dew. She reached up with hasty hands to grasp the tight-fitting waist of his trousers and yanked them down to his boots. For several moments she gazed at the wonder of him—the slender hips that held an unearthly power to thrust violently into her, the corded thighs, the line of dark hair that ran from just below his navel to the thatch between his legs, the potent part of him that was both soft and hard, sweet and salty. Her hands went to his naked buttocks and pulled him hard up against her, locking him to her as she closed her mouth around him. His head fell back and his breath came in rapid bursts.

From somewhere beyond the tumultuous beating of her heart she thought she heard a growl, long, low and dangerous, rumble from above. His whole body tensed, and just as he was on the verge of the powerful release she knew him capable of, he pushed her away and pulled her roughly to her feet.

Green eyes burning strongly into hers, he said demandingly, "Tell me how you want it."

Her lips wet with his lust, she rasped, "The wolves."

He laughed, a low, licentious sound from deep in his throat. He kicked off his breeches and sent them flying across the room, followed by his boots. Spinning her around, he pushed her face down onto the mattress, winding his arms beneath her and pulling her hips and buttocks upwards. He ran his palms over her derriere and closed his teeth on the round flesh, nipping and biting the smooth white mounds.

"Oh!" she cried, her body shivering when he shoved himself between her legs, spreading them wide with his knees, and took full possession of her. She groaned, pressing her face into the rumpled sheets, feeling shameless, guilty excitement.

As he pumped into her, he reached around and beneath her to caress the nub that was throbbing and swollen from his intimate kisses. The rough massage that another woman would not have been able to sustain this one's otherworldly appetite craved...demanded.

Like two wild creatures of the night they twisted and writhed, pumping and thrashing together in a savage coupling.

She cried out when an explosion of violent pleasure washed over her, but she was too shaken to realize that the sound was not that of her own voice.

At the moment of his release a long, protracted howl pierce the night. His pumping gradually eased, and then he collapsed on top of her, falling to the side and pulling her along with him.

She spiraled back to earth from the ground-shaking sensations, yet when she tried to extricate herself, she found that she could not.

At her squirming, he opened his eyes. His voice was husky with sated lust. "You wanted to do it like the wolves." His chest rose and fell with difficulty as he fought to regain composure. "Wolves are locked together after intercourse. I hope you're not in a hurry. It will take a while for us to uncouple."

"Once before we did it like the wolves," she said breathlessly, recalling a scandalous night of pleasure back in London all those decades ago. "And we had no trouble disengaging."

"Ah, but that was as two immortals simulating the wolves."

"You mean we were really..." She dared not speak the outrageous thought.

"We were."

She shook her head incredulously. "I thought it was a dream."

"If it was a dream, then how do you explain this?" Grasped between his thumb and forefinger was a tuft of gray fur.

When he was finally able to withdraw, he held her tight against his chest "Did you like it?" he asked.

She squirmed in his embrace, ashamed to admit that she had never felt anything like it. "It was...different."

"You're a very wicked little wolf," he said in a low growl.

Pru opened her eyes to find him staring hard at her, smiling that sinful smile of his. Breaking the glance, she sat up. "I thought you told me that we transform into wolves only when we are irrationally angry."

He ran a finger along her spine, raising goose bumps. "Or irrationally aroused."

"Do many people do it like that?"

"I dare say they try. Although I sincerely doubt they are as literal about it as we are." He pulled her back down beside him. "You were made for it, you know."

"For acting like a wolf?" she chided.

"For fucking," he flatly replied.

"Now who is being wicked?"

"Not wicked. Just truthful."

"When did it ever suit you to be truthful?"

He withdrew his arm from around her, complaining, "I see you're back to your usual disagreeable self," and got up and walked naked to the window.

For many long minutes he stared out at the bayou, composed and thoughtful. Hazy light shimmered through the tangled branches of the cypress trees. What appeared to others as a dark and lifeless place was to his finely tuned senses alive with colors and sounds of creatures scurrying, scratching, chirping, and struggling as one fed upon another. He felt the faint rumblings of thirst from within. He hadn't fed since last night. Soon the urge would well up from the depth of his being and overwhelm him until he had no choice but to seek out a victim and drink the blood that sustained him. He expelled a fatalistic sigh and spoke against the window, his breath fanning the pane.

"What did you want to talk about?" he asked flatly.

She answered easily, "The other night."

He was not fooled by the insouciance of her tone. She could pretend that night was of little importance or concern, but they both knew better. "Oh, yes," he said, turning back to the room. "Your wanton display. Would you care to elaborate on the purpose of that?"

She rose from the bed and went in search of her dress. Lifting it from its heap on the floor, she expelled a disapproving sigh upon examining it. "A fine mess you've made of my dress," she huffed.

"You should talk," he countered. "I should make you repair the seams of my shirt and sew the buttons back on. And don't divert the subject. I asked you a question."

"What were *you* doing there?" she asked. "Have you been spying on me?"

He rolled his eyes at her answer to a question with a question. "I can hear the drums from my windows at night. I go there sometimes for a ready meal. No one notices if I drag one of them into the darkness for a taste of slave's blood. Your turn."

Adjusting the bodice over her full breasts, she replied, "How was I to know the rum was laced with jimson weed?"

"That would explain the way you danced—quite provocatively, I might add—but not what you were doing there in the first place."

She came to him and turned her back, sweeping her hair up off her shoulders. "I was hoping to get Sabine to trust me."

"So, you dressed like a voodoo harlot?" he said as he slid each button back into its slot. "And danced with a snake around your neck? Good Lord, Prudence." He made a face. "I hate snakes."

"I'd dance with Satan himself around my neck if it meant getting Sabine to chant the words." She smoothed the wrinkles from her skirts with the palms of her hands. "Now I'll have to find another way to get her to do it."

"Don't count on it," he said. "Your voodoo queen is dead."

His cold, flat words confirmed what she already suspected. She tried to summon a measure of grief, but the person she had known wasn't really Sabine Sejour. "And Lienore?"

He lifted his hands and fluttered his fingers as if to suggest she had flown away. "Your guess is as good as mine. She'll probably flit about until she finds another host."

"I'll find her," Pru tersely vowed, her features hardening. "If it takes me forever, I'll find her and make her say the words."

He knew that look, stubborn and resolute and beyond any warning he might give her. With a shrug he said, "Do what you must. Although, without the book, it may prove difficult."

"The book!" In the turmoil of her harrowing episode in the swamp, she'd forgotten all about it. The memory of handing the book to Christophe flooded back to her now. "It must still be there."

"It's not. I looked for it. It's gone."

The air went out of her in a sharp whoosh. "Gone?" she repeated, struggling to make sense of the singular word. She felt the hope seeping out of her, the way the blood seeped from her victims' veins when she fed from their throats. "It cannot be."

In a voice devoid of emotion he said simply, "Well, it is."

Clinging to the impossible belief that the thing she wanted above all else could still somehow be had, while in her heart she knew that all was lost, she said, "Christophe must have taken it with him."

"He didn't. After I brought you home, I went back to the bayou. He was still there, weeping over the voodoo queen. I watched for a while as he composed himself and then carried her body away. He did not have the book."

"What happened to it?" she demanded, her voice rising to a shrill pitch.

"Maybe Lienore found another body to jump into and carried it away. Maybe an alligator crawled out of the swamp and ate it. How the hell should I know?" He stomped across the room, snatched up his breeches and began putting them on. "You'd best get used to the fact that without the book there is no chant, and without the chant, there is no mortality." As he buttoned the fall front of his breeches, he cast a look downward and frowned. His still potent erection pressed against the fabric. "Look at it this way. It could be worse." Like still wanting to couple with a woman who, at the moment, clearly wanted nothing more to do with him.

She followed his gaze to the bulge in his breeches and gave him a warning look to maintain his distance. "I don't see how that's possible. We have lost the book, and there's a hunter close by."

He sat down on the edge of the bed to pull on his boots. In a bored tone, as if to placate her, he questioned, "How do you know this?"

"Christophe told me."

He looked up, his eyes brightening with interest. "Go on."

She swept her hair up off her shoulders and twisted it into a knot atop her head. "He knows the hunter."

Nicholas felt his ire rising. How could she be so damnably casual about something like this? "Who is the bastard? Who is he?"

"It's not a man. It's a woman."

"That's preposterous," he said. "The Sanctum is—"

"First born sons of first born sons," she said as she secured her hair in place with the pins she rescued from the floor. "But perhaps she is the daughter of a Sanctum member. Or the sister. Or the wife. Or the mother."

Perturbed, he said, "I get your point. We have to find out who she is."

"I already know who she is."

He rushed to her and circled her forearm with a powerful grip, spinning her around to face him. "Prudence, this is not the time for games. You must tell me all you know."

She winced from the painful pressure of his fingers biting into her flesh. "Her name is Delphine. She was the servant of—" She bit her lip. "You're not going to like it."

"There's a lot about life I don't like."

"She was Stede Bonham's servant."

The unexpected mention of the pirate's name took him aback. When she used him earlier to help her forget, he had known it was the pirate she wanted to purge from her system. But even after their lovemaking, looking at her now, with her eyes lowered and unable to meet his, and from the tone of her voice when she spoke that name, he knew he had failed in eradicating the pirate from her memory.

"He's not what you say he is," she said. "The black bag isn't his."

"I know," he replied stiffly.

Her gaze burned into his. "You knew and you didn't tell me?"

"I tried to."

"But you didn't try hard enough." She twisted her arm free and stalked away from him.

"What do you want from me?" he said sullenly. "Did you expect me to just hand you over to him? To stand by and watch you fall in love with someone who could never love you as much as I do?"

"You, you, you. Must everything be about you?"

"My life *is* about me."

"And my life is about me," she argued. "And I'll do with it whatever I please. And if that means falling in love with a man who will never love me back, so be it."

"When you were thrown from a window and lay dying in a puddle of water on a London street, it was I who gave you life. When you were nearly burnt to death in the distillery fire that your fiancé set, using you as bait to destroy me, it was I who saved you. At great peril to myself, I might add. Or perhaps you think it was pleasant for me to bear those hideous scars for as long as it took my flesh to rejuvenate."

"All right," she relented, "I owe you my life, and for that I thank you."

"It's not your thanks I want," he said broodingly.

"Nicholas, please, you ask for too much." She turned away in aguish, knowing she was hurting him.

He came up behind her and wrapped his arms around her, pulling her against his chest. Beneath his bare flesh she felt his heart thumping savagely against her back. His voice was a ragged breath at her ear.

"Perhaps I do ask for too much. But I have waited so long, so very long. I have watched people I loved come and go over the centuries. Each time it left me feeling bereft of hope. I had begun to think that I was destined to go through eternity alone, a pitiful, solitary creature not worthy of love. Until you. You revived my hope and gave me something to believe in. You're wrong, Prudence, when you say it's all about me. Since the day I met you my life has been all about you."

Her head fell back against his chest and she closed her eyes to the rise and fall of his breath. Into her being she breathed the scent of him, the sweet ambrosia of the vampire and the lingering scent of the mortal man he had once been. Were they destined to go through eternity battling and brawling, hating and loving each other? He understood her as no one else did. Not even her dear papa understood the emotions that drove her—the all-consuming obsession with mortality and the undeniable lust that drew her again and again into the vampire's arms. He was her lover, her savior, her creator. It would have been so much easier for them both if only she loved him.

"It is a mistake for you to love me," she said weakly.

"Perhaps. But it's a mistake worth making. There is one thing I would ask of you, though."

She turned in his embrace and looked up into his astonishingly green eyes that had the power to mesmerize as they had the first time they made love when he had charmed her with his eyes into acquiescing to his will. She needed no mesmerizing now as she felt desire surging anew within and would have given in to anything he demanded just to experience all over again the exquisite torture of his possession "What would you have me do?"

"Spend the night with me."

It was not what she expected.

He bent his head and nuzzled her neck, nipping at the tender flesh. His breath tickled her ear. "We could hunt together and then come back here. I want you to hear the piece I composed just for you. You can do your shopping in the morning."

She thought back to the piece for solo violoncello he had written and played for her all those years ago which he called A Bridge of Light, named for the London Bridge on which they'd met and the light she brought into his life, or so he said. There was an expectant, almost pleading, look in his eyes as he waited for her answer.

After a long moment of silence passed, she said, "I'll stay on one condition."

He laughed, a low, melodious sound from deep in his throat. He would have promised anything, even his soul, if he had one.

"There will be no more talk of love."

He hid his disappointment behind a casual reply. "Very well." He withdrew his arms and went to the *armoire* from which he withdrew a fresh shirt. "I'm thirsty," he said as he slipped it over his head. "You're looking a little more pallid than usual, so I'm guessing you haven't fed today. What do you say we find ourselves a nice fat throat to drink from?" Taking her by the hand, he grasped his coat from the back of a chair and led her from the room.

In the parlor he swirled her cloak around her shoulders and fastened the clasp at her neck.

She drew his hands away and looked at him earnestly. "Remember what I said."

"I give you my solemn vow that not a word about love will be spoken." He smiled stealthily to himself. He didn't need words to show her much he loved her.

***

As they strolled the narrow streets of New Orleans together, he imagined that others who saw them envied him for having such a beautiful woman on his arm, and that they whispered to themselves, "Look at that handsome couple. They must be very much in love." *Well,* he scoffed ironically to himself, *it was half-true.*

At the entrance to one of the myriad dark alleys, he stopped and told her, "Wait here."

He selected his victim, a nefarious chap concealed among the crepe myrtles waiting to pounce on unsuspecting passers-by and relieve them of their purses, subdued him and sank his fangs in deep. Returning to her, he smiled broadly and said, "I have a present for you." He led her into the alley and presented her with the prize in much the same way a cat drops its catch of a bird or a mouse at the feet of its master.

He watched with almost paternal pride as she drank from the neat round puncture wounds, making sweet little noises of contentment with each swallow. Dropping to his knees beside her, he lifted his victim's limp wrist to his mouth, pierced the flesh, and drank. *How quaint,* he thought with devilish delight. *We're just like any other couple out for an evening of fine dining.*

Infused with the elixir that kept their kind alive—if indeed *alive* was what they could be called—they returned to his cottage on the bayou and engaged in more heated lovemaking. Her boundless capacity for pleasure thrilled him. Although the mortal women he'd had over the centuries had often marveled at his prowess, their frail human bodies could not withstand more than one round of such fiercely punishing sex. It was not a bad way to die, he'd often thought with grim amusement. But Prudence, ah, what a gluttonous little creature she was. No mortal man could give her what she needed the way he could.

In all the centuries since his making he had used countless women to sate his unquenchable lust, but he had never loved one nor slept beside one as he did now. With his arm wound around her shoulders, hugging her possessively to his side, he watched her as she slept. He had no doubt that if he were to awaken her, she would submit to his overtures. But he did not awaken her. Instead, he rubbed his cheek against her hair. Relaxing his embrace, he sighed deeply, aching for her yet choosing not to do it, content just to hold her and dream about how it could be.

He fell into a deep, untroubled sleep. Sometime before dawn, when the sky was still dark and the birds were just beginning to stir in the treetops, he opened his eyes and reached for her, but she was gone, and with her went the dream.

He rose from the bed they had shared and stalked naked around the room, his steps making no sound against the floorboards despite his rising anger. Was this how it was destined to be with them, with her coming to him only when she had need of comfort or a favor, offering her body in return and nothing more? He damned her, but mostly he damned himself for wanting her and not knowing how to stop. A groan of anguish ripped from his throat, rising to a wail of grief that overflowed the small cottage and spilled out into the bayou. It rustled the moss hanging from the trees and skimmed across the still water, startling the creatures of the swamp with its dark and lonely sound.

At the window he pressed his cheek to the pane and looked out at nothing in particular. He had no idea how long he remained like that gazing into the darkness.

A curtain descended over him shutting out all conscious thought and leaving only that which could be felt—the coolness of the glass, the wind like a long and sad lament sifting into the room through a splintered timber, the breaking of his heart. For the first time since his making he felt truly and literally dead.

By degrees he became aware of a brightness infiltrating the tangled swamp, of creatures scurrying through the muck and decay, of insects burrowing through the earth. The awareness coalesced into thought. His face was serious, his mouth set in a moody scowl. *Ah, well,* he thought as he turned from the window, *what relationship doesn't have its ups and downs?*

He went to the parlor and removed his instrument from its velvet-lined case. Sitting naked behind it, he drew it to his breast and began to play the new sonata he had composed for her. But it was no use. He could not continue.

Something nagged at him. Prudence, yes, with her plump breasts and her legs spread invitingly. But it was more than that. He dropped his forehead to the violoncello and groaned. What was it? And then he remembered.

It was the story Prudence told of the woman hunter. What was her name? Delphine, yes, that was it.

The unease he'd felt listening to the story returned to him now as he sat naked in the moonlight.

The Sanctum was a well-guarded secret among its members. It was not likely that a member would reveal the true mission to his wife or sister or mother or daughter. No indeed. The women were never to know that their husbands and brothers and sons were cold-blooded killers. The hairs at the back of his neck stood on end, and every instinct he owned, every impulse he had honed to sharp perfection over the centuries, told him that if a hunter was close at hand, it was not Delphine.

Chapter 29

What was she thinking? To share a bed with him as if they were a happily wedded couple was sheer folly. What false hope must it have given him that they could romp through eternity together?

She had not asked for this existence. On the contrary, she had refused his dark gift when he offered it. Then there was the whole Lienore debacle when she'd been thrown from the window and lay dying in a puddle of stagnant water. All right, so she owed him her life, such as it was, but that was all she owed him. She certainly did not owe him her love, as if she had any control over that. And even if she could control on whom she lavished her love, it would not be that arrogant, selfish vampire.

She tried to imagine the way he must have been as a strapping mortal hunting wolves in his homeland, his handsome face dark and magnificent against the snowy Carpathians, those green eyes enchanting every girl in his village and capturing the heart of the girl who'd almost been his wife. She could picture his broad shoulders hauling firewood and snowflakes dusting his dark hair, and hear the sound of his laughter, infectious and carefree, before the demon came and turned him into a vengeful creature of the night.

Her heart twisted with wild emotion. What was it about him that she found so compelling? His pale beauty, of course. And his icy touch stoking the embers of her deepest desires. And the powerful surge of bloodlust that both fascinated and frightened her. Even the venom that often dripped from his words. And the casual arrogance.

It was all those things that drew her. But it was the look of desolation and the aching vulnerability that kept her coming back to him again and again. He possessed the strength, power, and killer instincts of a vampire combined with the fragility of an all-too-human heart.

Oh, what was she going to do with him, she lamented as she made her way to the French market to do a little shopping before heading home. She circled the coops of clucking fowl, baskets of live crabs, and barrels of pugnacious crawfish, and climbed the rickety wooden steps to the next level where market people hawked everything from fish to trinkets.

The sky was beginning to brighten above the river as she hurried away from the crowded stalls and chatter of people all talking at once. Her steps slowed when she reached a quieter part of town where, except for the heavy wagons that rumbled by, she could hear herself think.

So wrapped up in thought was she that she did not notice the emerging sunlight glittering on the round turrets of the cathedral beyond the Place d'Armes or the people lounging in the doorways of their shops. She walked with her head down, past dingy alleys where women were hanging the morning laundry, her head filled with thoughts of last night, when a figure that came bustling out from between the trees, startling her.

"Marie!"

Once again she was taken by the comely face so perfectly shaped, the diminutive nose a striking contrast to the generous mouth, the eyebrows thick and flat across the almond shape of her eyes, the parted black hair streaming behind her ears reaching to her waist. Delicate fingers clutched the woolen shawl she wore to ward off the early-morning chill. An empty basket swung on her arm.

The girl stopped abruptly, her flawless cheeks flushed from running. "I am so sorry," she said breathlessly. "I am in a hurry."

"Are you afraid all the food will be bought up before you get to the market?" Pru chided.

"He will be very hungry. I must be back before he awakens."

Flashing a smile to convey the warmth she did not feel, Pru said, "Then I will not keep you," and stepped stiffly aside.

"*Adieu*," Marie cried as she rushed past her. She stopped in the middle of the *banquette* and turned around and called out, "I forgot to tell you. If you are still looking for Delphine, she has found employment at a house on Rue Bourbon."

Pru froze with shock. Her heart gave a savage thump in her chest. It felt as if a giant hand had reached deep down inside of her and squeezed hard, making every breath an agonizing distress. Her thoughts flew in one direction.

Papa!

***

The emerging sun refracted off the stone crypts and mausoleums of the cemetery, lighting the narrow paths with pale morning light. Christophe stood before the crypt of his beloved. The inscription on the plaque read simply *Sabine Sejour, décédé le 31 Decembre 1803, âgée de Quarante-cinq ans*. Name, date of death, age. Nothing more to signify the life of the woman he had known and loved.

Followers had already scratched X's into the white stone, some in black with charcoal, others in rusty red using crumbling brick from other tombs. One follower had left an offering of a strand of beads hanging from a nail in the hope of securing a favor from the dead voodoo queen. In death, her spirit was as powerful as she had been in life.

But none of them knew her as he had known her, as a happy, carefree girl, a kind, charitable, almost saintly person. Her beauty was unrivaled. No one who saw her once ever forgot her. No doubt, that was how he lost her to Jean Laveau, her first husband, and then again to the Creole landowner who took her upriver. With the loss of her only daughter, Evangeline, her life seemed to spiral into darkness. When she returned to New Orleans, she was much changed. It wasn't just the voodoo. Something sinister had taken hold of her. She had become a stranger to him, and he, to her, was someone to despise. He had his suspicions, but it wasn't until that night on the bayou when he witnessed the terrible transformation that he realized what evil was at work within his beloved.

And now she was gone, and he was alone with his grief and his memories and his dreams of what might had been, while everything around him was changing at a rapid pace.

He cast a dispassionate glance at the tombs lining both sides of the path and sighed. With the recent purchase of Louisiana and impending statehood, the influx of all those Americans was likely to overcrowd the cemetery. He found those opportunity-seeking Americans pushy, pointlessly ambitious and greedy, but since they seemed to like the Faubourg St. Marie and had to be buried somewhere, why not bury them there?

There was no sense lingering. Nothing was going to bring his Sabine back to him, and besides, he had work to do. He turned away from the tomb, picked up his black bag and followed the narrow path out of the cemetery.

***

She ran through the streets that were just now coming alive with traffic, oblivious to the landaus of the planters who came to town with their families for a day of shopping and the wagons that rumbled by on great spoked wheels, the clopping hooves of horses splattering mud on her cloak. She darted this way and that to avoid the bustling bodies of pedestrians—sailors fresh off ships, Irish and German immigrants, black slaves, free people of color, and Americans everywhere.

She wished for transformation, prayed for the wings to sprout and turn her into a hideous little creature so that she could take flight and wing her way home even faster. But it wasn't anger that drove her—Nicholas had explained that the transformation was a result of abject anger—it was fear, growing huge and insurmountable.

When she reached her house on Rue Bourbon, she came to a dead stop, her heart pounding against the stress. For several moments she stood there, staring mutely at the gallery doors that were opened to the parlor, her head tilted as she strained to pick up the slightest sound. Then she heard it, a heartbeat, undetectable save to one who possessed the power to hear beyond any mortal's feeble ability. There came the faint scent of tea leaves brewing in the pot and the sound of tea pouring into a cup.

But Pru's sigh of relief stuck in her throat when there came to her ears the sound of a second heartbeat. Papa was not alone.

She fumbled with the latch on the wrought iron gate, flung it open and raced headlong up the walk, her shoes clicking frantically against the flagstones. The front door crashed open with the thrust of her palm and slammed back against the wall. Her mind filling with imminent disaster, she flew up the stairs in a horrific wind that blew up the curtains over the tall leaded windows and rustled the tapestries that hung on the staircase wall.

The glass panes in the French doors nearly shattered when she burst into the parlor to find papa seated in his favorite arm chair, a bent figure hovering over him.

"Get away from him!"

She flew across the room, hands outstretched, ready to tear the vampire killer away from her papa.

"Pruddy!" James sprang to his feet. "What is the meaning of this? That is no way to speak to Delphine. You must apologize at once."

Pru stopped short. Her wild gaze slid from her papa's angry face to Delphine's mortified expression, and dropped to Delphine's hand frozen in mid-motion holding not an implement of death but a cup of tea.

"I—I—," she stammered, not knowing what to say. Her mind raced. Surely, if Delphine had meant to slay papa, she would have done it when they were alone and had the chance. She came forward and took the teacup from Delphine's hand. "It's just that I always take care of that," she said impulsively. She lifted the cup to her nose and sniffed it, but detected nothing amiss in the aromatic brew. "Here you are, Papa," she said, handing him the cup and noting the sharp disapproval in his eyes.

"Delphine, I didn't realize it was you. I thought…Please forgive me. I didn't mean…" Her words trailed off into awkward silence. She cast a guilty look downward, only now realizing that the basket was still swinging from her arm. "Here," she said, forcing civility into her tone as she handed the basket to Delphine. "Why don't you take this to the kitchen?"

The floorboards creaked beneath Delphine's feet as she hurried from the room.

When they were alone, unable to meet her papa's potent, silent eyes, Pru inquired, "When did this happen?"

"If you are referring to Delphine, we were quite fortunate that she heard we were in need of help and came to us to offer her services."

"Fortunate, indeed," Pru mumbled. "Do you know anything about her?"

James sat back down and picked up his newspaper. "She needed employment and we needed help. What more is there to know?"

"Her background. Her references."

"You can wipe that suspicious look off your face, Pruddy," he said admonishingly. "And that little display you put on was quite unbecoming. I would suggest you smooth things over with her."

"Of course, Papa," she said helplessly.

She found Delphine in the kitchen. Summoning her sweetest voice, she said, "You really must forgive me. I haven't been myself lately."

"I do not blame you. Nothing has been the same since she came," Delphine grumbled as she plucked the feathers from the chicken Pru had brought home.

Puzzled, Pru asked, "Who?"

"Marie. She is not as timid as she looks. I had it with her orders, so I left." She looked up at Pru from over the chicken. "I would not be myself if my man was stolen by her."

Pru made a sound of despair. "I had hoped things would have been different between me and Stede, but—" She expelled a fatalistic sigh. "*C'est la vie.*"

"You take it very well," Delphine observed. "I would scratch her eyes out."

"That sort of thing is not in my nature."

"*Eh, bien.* You would not harm a fly."

Pru watched her closely as feathers fluttered to the floor. "You can tell that about me?"

"*Oui.* And your *père*, too. You are good people. I am, how do you say it, lucky to be here."

"Did Babette tell you we were in need of help?"

"Babette?" Delphine shook her head. "I do not know this Babette. *Mon frère* told me."

"Your brother? How did he know?"

"He heard it from your *père*."

"I thought—" Pru was suddenly confused. "I was under the impression that your brother lives upriver."

"He lives on Rue Condè. Near the ballroom."

The ballroom where her papa enjoyed the fancy-dress balls. Yes, she supposed it was possible that he had met Delphine's brother there and mentioned it to him. "I must have misunderstood Christophe."

"Christophe? Ach, that weasel. I would not listen to a thing he says. I never liked that one."

"What makes you say that?"

"He is always sneaking around. Especially when Monsieur is on the island. Once, when I go to Monsieur's room to change the sheets, I catch Christophe at the *armoire*. I ask him, what are you doing there? He closed the doors quickly and left. I thought maybe he was stealing something. Every time Monsieur leaves, something goes missing." She shook her head as she placed the plucked chicken into a pot. "I do not trust him."

At the mention of the *armoire*, unspeakable fear raced up and down Pru's spine. Was Christophe stealing from the *armoire* or placing something at the back? "Does Christophe have any brothers?"

"*Trois* that I know of. One lives in Paris, one died when the fever came through last year, and one was killed in a duel with an *Amèricaine*."

"Were any of them older than him?"

"Younger, I think."

Wetting her lips, Pru dared to ask, "Do you know if his father had brothers?"

"*Ma foi*, so many questions about Christophe," Delphine complained.

Pru leaned forward and placed a hand on her arm. "Please, Delphine." She tried hard to keep the urgency from her tone. "It's important."

Delphine glanced at the pale fingers encircling her arm. "So cold."

Drawing her hand back, Pru said, "I'm sorry. It's an affliction that runs in the family."

"*Ce n'est rien.* His *père* died a few years ago. At the funeral there was only Christophe. The old man had a younger brother who did not survive him."

Pru fought to control the wild terror sweeping through her at the realization that Christophe was the first born son of a first born son. She saw it all now with sudden clarity—the way those watery blue eyes scrutinized her, luring her to the bayou on the false pretense of helping her get Sabine to chant the words, and lying about Delphine to throw suspicion off himself.

"Where will I find Christophe?" Pru asked.

Delphine swung the pot over the fire. "He has a cottage on Rue d'Orleans, but he spends much of his time at *La Bourse de Maspero* complaining about the *Amèricaines* while he plays dominoes and smokes cigars."

Pru walked numbly to the doorway, pausing only to utter from over her shoulder, "Papa likes red beans and rice on Mondays."

Chapter 30

*D*elphine hurried to answer the pounding on the door.

Nicholas burst in, yelling, "Prudence!" in a voice that shook the house like thunder.

"She is not here."

He turned on her fiercely. "Who are you?"

Unnerved, scarcely able to eke out the words, she stammered, "I—I am Delphine."

Bending his head close, he sniffed the air surrounding her. Detecting no trace of evil, with green eyes hot and intense upon her, he demanded, "Do you know where she went?"

She replied with a faint trembling in her chin. "Sh—she said something about taking care of business on Rue d'Orleans."

Abruptly, he asked, "Where is the master of this house?"

Before Delphine could voice a reply, the parlor doors swung open and James poked his head out. "What is going on out here?" His eyes lit up at the sight of his friend. "Nicholas. I was not expecting you." But his pleasure was quickly dashed by the look of distress upon that handsome face. "Is something wrong?"

"I must speak with you at once," Nicholas said urgently.

"By all means. Come into the parlor. Delphine, would you brew a pot of tea?"

"There's no time for that," Nicholas cut in. Shooting a look at the woman who stood by in mute silence, he said, "Pack a bag for Monsieur Hightower. Only the essentials. And be quick about it."

"I'm not going anywhere," James objected. "What is the meaning of this?"

"I'll explain everything," Nicholas said. Turning him toward the French doors, he led him into the parlor.

James sat down, elbows resting on the arms of the chair, hands steepled, listening intently and muttering fearful conjectures as Nicholas told him of the danger they were in. Finally, he jumped to his feet. "A hunter!" he cried. "This is terrible. We must do something."

"I have a carriage waiting outside," Nicholas said.

"Where are we going?"

"*We* are not going anywhere. You are. I made the arrangements before I came here."

"But—"

"Where do you keep your decanter?"

James nodded toward a rosewood cabinet and voiced a frantic thought. "What about Pruddy?"

Nicholas moved across the room like a quick and silent wind and pulled open the cabinet door. "Don't worry about Prudence. I'll find her. Come. You must leave at once. There is no time to waste."

"My instrument," James cried.

"I'll get it." He dashed off to the music room and returned with the case containing James's violoncello.

Delphine had a small tapestry bag packed and was waiting by the front door when they emerged from the parlor.

Lifting the bag from her hand, Nicholas said brusquely, "Return to your home and wait until you receive word to resume your duties. You will be paid in the interim. Do you know where I can find Christophe?"

"He has a cottage where the old fort used to be. At the end of Rue d'Orleans." She shook her head. "I do not understand all these questions about Christophe."

His suspicion was aroused. "Has Prudence been asking questions about him?"

"*Oui*. She asked many questions."

Alarm shot through Nicholas like a hard-driven nail. There could be no doubt about Pru's business on Rue d'Orleans and the danger she was walking into.

Outside, the sky had lost its dusky glow, and the lamp lighter was lighting the wicks on the whale oil lamps, throwing pale light onto the street. Nicholas tried not to convey his growing fears to James as he held the carriage door open for him, pushing the violoncello case in after him. In a level tone he said, "This carriage will take you to a house on the outskirts of the city. From there, you will be put aboard a ship and taken to a safe place." He thrust the decanter of chicken blood into his hands. "When this is exhausted, I'm afraid you'll have to do your own hunting."

"I'm perfectly capable," James irritably replied. "I'm not an invalid, you know."

"Of course not. I meant no offense."

"Besides," James added grudgingly, "I had a good teacher."

Nicholas allowed the compliment to go without comment. "When the danger has passed, I will come to collect you." He started to draw away from the coach.

"You will protect my girl, won't you?"

The desperate plea held him to his spot. Looking strongly into James's eyes, he said, "I give you my solemn vow that I will protect her with my life."

James gave him a little smile. "You must love her very much."

"Is it that obvious?" Nicholas asked ruefully.

"Only to another who loves her as strongly. Be good to her, my friend. Perhaps in time she will come around."

With that wish in mind, Nicholas tapped on the carriage door, signaling the driver.

James slid forward on the seat as the wheels began to turn and thrust his head out the window. "You did not say the name of the ship."

Standing beneath the street lamp, an otherworldly light shone on Nicholas's face as he called after the carriage rattling unevenly down Rue Bourbon, "The *Marie's Fortune*."

Chapter 31

"*I*'ve been waiting for you."

Christophe froze in the doorway at the honeyed voice that spoke from out of the darkness. As his eyes gradually adjusted to the absence of light inside the cottage, they perceived a woman seated in an armchair by the fireplace. His gaze darted anxiously around the room.

"Looking for this?" Pru asked, drumming her fingers against the black bag in her lap. "I didn't think a hunter went anywhere without the tools of his trade."

Closing the door behind him, he walked into the room. Without removing his coat, he went to a lamp on small round table and carefully lifted the flint glass shade from its weighted brass base. "How did you know where to find me?" he asked as he lit the wick and replaced the shade, releasing the unpleasant odor of whale oil into the room.

"Delphine told me. You remember Delphine, don't you? She's the one you warned me about."

"Why would I warn you about Delphine?" he said evasively.

"Oh, come now, Christophe. Don't pretend you don't know what I am."

His pretence dropped like a load of bricks. "Yes," he sneered, "I know what you are."

"I'm curious how you found out."

"Sabine told me." Even now, he could not utter that name without a wince.

"I find that difficult to believe."

"Not in so many words. I went to her cottage to pick up the green drink for Monsieur Bonham, and she said something about a blood drinker who had ordered a love potion. When I saw you at her cottage the night we went to the bayou, you said the love potion she gave you did not work. I merely put two and two together."

"Was it your plan to get the entity inhabiting Sabine to jump into me?"

"I didn't know about that until later that night. My first thought was to help you get Sabine to chant the words."

"How very generous of you," she said sarcastically.

"It was not for your benefit. When I realized that my Sabine was not herself and that something evil had taken hold of her, I thought I could get her back by enticing that...that thing...to leave her. You were a likely target."

"Alas, the best laid plans do not always work out, do they? There was one tiny thing I neglected to tell you, however. When Lienore, that's her name, you see, leaves the host, well, you saw what happens. How does it feel to know you killed the one you love? Although, she wasn't really the one you love." She sighed. "It's all so confusing, isn't it?"

"You told me getting her to chant the words would bring back what I had lost."

"I lied," she said coldly. "Just as you lied about Delphine. She's not the hunter. You are."

"Now that you know, what are you going to do?" he asked

"Hmm, that is a dilemma. I certainly can't trust you to be a good boy and not do me harm."

"It's not you I want to destroy."

"Ah, yes. Nicholas. You are, after all, the first born son of a first born son, and the Sanctum has been after him for centuries. What makes you think I will let you destroy him? Not that I believe it's only him you want to destroy. No, it appears I may have to kill you."

"Not unless I kill you first."

"And how would you do that when your killing tools are in this bag? Oh, by the way, all this garlic you have hanging about the walls and from your bedposts is a waste of time. As you can see, it didn't keep me away"

With a calculated look, he said, "You're right. My tools are in the bag. But this isn't." He reached into the pocket of his coat and opened his palm to reveal a small white wafer.

Pru hissed at the sight of the Holy Eucharist. Unspoken fury filled her veins, but she was determined not to reveal to him the extent of her fear of the powerful Host. "You fool," she spat. "What you hold in your hand does more damage to you than to me. The Eucharist can be used only in the ways that God permits, not to your own advantage. By profaning the Host, you consign your soul to eternal damnation and risk excommunication."

The lamp light flickered along the edges of the holy symbol as he brandished it before her, noting with perverse satisfaction the way she recoiled, her back pressing against the pillows of the chair. "I am forgiven for what I do."

"Sins are sins and cannot be forgiven in advance, only when you repent for having committed them. Do you consider yourself a good Catholic?"

"Of course."

"Then your use of the Eucharist as a means to threaten me is an offense against Christ."

"You dare speak to me about what is offensive to our Lord? You, a creature of wickedness. Of selfish passions and evil ambition."

"I am what God made me."

"You are from Satan."

"And God made Satan."

"You delight in cruelty and blood."

"I do not kill out of malice." *The nun-killer and the padre notwithstanding*, she thought with malicious irony. "Neither I nor Nicholas are a threat to you." Another lie. Nicholas would have devoured him the instant he walked in the room.

"Now it is I who do not believe you," he said.

"Do you have children?" she asked.

"No."

Without a first born son, his obligation to the Sanctum would end with him. There was always the possibility that he would produce a male heir in the future, but by the time that offspring reached maturity, she and papa would be long gone from this place.

"I will strike a bargain with you," she said. "In return for letting you live tonight, you will swear on the sacred Host that you will leave me and my kind alone."

She studied his face. He looked confused and disturbed. A moment passed in which he appeared to be thinking.

"Sabine treated me with kindness," she said, pressing her advantage. "She knew that I did not choose to be a creature of the night, an exile from humanity, that I am also a victim. Perhaps she took pity on me because I am deprived of the light created by God." This last part was not entirely true for she was quite able to get around during the daylight hours provided the sun was not shining too brightly, but she wasn't about to tell him that. "She even looked upon me as a daughter and asked that I call her *maman*." Her eyes were steady on him as she spoke. "There are worse dangers hiding in the night. You saw it yourself in the bayou. We are not so very different. You longed for love from Sabine, I from Stede, and we have both been deeply wounded by the loss of that love. If you agree to the bargain, I give you my word that I will leave you here tonight with your life intact."

"What about that green-eyed devil?"

"I will speak to Nicholas on your behalf."

"You lied before. How do I know you are not lying now?"

"You don't. It's a risk you must take if you value your life. Besides," she slyly added, "if you kill me, you will have to answer to Nicholas as well as to Stede."

His face paled in the lamplight.

"Nicholas is very clever," she went on matter-of-factly. "He will have figured out by now that it is you and not Delphine who is the hunter. If you kill me, he will no doubt tell Stede. I would not call them friends in the true sense of the word. Let's just say there is an understanding between them. So, you see, Christophe, you can die by having the blood drained from your body by Nicholas or by being run through with a sword by Stede. Or, you can agree to the bargain." She shifted in the chair and turned her face toward the window. "Be quick about it. Daylight approaches and I must be going."

She could hear the frantic rhythmic beating of his heart as he contemplated the offer and the consequences of refusing.

He turned slowly and looked at her. A shudder rippled through his body at the eerie stillness about her, like that of death. And yet there was also something else that gave him reason to pause and question, "Are they all like you? So…so… He cast about for a word to describe her.

"Human?" she suggested.

He managed a broken nod.

"I find it difficult to detach myself from human pain and misery. Perhaps it is because I have only been in this state for a brief time, not yet a century, and am still in touch with my mortal self." She shrugged against the darkness. "Who knows? In any event, I would advise you to take advantage of the human nature I still possess."

His voice barely rose above a whisper. "I will agree to the bargain."

Her gaze followed discreetly as he returned the wafer to his pocket. A savage sense of triumph swept through her. She rose from the chair and floated toward him. Lifting her hand, she stroked his cheek with a cold finger. "You have chosen wisely, Christophe." He trembled and flinched away from her touch. Hopeful that she had inspired sufficient fear in him to keep him at bay, she feigned a sweet smile and said, "Just remember our bargain."

Outside, the moon was large in the pre-dawn sky. Pru picked her way around the ditches that gurgled with black slush from yesterday's rain, wondering how long Christophe would hold to his part of the bargain. She didn't trust him and would have killed him right then and there had he not used the Sacrament against her. Her powers were not yet strong enough to shield her against the Consecrated Host. The religious symbol which she had accepted willingly in holy communion when mortal was now used as a powerful weapon against her. As much as she hated to do so, it had been best to bargain with him in order to gain time. New Orleans had seemed like a good place to reside, for a while at least, but now, despite her papa's fondness for masquerades and fancy-dress balls, it was time to leave.

She returned home feeling tired and weak. The thirst burned within, the grinding in her stomach a familiar pain from not having fed, but she was in no mood to hunt. She went to the mahogany cabinet where her papa kept his decanter of chicken blood, thinking a few swallows would temporarily alleviate the unholy craving she had for human blood, but the cabinet was empty.

Upstairs, her papa's bedroom was vacant, as well, the bed undisturbed. Perhaps he'd gone to one of the cabarets along the river's edge as he sometimes did, bringing along the decanter secreted under his coat. Tomorrow evening, after he had rested during the daylight hours, she would sit him down and explain why they had to leave New Orleans. Papa would understand.

In her room she fell onto the bed fully clothed, too tired even to remove her garments, and slipped into a restless sleep.

***

Her mind and body awoke in the same instant. Turning her head on the pillow she looked toward the window. Moonlight streamed over her face through a slit in the velvet drapes. She was about to roll over and go back to sleep when there drifted to her nostrils a familiar potent scent.

He was sitting in an armchair by the door, green eyes blazing out of the darkness, his shadow merging with the shadows on the wall.

She swung her legs over the side of the bed and got up. "How long have you been sitting there?"

"Long enough. Do you know you make the most delightful noises when you sleep?"

"I do not."

"How would you know?"

With a roll of the eyes she trudged to the dressing table and lit a candle. "Never mind that," she said, pulling out the stool and sitting down.

"You haven't fed," he observed. "I can tell by your color."

"We have more important things to discuss than my sleeping or eating habits."

"I know. What did you do with him?"

"With who?"

"Christophe."

"Oh, him." She pulled a tortoise shell brush through her hair, working out the tangles.

"Yes, him. I went to his cottage. He's not there. So you must have disposed of the body somewhere. Although from the look of you, you obviously didn't drain it. When was the last time you fed?"

"I don't remember," she replied wearily.

"And yet you were strong enough to kill him. I'm impressed."

"I didn't kill him," she admitted.

He got up and came to her, his boots barely touching the floorboards. "If you didn't kill him, what did you do with him?"

"I bargained with him."

"You what!"

"I told him I would let him live if he gave his word not to harm us and that I would speak to you in his behalf."

"Are you insane? You don't bargain with a sanctioned hunter."

Her eyes flared to life. "I had no choice. He threatened me with the Consecrated Host. I don't know what came over to me, Nicholas. When I saw it, I felt the most dreadful fear. It wasn't just an emotional reaction. It was more like a physical pain, in here." She rapped a clenched fist against her abdomen.

"Ah, well, even I would have difficulty with that," he conceded. "It's one of the few things that can stop a vampire in his...or her...tracks."

"So, you don't blame me, then, for not killing him when I had the chance?"

He ran a cold finger over her porcelain cheek. "Not at all. Leave it to me. I'll take care of it."

"If you can find him."

The rhythmic stroking of her cheek ceased. With typical arrogance, he said, "I'll find him."

A sudden thought brought Pru's hand to her mouth to capture a gasp. "Papa! He wasn't here when I got home. He must be at one of the cabarets. I have to find him before Christophe does. I don't trust Christophe to keep the bargain."

Nicholas laughed. "You little hypocrite. The way you are not keeping to your end of the bargain?"

"I'm a vampire of my word," she said indignantly. "I told him I would speak to you about it, and I have."

"You also told him you would not kill him."

"That's right. I told him *I* would not kill him. I didn't say anything about what you might do."

He gave her a cunning smile. "What a clever little vampire you are. Just my type." His arm reached out to snag her about the waist and draw her to her feet.

She recognized the hunger in his eyes and put her palms against his chest to keep him at bay. "How can you think of such a thing at a time like this? We have to find Papa. I won't rest easily until I know he is safe."

Bringing his face close to kiss her, he said, "He's already safe."

Pru twisted her head from side to side to avoid his lips. "What do you mean he's already safe?"

"Not now," he breathed against her hair.

The moment was splintered by a display of strength that surprised him when she pushed him away and said in a threatening voice, "Now!"

His face lost all trace of humor. He looked at her, green eyes lingering for a moment on her lips that were rigid with determination, and then turned away from her, muttering something unintelligible under his breath as he walked to the window and parted the drapes. For many long moments he stared moodily down at the street below. At length, he said, "I went to see your pirate." He heard her soft intake of breath behind him and knew that the mere mention of the pirate would elicit the response he'd been dreading. "I arranged for your father to be put aboard a ship and taken to safety."

"Stede? Stede did that for me?"

"I prefer to think he did it for me," Nicholas replied. "To repay his debt to me for saving him from the Spaniards."

"Yes, yes, of course. It doesn't matter who he did it for, only that he did. What did you tell him?"

"That your father is in danger from those to whom he owes some gambling debts."

"Nicholas, you know Papa doesn't gamble."

"Would you have preferred that I tell him the truth?"

"I would prefer that you start explaining."

"When you left my cottage, I got to thinking about what you had said. It didn't make sense that the hunter was a woman, and what doesn't make sense cannot be true. That meant the hunter was out there somewhere stalking us. I might add it's a wonder I was capable of thinking clearly after our extraordinary round of lovemaking."

Pru shivered, besieged by scalding memories of their night together, and said tersely, "Go on."

"So, I went to see your pirate—"

"He has a name," she cut in.

"So, I went to see your pirate," he went on deliberately, "and made arrangements for your father to be put aboard the ship. Let me see now, what is her name?"

"You know very well what her name is."

"Your pirate—" He stopped at the glaring look she shot at him and acquiesced with a slight inclination of the head. "Stede agreed to take him aboard the *Marie's Fortune*. She's being outfitted for a voyage. Meanwhile, she is anchored in a secluded place—he did not say where—but assured me your father would be safe. I then came here to find you, but Delphine told me you'd gone to Rue d'Orleans. When I learned that is where Christophe lives, I knew what you were up to. I put your dear papa aboard a carriage that would take him to Stede and, from there, to the ship. By the time I got to Christophe's cottage, you and he were gone. Assuming you had killed him and disposed of the body, I returned here to find you asleep. End of story."

"This story won't be over until you kill him," she said.

"I have to find him first."

"Try Maspero's Exchange on Rue de Chartres. According to Delphine, he spends much of his time there."

"I know the place," Nicholas said. "Merchants and brokers transact much of their business there. What would someone like Christophe be doing there?"

"Delphine said he sometimes steals items from Stede. Perhaps that is where he sells them."

"Then that's where I'll begin my search. But first, I'm hungry."

Her gaze traversed his face. In the flickering candlelight his cheeks bore a faint rosy, albeit temporary, tint, an indication that he had recently fed

He smiled licentiously. "It's not blood I'm hungry for," he said, reading her thoughts. "It's you. I won't take no for an answer. Besides, it's the least you can do after I made safe arrangements for your father."

"Doesn't it bother you that I will give myself to you only in return for a favor," she asked, "and never out of love?"

His arms went around her, crushing her to him, and his mouth covered hers in a savage kiss, and although he did not answer her question, she knew by the fierceness of his response that it bothered him deeply.

She owed him her thanks for getting her papa to safety and for so much more, yet while the love he craved would never be his, at least she could give him this. She melted against him, responding instantly, knowing in a distant part of herself that it was as much for herself as it was for him.

She shuddered at the sound of his labored breath when his lips moved across her cheek to her ear. Her body hummed with need and fulfillment. His mouth was suddenly everywhere—tasting, nipping, ravishing her cool white flesh with a wildness about him such as she had never glimpsed before.

Her desire changed from dreamy to desperate. She moaned, digging her nails into his shoulders, pulling him closer. Was it carnal satisfaction that made her feel like this, or was it something more?

She heard the seams of her garments ripping beneath his frantic hands and didn't care. Clothing could be replaced, but nothing could take the place of this feeling of wild abandon that she experienced only in the vampire's arms. There had never been any control in their lovemaking, and this night was no different.

Moonlight filtered into the bedroom sending shadowed light across her naked body as he swept her in his arms and carried her to the bed. He laid her down on the feather mattress, his mouth finding hers again as he settled on top on her. Her need grew as his hands moved over her body, cupping and lifting her breasts so that he could kiss the soft undersides, raking along her waist and the curve of her hips, up and down the inside of each silken thigh, coming to rest upon that place that burned like a wildfire out of control.

She moaned his name and reached for him, wrapping her fingers around his hardness, feeling it throbbing to her touch and thrilling to the sound of his strangled gasp when she pushed him onto his back and drew him into her mouth. Yes, she would pleasure him this way, not because he demanded it but because she wanted to, because he tasted so sublimely sweet, because it made her feel powerful to have him writhing against the mattress, because only with him could she be as wanton as this without being judged.

Lifting her face, she ran her mouth up along his belly to his chest—tasting, licking, savoring the coolness, swirling her tongue around his hard little nipples as she straddled him. She leaned forward and kissed him. His tongue met hers in a heated union. Reaching down, she grasped his phallus and rubbed its tip around her entry, teasing and eliciting an unintelligible epithet from him before coming down upon it.

There was no need for soft motions that built in rhythm and speed. The instant she felt it go in she began to move on top of him, pumping her hips in a beat that grew more frantic, like the voodoo drums in the bayou. With his hands about her waist, fingers biting into the tender flesh, he used his preternatural strength to lift her and bring her down hard, over and over again, succumbing to their mutual need to possess and be possessed.

Lifting his head, he buried his face in her pendulous breasts and tugged at the hardened nipples with his teeth, eliciting a moan from her.

"Am I hurting you?" he rasped without stopping.

She grasped the back of his head and held him there. "More."

Her response enflamed him beyond rational thought. Acting now on pure instinct, he pulled her off him and flipped her onto her back. Grasping her ankles, he drew them up over his shoulders and brought his mouth forward. There was no need to go slowly. He craved the sweet, succulent taste of her, and her fingers digging into his hair demanded complete ravishment. Her body strained and arched as her breathless voice begged for more.

When she thought she would explode from the wicked pleasure, he lifted his head, and without further ceremony, plunged into her. With a sharp cry, she wrapped her legs around him, holding his body prisoner to hers.

The moonlight fell across their writhing bodies as release came upon them simultaneously, and the midnight air filled with the sounds of two wild things coming together in a tangle of hot, torrid need, each gasping with shock over the power and strength of the other.

She lay beneath him exhausted, but hungering for more, always for more. Dizzily she wondered where she would ever find another man with his strength. What other man could strip her of all inhibition with his savagery?

Making love with him was like making war. It was passion and pain, euphoria and torment. It reduced her to the most elemental instinct, making her no better than any wild animal, incapable of resisting.

Through the darkness he could see the pale cloud of her hair fanned across his shoulder as she lay with her head resting against him, and her moonlit flesh gleaming like marble, and tightened his hold on her.

"After I put an end to Christophe, I'll come back for you. We can leave this place and start a life somewhere else."

She turned her head to look at him. He had an expression on his face that she recognized only too well—obstinate, resolute, possessive. He had taken her to the edge of reason and now he wanted to take her away. Her lips, moist and swollen from his kisses, parted. "I'm not going anywhere with you," she said, disentangling herself from his embrace and sitting up.

"After what just happened here?" Disbelief was written in his eyes. "After what happens every time we're together? Would you let any other man do to you the things I do?"

"No," she said with a pout. "I don't know. Please leave me alone."

"Not until you admit that we were meant for each other."

She shrugged away from him, but he caught her roughly by the wrist before she could leave the bed. "You are mine. You will always be mine. I'll never let you go."

Anger stole in, chasing away the passion and dreamy reverie of only minutes ago. "Damn you," she hissed. "You cannot make me love you." Twisting free of his grip, she sprang from the bed and stalked away. "If such a thing were possible, I would have had Stede's love long before tonight." She heard his sharp intake of breath and knew she had wounded him. "Oh, why do you force me to be unkind?"

His mouth was set in moody shadow, and there was nothing in his eyes. Woodenly, she said, "Hadn't you better get dressed and tend to Christophe? We can finish this discussion later."

She watched him rise from the bed and dress in brooding silence. Even now, with so much unresolved between them, knowing she could not give him what he wished for, she could not will her eyes away from him.

He was a perfect specimen, with symmetry of muscles, a striking combination of hardness and softness, of unspeakable power and unexpected vulnerability. Hardening herself against his magnificent appeal, she went to the window, biting back a sob as she turned her back to him.

Angry and hurt, he left the room without saying another word. Moments later she heard the downstairs door slam shut.

She watched from the tall window as he appeared on the street below and stood motionless beneath the street lamp. From over his shoulder he aimed a glance at the window, his face set in a scowl, green eyes radiating up at her. Placing a palm against the pane, she gave him a half smile and offered a silent apology for her deception, for she had no intention of continuing their discussion later, or ever. They had made love tonight with wild impatience, as if it had been their first time when, in reality, only she knew that it had been their last.

When his shadow disappeared around the corner, Pru pulled a tapestry satchel from beneath the bed. Then she rushed to the *armoire* and began to pull garments from their hooks, stuffing them into the satchel together with articles hastily gathered from the dressing table. Snatching her cloak, she swirled it around her shoulders and hurried from the house.

Outside, she paused at the wrought iron gate to look back at the house she and papa had lived in these last months. Come spring, the blossoms on the Spanish lime tree would fill the air with their sweet fragrance, but she would not be here to smell it. The branches would explode with the small green fruit, but she would not be here to see it. With a mixture of regret and relief, she turned away. There was no time to lose. Nicholas didn't know where Stede's ship was anchored, but she did. She had to get to Grand Terre before the *Marie's Fortune* set sail.

Chapter 32

*N*icholas sat at a table in the corner with his face turned toward the brick wall, suppressing a yawn.

Tables were pushed together so that a group of newsmen could discuss the daily activities of the city. He had no interest in their discussions. What did he care about the bands of robbers roaming the streets, or the feeble efforts of the Civil Guard to check their depredations, or the battalions of men patrolling night and day to protect the city from looting and rioting, possibly the only endeavor the Creole and American residents undertook together?

He listened with a bored expression as the patrons of Maspero's expressed their discontent over the new statutes imposed by the United States regulating the conduct of the people. There was to be no cursing. Driving carts on Sunday was forbidden. Slaves, soldiers and sailors were not permitted on the streets after eight o'clock without a written pass from a master or commanding officer. The only thing that half-interested him was talk of the pillories, for on more than one occasion he'd found an easy meal in a thief whose head and hands were imprisoned and in no position to put up a struggle.

Yes, he could move about these narrow streets virtually unnoticed beneath the oil-dripping lamps, with enough dark alleys in which to hide, and true, there was no city in America quite like it, but with the coming of the Americans, New Orleans was fast become too confining to someone like him who, for centuries, enjoyed the freedom to roam at will without answering to anyone.

Frankly, he'd had it with having to pay six and a quarter cents for a measly four buckets of water brought from the Mississippi and sold from carts and wagons. And with the single newspaper in town filled with proclamations, business advertisements, bills of lading, and only an occasional item of foreign or local news. And except for *Le Thèâtre St. Pierre*, with the woefully lacking performing arts. And with all those flatboat bullies, the ferocious brawlers who swarmed into New Orleans from the western country. And with the screaming orgies and writhing snakes of the voodoo ceremonies in the bayou. He'd been in this uncivilized place long enough. It was time to move on.

As soon as Christophe was dispatched, he would find out where Stede was keeping James and then return to the house on Rue Bourbon to collect Pru, and the three of them would leave this soggy place. She could argue against it all she wanted, but in the end she would see that it was futile to deny the irrefutable fact that they belonged together, now and forever.

He glanced up at the beams in the ceiling and heaved an impatient sigh. He'd been here for over an hour and his quarry had not shown himself. He rose to leave his spot against the wall when the tavern door swung open and a tall, lanky figure entered. He sank slowly back into his chair and watched surreptitiously from over the rim of his tankard of ale as his prey settled himself at the bar and withdraw items from his coat. Apparently, Delphine was right, he was selling objects stolen from the pirate. Ironic, considering the items were part of the pirate's booty stolen from some unfortunate Spanish ship.

The hour passed. Beyond the walls of the coffeehouse the cathedral bells began to ring. Finally, his prey pushed himself away from the bar and left with the coins from his illicit sales jingling in his pocket, unaware of the footsteps just a few heartbeats behind him.

Christophe walked north along Rue de Chartres, heading toward the old French city, past whitewashed walls and the tall wavering fronds of banana trees rustling in great courtyards. Candlelight streamed from the high windows of the houses and played across the plaster ceilings within. At one point he stopped and turned around, thinking he heard something behind him, but saw only a swirling mist rising from the *banquette*.

At the corner of Rue Bourbon he paused to glance around, then proceeded down the street, his steps growing quicker and more determined. He stopped before one of the old houses, fingers wrapping around the wrought iron gate as he gazed up at the second floor gallery shaded by the leaves of a Spanish lime tree. The rusted iron hinges squealed when he pushed the gate open and entered the courtyard. He paused to draw the stake and mallet from beneath his coat before quietly opening the front door and stepping inside.

Concealed behind a hedge of crepe myrtles, Nicholas was not surprised that Christophe was not keeping to his end of the bargain. The concept of live and let live was lost on the Sanctum, he thought with rankling hatred. With the speed and dexterity of an alley cat, he sprang over the wrought iron fence. But it was no ordinary feline that leapt into the air as if sprouting wings and landed in a crouch on the second floor gallery. Without making a sound he entered the house through the French doors, moving like the wind across the parlor floor and up the staircase. His preternatural senses detected Christophe's soft tip-toe steps and the rapid beating of his heart and smelled the blood flowing anxiously through his veins, while his cat-like eyes pierced the darkness of the hallway leading to Prudence's room. He strained to pick up the sound of her, but heard no telltale sign of her breathing nor of the little noises she made during sleep about which he had teased her. Something was amiss, but he could not dwell on it while Christophe was so dangerously close to his beloved.

He watched through the shadows, his own shadow merging with the those thrown up on the wall by the hazy moonlight beyond the window. His rancor grew as Christophe placed a hand on the doorknob and gave it a turn. His lips drew back in a snarl over his lengthening teeth. He was about to pounce when Christophe backed out of the room.

Relief and bewilderment flooded through Nicholas. Prudence wasn't in her bed, but where was she? He ducked behind the longcase clock in the hall, his hatred boiling over as Christophe went back downstairs and left the house.

Outside, a cabriole rolled past with a thud of horses' hooves and the churning of wooden wheels. Swearing under his breath, Christophe shoved the stake and mallet back beneath his coat as he hurried along Rue Bourbon.

Suddenly, a gust of wind rushed past him, not the gentle breeze from the river that made the lanterns hanging from the lamp posts sway, but something cold and dark, like the savage currents of air that signaled the approach of a violent storm. He glanced skyward, but the heavens were clear, with no sign of a storm brewing among the stars. He shivered, pulling his coat tighter around himself, quickening his steps. By the time he reached his modest one-story cottage on Rue d'Orleans he was running.

Panting, he rushed through the hall-parlor and went immediately to the bedroom where he pulled the black bag from under the bed and replaced the stake and mallet, then removed his coat and tossed it irritably onto the moss-filled mattress.

Back in the hall-parlor, without bothering to light a candle, he went to the mahogany *armoire*, took out a dark green bottle, pulled out the cork with his teeth and drank without ceremony. With the bottle grasped in his hand, he glanced at the French ivory crucifix on the wall beside the *armoire*, crossed himself, and was about to turn away when there drifted into his nostrils a sweet fragrance. It reminded him of the aroma that sometimes drifted downriver from the plantation of Monsieur de Borè when the cane was being refined. But the scent that filled the small room was not that of sugar, nor of perfume, nor of the oleander outside his window. It was unlike anything he had ever smelled before. Beneath the warm, sweet redolence was a distinctly forbidding essence of something sharp and cold and dangerous.

He began to tremble, and tiny beads of sweat broke out on his forehead.

He heard the sound of breathing close by. Sweeping the darkened room with his gaze, he saw nothing. He whirled in all directions at the soft brush of footsteps coming closer. A cold breath touched his cheek, sending convulsive shivers down his spine.

"Wh—who are you?" he breathed hoarsely. "Show yourself."

The figure of a man moved into the light of the moon whose rays slanted in through the window. For several moments he stood before Christophe, dark hair falling across his forehead, light shining in his eyes that were green and blindingly bright. He smiled, a mere travesty of a grin, before his lips curled back to reveal his magnificent teeth.

Christophe gasped. A low strangled cry rose from his throat at the sight of the sharp canines, and he coughed violently at the breath that fanned his cheek, now like the stench of swamp decay, when the man…the creature…spoke.

"It isn't nice to go back on a bargain."

Claw-like fingers reached for Christophe's throat, and drawing him dangerously close, he sniffed the air about the blond head. "I can smell your fear. You are right to be afraid." Slowly, he lifted Christophe off the floor so that his feet dangled in mid-air. He held him there long enough to have him gasping for breath but just shy of choking the life out of him before lowering him to the planks. With the glint of the moon in his eyes, he asked, "Do you know who I am?"

Every muscle in Christophe's body was rigid with fear. "Sh—she told me she would speak to you."

"And she did." The talon grip relaxed and drew away. "I might have been persuaded to let you live," Nicholas said, "had you not tried to kill her tonight."

"I—I did not," Christophe choked, the lie knotted in his throat, his heart beating hard against his chest.

"Oh, but you did," came the smooth reply. "I was there. I saw you.

"I cannot help it," Christophe cried. "I took an oath."

Nicholas moved away and sauntered about the room, noting with benign disinterest the dried Easter Sago palms tucked behind the 18th century crucifix. "And how did a good Catholic like you become a member of the Sanctum?" He could hear Christophe's strained breath behind him. "Go on. You have my full attention."

"*Mon père.*"

"Yes, yes, your father," Nicholas droned. "Tell me something I do not know."

Christophe's frightened gaze darted wildly to the doorway. If he could make it to his bedroom where he'd left the black bag and to his coat whose pocket held the Consecrated Host, he might be able to subdue the vampire and destroy him. "When m*on père* was a young man, he fell in love with a beautiful girl from Saint-Domingue," he began as he edged cautiously toward the door. "But she was found one night in the swamp with her throat bitten and her blood drained. That was when he took the oath."

"You did not have to follow in his steps," said Nicholas.

"She was my mother," Christophe tersely replied.

"I see. And so, a first born son of a first born son becomes a killer no better than the one who took your mother's life."

"I am no worse than you."

"Ah, but there is a difference. I do not kill innocents. Prudence has done nothing to harm you," Nicholas said, his calm deserting him as he turned back to Christophe.

"She is one of your kind."

"Not of her choosing, but that is neither here nor there."

"She is a killer."

"Oh, yes. Make no mistake about that. She is lethal. Although I suspect even she is not fully aware of what she is capable of. I, on the other hand, know precisely how deadly I can be." He moved smoothly toward Christophe. "If I were to let you live, would you try again to kill her?"

Christophe backed away from the menace in those green eyes. "N—no. I would not. I give you my word."

"Your word?" The vampire laughed, shaking the walls with the force of the sound. The laughter died as abruptly as an extinguished wick. His voice was a low hiss. "I can smell the lie on you. Unlike Prudence, I am not so trusting. You will try again. After all, you took the oath," he mocked. "There is just one more thing I must know before I kill you. What was that you drank?"

Christophe had forgotten about the bottle still grasped in his hand. His words eked out. "*La fèe verte.*"

"I have a fondness for blood flavored with sherry," Nicholas mused. "But absinthe? Not so much."

Acting purely on impulse, Christophe flung the bottle at the vampire, hitting him squarely in the head, causing him to stumble backwards, and in that instant Christophe rushed toward the door.

The vampire lunged, catching him by the arm, twisting so fiercely that his shoulder was wrenched from its socket. Christophe screamed in pain and fell against the wall. With frantic, sobbing breaths he struggled against the iron hand that held him. Talon-like fingers dug into his crinkly blond hair, forcing his head back. At the touch of fangs against the flesh of his throat, he ground his eyes shut, awaiting the bite that would suck his absinthe-laced blood from his body. But the death bite did not come.

Still locked in the vampire's inhuman grip, Christophe opened his eyes, and what he saw compounded his terror. The face of the thing that held him was handsome and serene, the smile almost luminous, the eyes more beautiful than anything he had ever seen. Christophe opened his mouth to speak, but no words passed his lips. Somewhere in the tumult of his mind he thought he heard the vampire speak.

"Well, perhaps just a taste, after all."

A great shuddering moan escaped Christophe's lips as the fangs sank into the pulsing flesh, followed by a horrifying sound, like that of a cat lapping at a dish of milk. But it wasn't milk; it was blood—his own blood flowing out of his body and into the vampire's mouth. A dry, rasping sound emerged from his throat. His struggles weakened. And then the terrible sucking stopped.

A bubble of blood appeared at the corner of Christophe's mouth, and then seeped from the wounds in his throat, spilling out of his jugular onto the floorboards.

He felt himself being lowered. The floor was wet and sticky beneath his back. The vampire knelt beside him, an unnatural light gleaming in his eyes. He moved his fingers through Christophe's crinkled hair and slid his hands downward to frame his face. His touch was cold but gentle, almost a caress, it seemed.

Christophe tried to raise his head, but in his weakened state the only thing he could move was his eyes. His lids fluttered and strained to see past the beautiful face hovering inches above his own. The last thing he saw was the French crucifix on the wall before the hands on his face tightened and with one quick motion snapped his neck.

Nicholas rose and glared down at the dead body lying in a pool of its own blood. "Absinthe," he said with a grimace. "I never did like the taste of that stuff."

He left the cottage on Rue d'Orleans, the taste of blood and absinthe lingering on his tongue. By the time the quadroon's body was discovered, it would have decomposed beyond recognition, with no telltale sign of the puncture wounds on the throat. He could have buried it in the swamp, but he was anxious to get back to Rue Bourbon and to Prudence.

The moonlight filtered through the limbs of the Spanish lime tree as he hurried along the flagstones to the front door. He didn't wait for her to answer his knock. Pressing his fingers to the door, he pushed it open and entered the house.

There was an eerie stillness about the rooms. The crystal chandeliers were unlit, the Oriental carpets bearing no trace of footsteps having tread on them. The silk screens painted with flowers and birds stood like lonely sentinels. He went from room to room, searching for a sign of treachery, detecting nothing in the cold, still air. The music room that had rang with the melodious chords of the violoncello was now deathly quiet. The parlor, once so lively with conversation, even if it was verbal sparring with Prudence, had a ghostliness about it. The hairs at the back of his neck stood on end. Something was not right.

He took the stairs two at a time. Even he, so accustomed to the cold that ravaged his body, shivered at the icy fingers running up and down his spine as he raced to her room. He somehow knew even before he saw the empty bed that she would not be there. One thought tore through his mind. The window.

He stood in the middle of the room, not daring to look toward the window for fear of finding the panes shattered like before. Drawing in a ragged breath he turned his face toward it. It was not broken. An immense sigh of relief shuddered through him. And yet, something, he knew not what, caused the breath to tighten in his chest. His gaze flew to the dressing table and flared wide to find it empty of the articles with which she primped. He went to the *armoire* and threw open the doors. Her clothes were missing from their hooks.

Nicholas stumbled backwards. He threw his fist up to his mouth but could not stifle the audible groan. He stood rooted to his spot, trying desperately to make sense of it as his heart heaved in his chest.

It could have been minutes; it could have been hours. Gradually, movement returned to his limbs, and with it came the chilling realization that she was gone.

He turned and left the room. Outside, the leaves on the Spanish lime tree shuddered in the wind as he walked away from the house on Rue Bourbon.

***

"Nicholas, *mon ami*! How good it is to see you."

But Marie's elation at seeing her friend and former lover was short-lived when he pushed past her, demanding, "Is she here? Where is she?"

"I do not understand," she said, hurrying after him as he stormed from room to room.

"Prudence. Is she here?" he snapped, his anger radiating through his distress.

"No, she is not. I have not seen her in many days."

She practically slammed into him when he stopped abruptly and shrank back when he whirled to face her.

"Where is that miserable pirate?"

"Stede?" Marie's face paled. "He left two days ago."

"Do you know where he went?"

"He does not tell me where he goes, but—"

"But what? Marie, if you know anything, you must tell me."

"I heard him talking to one of his men. He told the man to get the ship ready. The *Marie's Fortune*. He named it after me."

"Did she go with him?" His tone was accusing, the look in his eyes beseeching.

Meekly, the girl replied, "I do not know."

"Where is the ship now?"

Was it true? Had Stede run off with Prudence? Marie bit a corner of her lip, hesitating. Would he do such a thing to her? Her chin trembled and she struggled in vain to keep the tears at bay as her hands ran over her softly swelling belly beneath her dress. "On the south side of Grand Terre," she said. "That is where you will find the ship."

He left her standing there, her heart on the verge of breaking.

Anger in him built to a deafening crescendo, blocking out all thought. The moon was large over the moss-draped cypresses as a tiny winged creature took flight, winging its way over the swamp and across the water.

***

The *Marie's Fortune* was sailing before a light breeze. On deck, Pru stood at the bulwark, arms resting on the rail, lost in thought as she watched the dolphins swimming alongside the ship.

Nicholas would have discovered her absence by now. If she knew him, he wasn't taking it very well. She felt guilty for her surreptitious flight in the middle of the night, but what choice did she have? She had no doubt that he would kill Christophe and then return for her. His words rankled in her mind. "You are mine," he said. "You will always be mine." She could not deny the unbridled passion she felt in his arms, but neither could she give him what he wanted—her love. Love was just an inconvenience of the heart. Look what it had gotten her. She had gone to great lengths to secure a man's love only to have him fall in love with another woman. No, she was not likely to ever fall in love again, and certainly not with the vampire who swore he'd never let her go.

"How is your father?"

At the sound of Stede's voice, she turned and hid her thoughts behind a smile. "Not much better, I'm afraid. This voyage has him looking rather green."

He came to stand beside her at the rail, the wide sleeves of his shirt billowing in the sea breeze. "The best thing for seasickness is to fix your eyesight on a spot on the horizon."

"I doubt I can convince him to come topside," she said. "He has refused to leave his bunk for two days now." Her one consolation was that if papa insisted on remaining below deck, at least he'd be resting on native soil, thanks to her foresight in scooping up several handfuls before leaving the house.

"A small price to pay for avoiding a gambling debt."

She hated perpetuating the lie Nicholas told him about papa, but it was better than the truth of what they were running from. "He gave me his word he will never enter another gambling house for as long as he lives." And that would be a very long time, she thought with wry amusement.

"You know, I've been thinking," he said as he gazed out upon the blue-green Caribbean Sea. "What if I was to turn the *Marie's Fortune* into a gambling ship?"

"Aren't there already gambling houses on the water?"

"Yeah, sure, the flatboats. But that's not where the money is. It's in the pockets of the gentry. If given the choice, I'm thinking those fine gentlemen would rather gamble in luxury than side by side with the Kaintocks. Besides, the Mississippi current is so strong the flatboats can only move downstream, and until someone builds a boat that can move upriver under its own power, it takes a hell of a lot of poling against the current to get back upriver. Can't you just see it, Pru? A floating palace with a cafè on board and maybe even a little cabaret below deck. Ha! Imagine it. Me, a legitimate entrepreneur." He threw his head back and laughed, the sound skimming across the water.

Pru looked at his profile etched against the blue sky. These were the same features that had captured her heart, yet something was different, and with a start she realized that the difference resided within herself. The pain of despair she'd felt over losing him had eased to mild discomfort, and the love she'd once had for him had somehow changed to simple affection. She suppressed a laugh of self-deprecation. After all the trouble she'd gone through to win his love—even resorting to a voodoo love potion—this was what it had come to.

Sweeping the burnished strands of hair from her eyes, she asked, "Where are we headed?"

"Port Royal off the southern coast of Jamaica. The town's not what it used to be. In its heyday it was the place for enterprising men much like me to set up shop, being so close to Spanish shipping lanes. The locals tell stories about how a big earthquake over a hundred years ago dumped most of the city into the harbor. These days it's pretty much just a fishing village, but it has a natural deepwater harbor good for protecting ships at anchor. I'll drop you and your father off there. Here, you'll need this." Into her hand he pressed a pouch jingling with coins. "This should buy you passage aboard another ship."

"I can't tell you how grateful I am for this, Stede."

"There's no need, Pru. When you showed up at Grand Terre, I knew right off something was wrong. Is it him?"

"Partly," she admitted. "Nicholas will find you and demand to know where you've taken me. What will you tell him?"

"The truth. Port Royal. From there, who knows?

"What about you? Where are you off to?"

"Back to Nawlins. To Marie. She's been talking some nonsense lately about getting married. I never figured I was the marrying kind, but—" He shrugged. "She's carrying my babe, so, yeah, why not?"

She would miss this pirate with the bright gray eyes and happy-go-lucky nature and the lilting cadence of his speech that marked him as a man of this time and place.

"I'm happy for you and Marie," she said, and though she meant it, she could not help but feel a bit sorry for herself.

Stede and Marie had a future ahead of them filled with children and grandchildren. Fortune was not so kind to her, however. Where was the love for which she hungered? In which direction did her future lie? Was her wish for mortality destined to remain an unanswered prayer?

***

Nicholas returned to his cottage at the bend in the bayou, inconsolable with grief and pain and rage. When he'd gotten to the island, the ship, and Prudence, were gone. He had lost the one true love of his life. He howled a lost and lonely lament, the sound infiltrating every dark corner of the swamp.

Long into the night he sat on the floor, his back pressed against the wall of cypress timber, looking at nothing, feeling nothing. Even his pain had drained out of him, leaving a hollow shell in which the beats of his broken heart echoed. Little by little the blood thirst came upon him. It started in the pit of his belly and worked its way insidiously into his throat, but he made no move to sate it. He didn't want to hunt, tonight or ever. He wanted the one thing that someone like him would never have—peace. Peace of mind. Peace of heart. The peace that comes to all mortals in their final moments. If he could will himself into eternal sleep, he would have done so, if only to be released from the prison of immortality. The one bright spot in his life over all these centuries had been snuffed out like a tallow candle as if it had never existed. What was left for him now except bitter memories of love unrequited and a life half-lived in darkness?

Prudence.

Her name formed like a prayer in his mind. He hated her beyond endurance. He loved her beyond belief. With her, he could embrace life. Without her, he could only endure it. Aching for redemption and deliverance, he knew he would never find it now.

Somewhere in the wide world was the only being who had ever seen that part of him that was lost forever—his soul. If only there was a way to get her back. But where was she? Where would he even begin to look? A great sigh racked his body. She was gone.

Gone.

He closed his eyes, shuddering inside, holding back the threatening tide of emotion.

And then, when all seemed lost, a glimmer of hope pierced his consciousness like a dim ray of light in a dark and lonely place. Perhaps there was a way to get her back, after all.

He pushed himself up from the floor and went to his bedroom. Grasping the brass handles of the top drawer of the chifferobe, he slid it open. There it was, just waiting for the right time to be of use to him. He lifted it out and smiled wickedly. If it took him until the end of the world he would find her. And when he did, he would use this—the Book of Chants he'd told Prudence was lost in the swamp—to lure her back to him with the promise of the one thing she desired above all others.

Mortality.

http://www.nancymorse.com
Historical and Contemporary Romance
Where Love Is Always An Adventure

Printed in Great Britain
by Amazon

48253356R00155